Also By The Authors

Serpentine

Majestic

Headhunter

Skeleton

MetroCafe

Mule

The Ascendant

Letters From A Killer

sands press
Brockville, Ontario

Letters From A Killer

*Peter Parkin &
Alison Darby*

sands press

sands press

A Division of 10361976 Canada Inc.
300 Central Avenue West
Brockville, Ontario
K6V 5V2

Toll Free 1-800-563-0911 or 613-345-2687
http://www.sandspress.com

ISBN 978-1-988281-77-3
Copyright © 2018 Peter Parkin
Website: www.peterparkin.com
All Rights Reserved

Edited by Laurie Carter
Publisher: Sands Press
Author Agent: Sparks Literary Consultants

For information on bulk purchases of this book or any book published by Sands Press, please call 1-800-563-0911.

1st Printing November 2019

To book an author for your live event, please call: 1-800-563-0911

Sands Press is a literary publisher interested in new and established authors wishing to develop and market their product. For more information please visit our website at www.sandspress.com.

Chapter 1

His hands trembled as he held the letter. Reading had always been a pleasurable experience for Brad. But, this time, with this particular document, he wasn't quite sure what he was feeling. Was he getting pleasure from this? Or was it morbid fascination? Probably a mixture of both, he decided, as he took a badly needed sip of water. His throat was as dry as sandpaper, and he knew what that usually meant. He was in trouble.

Not imminent trouble, he was fairly sure. But, he knew it would come eventually. Brad had been cursed with the need to know. To discover the answers, to force the illogical into the realm of the logical. Not an easy thing to do. But, for an investigative reporter like Brad, it came naturally.

He wrote under the byline Bradley Crawford. And he sold himself to the highest bidder—kind of a prostitute, if there ever was such a thing in the world of journalism.

Brad never had any trouble selling his stories. And they really couldn't even be described as "stories." More accurately, they were exposés. Brad exposed things. Tore them open. Researched them meticulously. Left no stone unturned. He was a hated and feared man in many circles. Sometimes, he had to wear a disguise and assume fake personas in order to get people to talk to him. He was a detective in the truest sense of the word.

He wasn't hated in all circles, of course. Editors and publishers loved him. Because very few could do what Brad could. A Pulitzer Prize winning journalist—not once, but twice.

The first time, he'd brought an American city to its knees with his shocking disclosures of corruption in the mayor's office.

The second time, only three years after his first win, he'd uncovered the collusion between certain U.S. border control officers and traffickers of illegal Mexican immigrants. Massive payoffs, in both cash and drugs, which resulted in reportedly 25,000 pathetic and desperate souls escaping into the not so welcoming arms of the United States of America over a period of two years. Through covert tunnels and overcrowded trucks.

After both exposés, Brad had received death threats. Being Canadian, he wasn't as easy to reach—but, despite that sense of comfort, he still kept his head up. Living in Toronto gave him the luxury of being far enough away from those two stories that he didn't have to eat and sleep the details. But, once his exposés were published, he was either the toast of the town wherever he went, or the goat who didn't know to leave well enough alone. Depended on the audience.

Notoriety was just something that came with Brad's chosen profession. History hadn't seen too many people quite like him. And, in these modern times, a true reporter was a rarity indeed. The mainstream media wasn't an easy nut to crack. Doors closed fast, and voices became mute. No one seemed to want to ask the tough questions anymore, to tell the public those truths that a legitimate "free press" should want to tell. That eagerness and excitement to publish a controversial story seemed to have faded with time.

The most notorious journalists prior to Brad were Woodward and Bernstein, made famous by the movie, *All the President's Men*. After that story came out, resulting in the virtual impeachment of Richard Nixon, the news world seemed to change dramatically. Cement walls started popping up everywhere, and the flavor of stories started to change. They became more about scandal and salaciousness rather than hard news.

Rather than holding people accountable.

Brad was old fashioned—he still believed in accountability and still believed that people should care about that.

But with the current state of affairs in the world, it seemed that the news was now sanitized. And the messages seemed disingenuous. There was so much clutter now—it seemed as if there was no room

2

for real news anymore because all of the room was being taken up by stories about celebrities like Beyoncé and JayZ, and whether or not their marriage was really over. *Who gives a shit?*

Apparently, a lot of people give a shit.

Brad still loved what he did—and he had this "missionary zeal" still etched into his brain; had convinced himself that people still cared about hearing the truth, and still cared about those in power being held accountable.

And if not for people like Brad, who in God's name would hold their fingers to the fire? If not for courageous journalists, how would anyone hear the real news, know the real truth? But in the back of Brad's mind, he did indeed wonder if anyone really cared anymore. As long as the lies and deceit didn't affect their singular little worlds, then life was a happy journey.

He knew he was an idealist, and knew also that he had this old-fashioned sense of truth and justice. That was just Bradley Crawford in a nutshell. And he liked who he was.

Brad also liked how rich he was. Being a famous journalist had earned him a huge income over the years. Even before he became freelance, he'd made his mark. Worked his way up the ladder after graduating from the University of Toronto with a master's of journalism. Moved up fast, becoming managing editor at the *Toronto Times* before the tender age of thirty. Then he floated a massive loan and executed a leveraged buyout of that national newspaper before his thirty-fifth birthday party. And what a party that was...

Brad changed the nature of the paper during his tenure as publisher—transformed it from one that relied mainly on fluff stories to a controversial ball-breaker. And he'd even selfishly held onto his job as managing editor while acting as publisher—he wanted to influence the stories, because, after all, it was his fucking newspaper. And he was determined to put his stamp on it.

Five years later, Brad sold the newspaper and pocketed a capital gain of thirty million. Then he was free. Free to pursue. Free to dig and provoke. And free to sell his particular brand of expertise to whoever was willing to pay him.

While Brad was indeed a rich man now, he still expected to be paid. He liked money. And he liked being able to command his worth. Because no one did it better than him.

He turned his attention back to the two-page letter in his hands.

What was this man saying? Why had such an obviously articulate man written what amounted to no more than just a fluffy wishy-washy letter? A letter full of crap—not even worth the effort. But...there were indeed subtle nuances. Was he trying to say something without coming right out and saying it?

Brad knew that was why his hands were trembling. This nonsensical letter was actually making sense somewhere in his brain. He'd seen enough cryptic phrases in his professional life to understand that the man was talking in code. And doing it from behind the walls of a medium security prison in the great state of Georgia.

He looked up and stared off into space—well, not really in space. Towards the window in the living room of the rented cottage. Which now acted as a mirror because of the darkness that had descended outside. He felt himself falling off into a daydream:

A doomed and dying man, in solitary confinement, hunched over his tiny little desk in a four foot by ten foot cell. Writing like a madman, using his considerable covert skills acquired during his days at the CIA by scribbling in code. Knowing that all of his mail was screened before it was allowed to leave the confines of the pigpen that was now his home. Wondering what he could say, should say— what legacy he could leave behind. And if anyone would care. Brad could see him stretching his considerable muscles, pushing back his thick blonde hair, smiling his sardonic smile as he considered how he was outsmarting his screeners; or as he referred to them in the letter—his "keepers."

The handsome and gentle face that belied the sordid resume: one that contained ten convictions for murder and a suspected forty more. Forty murders that were never proven as they had taken place in foreign lands. The handsome face that could have easily graced the silver screen, but instead was overcome with joy every once in a while, whenever he thought of the son who enjoyed that honor in his place. A son who was now more famous than the father. He probably thought that was only fitting. After all, his son was a bona fide movie star now, and Hal Winters was only the most infamous hitman America had ever created. Some things weren't worth celebrating.

Brad was sure that such thoughts went through the twisted brain of Hal Winters in his dying days.

Suddenly, Brad was jarred out of his daydream. A reflection in the window glass—movement behind him coming from the kitchen. A glamorous image right out of a 50s movie, complete with the sultry pose and the elegant silk nightgown shimmering in the dim moonlight illuminating the room.

Then he heard her voice, which interrupted the film noir fantasy that was filling his imagination. Brad liked fantasies.

"What on earth are you doing?" She giggled. "Sitting there, staring out the window. You can't see anything, darling. It's pitch black outside."

Brad turned his head to face her. "Ah...but I did see you. And while I think you're a gorgeous babe, you've never looked more gorgeous than you did a second ago reflected in the window pane."

In her usual fun-loving way, his beautiful brunette with the voluptuous figure slipped over the back of the couch and executed a soft landing in a perfectly seductive pose. In that same instant Brad rolled onto the floor to give her all the space she needed. Then he knelt on the floor beside the lips that were puckered and waiting. He gently kissed them.

"I thought you were fast asleep, Kristy. The last I heard from you were snores that would awaken the dead."

She leaned in close and kissed him back. "Yeah, right. You love to exaggerate. The only one who snores in this family is you."

Brad lifted himself off the floor and snuggled in beside her on the massive sofa. "I'm so glad I married you. Know why?"

She smiled. "No. But, I'm waiting with bated breath."

"Because at this time of night I can always count on you to make me a sandwich if I say I'm hungry."

"Are you hungry, Brad?"

"Yes, dear, desperately so."

She tickled him under the arms. "Then you'll have to divorce me. I'm done making sandwiches for you at any time of day or night!"

Brad made a face, but she wasn't buying it.

"You're hungry because your brain is trapped in another mystery. Am I right?"

Brad sat up on the edge of the couch. Reached over and picked up the letter that he'd dropped on the floor. "Yeah, I think you're right."

Kristy sat up too, crossed her legs, and tucked her feet underneath her bum. Brad looked at her—amazed that she was able to do that so easily. At fifty years of age, he couldn't even imagine doing that; in fact, he hadn't been able to do that even when he was in his twenties. Having been a triathlete for most of his life, Brad was in very good shape, but his joints had never been able to move the way Kristy's could. The bonus was that their times in the bedroom would usually get pretty interesting. She was double-jointed, which added all sorts of interesting possibilities. For just an instant, a wonderful instant, Brad could feel a stiffening in his crotch as one particular memory popped into his head.

Kristy leaned over his left shoulder and peered down at the letter in his hand. She gently rubbed his arm. "Come to bed and play. I'll even let you pick the fantasy. You won't figure that letter out tonight. Maybe in the morning some brainstorms will come to you."

Brad nodded. "I'm puzzled as to why he let me have this. It's an original too—not a copy."

Kristy snuggled her chin up against his. "He recognized you as soon as we pulled into the driveway. Because of who you are, he was more than happy to take down the vacancy sign."

"Yeah, that's true. He did seem kind of thrilled to have us stay. I can't believe that he and his wife live in that little cabin over there while we're staying here in their house in relative luxury."

"Well, it sounds like they just do that during the season. Here in the Campbell River area of Vancouver Island, summer comes to a quick end. So, I guess they make really good money for the sacrifice of living in that tiny cabin for three or four months."

Brad rubbed Kristy's bare knee. "It's strange—almost as if he followed us to that pub the other night. And I still haven't seen his wife, have you?"

"No, but I know she's in there. I heard some pots and pans banging around in that little kitchen."

"I guess so—weird though, that she hasn't made an appearance yet. I mean, they're only fifty yards away from us. You would think she'd pop over for a quick 'Hi.'"

Kristy kissed Brad on the cheek. "So, how about that offer to come to bed?"

Brad smiled. "In a few minutes. My brain's still going 150 miles an hour. Back to that pub—he seemed to know we were there. He just came in the front door and walked right over to us. Sat down in our booth with that bundle of letters in his hand."

Kristy frowned. "A bit weird, yeah. But, he knew you were a newsman, and there's only one restaurant within ten miles so he probably assumed we'd be there for dinner."

"But, that bundle of letters?"

Kristy chuckled. "Funny how he asked you to choose a number between one and twenty. You chose nine, and he gave you envelope number nine from the pile. What made you choose nine?"

"Just numerology—it's supposed to be my number. But, I wonder what's in the other nineteen."

"He said they were all from Hal Winters."

"Yes, but the letter he gave me isn't addressed to our landlord. It was sent to someone in England—an address in Coventry. Remember, I asked him how he got those letters and he just shook his head and went silent?"

Kristy shifted to the edge of the couch. "I don't know—he must be hoping you'll look into it. But, what can you do now, anyway? The killer's long dead. His death is old news."

Brad turned and gazed into Kristy's green eyes. "Hon, you must know by now that nothing is ever really old news. Everything connects somewhere along the line, and just finds a way to regurgitate."

She ran a hand through his thick hair. "You need a haircut, dear. Let me do it for you tomorrow."

Brad laughed. "No goddamn way! I remember the first time you tried that. It was a disaster."

Kristy protested. "But, I had the wrong scissors. You can trust me now."

"No, I can't. I'll just trust you to keep editing my stuff—you do a splendid job at that, and at least I know that's what you're trained to do."

Brad kissed her on the lips. They both laid their heads back against the couch and began necking like teenagers. He was starting to think that her fantasy in the bedroom suggestion might indeed be a good idea right about now. With some double-jointed extras?

A sudden noise cut short his dreamy thoughts.

They stopped kissing and listened.

Kristy whispered, "What was that?"

The noise came again.

"It sounds like a dog barking."

"Maybe it's at a neighbor's house?"

Brad shook his head. "No, this estate sits on twenty acres of land. There are no neighbors within earshot. Our hosts must have a dog."

A different noise shattered the quiet.

"Jesus, that sounded like a gunshot!"

Brad held onto Kristy's hand. It was trembling. "Maybe they're shooting at gophers or a fox, something like that."

Another sharp report!

In a shaky voice, Kristy whispered, "Brad, let's just...go to bed and snuggle...under the covers. I'm...sure it's nothing."

He pulled her up by the hand and stuffed the letter into his pocket. "You're right—let's go."

Hand in hand, they were heading towards the back bedroom when there was a soft knock at the door.

They stopped dead in their tracks. Brad called out, "Yes, who is it?"

"It's me, Brad. Your landlord, Colin."

Brad squeezed Kristy's hand. "Not to worry, it's only Colin."

He walked to the front door and opened it wide. "Colin, you're burning the midnight oil, too. Wanna join us for a nightcap?" Brad sensed that Kristy had followed him to the door, and was breathing down his neck right behind him.

As he adjusted his eyes to the dark outside, he could tell that Colin's face was aghast. Pale, with tear-streaked cheeks.

"Colin, what's wrong? Are you okay?"

"I...n-need...that...l-letter...b-back."

Brad just stared at him, shocked at what he was seeing and what he was hearing. He reacted on journalistic instinct. "I'm sorry, I can't do that, Colin. You gave it to me. You can make a copy if you want, but I'm a journalist. I can't give it up."

Suddenly, another figure appeared behind Colin. And, the instant he appeared, Colin lurched forward into the living room. Shoved hard from behind.

Brad didn't hesitate—danger signals went off in his brain. He leaned his torso back, so far back that he could feel his head touching Kristy's chest. Then he shot his right foot out at lightning speed against the shadowy figure rushing through the open doorway. He caught him on the chin, causing the man to grunt and fly back against the door frame. But, the man steadied himself almost instantly.

Brad's stomach did somersaults. There was now a large pistol in the man's hand and he was raising it to chest level.

Brad went into action again. He lunged forward and used both of his hands to grab the man's wrist and slam it down on top of his raised knee. The gun came free and slid along the hardwood floor towards Kristy. At the same instant, Brad thrust his right elbow up into the man's face, giving his chin one more hard hit. The man went down, but once again recovered quickly. He reached underneath his suit jacket and pulled out another pistol.

Brad spun around, grabbing Kristy in the process, and ran towards the couch. He threw her over to the other side and dove after her. He suddenly felt something cold in his hand. Kristy had retrieved the first pistol and was shoving it into his palm. Brad said a silent prayer of thanks.

With one hand, he shoved Kristy's head to the floor and held it there. The other hand squeezed the pistol grip and a nervous thumb flicked the safety. He carefully raised his head up to peek over the back of the sofa. The stranger had dragged the hapless Colin up off the floor and was holding him in front as a shield. He started firing.

And he kept firing. The gun was tearing both the couch and the room to pieces. From the tiny angle that Brad had, there was no way he could get a clear shot at the man. Colin's bulk was completely blocking him, except for the man's head and gun hand. And Brad just wasn't that good a shot.

The killer advanced closer and closer to the couch, a sinister smile on his face. He seemed confident about the outcome.

Brad knew the man wanted the letter. That's all he wanted. And it probably didn't matter to him if everyone in the room was left dead or alive. From the look on Colin's face when he'd appeared at the door, Brad deduced that those sounds they'd heard earlier were indeed gunshots. He knew in his gut that Colin's wife was already dead, killed as leverage to make Colin hand over the letters. But, there was one letter he hadn't been able to hand over. And that's why the two of them had made a visit to the cottage next door.

It was kill or be killed. Brad had no other choice.

The man was about eight feet away now, and nearly ready to drag Colin around in front of him to the back of the couch where Brad and Kristy had taken refuge.

Brad took a deep breath and muttered, "God, forgive me." He jumped up from behind the couch and aimed his pistol right at Colin's left chest area, knowing full well that at this close range the bullet would drill right through the hearts of both men. He willed himself to pull the trigger and the gun shuddered in his hand. The blast was deafening, more deafening than Brad had ever experienced at a shooting range. Probably because for the very first time he was aiming at living, breathing people. The blast had meaning this time.

At that instant, everything seemed to slow down. The look of shock and horror on Colin's face as the grim reality registered. The stranger's pistol firing wildly towards the ceiling as the life essence eked irreversibly out of his body. The chests of both men ripped open by the blast. Blood spurting out like fountains.

Brad swallowed hard. Then he slowly made the sign of the cross.

Chapter 2

Compared with the horror of the last few moments—moments that had seemed almost surreal—the silence and relative calm now was just plain eerie. Brad stood frozen with the gun shaking in his hand, and stared unbelieving at what he'd just done. The bodies of both men lay on the floor, twitching. Colin on top of the stranger, lying face up, staring at the ceiling.

Brad shook his head, trying to convince himself that this was just a bad dream. Alas, it wasn't.

And the bodies were still twitching.

Suddenly, Colin gasped. Actually, more like a long exhale. Brad forced himself to move. He dropped the gun and dashed over to the bodies, grabbing a pillow from the couch along the way. He knelt down beside Colin and raised his head up, sliding the pillow underneath. The man's eyes were rolling, trying hard to focus.

His lips pursed, trying to form words. Brad reached over and dragged a blanket off the side chair, stuffing it into Colin's massive chest wound. He applied pressure and stared into his landlord's eyes. They were semi-focused now, and it felt to Brad as if the man was staring right into his soul. Judging it, condemning it. A soul that right now felt about as empty as a soul could feel.

Suddenly, Colin seemed to smile—maybe it was just the gas escaping through his mouth and nose, but to Brad it seemed like a genuine smile. Maybe his conscience just wanted it to be. A raspy noise came from deep down in his throat, and then words. Slowly, quietly, but they were real words. Brad leaned down and put his right ear close to Colin's lips. It was barely a whisper.

"Check...Katy."

His wife!

"I will, Colin. Hang on—we're going to get some help."

Brad turned his head back toward the couch and yelled. "Kristy, phone 911!" He couldn't see her, but knew she was still down on the floor.

He felt a weak tug on his shirtsleeve. Colin was trying to get his attention again.

He whispered, "Letters...pocket."

Suddenly, Colin's head raised slightly and blood began streaming out of his mouth and nose. Brad looked on in horror as the man's eyes rolled up into his forehead—then the head fell back down onto the pillow again as a massive sigh erupted from his lungs.

Brad knew he was gone. He put his fingers up against the side of his throat and on the inside of his wrist. Nothing.

He leaned back on his haunches and just stared for a few seconds, hearing his stomach gurgling with panic. He looked behind him—Kristy was standing up now, one hand holding the phone, the other hand covering her eyes.

Brad reached underneath Colin and checked the pulse of the stranger. Dead as well.

He stood and walked back to Kristy, took the phone out of her hand and wrapped his arms around her. "Did you phone 911?" he whispered.

"No," she sobbed, shaking her head.

"I have to go check on Colin's wife. I'll take the phone with me. Are you okay here until I get back?"

Kristy shook her head violently. "No! I'm...staying with you!"

Brad grabbed her by the hand and pulled in the direction of the door. "Okay, let's hurry!"

Out the door they ran, both breathing heavily. A light drizzle was falling, typical of late summer on Vancouver Island.

They dashed in the direction of the tiny cabin, illuminated by a single table lamp in the miniature living room.

Brad led the way up onto the wooden porch and pushed open the front door. The sight that greeted them wasn't much better than the one they had just left behind. A once beautiful Border collie was lying on its side in a pool of blood, just to the left of the foyer. As their eyes adjusted to the dim light, they saw Colin's wife, Katy. Sitting in an easy chair, eye glasses riding down over the bridge of her nose, a book lying face down in her lap.

And a bullet hole in the center of her forehead.

Her face was streaked with blood and for one weird moment Brad was reminded of the scene from the movie, *Carrie*, the one with Sissy Spacek's face smeared in pig's blood.

Kristy put her hands over her eyes and started to sob. Brad walked over to the very dead Katy. It was clearly a moot point, but he checked her pulse anyway—only because Colin, in the throes of death, had asked him to.

Then, acting purely on survival instinct, Brad headed towards the little office in the rear of the cabin. "Stay here, Kristy, I'll be right back."

He knew what he was looking for—evidence that he and Kristy had checked in. He'd asked Colin, when they'd arrived three days ago, to keep his visit incognito. Being a famous journalist, Brad was accustomed to wearing disguises and registering under phony names. But, he hadn't worn a disguise that day, and Colin had recognized him as soon as he'd gotten out of his car. Seemed thrilled, a little star-struck. But, Brad had begged him to keep him off his records, to not tell anyone who he was, and then rewarded him with an up-front cash payment for the five days they'd planned to stay—along with a three-day bonus.

Despite the horror they'd just experienced, Brad was thinking rationally—and with self-preservation in mind. If their names were written down anywhere, he'd eliminate that evidence. Now that he'd determined there were no lives left to save, nothing would be gained by reporting this. In fact, a little voice was telling him that everything would be lost if they did report it. Instinct and gut feel were guiding him. It was the letter—he knew it was trouble. There was something about that one letter and the other nineteen.

There were several folders and papers on the desk. Brad leafed through them, scanning them quickly with his trained eyes. Nothing. Then, he went through all the drawers in the desk. Again, nothing with their names. Brad noticed that Colin's computer was still on. He punched one of the keys and the screen lit up, but the CPU was locked and a prompt for a password appeared. Brad cursed under his breath. He just had to hope that there was nothing on the computer, but from what he could tell, Colin ran an old-fashioned little operation. Seemed to be all paper—the folders contained lists of prior guests and future guests. But, luckily, didn't seem to list the current guests.

Brad started to turn away from the desk, but then stopped himself. *Safer to just take the damn laptop.* He unplugged it, shoved it inside its padded case that was lying on the floor, and stuffed it under his arm.

Brad took one last glance around the office and saw a calendar hanging on the wall. He walked over to it. In the square for the day he and Kristy had arrived, August twentieth, was written in black marker pen: "Bradley Crawford! Wow!"

Brad cursed again. He ripped the entire month of August off the calendar and shoved the page into his back pocket.

Before leaving the office, he took a quick peek in the garbage can. Some rolled up pieces of paper and chewing gum wrappers. Brad unrolled each sheet and gave them a quick once-over. All clear. Then he noticed that at the bottom of the can was a large brown envelope— legal size. He pulled it out and saw that it was addressed to Colin. He flipped it over and looked at the return address—no name, just a post office box in McLean, Virginia. Strange, he thought. An envelope addressed to an innkeeper on Vancouver Island, Canada, from an address in Virginia? And it was postmarked only ten days ago, so Colin had just received it.

Then it occurred to him. This envelope was just big enough to hold a pile of letters.

He folded the envelope and stuffed that in his back pocket as well. He dashed to the outer cabin where Kristy stood with her hands still over her eyes. He spun her around toward the door. "We have to go, Kristy!"

Her body obeyed the spin. Then she muttered, "Aren't we calling

911?"

"No point."

"The police?"

Brad opened the door and nudged her outside. "No point in that either. In fact, better that we don't."

Kristy protested. "But…they're all dead!"

He grabbed her by the hand and pulled her back toward the cottage in a jog. "Not our fault. And not our problem. If we contact the police, it'll become our problem."

"But…Brad…"

"I'll explain more later. Right now, we have to get off this island before we won't be able to."

He pushed open the door to the cottage. "Kristy, pack our stuff together—fast! Don't leave anything behind!" He ran over and knelt once again beside Colin's body.

"What…are you doing?"

Brad looked up. "Before he died, Colin mentioned the letters— said they were in his pocket. I'm going to take them."

Kristy just stared at him.

"Kristy, trust me. It's what we have to do. Please—just pack!"

She ran to the bedroom, and Brad immediately started rifling through Colin's pockets. Checked his sport jacket, inside and out. Then lifted him slightly and shoved his hands into the back pockets of his pants. Pants that were moist—Brad shuddered, knowing why. Then he checked the front pockets. Nothing.

He scratched his head. Did Colin mean the pocket of something hanging in his closet back in the cabin?

Then it dawned on him. He meant the killer's pocket! Of course, the man had already taken them from Colin and came over to the cottage looking for the one missing letter.

Brad gently eased Colin over onto his side so he could gain clear access to the killer. He reached inside the man's jacket—sure enough, he felt a handful of letters in one of the pockets. Brad pulled them out and counted them. Nine. There were still ten more. He slipped his hand into the opposite inside pocket and pulled out some more. Five.

So, five to go. He lifted the man's bum up—moist as well—and felt inside the rear pockets. One held a wallet and the other one held the remaining letters.

Brad stood up and walked over to the closet, pulled out his briefcase and flipped it open. He stuffed the nineteen letters inside, then pulled the one he'd been given out of his back pocket and added it to the safe confines of his alligator leather case. He also threw in the envelope from McLean, Virginia, and the August page from Colin's calendar.

Done.

Kristy came running out of the bedroom, fully dressed, with their two small duffel bags. Brad went back to the killer's body. He knelt down and removed the man's wallet from his back pocket.

Kristy was still breathing hard. "Did you...find the letters?"

"Yeah, I got 'em."

She dropped the suitcases to the floor. "What are you doing now?"

"Finding out who this prick is."

Brad flipped open the wallet—the thing inside was glaring at him as if angry. The famous seal of the Central Intelligence Agency embossed on a laminated card attached to the inside flap of the wallet. The dead agent's name was Richard Reinhardt.

He stuffed the wallet back in the man's pocket and jumped to his feet. "Okay, let's get outta here—fast!"

"Who was he?"

"Tell ya later."

Brad grabbed his briefcase, computer case, car keys, and yanked open the door. Kristy carried the two duffel bags, and they ran to their Audi Q5. Everything went into the trunk. As he slammed the hatch shut, Brad was reminded by the image of his Ontario license plate that they had one hell of a long drive back across Canada.

"Shit! Forgot something!" Brad ran back to the cottage, and yelled back to Kristy, "Get in the car, hon, I'll be right back."

He dashed inside and over to the couch. Picked up the pistol he'd dropped after the shooting. Shoved it into his waistband and took one last glance around the cottage. Then, he reluctantly allowed himself one final look at the two mannequins of death sprawled out over the hardwood floor. Shaking his head in disbelief, Brad ran through the doorway for the last time and jumped into the driver's seat of the Audi.

Cranked the engine and floored the SUV down the dirt path towards the freedom of the open highway, not more than a mile away.

Kristy leaned back against the headrest. "This is like a nightmare. I keep hoping I'll wake up and discover that it was all just a dream."

"Me, too." Brad flipped on the high beams and glued his eyes to the road.

Kristy turned her head toward him. "Where was that guy's car? I only saw Colin's as we pulled away."

Brad frowned. "Don't know. Good question. Maybe he ditched it farther out and hiked in—so his headlights wouldn't give him away?"

"Maybe."

Kristy touched his arm. "Brad...what about our fingerprints?"

Brad shook his head. "Not a worry. Neither of us are fingerprinted in any database, so they wouldn't be able to match us. And I checked Colin's office—our names aren't written down anywhere. Well, except for his calendar, and I took that page with me. And I took his computer."

Kristy sighed with relief. "I feel like a fugitive."

"We're not—well, we are, but we're not guilty of anything. It was self defense—but I have a strange feeling that we'd be hung out to dry anyway. So, best for us to run. It was all because of those letters and, ironically, I think our survival now also depends on those letters."

"Why? Who was that madman?"

Brad swallowed hard. "CIA."

Kristy put her hand up to her mouth. "Oh, God. What are we into?"

"Don't know—but right now, let's just get our asses back to Toronto. We have a three-day drive ahead of us. And...I never want to see Vancouver Island again."

Brad gunned the car around a tight turn in the dirt road, and the Audi's rear end spun off. He turned into the skid and the car straightened out again. He breezed through the next turn and was comforted knowing that the highway should be just about a half mile ahead.

Suddenly there were lights!

The headlights of another car, coming from a side road. The black vehicle pulled out onto the driveway and stopped, blocking their passage. Brad slammed on the brakes and the car skidded to a stop just inches from impact.

The driver's door opened. A short burly man jumped out and ran towards them. His figure was illuminated in the Audi's high beams, and he held one hand up shielding his eyes. And in the other hand...

Kristy gasped. "Brad, he has a gun!"

Brad slipped the pistol out of his belt. Then he positioned it on his lap pointed towards the driver's door; the door that within seconds would be yanked open by yet another killer.

Brad slipped his index finger against the trigger and, for the second time that evening, flipped off the safety with his thumb. He prayed that the darkness would hide the shiny black weapon that was now poised on his crotch.

The man was at the window now and Brad heard the flip of the handle. A rush of damp air swept through the car as the door was tugged open.

And there the thug stood in all his over-confident glory, gun pointed straight at Brad's head. He snarled, "Get the fuck out! Both of you!"

Brad held his breath and pulled the trigger.

Chapter 3

September 11, 2001—It was a bright and sunny day. The kind of day people pray for when they know they're going to be flying. It was calm, too, very little chance of turbulence for four particular jumbo jets that would be winging their way towards the west coast of the United States of America.

Three of the four jets were heading to Los Angeles, and the destination of the fourth was San Francisco. At least, those were the planned destinations of these four infamous planes.

Despite being a picture-perfect day, it was strange in many respects. On this very day, a simulated Air Force exercise was underway—in fact, very much underway at the time these planes were destined to take off. And the exercise was being undertaken on the east coast of the United States, right in the general vicinity of where these four planes were readying for their journeys.

It wasn't a normal everyday simulation—no, not on this day. What will go down in the annals of history is the incredible coincidence of the Air Force simulating attacks by jumbo jets on the World Trade Center towers—on September 11.

The purpose was to test the military response to hijackings: how they'd respond, how long they would take to respond, what the military radar systems would look like. All that jazz. And, of course, as with any simulation, the radar would be rigged to show false blips. Just to test to see how controllers would react and how Air Force commanders would respond. Today was purported to be a safe and controlled learning exercise for the mighty military machine of the United States of America. For the protection and security of Americans everywhere.

Hundreds of military personnel were involved in the simulation on September 11, and every single one of them believed in the importance of what they were doing. And what civilian would disagree? There was, without a doubt, an ongoing imminent fear of terrorist attacks emanating from the Middle East—the threats had been persistent and mind numbing for at least the last decade, and especially so since the World Trade Center had been crippled by a car bomb in 1993. The public was scared, and so was the military. Tests had to be conducted.

But it wasn't just going to be simulated images on radar during this massive exercise. No, it was decided that there would be a "real life" test as well. And who could disagree? How would the Pentagon know if they could really respond properly to the unthinkable unless they had actual live test cases?

They had to know.

The only people who knew about the live test, other than the top brass, were the eight pilots who were chosen to replace the actual pilots on the United Airlines and American Airlines jets. These eight pilots—four pretend captains and four pretend first officers—were honored to have been chosen. And they were chosen not only for their calm professionalism, but also for their expertise in flying virtually any airplane ever created. Flying 767s and 757s was child's play for these professionals. Five of them were Air Force pilots—in fact, two of them were in the astronaut training program. The other three were CIA officers of the highest order—officers who had served all over the world, not only in flying planes for the C.I.A., but also in black ops field assignments. The kinds of things that weren't normally discussed at cocktail parties.

Two of the jets would be taking off from Logan International Airport in Boston, one would depart from Dulles International in Washington, and the fourth would leave from Newark International. This would give the Air Force and the radar specialists a real test— four "hijacked" planes that they would be forced to plan a response to, and all of them departing fairly close together to test the military's ability to respond within a tight time frame.

This was the story each of the eight substitute pilots were told, and none of them had any reason to suspect that they weren't being told the truth. They were assured that any response from the military exercise would be "test mode" only, and that they and their passengers would never be in harm's way.

These jets, however, had a strange passenger manifest—in fact, it was only a partial manifest. The total number of seats collectively available on the four jumbo jets was 684—yet only 232 were occupied on this particular day. An occupancy rate of only thirty-three percent— unheard of for a transcontinental flight to even take off with such a low rate of passenger bottoms. But all four jets would take off anyway. This was, after all, just an exercise.

The fleet of test planes left their airports as planned, and began their treks to the west coast. They were all supposed to leave within a twenty-one-minute window, and three of them did just that. But, one plane, which was scheduled to have been the second plane to depart within that time frame, was actually delayed forty minutes. So, suddenly the test was somewhat skewed.

Each of the substitute captains received instructions over military frequencies while en route, unheard by civilian control towers in New York, New Jersey, Boston, or Washington. This was, of course, part of the test. The control towers couldn't know what the planes were planning to do as that would ruin the integrity of a true test.

Not long after takeoff, the government pilots in charge of the four planes were instructed to change course and head back towards the east coast. Their job was to simulate hijackings to challenge the capabilities of civilian air traffic controllers, military radar specialists, and of course the vaunted air defence system of the mighty Air Force.

The pilots did as they were instructed.

Shortly thereafter, they received new instructions. They were to turn off their aircraft transponders—which, at that point, would make their "squawks" impossible to identify. Controllers on the ground would no longer know the identities of the four aircraft. They could only guess. Also, with the transponders off, there would be no way of knowing the altitude the planes were flying at.

Military commanders on the ground then advised the pilots that the images of their jets on radar would be substituted with bogus images—created solely through technology trickery. It would appear to the ground as if their planes were heading towards high-level targets in New York and Washington. This was all just part of the test.

Most likely, each of the pilots would have shrugged with indifference, thinking that, of course, this was just part and parcel of a true test.

Just mere minutes after the last instruction, the substitute pilots of three of the jets were commanded to change course once again. Instead of heading back towards the east coast, they were to resume a heading due west, which was their intended direction from the beginning.

But, instead of Los Angeles and San Francisco, they were to land at Denver International Airport. They were told that an actual terrorist attack was underway and that the World Trade Center had been hit by hijacked planes. The pilots asked if this was "real world" or "simulation." They were told it was real world, as real as it could possibly get. Speculation was that terrorists planned these attacks deliberately to coincide with the day of the Air Force simulation, knowing that there would be confusion as to what was real and what was not. They must have been in possession of very good intelligence.

The pilots were told that every plane in the air across the continent was being grounded at the closest airports, but, due to the size of these particular test jets, the most capable and safest airport for them to land at would be Denver International. Clearance had already been obtained by the military to allow the three jets to land.

The pilots acquiesced. They couldn't argue with the orders. Safety of their passengers was paramount, and if terrorist attacks had occurred in New York, more might be in the works. Deep down inside, the pilots were horrified and saddened at the news they'd been given— but their military and CIA training had conditioned them to accept tragic news with calm resolution. Their missions were paramount— sad thoughts could come later.

The fourth plane was a different story entirely. Its pilots would not be given orders to divert to Denver. That plane, a United Airlines 757-200 with a mere 37 souls in a cabin with a capacity of 182, had become a problem. It had left forty minutes late, which had thrown a hitch in the planned timeline. Because it left so late, passengers had already been in touch with family and friends on the ground by using the jet's seatback air phones. That alone wouldn't have been a problem if it hadn't been for the fact that the plane had already changed direction back towards the east in line with instructions from the military for the test. So, naturally there was nervous tension amongst the passengers.

The air phones proved to be wonderful conduits into the world of terror. An uprising began its slow boil. The substitute pilots reported to the ground that the test was being put in jeopardy by their passengers. They asked permission to tell the passengers that their plane was merely in a pre-planned test pattern, that they hadn't been hijacked, and that there was no reason for concern.

The commanders on the ground replied, "Negative. This military simulation is classified and cannot be disclosed to anyone. Await further instructions." Those instructions never came. In fact, the pilots never heard from the ground again.

By that time, the eighty-percent empty jumbo jet was flying over the great state of Pennsylvania, not far from the town of Shanksville.

And the passengers were scared out of their minds. They had not only heard from loved ones that the Twin Towers had been hit, but now they'd heard that the Pentagon had also been attacked. The airplane cabin was erupting in absolute uncontrollable chaos.

Several male passengers began their rush toward the cockpit.

But they didn't even get past the galley.

It was 10:06 a.m. and the three other test planes were already more than halfway to their safe destination in Denver.

A Sidewinder missile fired from an F15 fighter jet streaking across the sky two miles distant, slammed into the airframe of Flight 93. The massive jet became an instant fireball.

Just to make sure that the plane was really and truly dead, a twin of the first Sidewinder hit it again milliseconds after its brother—a cruel display of overkill as the ball of fire made its tragic descent.

Flight 93's legacy would be that it was the one and only airplane that crashed or was destroyed on that fateful day of September 11, 2001.

Chapter 4

Brad took his tall glass of scotch onto the balcony and stretched out on one of the padded chaise lounges. Kristy occupied the other and had already been parked there for an hour, soaking up the late afternoon sunshine. She glanced up from her book and flashed him a weak smile.

"How are you doing?"

"I dunno." He held up his glass. "I'm hoping this will help. Do you want one?"

She shook her head. "No. I want my wits about me in case we get a knock on the door."

Brad winced. "I know what you mean."

He glanced out over the lake. He hadn't yet told Kristy the latest—what he'd just read in the news on his computer.

It had been five days since they'd "escaped" from Vancouver Island—three of those days were spent in the car, in an obsessive quest to just get home to Toronto as fast as humanly possible.

Almost 3,000 miles of stressful driving, pushing the speed limit as often as they safely could. They knew they wouldn't feel any semblance of security again until they were back in the familiar confines of their thirty-eighth floor home. And they'd just wanted to put as much distance as possible between themselves and the nightmare at Campbell River.

Brad gazed out over Lake Ontario. It was a beautiful day, sunny and warm. A slight but steady breeze had brought the boats out today. So pretty to look at, with their multi-colored sails contrasting with the shimmering blue waters of Toronto Harbour.

He watched the ferries crisscrossing between the harbourfront and the Toronto Islands. Sometimes, he envied the people who lived over there. Very few did, but those lucky few enjoyed the ultimate in seclusion. He and Kristy could use some of that right now.

Brad smiled as he remembered back to his days as a teenager growing up in Toronto. Kind of wild and carefree, but with very little money to indulge his inner wild child. His parents had actually had the audacity to insist he get a part-time job—no allowance for him. Once he was old enough to work, he was expected to do just that. Brad had had a tough time with that rule. Working would have meant giving up his free time, time that was intended to be spent partying.

One summer, he and his four closest buddies decided that they wanted—no, *needed*—to go to the Mariposa Festival which was being held on one of the Toronto Islands. None of them could afford the admission to the famous folk festival—they had just enough money for the ferry ride to the main island. So, that's where they went, carrying plastic garbage bags.

Once on the main island, they waited until the cover of darkness, then stripped down naked and stuffed their clothes in the garbage bags, tying them as tightly as they could. They slipped into the dark, slimy, oily waters of Toronto harbour and swam the half mile across the bay to the edge of the festival grounds, pulling their garbage-bagged clothes along with them.

Brad chuckled as he remembered how proud they were, how they felt like commandos, frogmen. And most of all, how proud they were that they'd snuck into that concert free of charge. It turned out to be the most enjoyable concert any of them would ever remember. Not because the music was all that good, or the atmosphere either. But, because they had been so creative in how they'd crashed it. And, he guessed, it was mainly because they'd done something they weren't supposed to do, and for a teenager that was usually thrill enough. He knew that if they'd paid to get into that concert it wouldn't have been half as enjoyable.

Brad snapped out of his trip down memory lane. Back to reality.

It was a relief when he and Kristy had finally arrived back in Toronto, and they'd spent the last two days just relaxing—or at least trying to relax. Neither of them were sleeping much during the night. Instead, they were falling asleep at odd times during the day and in odd places, like out on their oversized balcony with the fresh breeze from the lake caressing their faces. It was soothing, and it was different. Brad had even ventured out at around 3:00 that morning and managed to drift off for about an hour.

They felt safe up on the thirty-eighth floor. It was a penthouse apartment in downtown Toronto's prestigious Harbour Square condominium complex. While it was an apartment, it seemed more like a house. A split-level, with the kitchen, living room, dining room, study and a bathroom on the main floor; three bedrooms and three more bathrooms on the second floor.

They had two balconies—the one they were sitting on right now was a wrap-around off the dining room, facing south and southwest across Lake Ontario. On the second floor, right off the master bedroom, was the other balcony—that one faced north across the cityscape.

It was easy to forget that it was an apartment, with a total of 2,400 square feet of luxury space. Bigger than they needed, but both he and Kristy liked space, so it suited them. And they didn't want to bother with lawn maintenance and the usual chores that went along with owning property at street level.

But, they paid dearly for the luxury—monthly maintenance fees were $1,600, and annual property taxes topped out at around $8,000. Not cheap, but they consoled themselves with knowing it was a good investment. Five years ago, they'd bought the unit for a cool two million, and recently a realtor had appraised it for them at almost three.

So, that made them feel better about the expenses. Much better.

Where they lived had everything at their fingertips, including a free daily shuttle bus that took residents to the trendy St. Lawrence Market and back. Just for those unique food items you couldn't find in your typical grocery store. And for the buzz—St. Lawrence always had a buzz about it, which made it fun.

The apartment building had a huge indoor pool, just three levels below their floor, and it was open twenty-four hours a day, which was a unique feature. It also had a gym, squash court, car wash, library, billiard/TV room, sauna/steam room, and a party room. Brad liked the fact that they had two underground parking spots, which meant their cars were always warm and snow-free in the winter months. And, the building had twenty-four-hour security, which was a real plus. *Especially now*, Brad thought wryly.

He watched as a plane circled for landing at the Island Airport. While Toronto's international airport was located about a forty-five-minute drive northwest of downtown, this small airport on the island served some inter-city traffic within the province. It was large enough to handle smaller jets, and a lot of private corporate jets utilized the island as well. It gave easy access to the Toronto office towers.

There was always something to watch sitting out on this balcony. Never a dull moment. And they were so high up that it felt safe—Brad knew this was really just more illusion than reality, but it did indeed feel that way.

He looked over at Kristy. She'd dozed off, book lying in her lap and glasses riding the bridge of her nose. Brad shuddered. Seeing his wife that way instantly brought back the image of Colin's wife Katy, with a bullet hole in her forehead. Shot where she sat. Shot in the act of doing one of the most peaceful non-threatening things in the world—reading a book.

A fucking book!

What had been so important that it justified killing a harmless lady? If Colin had just handed over the letters to agent Richard Reinhardt of the CIA, would he have let them live? Why had Colin resisted? The man must have asked for the letters first—Brad was sure he didn't just come in firing. Colin must have said no. Then the dog was shot. Colin still must have hesitated. Mr. Reinhardt didn't wait too long—Brad remembered there were only about ten seconds between the two shots they'd heard.

At that point, a horrified Colin, upon seeing his wife shot in the forehead, must have handed over the letters. But, how would Reinhardt have known there was one missing? He must have had firm information that there were twenty letters—so he counted them and knew there was one more.

Colin must have capitulated again—out of sheer terror and fear for his own life—and led Reinhardt right to the front door of their cottage.

Brad walked into the study, opened his bar cabinet, and poured himself another tall scotch. He sucked back a mouthful and gasped. Then sucked back another.

They'd left four dead people behind them back on Vancouver Island. And Brad had killed three of those people. The guy out on the road was dead before he hit the ground, Brad was sure. The bullet went right through the upper half of his forehead. Not that Brad had planned it that way—his gun had been sitting poised on his crotch, aiming for normal chest level. But, the guy was so short that chest level meant head level.

After the guy went down, Brad jumped out of the car and checked for a pulse. Once that proved fruitless, he searched the man for identification. A card in his wallet identified him as a private investigator out of Seattle.

So, two dead gunmen—one with the CIA and the other a private detective. Both of them Americans, with guns, in Canada. How had they pulled that off?

Brad hadn't completely reconciled in his mind yet that he'd actually killed three people. It was the kind of thing that was unsettling to think about, to think that he'd snuffed out three lives. He knew he'd had no other choice, that he'd done the right thing. But, all the same, it was still tough to think about. And what bothered him the most was that innocent Colin was one of the three he'd killed. Just for being a human shield. The poor man had already gone through the horror of seeing his wife shot through the head. And then a friendly face iced the cake and shot him through the heart.

Brad wondered if vibes were different during the day that you were going to die. Had Colin, or Katy, awakened that morning with weird feelings? Premonitions? Or just random thoughts that something was out of whack? Did they have any kind of psychic inkling that they had only a few hours left to live? Did they kiss each other harder, give more hugs, and tell each other how they felt? Perhaps reminisce a bit?

Killing people was bad enough. Watching them die was even

worse.

And feeling with his own hands the human body's natural reaction to death in the seats of their pants had been horrifying. It brought the indignity of death home to roost, and just added volumes to that sick feeling of his own mortality.

Brad shuddered, then shook his head and walked back out to the balcony. Kristy was still dozing.

It was time to tell her.

He placed his glass of scotch on a table, then leaned over and gently kissed Kristy's lips. He pulled back quickly as she gasped and lurched upward in her chair, almost knocking out his teeth.

Her right hand flew to her heart as she exclaimed, "Oh, God, don't wake me suddenly like that. You scared me!"

"I'm sorry, hon." He picked up his glass and handed it to her. "Wanna sip?"

She reached for it eagerly. "Yes! Now I do, for sure."

"Take a good long one. I have something to tell you."

Kristy frowned at him. "Oh, no. Do I want to hear this?"

"Probably not. But, you have to."

She sat up straight, folded her arms across her chest, and braced herself. Then she nodded. "Okay, hit me with it."

Brad took the scotch out of Kristy's hand, and stole another sip for himself.

"The news headlines. Finally, after five full days, there's something about what happened. First of all, they identify Colin as being Colin Wentworth. Dual citizenship, Canadian and British. It was reported in the news that he was a retired British intelligent agent with MI5; retired five years ago."

Kristy nodded, a surprised look on her face. "I would never have thought of him like that."

"No, me neither. I guess we have stereotypes in our minds. But, here's what's wrong with that news report. Do you remember that Colin told us he'd moved to British Columbia twenty years ago?"

"Yes, I commented to him that I thought he would have lost his British accent after all that time in Canada, but he hadn't."

"Well, here's what's wrong. If he worked for MI5, he would have been based in the U.K., because MI5 is the domestic intelligence agency for the Brits. They don't work abroad. They're kind of the equivalent of the FBI in the U.S. and the RCMP here in Canada."

Kristy stared at Brad, listening intently.

Brad continued. "But, he lived here for the last twenty years. Which means he wasn't MI5. Colin must have been MI6, the ultra-secret foreign intelligence service for the U.K. They all work *outside* of the U.K., not *inside* it. Made famous by the James Bond movies, although Colin hardly looked the 007 type. Basically, MI6 is the British equivalent of the CIA.

"And, like the CIA, its operatives are seldom identified, which is probably why it was reported that he was MI5 instead of MI6. But, they made a mistake—that story doesn't wash if he retired only five years ago, but has lived here for twenty years. That means he worked in intelligence here in Canada for fifteen years—which has to make him MI6."

Kristy bit her lip. "So, he was into something—or connected to something."

Brad nodded. "Or knew somebody—or tripped over something. And, maybe, just maybe, Colin hadn't really retired after all."

Kristy nodded, and then squeezed her arms tighter around her chest. "Okay, what did the news say about the killings? You haven't told me that part yet, and I'm wondering..."

Brad squeezed her hand. "This is where it gets really weird. The news story described the incident as a murder/suicide. The police concluded that Colin—who they say was suffering from severe depression—shot his wife, the dog, and then himself. There's no mention at all of the other two dead men."

Chapter 5

It was a dark, gloomy day in McLean, Virginia. Just the kind of day that Sean Russell hated. Sure, most people hated gloomy days, but in Sean's job the sun was needed to offset the gloominess of everything he had to face, day in and day out. He always prayed for a sunny day as soon as the morning alarm went off.

Today, it was just going to be double gloomy. He knew it.

He looked out the window at the surrounding countryside— officially, his office was located in McLean, but where Sean worked they all just referred to it as "Langley." At least where their little world was based. This was CIA headquarters and Langley used to be a separate little hamlet until it got absorbed into McLean a few years ago. But as far as Sean was concerned, it was still just Langley.

Langley was only eight miles away from Washington, D.C., which was handy for the countless meetings Sean had to attend there. And the entire postal district of McLean was actually the wealthiest in all of the Washington area. Sean wasn't surprised—plenty of filthy rich people lived there, from senators to former vice presidents of the United States. He figured that even when they retired, they didn't want to be too far from the seat of power. Power was addictive, and it was probably tough for any one of those clowns to truly retire.

Sean was forty-five years old now. No wife, no kids—no surprise. The job had consumed him ever since college. After graduating at the top of his class with a law degree from New York University twenty years ago, he had been swarmed by recruiters—the most aggressive being the Central Intelligence Agency. Tough to resist that glamour. So, he'd succumbed, and his career with the Agency had been nothing short of meteoric. Stints in Bolivia, Brazil, Venezuela, Africa, Iran, and even Russia, had enriched him with more experience than most active members. Experience with a lot of things—not just intelligence gathering. As well as the advantage of having learned several languages, including Russian and Spanish. He tended to use those two the most.

But, it was exhausting—he couldn't date anyone, he just never had the time. Correction, he just never made the time.

More than anything else, Sean wanted to be in love again. The last time for him—the only time for him—was not long after graduation from college. He'd been at the Agency "school" for a year already when they first met. Then they moved in, totally smitten with each other.

Her name was Jannat, and she was a Muslim. Her family ties went back to Iran. They'd been together for two years when it happened.

Sean had just finished his extensive training when his superior summoned him. He remembered the date well—because it was the end of his life as he knew it.

It was June 21, 1996. He'd just been through three years of the most rigorous training any human being could endure. Everything had been fast-tracked, and every day had been fourteen hours long. Despite that, Jannat had waited patiently for him every night, and even cooked him late meals when he finally staggered in through the front door of their cute little apartment in Langley.

During those three years, he'd become an expert in Tae Kwando, a marksman, fluent in three foreign languages, and conditioned to withstand torture for days on end. He knew each of the four corners of the Earth just from mental barrage and sleep study exercises, and he had learned to function alertly after being kept awake for up to seven days straight.

After the three years of training, Sean was a machine. And was suitably brainwashed into wanting to be a CIA agent more than anything else in the world.

Which was probably why his superior had waited until that training was over and Sean's mindset was right where they wanted it to be, before they called him in to that special meeting.

He remembered the conversation like it was yesterday:

"Congratulations on finishing your training, Sean. You're now ready for your first posting."

"Thank you, sir. I look forward to it."

The man's gaze changed immediately to solid impenetrable steel.

"You live with an Iranian woman."

"Well, she's actually American, sir. She has some family back in Iran, but she's a second generation American."

"No, she's a fucking Iranian. And she has a Persian name."

Sean remembered the beads of sweat that immediately started dripping from his forehead at that remark.

"Sir, where is this conversation going?"

The man sat back in his chair and crossed his arms over his chest.

"Are you familiar with the Iranian hostage crisis back in 1979?"

"I was only ten years old then, sir, but yes, I did study it in college."

"What's your recollection of it?"

"Fifty-two Americans from our embassy were held hostage for two years by Iranian student radicals. We had installed, propped up and supported the Shah of Iran, and when the revolution forced him out of power, we whisked him out of the country and provided asylum for him in America. The Iranians insisted we return him to Iran to face charges for corruption and brutal acts against the citizens of Iran. When we refused, the students took over our embassy."

"Correct. This is now 1996. Iran is our sworn enemy."

"Maybe we can change that, sir."

He nodded. "Did you tell...Jannat...that you work for the CIA?"

"No, of course not. I'm well aware of the protocol—we're not to ever confirm to anyone who we actually work for."

Sean's boss scratched his chin. "It's come to our attention that she has been telling friends that you work for the CIA."

"I can't control what she says or thinks. And, I think it's reasonable to expect that anyone close to a CIA agent has their suspicions. How can you possibly prevent that? It's not a normal life, nor a normal occupation. Jannat knows that I'm a lawyer and as far as she knows from me, I've been struggling to build my law career with an up-and-coming law firm in Washington. A name you told me I 'officially' work for, and one that actually does exist as a front."

The imposing man stood and walked around the desk. He stared down at Sean.

"Your first posting will be Iran. If you insist on staying with this woman, we will need to clear her as a security risk. Which means we will need to interrogate her for a period of time. Well, we won't do it, of course—we'll assign that task to a contractor. She won't be able to accompany you to Iran, though. You will be allowed visits back to America twice a year to see her. And, as far as she's concerned, you will be practicing law in the Brussels office of that Washington law firm."

Sean had heard only one thing. "What do you mean 'interrogate her?'"

"I think you know what I mean."

"Who would do this? How would it be explained to her?"

"As I said, Jannat is a Persian name—and it means 'paradise.' All these jihadists refer to paradise before they commit their suicide attacks. It's a concern to us that you're with such a woman. We won't interrogate her as the CIA. We have other people who do that for us in covert situations where identities have to be kept secret. In this case, we would be attempting to keep your identity secret from her. She wouldn't know who she was being questioned by—it would probably be disguised as a home invasion to see if we can get her to crack. We'd position it more as a 'racial' thing, an aggressive act against a visible minority. Get my drift?"

Sean was in shock. He knew exactly what he meant; got his 'drift.' He stood to face the man, eye to eye. "No, I can't let you do that. I'll break it off with her tonight."

He put his hand on Sean's shoulder and squeezed it. "I think you've made the right decision. Yes, do that tonight. Tomorrow we'll discuss the details of your posting."

Sean wiped a tear from his eye as he remembered back to that night. The look on her face when he'd told her that he was in love with someone else. That he'd been carrying on an affair for the last three months, and that he wanted Jannat out of the apartment that very night. She cried and he resisted the undeniable urge to comfort her.

He wanted to swoop her into his arms and tell her to forget everything he'd said. But, he couldn't. He needed her to hate him, and to get away from him as fast as she could, as far away as she could. The image of Jannat being "interrogated" in the way he knew the CIA and their contractors were capable of was more than he could bear.

He knew that his boss had forced his hand. That man knew exactly what decision Sean was going to make. And even if Sean had agreed to allow them to do that to the woman he loved, he knew that after she'd been put through the most horrific experience of her life they would still have disqualified her. He'd been naïve to think that they would ever let him function as an agent with his lover being one of their sworn enemies.

She packed her bags that night and left to stay with a friend. Sean never heard from her or saw her again. It had been eighteen years now, and he wondered almost every day how her life had turned out.

Sean knew full well how his own life had turned out. He was director of the most secretive CIA unit, the Special Activities Division. A division that did everything that no one else could do, or was capable of doing. And virtually all of it was done as covertly as could be imagined. His salary was off the charts and his brain was stimulated every single day. But, most days, it was just gloomy stimulation, just like the skies outside this day. Stuff that just wasn't nice. But, it was such a part of his life now—really, the only life he had—that he was in it up to his neck.

He wondered if life would have been different if…

Sean glanced at his watch. The young lad would be here any minute now. He'd been under house arrest for several days, and it was Sean's turn to take a run at him. There was a time bomb on the horizon, and it was Sean's job to make sure it didn't blow up.

*****

The kid looked like a nerd; a clone of the NSA's Edward Snowden. Sean wondered how these nerdy-looking guys got the nerve to do what they did.

He motioned for the armed guards to leave the room, then in a stern voice ordered Steven Wilmot to sit in one of the guest chairs.

35

"You've been detained now for eight days, Steven. You haven't said a word about what you did. But, I think you've just been talking to the wrong people so far."

The kid winced. "I don't think I should say anything. I want a lawyer."

"The people who have interrogated you so far weren't authorized to tell you what I'm going to tell you. So, brace yourself, Steven. This is the way it's going to be—you won't be allowed to call a lawyer or anyone else for that matter. Before you leave this office, I'll arrest you under the Patriot Act as a traitor and a terrorist, which means indefinite incarceration without a trial. How do you feel about that?"

Steven's brow was getting wetter with each word Sean uttered. "You...can't do that."

Sean smiled. "I can do whatever I want, Steven. I'm the CIA. And the law allows me to do what I just told you. We can thank 9/11 for the Patriot Act. A wonderful piece of broad legislation—so broad I can interpret it pretty much any way I want. No one will ever hear from you again, Steven."

"I want a lawyer."

Sean stood. "You haven't heard a thing I've said. Okay, then, have it your way." Sean walked toward the door. "I'll call the guards back in. Within minutes, you'll be on your way to a military prison for the rest of your life."

"No! Don't! Okay, I'll tell you everything!"

Sean strode back to his chair and sat down. "Don't fuck with me, Steven. I'll be fair with you if you're honest with me. You'll be allowed to go free today—but you have to tell me what happened."

The kid wrung his hands together as he chose his words. "I was contacted by Brock Winters."

"The actor?"

"Yes. I don't know how he got my name. He told me he wanted a bunch of letters that his dad had written while he was in prison. He even knew what safe they were in, and the combination of the safe."

Sean was writing notes. "What did he offer you?"

"Half a million."

Sean whistled. "I can see why you were motivated."

"Yes. Well, I figured that these were just letters from a killer, and who the hell would really care? And if his son wanted Hal Winters' letters, well, why not? I knew Hal Winters had worked for the CIA, so it was logical that documents from him would be kept here. So I didn't doubt what Brock was telling me."

"Correction. Hal Winters *allegedly* worked for the CIA—don't jump to conclusions."

"Right—I know about all that secrecy stuff. Doesn't matter—the letters were in the vault. I got them out, contacted Brock and asked him where he wanted me to send them."

"Is that when Brock deposited the money to your bank account?"

"Yes, I verified the deposit before I relinquished the letters."

Sean made a couple more notes on his pad. "Okay, so why did he ask you to send the letters to a Colin Wentworth in Canada?"

"I don't know—but he was insistent on that. He said Colin was expecting them. Who is he, do you know?"

"I'm asking the questions here, Steven."

Steven lowered his head and nodded.

"And then you confided in someone—or, should I say, bragged to someone."

"I was drinking. A girl who works here at the Agency, same floor as me, came over to my table at the bar. I got a bit carried away."

"That's who told us what you did, Steven. Never trust a pretty girl, son. And, in her case, her job is a lot higher up than your analyst position. She's what the police would call Internal Affairs. Her job is to spy on people like you, get you drunk, and even fuck you if that's what it would have taken. Did she fuck you, Steven?"

Steven Wilmot stared at Sean, naïve shock written all over his face.

Sean waved his hand. "You don't have to answer that last question. It was rhetorical."

As he made the final notations on his pad, Sean realized that the puzzle was now complete, at least as to how it happened. He had discovered who had made the request of his analyst—a famous movie star who obviously had friends in high places. And the two men Sean had assigned to retrieve the letters were dead. Whoever killed them had the letters. Who was this person? He had to find out. And he had to get those letters back before it was too late.

He got up, walked over to the door and motioned the guards back into the room. "He's on the next Company plane to Charlotte. Get him to the airfield on time. Papers are down at the front desk."

Steven jumped to his feet, stammering, "But...y-you promised m-me I could g-go free!"

A wry smile came over Sean's face as he addressed the young man for the last time. "We lie for a living here, son."

Chapter 6

The third cup of coffee was always the worst. It was usually the one drunk purely out of blind habit and obsessive concentration, but the one that also tasted rancid. Brad made a face and pushed it aside. He walked out of his office, over to the kitchen sink, and twisted the brushed nickel handle of his purified water dispenser. Poured a glass, rinsed out his mouth, then poured another one and swallowed it all in one guzzle.

Feeling suitably refreshed, he strode back into his office and sat down once again in front of his computer. Piled up neatly on one corner of his desk were twenty letters from a killer. He hadn't started poring over them yet. First things first—he wanted to know the killer.

Luckily, there was a lot of information splashed over the Internet about Hal Winters. Most of it was hearsay. Interviews with other government operators, mostly retired.

All evidence pointed to him being a lifelong CIA agent, who worked for the Special Activities Division for most of his career. This clandestine group was apparently known in most circles as being charged with working above the law, its agents being assigned contracts that were dangerous, mostly illegal, and untraceable. This division actually worked within the United States as well, whereas the CIA charter forbade such domestic work. That was the purview of the FBI —but the CIA ignored their jurisdiction when it suited their purposes. The two organizations generally despised each other.

Brad never put much faith in the alternative news sources—some of it was just sensational and simply untrue. The stories they covered were oftentimes ridiculous—photos of aliens popping up in forests alongside Sasquatch, ghosts jumping out of nowhere in front of cars racing down the interstates, junior versions of Godzilla roaming the jungles of Brazil. Most of it was just good entertaining fun; nothing more, nothing less.

But, Brad's acute journalistic instincts allowed him to wade through the crap. He could easily sift out the nonsense and find the real stories that seemed to have some truth to them. And these fringe news outlets sometimes offered the only opportunity for the truth to be told—he knew that full well. These organizations, viciously labelled by governments as conspiracy nutcase tabloids, were actually solid news sources for stories that the mainstream media avoided. These stories had to find a home somewhere, and frustrated journalists sometimes just had no choice but to lodge them there and hope to hell that someone with any semblance of a brain would read them.

So, a lot of good solid stories were mixed in with the sensational nutty stuff.

Brad noticed that there was a distinct difference between what the alternative sources reported about Hal Winters, and what the mainstream news wrote about him. The difference was striking.

The mainstream news outlets seemed to concentrate only on the sensational and horrific act that Winters had pled guilty to. The act he'd committed on the day that he'd apparently gone crazy: September 15, 2001.

It was at one of the largest shopping malls in the United States— the Mall of America, in Minneapolis/St. Paul. He had been cornered in a men's clothing store, which he'd apparently walked into disguised in an airline captain's uniform. A strange story, especially since it occurred only four days after the horrific terrorist attacks in New York City and Washington. Anyone "disguised" in an airline uniform would get major headlines.

According to the news reports, witnesses in the store who'd survived the ordeal told of a man who came into the store looking a certain way, and then tried to leave looking like someone else. Left his airline clothes behind in the change room, and walked to the check-out counter wearing jeans and a Minnesota Vikings T-shirt. Paid for the clothes and turned to walk out.

But, he didn't make it. Four men dressed in plainclothes rushed into the store from the mall area, guns drawn. They ordered Winters to raise his hands in the air, but instead he dropped to the floor behind the counter and pulled a pistol out of his waistband—a gun that had been covered up by the Vikings T-Shirt.

The four men began firing and Winters fired back, killing two of them in short order. One witness reported hearing Winters shout: "If you kill me, the truth will come out!" A few more shots rang out until Winters' pistol finally ran out of bullets.

He threw his pistol out from behind the counter and lay on the floor face down, hands outstretched, waiting for the remaining two gunmen to come and get him.

Winters was handcuffed and hauled quickly out of the store. In addition to the two dead gunmen, the floor was littered with eight dead customers. The mainstream news reported that the officers on the scene said that Winters started shooting people indiscriminately— apparently screaming obscenities about government tyranny at the top of his lungs. The fringe news sites reported a different story—that the only thing Winters shouted was: "If you kill me, the truth will come out!"

The mainstream news insisted in their reporting that Winters was a terrorist, caught up in the maelstrom of 9/11, a man fantasizing about being an airline captain and had probably failed in his attempt to take over a jetliner—thus the reason for him being dressed in an airline captain's uniform. They reported that he fired his gun at anyone in the store who moved. He was a mass murderer. A terrorist of the most dangerous type—an American, a domestic.

The fringe news outlets, on the other hand, reported that Hal Winters was a crack shot, a marksman, and the only two people he'd killed that day were two of the unidentified gunmen who apparently started shooting first.

One fringe outlet published a particularly intelligent analysis of the event—including witness statements. People hiding out in the mall area during the shootout reported seeing one of the four gunmen taking direct aim at several customers in the store and shooting them.

Then shooting one of them again once they had Winters in custody. In other words, one of them appeared to be still alive until that second shot was fired. Witnesses at first thought that the man on the ground who was shot twice had been one of the perps, which explained in their minds why he was shot again. But, he was simply a customer who had a bag at his side filled with sports jerseys for his son's tenth birthday.

The fringe news report also raised the fact that no autopsies were done on any of the victims—at least the reports weren't available for viewing when they were requested. Nothing official that said which gun or guns the fatal bullets had come from.

It was an open and shut case. Hal Winters had killed all ten victims and was sent to a federal penitentiary in Georgia for the rest of his life. And he pled guilty, avoiding a trial.

Brad tended to believe the alternative news sources' version of events. But, the fact that the man had pled guilty left a seed of doubt in his mind. Why had he done that?

And what "truth" was Winters referring to when he shouted out to the officers? The fact that all four of the gunmen were in plainclothes made Brad think they were probably FBI.

The mainstream news reports identified Hal Winters as the father of the well-known movie star, Brock Winters. They also identified him as a former mob hit man and a military sharpshooter. They alluded to the fact that he'd worked for the American intelligence services for many years, but didn't say who he was working for at the time of his arrest.

The fringe news services on the other hand, identified him as a lifelong CIA agent, who had performed double duty for a period of several years as a sniper with the military. "Inside sources" reported that Hal Winters was probably the most prolific hit man the CIA had ever produced, being linked to at least forty assassinations in mainly foreign lands, but including a handful of high profile hits at home in the United States as well. Never proven, just "linked."

Yet, during his entire life, despite all the killings he'd apparently participated in, the only convictions against him were the ten dead people in the Mall of America.

The mainstream news seemed to revel in writing about how he had been impersonating a pilot that fateful day, most likely considering a terrorist attack of some sort.

The fringe news gave a slightly more detailed background on the man. One of the skills taught to him by the military and the CIA was flying. Hal Winters apparently had been a Top Gun fighter pilot during a stint with the Navy, then spent several years flying jets for the CIA in their covert drug running operations between Columbia, Mexico, the Caribbean and Florida; a front that was made famous in the movie, *Air America*, starring Mel Gibson and Robert Downey Jr. Air America was used in its early years as a cargo and human airlift operation in Asia, including parts of China and Vietnam. These planes were allowed to get into places covertly, places where the U.S. Air Force wasn't. In later years this airlift fleet moved to the Americas and became a covert participant in the drug wars, busting some of the more violent cartels, but also raising some serious revenue for the CIA.

Another aspect of Hal Winters' skills disclosed by the fringe news was the fact that the man reportedly was trained and rated to fly virtually anything—from fighter jets, the Air America jets, stealth bombers, and helicopters, right up to jumbo passenger jets. It was reported that he was one of the test pilots for the Concorde when it was in its early stages of development. No French pilots were courageous enough to do it, so France called upon the U.S. to volunteer some of their best. Hal Winters was one of those "volunteers."

Another surprising facet of his career, reportedly, was that he'd functioned several times as an armed Air Marshal on American flights where there were hints of hijackings. He was a double threat in that role, because not only was he trained to defend the cabin from hijackers, but if something happened to the pilots he could sit in the cockpit and take over.

None of these facts about Hal Winters was reported by the mainstream press. What they concentrated on was that he was a wingnut who went crazy and shot up a store on September 15, 2001. And was disguised as a pilot. That little point alone scared the shit out of people, which is one thing that the major news outlets loved to do, Brad knew full well.

Brad rubbed his eyes. Staring at his computer for hours on end was taking its toll. He got up and walked into the living room where Kristy was watching a soap opera on TV.

"So, who's fucking who today, Kristy?"

She chuckled. "Don't be cruel. These stories aren't always that shallow. Once in a while they deal with some heavy topics."

Brad dropped down onto the couch and stretched out his legs. "Oh, yeah? Like which of the four rich sons is having an affair with his aunt who he doesn't know is his aunt and she doesn't know he's her nephew?"

"Very funny. You should watch with me once in a while. It might change your mind."

Brad yawned. "I don't think so, hon. I'd be too judgemental and that would just ruin your enjoyment."

Kristy put the show on pause, then crawled over on top of Brad, laying her head on his chest. He wrapped his arms around her and squeezed tight.

She whispered. "Did you find out anything interesting about Hal Winters?"

Brad whispered back. "You bet I did, and it makes your scandalous soap operas look pretty darn boring in comparison."

Chapter 7

September 11, 2001...Hal Winters' bum was getting sore. It had been years since he'd flown one of these 767s. Sure, he'd been in a simulator many times over the years since, but only for an hour or two, just to keep his skills sharp. But, this time, it was a bit more than he was used to. Maybe just age finally catching up with him.

He thought it weird that the cockpits of fighter jets had always seemed more comfortable to him than these luxury jumbo jets. The seats just seemed to hug the hips better in those sleek little machines.

They were approaching Denver now. He picked up the intercom microphone and announced to the passengers, "This is your Captain speaking. Sorry for the diversion, folks, but Denver International is our destination. We've been asked to divert there due to some complications with air traffic today. Hopefully, you won't be stuck in Denver for too long. We'll try to take off again in short order and continue along to our original destination, Los Angeles. At this time, I would ask that you all buckle up as we begin our descent. Thank you."

Hal inserted the mike back into its holder and turned to his co-pilot. "Start pre-landing checklist. I've got the aircraft—starting descent from 35,000 feet. Check."

The first officer answered, "Check, you have the aircraft," and began leafing through the 767 landing checklist chart. Hal took the plane off auto-pilot, grasped onto the yoke with both hands and began guiding the jet down through the levels of altitude.

His partner glanced over at him. "You didn't have to do that—could have just left it on auto-pilot and punched in the coordinates."

Hal smiled. "Yeah, I know—but I still like to have the 'feel' of the plane in my hands, know what I mean? Old-fashioned, I guess."

The first officer smiled back. "Yeah, I'm kinda like that, too. What's the fun of flying if you don't actually fly the damn thing, right?"

Hal lifted his right hand off the yoke and held it out to his partner. "I'm Hal Winters. And I'm assuming that, considering our assignment today, it's okay for me to tell you I'm CIA."

The man shook his hand. "We were instructed not to introduce ourselves—but what the hell. I'm Dave Tuckett, Colonel, U.S. Air Force. Yeah, I was told that out of us eight substitute pilots today, three would be CIA." He chuckled. "Your secret's safe with me."

Hal slapped him on the shoulder. "Good to hear. And pleased to meet you. We've sure had a weird day, huh?"

Dave frowned. "God, I can't figure this one out. On the very day that we're testing the ability to respond to hijackings, there are actual hijackings? What are the odds of that?"

Hal grimaced. "I don't know about you, Dave, but I don't play the odds too often. There's something strange about this whole thing. For one, why are we landing in Denver—why not just go all the way to our destination? Los Angeles isn't that much farther, maybe an hour?"

"They said something about it being safer in Denver today for our size of jet?"

"Yeah, I don't get that. But we're not paid to question, are we? We're just paid to do what we're told—so that's what we're gonna do. I guess the other three test planes are being instructed to land in Denver too. American Airlines 11 should have landed already. Not far behind us will be AA 77 and United 93."

Hal guided the plane down to 15,000 feet after getting a quick clearance from the air traffic controllers in Denver. They advised him to just proceed at the rate of descent that he was currently on.

A few minutes later, with the airport in view a few miles distant, Hal clicked on his headset. "Denver Tower, this is United Flight 175. Confirm runway information, please. Out."

"Roger, 175. Confirm runway 13 left. You are clear to land. No further permissions needed. Out."

"Roger, Tower. Out."

Hal clicked off—then reached inside his jacket pocket and pulled out his cellphone.

He turned to Dave and said, "Hope you don't mind if I break the rules here. I'm curious as hell about what's been goin' on, and we've been kept on radio silence by our military bosses for a couple of hours now."

"No problem, Hal. I'm curious, too."

Hal put the plane back on auto-pilot and tapped his fingers on the instrument panel, putting in the exact coordinates and rate of descent.

"We'll let the plane take over again for a few minutes."

He glanced down at his screen, put in his password, and clicked on his inbox. "I get news headlines sent directly to me. Always up to date that way—to the exact second. It's great."

Dave engaged the flaps, then glanced over at Hal. "Ready for landing gear?"

Hal's mind was elsewhere now, but he managed to say, "Roger. Landing gear."

He then picked up the mike for the intercom. "Prepare for landing. Attendants, take your seats." Then he flipped the button to engage the seat belt sign.

Hal looked back down at his phone, and shook his head from side to side. "Dave, there's something really wrong here."

"What? What's wrong?"

"It says here that passenger jets hit the two World Trade Center Towers in New York, and another one hit the Pentagon. And the two towers have now collapsed."

"Jesus! Collapsed? And the Pentagon was hit, too?"

Hal answered in a soft voice, "Yes."

"Well, they already told us planes had hit the towers. So, it's worse than we thought. I can't believe the towers collapsed. That's unreal. And it took some balls for someone to hit the Pentagon."

Hal scrolled down on his phone.

Suddenly, he gasped.

Turned his head and glared into Dave's eyes. "It's a lot worse, Dave. It says here that our flight, 175, hit the South Tower. And that two of the other test planes in our group, 11, and 77, hit the North

Tower and the Pentagon. And the fourth plane in our little team, 93, crashed in Pennsylvania."

"That's ridiculous! There has to be some mistake. You know how reporting can be screwed up big time in a crisis."

Hal nodded and sighed. "True. You're probably right. Does seem kinda strange, though, don't you think?"

He turned his attention back to the instrument panel, and switched off the auto-pilot.

A few minutes later, Hal expertly guided the plane down for a soft landing onto runway 13. He heard the Tower buzz his headset. He clicked back on.

"Flight 175—follow runway 13 to the end, then take ramp 13A to your starboard and proceed to follow the flags."

Both of the pilots were silent as Hal proceeded along as instructed. Runway 13 was one of the longest at the monstrous Denver airport.

He took the plane to the very end, then turned starboard onto ramp 13A. Hal saw the flag bearers about 300 feet ahead.

Then he saw something else—something so bizarre that it made his stomach churn. Ramp 13A came to a dead end at a large grassy mound. And as they approached, the mound began to open upward. The fucking hill was opening up like a trap door, and he could see a dark abyss beyond its opening.

"Apply brakes!"

Dave obeyed the command, and the plane crawled to a stop. The flag bearers ahead were waving frantically now. Hal could see that they weren't normal airport flag bearers. They were dressed in military uniforms.

"Hal, what the fuck is that tunnel?"

Hal winced. "I don't know, Dave, but I don't like this. Wanna know why I don't like this?"

"Yeah."

"We're all dead. We were supposed to have crashed into the South Tower. We don't exist anymore. I thought it was strange when I realized we were flying only fifty-six passengers out of a total capacity of 168. That alone was strange for a jumbo jet. Now they're reporting in the news that all fifty-six are dead, plus the nine crew. It's not a news-reporting mistake. We're not supposed to surface again. Ergo, this tunnel to who knows where."

"What the fuck is going on?"

"I don't know what the hell hit the South Tower, but we know that it sure wasn't us. I suspect that we, and the other three test planes, were just props in a stage show. That's what this is starting to feel like. And they can't possibly allow us to be seen again. Because we're supposed to be dead. We were apparently hijacked and then deliberately flown into that tower."

Dave gulped and, in a strained voice, asked, "Plan?"

"The only one that comes to mind is that we'd better fucking run for our lives. My instincts are telling me that we're all in deep doo-doo. Are you packing?"

Dave pulled back his jacket, displaying his sidearm.

"Okay, me, too. We have to get everyone off this plane. Then we run."

Hal unfastened his seat belt and ignored the frantic flag bearers up ahead waving them towards the ominous mouth of the tunnel to nowhere.

"Let's go!"

They both rushed out of the cockpit and into the first galley. A huddle of flight attendants were standing there, talking in hushed tones.

The head steward spoke. "Captain, why have you stopped the plane out here, so far from the terminal?"

Hal addressed the group. "Listen to me carefully. We don't have much time. We have an emergency. Open all six exit doors and evacuate the passengers."

"But…we can't sir. The bridges haven't pulled up. And the doors are armed for the inflatable slides."

"I know. Don't disarm them. Just open the doors and let the slides inflate. Then organize the fastest emergency exit you've ever trained for."

"Sir, what do we tell the passengers?"

"Tell them to run for the open fields and not to stop for anyone. And to keep running. Get as far away from this goddamn airport as they can."

"But—"

"Do it! Now! It's a matter of life or death!"

The flight attendants didn't wait to be yelled at again. They moved fast, their professional training rising to the surface of their consciousness. The doors were opened and the slides inflated. Then, one by one, the passengers disembarked. There wasn't much panic— just a lot of puzzled faces. Within mere minutes all of the passengers were out on the tarmac and, true to their instructions, were running towards the vast open fields that surrounded the Denver airport.

After the passengers were all out safely, the attendants came back to the front of the plane where Hal and Dave were standing. "Sir, what now?"

"Now it's your turn. Go! Follow your passengers!"

The attendants slid out through the front left exit door and hit the tarmac, one by one. Off they ran in the same direction as the confused passengers.

Hal turned to Dave. "Follow my lead, Colonel. Let me do the talking." He nodded down at the tarmac. "I see we have company already."

A military Jeep had pulled up just next to the nose of the jumbo jet. Two armed officers got out and walked over to the edge of the slide.

"Okay. But, Hal, those are supposed to be the good guys."

Hal put both his hands on the sides of Dave's head, and shook it hard. "You're young, around thirty?"

Dave nodded, shocked at the force Hal was exerting on his head.

"I'm a lot older, and I've seen more than you'll see in a lifetime. Right now, except for us, there are no good guys. Trust me on this. You, me, and our passengers and crew, are the only good guys on this tarmac. I think your instincts are telling you the same thing, but you're just too young and patriotic to listen to them. So—listen to mine if you want to live. And be prepared to use your weapon. Even against the good guys."

Dave nodded, a look of abject astonishment on his face. Hal slapped him on the back. "Okay, let's go. You first."

Dave swung himself through the door, then slid down to the pavement. Hal followed three seconds later.

Once at the bottom, Hal led the way over to the two officers who were standing just a few feet away.

One of them spoke. "Captain, what's the problem?" He nodded his head off towards the tunnel. "You were supposed to follow the flags. And...the passengers. Why were they all running away?"

Hal glanced back in the direction of where his charges had gone. His heart sank, as he saw a column of military vehicles cutting off their escape. They were now huddled together at the far end of the runway. Sadly, they'd never reached the relative safety of the fields. Hal nudged Dave to take a look back, too. His face instantly lost its color in seeing the dozen or so Jeeps surrounding the passengers and crew.

Hal turned back to the officer. "We had an emergency onboard the plane—smoke in the cabin. We couldn't risk it."

"Oh, I see. Well, get into the Jeep and we'll take you over to Registration."

Hal took his cap off and smoothed back his thick blonde hair. "Registration? What's that? Why don't we just wander over to the terminal?"

"No, sir. That's not the plan for today. It's a dangerous day today, due to the terrorist attacks back east. We need to take you to Registration."

"You still haven't told me what that is."

"Not my place to say, sir. Follow us, please."

The officer turned, but was only able to move one step before he felt the cold steel of Hal's pistol against the back of his head. Dave followed Hal's lead, and rammed his gun against the other officer's forehead. With their free hands, they yanked the soldiers' pistols out of their holsters.

Hal's voice took on a different tone now, borne from decades of experience as a trained killer. "This is what you're both going to do.

Run towards your fucking tunnel and don't stop. If you stop, I'll kill you. And trust me, even with a pistol I can hit you within 100 yards."

The two young officers turned and ran. No more orders, no more questions. They didn't even turn their heads to glance back; not once.

Hal yelled at Dave. "Okay, into the Jeep! Let's get outta here!"

They ran to the Jeep and jumped in, Hal at the wheel.

Dave asked, "What about the passengers and crew?"

"Can't do anything for them now. We did our best."

Hal slipped the vehicle into gear and sped off toward the fields farthest away from the military vehicles that had surrounded the hapless travelers of Flight 175. He put his foot to the floor, skidded off the tarmac and into the tall grass.

Dave opened his window and shoved his head outside. "Hal, there's a vehicle gaining on us!"

"Shoot his tires out!"

"Can't be accurate with this pistol."

"I noticed a rifle in a rear rack. Use that."

Dave reached behind him and yanked it out of its holder. "Yeah, this'll work."

He swung the rifle out the window and took aim at the front tires of the military SUV creeping up behind them. Just as he pulled the trigger, Hal heard another shot. It smashed through the rear window. There was a sickening groan...then silence.

He glanced over at the very dead Colonel Dave Tuckett, half of his head cruelly abandoned somewhere in the grass behind them. He was slumped over the door frame, rifle still cradled in the crook of his arm.

Hal cursed, then slammed on the brakes. The Jeep skidded in the grass and came to a stop. He pulled the rifle off Dave's arm, shoved open his door, and dove to the grass. Lying near the left rear wheel, he assumed a very familiar sniper position. Hidden from view, he waited until company arrived.

And they did. Both officers jumped out of the SUV, one with a rifle, the other with a pistol. They cautiously approached the Jeep, probably thinking that both the occupants were either injured or dead.

Hal noticed that both were wearing body armor, and their helmets left only about four square inches of forehead. With their hearts protected, Hal had only one choice. But, four square inches of forehead was more than enough for his skills.

He pulled the trigger twice. In rapid succession, the soldiers went down.

Threat eliminated.

Mission accomplished—as with so many others in years gone by.

Hal calmly walked around to the passenger side of the Jeep. Opened the door, pulled Dave's body out, and laid it gently on the ground. Then he saluted.

He jumped back in the Jeep and roared off in the direction of the highway that he knew wasn't far off.

But, first, he had a perimeter gate to crash. He took that down in short order. The metal rods flew up and over the powerful steel hood of the military Jeep, and on the other side of the crushed gate the vehicle enjoyed the welcome feel of solid pavement again.

Hal Winters headed east. Back in the direction he'd flown from just a few hours before. Back when life seemed simpler than it did right now.

And, surprisingly, considering Hal's occupation, the world itself seemed a lot safer and saner a few hours ago than it did right now.

Hal blinked his eyes three times. Then rolled his head around and around, stretching the muscles in his strong neck.

There were four things he had to do next. His powerful mind was thinking fast. He was on auto-pilot.

First, he had to get rid of this Jeep and steal another car—quickly.

Second, he had to drive as far away as possible; as fast as he could without attracting unwanted attention.

Third, he had to find a large shopping mall where he could disappear into the crowd while he shopped for new clothes.

Finally, he had to write a letter and mail it along with a certain little cassette tape.

Chapter 8

September 18, 2001...Hal Winters glanced around at the dingy little world he was now confined to. It was tight, really tight, and bars separated him from the hustle and bustle he could hear going on outside his cell.

Hal knew he was still in Minneapolis. After they'd hauled him out of the Mall of America in handcuffs, it had only been a short car ride to this holding cell. Somewhere in the center of the city.

But he knew he wouldn't be here long. He was too high profile a prisoner to stay in this low-profile facility. They'd want him locked up good and solid. With thick walls on the perimeter of even thicker interior walls, armed guards and high-tech monitoring.

Particularly since he knew enough to blow the lid off the greatest deception ever pulled over the eyes of the world.

Hal struggled to his feet. It hurt to perform even that simple task. They'd kicked him in the balls so many times he'd lost count. He was afraid to pull down his pants to take a look at the damage they'd inflicted. He'd already peed his pants several times, just from the inability to hold it—brutal force against the nether-regions will do that to a man. He knew that full well, having done it to a few prisoners himself over the years, under the explicit orders and benevolent authorization of the Central Intelligence Agency.

He staggered over to the little mirror hanging on the wall and took a look at his face. He muttered to himself, "Hmm...not so handsome anymore, am I?" Then he chuckled and grumbled, "Well, I'm fifty years old now, what do I expect?" What stood out the most reflecting back at him from the mirror were his eyes. Both of them swollen up like apples, with the color of over-ripe plums. He opened his mouth—

two of his lower front teeth were missing, and his right jaw seemed somewhat crooked. He muttered again, "If they decide to let me live, Uncle Sam's crappy health care system owes me some cosmetic work."

Hal picked up a dirty paper cup, turned the handle of the rusted tap and poured himself a glass of something that resembled water, although it looked more like stagnant pond scum. It would have to do. He tilted his head back, took a sip and gargled. Then he spit it out. Another tooth tinkled into the sink, accompanied by blood-red rinse.

Hal sat back down on the metal cot and gently rubbed his swollen jaw. And listened to the footsteps that were stomping down the hallway. He could tell there were two sets of feet making the authoritative stomping—they wanted him to know they were coming.

He reluctantly looked down at his crotch. "Brace yourselves, boys. More lovin' comin' your way."

There was a jangle of keys and the cage door opened. Two goons walked in—they looked like the same stooges who had kicked the shit out of him non-stop for the last three days, but he couldn't be sure. His eyes were looking out through narrow slits now, and were a bit blurry from the bloodshot souvenirs of his beatings.

But, he held his head high.

They stood over him, trying their damnedest to intimidate him. Clearly, they were forgetting who he was, and forgetting the fact that he had been trained even better than they had been. Hal was a legend, but it was hard to get respect from the young studs the CIA hired these days.

Hal Winters could withstand torture. He had been taught to be in total control at all times, within his mind and his body. Even though he was in his fifties, he had the stamina and physical abilities of a thirty-year-old.

"Well, Mr. Winters. Do we have to beat the shit out of you again, or are you going to talk to us now?"

Hal spread his arms out wide with palms up, in a gesture of cooperation. "I have been talking to you guys. I don't know what else you want from me."

One of the goons took a step closer. "You know what we want.

You said that if we killed you, the truth would come out. What truth?"

Hal sighed. "You know what, boys? To spare my balls another beating, I'm going to open up to you. Only because you have such great bedside manners. That jumbo jet I was commanding had its own flight recorder, which obviously I couldn't take with me. But—I had my own flight recorder—in the pocket of that United Airlines uniform that I was proudly wearing on that fateful...no, correction... "fakeful"... day. You know the kind of slick little instrument I'm talking about— I'm sure you've used them before. Well, it caught everything—the orders from the ground, the conversations about how the 'test' was to be conducted. And the conversations between me and my co-pilot. Everything a conniving person like me would need to show the world that flight 175 did not crash into the South Tower that day. Instead, it ended up at Denver International Airport and was ordered to pull into some monstrous fucking tunnel."

The second goon brought his hands to his hips and took a military stance, feet wide apart. "Where is that tape?"

Hal rubbed his sore jaw. "You see, that's the funny part, boys. Ironic that the U.S. Postal Service has acted as my agent here. Isn't that hilarious? It has probably already arrived at its destination, courtesy of the government we're all so loyal to."

A heavy foot struck Hal in the face. He heard the bones in his nose crunch with the impact. Blood was dripping into his mouth, the salty taste from being mixed with his sweat strangely soothing.

Hal glared up at the guy. "I'm in the driver's seat, you prick. And if you do that again, I'll kill you."

Both goons laughed, mockingly, just as two more men arrived at the gate to Hal's cell. He glanced through the bars at them and grinned. "I'm sure you've been listening in on this little conversation. Call off your boys. Our friendly little chat is over."

One of them, dressed to the nines in a silk suit, asked in a quietly menacing voice, "Who did you send it to?"

"Someone who's been instructed to provide copies to every media outlet in the world, if anything happens to me, my sons, or my ex-wife. You decide."

The silk suit guy nodded at the goon who had just broken Hal's nose. A foot came flying at his face once again. This time Hal grabbed it in mid-air and twisted it in a 180-degree arc, forcing the man to the ground face-down. Hal moved fast. He leaped on top of the prone figure, raised his right hand—stretching his index and middle fingers out in the shape of a dagger—and rammed them down and through the base of the man's skull. The beast gasped, quivered, and then went limp.

Hal got to his feet, staring down at the eerily still figure. "I warned you, asshole."

Suddenly, the other goon rushed at him. Hal flipped his hand up and smashed him flat in the face. The man went down hard. Hal pounced on him, and put his open hand on the man's crotch. "Kicking doesn't do much permanent damage to the balls, you prick. But, this does."

Hal squeezed his hand into the tightest fist he'd ever formed, and he felt the man's sack crush in his grasp in cadence with the most blood-curdling sound of agony he'd ever heard in his life.

He then stood and stared at the two suits standing dispassionately on the outside of the cell.

"Your call. You know who I am, and you know who you're dealing with. If you want your little secret kept from the world, you had better fucking keep me and my family alive. Enough of this kicking me in the balls crap. Let's make a deal, huh?"

Silk suit man spoke, in a tone that was less threatening than it had been a few minutes before. "Plead guilty to the killings at the mall. Avoid a public trial. We'll send you to a medium security pen in Georgia."

Hal nodded. "Agreed. And I expect to be treated with respect. And to be allowed communication with the outside world, subject to your usual screening. I'll have a few more reasonable demands when I can think clearer. Right now, my balls hurt like hell and my brain is dull. I need new teeth and my jaw has to be re-set. I want my movie star looks back. If I'm gonna be your star prisoner in Georgia—the so-called 'Mall of America Mass Murderer'—I have to look good for the Press."

Silk suit man grimaced. "Your sarcastic sense of humor isn't appreciated right now."

Hal grinned. "Oh, sure it is. C'mon, gimme a smile."

"Fuck off."

Hal chuckled. "Okay, be a grump." Then, in an instant, Hal lowered his voice to a growl. "You'd better fucking keep me and my family alive."

Silk suit nodded slowly, grudgingly. "We'll keep you alive."

Chapter 9

The first letter was dated December 7, 2001. Almost three months after the infamous Hal Winters had been nabbed at the Mall of America for the mass murder of ten people. And only two months after he'd pled guilty to the murders—no trial, no testimony, no attempt at freedom.

Brad thought this was very odd indeed. A cunning and calculating man such as Winters—or at least that's how he'd been portrayed in everything written about him—didn't even try to defend himself?

He was immediately incarcerated at the Atlanta Federal Penitentiary. They threw away the key. Ten life sentences pretty much guaranteed he'd never see a sunrise or sunset again. He wouldn't even get to see the spring peach blossoms in the lovely state of Georgia.

This prison had hosted some pretty bad dudes. Sounded like Hal was in good company. Al Capone, the head of the so-called Chicago Outfit, had graced the pen with his presence until he was transferred to Alcatraz Island. And Jimmy Burke, portrayed so brilliantly by Robert De Niro in *Goodfellas*, was another one of the prison's famous residents.

Brad scanned over a few more of the criminal names who had lived and died in the Atlanta facility. It seemed, by the list at least, that the prison was a popular choice for Mafia figures. So, of course, it made sense that Hal Winters had been sent there—the official stories seemed to have condemned him to being a Mafia hit man more than a CIA assassin. Brad doubted that fairy tale.

But what surprised Brad the most was that the Atlanta prison was only medium security. For someone who'd been convicted of mass murder, a crazy man who shot up a store in one of America's largest malls, and someone who the authorities and the press persisted in hinting was a potential terrorist because he'd been dressed in a pilot's uniform, Brad figured he would have been sent to a maximum security facility.

So, that didn't make sense, and neither did the fact that he'd pled guilty. Were the two anomalies related? Was that part of his deal for pleading guilty? Did he insist that he be placed in a medium security prison? One that would allow him regular visitors as well as the freedom to send letters to friends and family?

And why indeed had Hal Winters been dressed in a pilot's uniform? And why did this incident in the Mall of America happen just four days after the 9/11 horrors? Was there any significance to that? Or just coincidence?

The timing of this whole thing seemed incredible to Brad's sharp journalistic mind. There was a story here—he just didn't know what it was yet.

He spread the twenty letters out across his desk. Then, just as quickly, he shifted them all back into a neat little pile, pulled the very first letter off the top and laid it on the desk in front of him. Brad decided that the best way to proceed was not to let his mind be affected or tainted by any of the future letters. Best to start at the beginning.

He put on his reading glasses. Right away, he was struck by how neat the man's handwriting was, perfectly drawn letters, impeccable spelling, words sitting perfectly on the lines of the page. This seemed paradoxical to Brad—he never would have imagined a killer being so precise in his letter-writing.

He was just caught up in typecasting, he guessed. A natural thing to do—someone who killed other human beings would be imagined as being a slob, evil as hell, and cavalier in how he presented himself. Not so with this Hal Winters character—he appeared educated and quite proper, including his choice of words. The man was indeed articulate.

Brad turned on his desk lamp and began to read the first letter, dated December 7, 2001:

Dearest Richard:

This is my first letter as a guest of the Atlanta Federal

Penitentiary, and I decided that I would favor you. Aren't you the lucky one? I'm being treated just fine; in fact, I seem to be somewhat of a celebrity here. I have my own cell, and the food is actually pretty good.

I get to go out in the yard a couple of times a day and socialize with the other outcasts of society. And, eating in the dining room is a bit of a treat—the contact with other guests is soothing to my brain, which at times becomes quite stale spending so much time alone.

I have a window in my cell, and sometimes I think I'm seeing mirages; outside is just nothing but concrete due to the outer wall on the perimeter. But, I swear I can see lakes, and trees, and other tricks of the brain.

I know it's just wishful thinking on my part, that someday I may see those things again. Things that I miss so much, things that I probably took for granted when I had my freedom. In fact, I know I took them for granted—thought they'd always be there for my eyes to see, but now my eyes are just playing tricks on me. Seeing things that just aren't there. In reality, there's nothing but concrete, basketball hoops, and exercise equipment. Instead of those things, I'm seeing lakes and trees!

I hope you are well. I miss our chats—always very stimulating, and as you know, I tend to get bored quite easily.

I hope you'll be able to get over here from England sometime and pay me a visit. Would love to see you.

Your friend always,

Hal

Brad read the letter three times. It did seem like just a normal letter—nothing special going on, just a guy lamenting his loss of freedom. But amazingly articulate, and Brad was also touched by how there was really no moaning or complaining expressed in the letter. Hal seemed like someone at peace with himself, and at peace with where he was in his life. Just being realistic maybe? Or resigned?

All of the letters had been sent to a Richard Sterling in Coventry, England. Brad had done some searches on the Internet and so far, had found no reference to such a person in that particular town. As well as the letters themselves, that puzzled him, too. He wondered who Richard Sterling was, and why Hal Winters had written to him so many times. What was their relationship?

Of course, Winters could have written to dozens of people over the time he was incarcerated, right up until his death in 2011. But, these were the only letters Brad had. So, why were these letters so important? Why did Colin Wentworth have those letters in the first place, and why had he given Brad one of them? What did he want him to do with it?

Well, now Brad had all twenty, and his journalistic instinct told him there was a story here, especially considering the violence that had surrounded the letters back on Vancouver Island. There was something deadly sinister going on, and the letters perhaps held the key to unlock the mystery. Why did people have to die for these letters? Brad shivered as his mind shifted back to the bloody scenes in the cottage and the cabin.

He went into the kitchen and poured himself his third cup of coffee. It was still early in the morning, and he usually needed about five cups before noon in order to function like a normal human being. Kristy had gone out shopping, so it was nice and quiet in the apartment for him to concentrate.

Brad sat back down at his desk, opened the drawer and pulled out a legal pad. He clicked his pen nervously as he scanned the first letter once again. He wrote a title at the top of the first page of his notepad: Letter Number One, December 7, 2001.

Then he began jotting down words and phrases that seemed out of place, words that might mean something: *guest; favor; lucky; celebrity; socialize; outcasts; treat; soothing; stale; mirages; tricks of the brain; wishful; eyes are playing tricks; seeing things that just aren't there; basketball; exercise; lakes,* and *trees.*

Brad didn't know what to make of it all at this point—any one of the words or phrases could be a clue to something, or they could be nothing at all. They could just simply be part of a well-written, friendly letter.

He decided to move on. The letters could mean something collectively rather than individually, so Brad wanted to resist the common journalistic trap of analysis paralysis. He needed to go through all of the letters one by one.

The next three, from what he could tell, said nothing at all. They were just short and to the point—no words or phrases worth noting. One simply wished a Merry Christmas to the Sterling family in 2002, another one wished Happy Easter in 2004, and then Merry Christmas again in 2005.

Letter number five was a bit different though. After more than a four-year lull, Hal Winters had suddenly become communicative again. The letter was dated July 2, 2006:

Dearest Richard:

It's been a while since I've written to you, and I do hope this letter finds you well. I'm doing fine for the nonce, but this darn depression is getting me down a bit. The guards have all been treating me fine though, and are sympathetic to my state of mind.

I couldn't ask for nicer keepers, and have actually become quite good friends with some of them. We have some good games of chess together in the late afternoons before chow-time.

One of my guard friends felt so bad for me because my radio broke. So, he bought me a new one—isn't that nice of him? Even though he's the guard, I'm the prisoner, and sometimes we're going in two different directions, there are a lot of things we do see eye to eye on. It's nice. Makes my time here more pleasant.

He even bought me a new deck of cards as well. I play a lot of solitaire, as you might imagine and I noticed that the ace of clubs was missing from my deck the other day. I got kinda frantic—can't play cards with a deck of fifty-one. So, Ian was good enough to buy me a new deck. I love these new cards—nice and shiny and slippery. The old deck had indeed gotten old in the tooth.

Anyway, back to the radio, I heard a song the other day that reminded me of Anne. Even though we divorced, I never stopped loving her, as you know. I was just a very poor husband—she deserved better.

I don't know where she lives now—I know you do and that she asked you not to tell me. So, could you at least pass along a message to her and tell her that I was listening to the tune "Annie's Song" and that I thought of her? Could you tell her that for me, old friend? Please? I know, it probably won't make a difference to her to hear that I was thinking about her—I guess I'm just living on the wings of a dream here. But, it would mean a lot to me.

Well, time for me to say goodbye for the nonce. I hope to hear from you soon.

Your friend always,

Hal

Brad sat up straight in his chair and rubbed his chin. This letter was indeed interesting—there were a lot of words and phrases that, in Brad's mind, seemed planned and out of context. Almost unnecessary. He couldn't really understand why he felt that way; maybe he was just looking for things that didn't exist.

But, his detective instincts told him that some of these expressions had real meaning. Deeply hidden behind the smoke screen of an innocent letter, but he had the distinct feeling that this letter—and the first one—weren't so innocent.

He picked up his pen and began jotting: *nonce; depression; keepers; chess; radio; two different directions; deck of cards; solitaire; Ace of Clubs; fifty-one; old in the tooth; Annie's Song; on the wings of a dream.*

He turned his head suddenly at the sound of Kristy coming through the door, several plastic bags in each hand. She was huffing and puffing.

"Brad, dear, could you go down to the car and get the rest of the bags? Please? I'm so tired from shopping and I just don't have the energy to go down forty floors to the garage again."

Brad got up from his chair and ran over to give Kristy a hug. "Of course, baby. What are you making for dinner tonight?"

"How about lamb chops?"

"Oh, wow! I'll definitely go down to the garage for you, then!"

She kissed him on the cheek. "What would you have said if my answer was liver and onions?"

Brad frowned. "I would have said, 'Let's go out for dinner.'"

"Clearly, you can be bought."

"Yes, food is indeed the key to a man's soul."

She smacked him on the bum. "Good thing I'm a good cook, then. How did your work on the letters go?"

Brad grabbed the car keys off the counter. "Really good, so far. But I'm gonna need some expert help. What I think I'm seeing is way above my pay grade."

Chapter 10

The flight from Washington's Reagan airport was smooth. A sunny and calm day, perfect for flying the friendly skies into Canada.

The Continental Airlines jet landed in Toronto on time, and now Sean Russell had about two hours to kill before his connecting flight to Calgary. Then on from there to Victoria which was located on Vancouver Island. He'd been to Canada many times before, and absolutely loved the country. He never failed to notice how much cleaner and more organized the airports were in Canada compared to America. In the States it was absolute chaos at the best of times.

He cleared customs and immigration quickly, and answered all of the prying questions about who he was and what he was doing in Canada. Didn't identify that he was with the CIA, of course. Not that he wouldn't be allowed to do that, it was just cleaner if he didn't. Particularly if something nasty happened when he was in another country—a CIA agent would be one of the first people they'd track down for a friendly little chat.

The general rule was that family members and acquaintances weren't allowed to know what an agent did for a living. They would only know the cover story. Sean, being a lawyer, used the "front" law firm in Washington as his cover for most of his assignments in and around the United States. For foreign adventures, there were other covers he could use if the lawyer front wouldn't fly.

He was permitted to use CIA credentials when on official assignments and when he had to pull rank. Or when dealing with other government officials within the U.S. or foreign countries. If the credentials worked to the CIA's advantage in opening tightly closed doors, then they were permitted to be used. And, of course, once an agent retired he could freely say what he had done for a living. The secrecy ended upon retirement—and upon death.

But, for this trip to Canada, Sean decided to use the cover identifying him as a diamond importer, only because it was believable. The CIA owned a diamond importing business as one of its fronts and, conveniently, one of its offices was located in the beautiful city of Victoria on Vancouver Island.

So, today, Sean was a diamond importer from Washington, and he answered that way when the customs and immigration people gave him the usual third degree. He breezed through without any trouble, but the friendly immigration lady was intrigued by his diamond business. She had some specific questions, of a personal nature. The lady flashed her engagement ring at Sean and asked his opinion. Sean took an authentic looking loupe out of his pocket and pretended to give the ring serious scrutiny. Then he smiled at her and gave the thumbs up sign.

"That's a quality diamond. Don't worry, your fiancé didn't cheap out on you."

She smiled at him, clearly relieved. "Oh, thank you so much. He's famous for taking shortcuts, so I was a little worried."

"Ha, ha…don't you worry. That's a very nice ring. I hope you'll both be very happy together."

Sean gave her a little wave of his hand and started walking through to the Domestic Connections wing in Terminal One of Toronto's Pearson Airport. He chuckled to himself, hoping he hadn't given that woman a bum steer. He didn't have a clue as to whether hers was a good diamond or not, or even if it was real. His cover was designed to simply open doors easily if confronted and challenged, but as a last resort he'd always use his official federal government identification. He seldom had to do that, because he was just pretty darn good at bluffing his way through.

His gate was a long way down at twenty-seven, so he hopped onto the moving sidewalk and let the machine do the work. Sean eyed the hordes of people as the track took him smoothly along to his destination. Marvelled at how unstressed they all looked. Relaxed, laughing. Two men in a hurry walked past him on the track and excused themselves. Canadians were very polite, as well as being relaxed. He knew that if he was in an airport in the States, those guys would have just rudely pushed past him without saying a word of apology.

He jumped off the track and strolled over to Gate 27. Saw an ice cream shop and bought himself a butterscotch ripple cone. Then he sat down and picked up a newspaper from the seat next to him. The top headline screamed "Ebola." And the one underneath was the latest on ISIS.'

He shook his head sadly. The world was in such chaos right now, and he knew that he and his colleagues had certainly done their level best to make it what it was. He had regrets, lots of them. While his job was stimulating, he knew at times it was rife with misguided deeds. Operations that would just get out of hand. But, ones that had certainly seemed like good ideas at the time.

One thing the CIA always overlooked was that it was difficult, if not impossible at times, to put the genie back in the bottle. Sometimes they just went too far—tried to manipulate things into a desired result, but instead got kicked in the ass.

If the populace ever discovered the truth about some of the tragic things that had happened over the last two decades, and *how* they'd happened, Sean was fairly certain the United States and most of Europe would become powder kegs.

Luckily, the media, such as the newspaper he was reading right now, was controlled. At least for now.

He and his colleagues dreaded the rise of the "alternative" news. Those outlets were gaining fast in recognition, earning more credibility—starting to be listened to. There were too many leaks now, and scores of mistakes—some very blatant ones. And the data being released about the NSA, a tiny bit at a time—some of it coming out of Russia—might prove hard to explain away if it continued at the pace it was leaking.

If the alternative media started getting some serious backing from powerful groups whose interests were perceived as no longer being served by the United States government, there would be hell to pay. If those alternative sources started streaming into the normal network channels, it would be dangerous. Right now, they existed in the shadows, in the dark—on YouTube and other fringe Internet sites. The CIA had done a pretty effective job of infiltrating those sites, putting spies on as commentators and contributing editors. These folks were able to provide disinformation, basically with the intent of destroying the credibility of the fringe news. In other words, they made up some things that were so outrageous that it made it hard for the public to believe the stuff that was actually accurate. This strategy had worked for at least a decade now, but it was starting to lose its glow. Some of the CIA's plants were being discovered, called out. The disinformation strategy had a shelf life, and that life was fast reaching its expiry date.

For the most part though, the fringe news was just good entertainment and that was all; most people didn't pay much attention to anything that didn't show up on mainstream news channels. Just like the average consumers always gravitated to the name brand foods at their grocery stores, even though generic versions were just as good, and cheaper.

The power of branding was strong, and that applied to the news media world, too. It was a trust thing. Viewers didn't know why they trusted, they just did because of the sheer power of branding.

The alternative news sources hadn't yet succeeded in branding themselves positively. But the CIA feared that could gradually—and maybe not so gradually—change. The information revolution was in acceleration mode, and it was virtually impossible to control or keep up with it anymore.

Danger lurked around every corner now. If the average citizen started paying attention to alternative news sources in an avalanche of curiosity, there would be hell to pay. Revolution at the very least. Blood in the streets. Americans killing Americans. Allies abandoning America.

Because there was just no telling what people would do if it finally resonated in their brains that they'd been lied to by the officials they'd been trusting, and by the name brand media that they had placed total faith in. The era of Walter Cronkite had ended long ago, but the public just hadn't caught on yet.

So, in essence, now the government ran the risk of blackmail—by foreign governments and by media moguls. And by the emerging alternative media moguls. There were enemies everywhere now, due to the information revolution. The CIA hadn't really anticipated this emerging trend very well—they should have, but they hadn't. They were more obsessed with causing mischief, than spending equal time planning for how they'd contain the truths about all that mischief.

Sean knew that his job would only get tougher—not only in intelligence collection and containment, but also in the "shoveling shit" department. So many things were coming to the surface now, ready to explode, that a lot of his time would be spent just putting out fires.

Putting out fires on things he'd had nothing to do with at the time they were set. Covering up for acts that happened back when he was still doing clandestine work over in the Middle East. Acts that were carried out when he was not included in the "need to know" group.

Now that he was so high up in the CIA almost nothing was excluded from him. He was considered need to know on virtually everything.

And a lot of it didn't sit well with him. He was a loyal government employee, but some of the things he knew about now, Sean wished he didn't know.

Like the story behind these letters from Hal Winters—the reason for his trip to Vancouver Island. He was going there to retrace the steps. And hopefully start the process in discovering who had killed his two men. And the name of the person who now had possession of the letters.

This was the shoveling shit part of the job that Sean hated the most. Schemes that he'd had no say in, and would have voted against, were now backfiring on the country. There were loose ends out there that were extremely dangerous. Explosive details that could never get out. And it was his job now to make sure they didn't.

Sean was becoming increasingly uncomfortable with that, and he didn't quite understand why at this stage in his life he was starting to feel that way. This had been his life for so long, but now feelings of dread were creeping up on him.

He snapped out of his daydream. An exotically beautiful woman walked by and smiled at him as she strolled along to the next gate. Duffle bag in hand, green eyes, long black hair—a vision of loveliness that jolted him into the past. She could have been a twin of Jannat. Of Middle Eastern descent for sure, but she dressed like a westerner, just like Jannat always had. Sean felt a twinge in his heart as he remembered back. Pictured her exotic face in his mind, felt her smooth skin against his naked body, laughing at her laughs, wincing at her teasing, loving her day in and day out.

Until he abandoned her. Threw her under the bus in favor of his career in the intelligence services. Cast her aside like useless garbage. Just for his career.

For this. Sitting in an airport getting ready to fly across Canada to shovel shit.

Sometimes, in fact at least once every single day, he really and truly hated himself.

Sean glanced down at his watch, then looked up and noticed that several Air Canada attendants were already at the counter preparing for boarding. The waiting area was full to the brim now.

A Middle Eastern family took the last four seats, right across from Sean. Mother, father, two little boys. The mother was wearing a hijab covering her head and flowing down over her chest area. She had a pretty face, and with the hijab framing that face Sean thought she looked like renditions of the Virgin Mary, which of course was the exact opposite end of the spectrum from her obvious religion.

Suddenly, two young men dressed in expensive pleated trousers and Greg Norman golf shirts rushed into the waiting area and slammed their duffle bags onto the floor in disgust. One of them cursed, "Damn! No seats left."

Sean glanced at them sideways while pretending to read his paper. One was bald and the other had thick hair worn down over his ears. He figured them to be in their mid-thirties.

Preppies. Probably heading to Calgary for a week of golfing heaven in the Rockies.

The other guy started cursing, loud enough for most people to hear. "Christ, it's still about half an hour before we board. I need a cigarette!"

The bald guy made a face. "Hell, surely you can control your habit for a few hours."

His friend laughed. "Yes, I can. But, stop calling me Shirley."

They both bust out laughing, while Sean rolled his eyes.

The bald guy suddenly walked over and stood in front of the Middle Eastern family.

"Would you please consider giving up your seats for a couple of hard-working Canadians?"

The father looked up at him. "We are Canadians too, sir."

The long-haired guy joined his friend and pointed at the mother. "Well, not really. Look at what she's wearing on her head. When you become Canadian, you don't continue to wear those things."

The mother kept her head down, but the father decided to stand and face the men eye to eye. "Excuse me, are we bothering you?"

"Yes, we'd like to sit down. Maybe you can all go sit on a camel or something?"

They both doubled over in laughter.

The father sat down again without responding. Sean saw that the mother was still staring at the floor, while the two little boys just looked perplexed. People around the family were starting to pay attention, but no one was making a move to defend them.

The bald guy spoke again. "Where are you from?"

The father replied politely. "We live here in Toronto."

"You're Arabs."

"We're Canadians."

"No, you're not *real* Canadians. *We're* real Canadians."

A small nerdy looking man sitting next to the Arab family suddenly jumped into the fray. "Hey, you can't say things like that to people. They're not bothering anyone."

The long-haired guy rammed his finger into the man's chest. "Shut the fuck up, buddy! We're not talking to you!"

A stunned hush came over the waiting area as passengers stopped what they were doing and saying, forced to watch the ugly drama unfolding. But, no one was showing any eagerness to intervene. They just—watched.

The bald guy addressed the father again. "Are you all on this flight to Calgary?"

"Yes, we are."

"Are we safe flying on the same plane with you? You're not ISIS, are you?"

His buddy was laughing so hard now that tears were rolling down his cheeks.

For the last few minutes, Sean had been promising himself he was going to keep a low profile and let somebody else intervene. But, he just couldn't take any more. The humiliation this poor little family was enduring was horrible. He'd been watching carefully and quietly, hoping the ugliness would end, that the idiots would get bored. But, it was apparent that wasn't going to happen. They seemed emboldened now.

As Sean rose to his feet, one of the little boys grabbed onto his mom's hand and squeezed it tight. He was shaking, and his face, despite being of Arab descent, looked very pale all of a sudden.

Sean put his hand on the shoulder of the bald guy. "Let's cool it, okay? There's no need for this."

The man whirled around, shoving Sean's hand off his shoulder. "Who the fuck are you?"

"Just a guy. Those seats are taken. Give it up. One of you can have my seat. I don't mind standing."

Both men made faces and chuckled, mocking him.

"Well, aren't you the gentleman? I don't want your seat—I want *their* seats."

"Okay, have it your way." Sean raised his arm high above his head and snapped his fingers, calling over to the Air Canada counter. "We need Security here, please!"

The attendant who had been trying hard to pretend nothing was going on, nodded, picked up his phone, and dialed.

"You gonna tattle on us, Mister?" More laughter.

"I don't have to tattle." Sean spread his arm out in a wide arc. "All these people here heard what you've been saying to this family. So why don't you just move along before Security arrives?"

All of a sudden, without warning, the bald guy swung his fist towards Sean's head. Sean ducked, grabbed the man's forearm with both hands, and in one fluid motion wrenched it behind his back. The man screamed out in pain as Sean held on tight, only one hand on the forearm now while the other one pulled back on his left shoulder, with Sean himself positioned safely to the rear.

The long-haired guy yelled and took a step forward—but that was as far as he got. The sight of Sean's right foot rising menacingly into position around the side of his friend stopped him in his tracks.

No longer was there silence in the waiting lounge. Sean knew that they were all talking about one thing, and only one thing. He noticed countless mobile phones held high in the air, and he wondered how much of what just happened had gone viral. He swallowed hard, confused as to what had possessed him to become so visible. He should have known better.

Sean whispered into the ear of baldy. "Are we okay, now? Can I let you go?"

The man nodded sheepishly and Sean released his arm, giving him a gentle shove towards his friend.

The Arab father came up to Sean and held out his hand, bowing slightly. "I don't know how to thank you, sir."

Sean took his hand, held it in both of his, and shook it warmly. "No thanks necessary, sir. I hope your wife and kids are okay."

The man motioned with his hand to his wife, apparently giving her permission to look up at Sean. She did, and she smiled her thanks. Sean could see the respectful gratitude in her eyes.

Suddenly, there were men on either side of him. Men in uniform, and Sean could tell by their badges that they were RCMP. Out of the corner of his eye, he saw the two preppies being led away by two other officers.

"We need to chat with you for a few minutes, sir. Could you come with us, please?"

Chapter 11

Sean slowly made his way through the Victoria airport, keeping an eye out for his contact. He'd been on a few assignments with him before. A guy named Bart Holgram; tall, skinny and bookish. He was the man who ran the CIA's diamond importing business in Victoria. But, in reality, like Sean, he knew very little about diamonds.

The longest stretch the two of them had worked together was in Libya back in the late 90s, working to undermine the Gaddafi government amongst the rank and file. Their job had been to gradually breed dissent, which eventually paid off during the civil war in 2011.

Bart was about sixty years old now, and was content to semi-retire as the CIA's man in Western Canada. Not very much of intelligence interest usually took place in Canada, being that it was one of America's closest friends. But, the coastal regions of British Columbia were strategic gateways to the Far East, so the area was of prime interest to the United States, what with the growing strength of China, and the threatened re-emergence of Japan.

Bart was still an American citizen, but had permanent residency status in Canada. And the RCMP knew who he really was. They looked the other way, and gave whatever cooperation the CIA needed. It was quid pro quo—they received the same courtesy down in the United States when matters of national security were at stake. The public wasn't generally aware of the close relationship the two intelligence forces had with each other, and it was best that it stayed that way. What they didn't know wouldn't hurt them.

As Sean walked through the terminal and saw passengers lazing around in their seats waiting for flights, he was reminded of his ordeal back in Toronto. On the one hand he still regretted getting involved, but on the other hand he was glad that he had.

The RCMP had pulled him off to a private office for interrogation after the incident. They simply wanted his side of the story, and they also took witness statements from the other passengers. Sean just stuck to the facts—told them what they needed to know and left it at that. They were respectful to him, and nothing they asked required him to disclose his true identity. After fifteen minutes, he was allowed to go, and just managed to catch his flight to Calgary. Then a quick connection there and now here he was—in beautiful Victoria.

Sean envied Bart—he could take living in a lush city like this. And it seemed peaceful and laid back; something he could really get used to one of these days in the not too distant future. He knew he couldn't do this job forever—his soul wouldn't survive it.

In fact, he wasn't even sure he had a soul anymore. He certainly had to dig much deeper than ever to find it, and lately he'd found himself digging more often. Perhaps it was age creeping up on him, or just the need to find a greater purpose. Something was nagging at him lately, causing him to question everything. Mid-life crisis maybe? Unfulfilled? Ashamed?

The CIA was very adept at brainwashing raw recruits from the outset, and then again during the early career years. After that, there was an ongoing psy-ops program that all agents had to undergo; year in, year out. Hypnosis, denial of comforts, films, and tape recordings filled with propaganda. It was generally effective. Very few agents went rogue. But, when they did, all hell broke loose. The agency went to herculean efforts to find them and bring them in—and they were generally never allowed to see the light of day again.

Sean didn't have any checked bags—just his carry-on duffle bag. Bart would give him the other stuff he needed. This was just a short trip. Sean wouldn't need much time to determine what he needed to know.

He looked out over the crowd towards the exit and saw Bart standing near the main doors. The tall geeky man waved and walked towards him.

"Hey, Sean. Good to see you, man."

Sean reached out and shook his hand. "Good to see you, too, Bart. God, it's been ages. The last time was in New Orleans, I think, shortly after Katrina blew in?"

"Yep, that was it. We were the lucky guys who had to clear out the office before anyone could get their hands on it."

Sean shook his head. "What a near disaster that was. My gosh, we were wading through water and sewage up to our waists! But, we got it all out of there, thank God. Would have been a disaster if the wrong eyes saw it."

Bart led the way out to the parking lot, talking as he walked. "We sure do have to clean up after ourselves sometimes, don't we?"

Sean shifted his duffel bag over to his left hand. "Yeah, no doubt. More often than not lately the job seems to be consumed with that."

"So, how do you like running the Special Activities Division? Better than being out in the field with guys like me?"

"I kind of miss the regular fieldwork. But, I do still allow myself to escape once in a while, like for this project here. I'd rather do this than shuffle administrative paper, that's for sure."

They reached Bart's car, a sporty little Ford Fusion. Bart opened the trunk and Sean dropped his bag inside.

Inside the car, Bart reached down underneath the seat and handed Sean a holster with pistol. Sean snapped it onto his belt. Then, Bart opened the glove compartment, withdrew a badge with a laminated identification card, and passed both over to him. "Today, you'll be Inspector Stephen Dixon of the RCMP. I'll be Special Constable Dave Creary." He chuckled. "Don't you just love how I've deferred to your seniority, even with fake credentials?"

Sean laughed and patted him on the shoulder. "Well done, Bart. You were always great at sucking up."

Bart pulled out of the parking lot and turned north on Highway 1. "We'll drive north a bit and then this road turns into Highway 19, which will take us all the way to the Campbell River area. It's about a two-and-a-half-hour drive, so I hope you're prepared to help kill time by spilling all the secrets of the SAD unit to me."

Sean looked out the window. "I think I'd rather just enjoy the scenery. Don't want to ruin it with all that crap."

Bart nodded. "Yeah, probably a good idea. I know you can't tell me much anyway."

"You got that right. Hey, thanks for cleaning everything up after the killings. Must have been quite the mess."

"No problem. I've seen worse. Sent our best crew up there, and we had good cooperation from our contacts here, so we managed to kill the story as well. Went smoothly."

Sean pulled a notepad and pen out of his pocket and began scribbling little reminders to himself. He looked over at Bart. "Did you know my two men who were killed?"

Bart shook his head. "No, never met them."

"They were good guys. A shame to lose them."

"Where were they from?"

"Richard worked out of Portland—out of the actual CIA district office—and Kevin was a lifelong Seattle boy. He ran a private investigation front operation we had there. Two guys I have to replace now—won't be easy."

For the next ninety minutes, the car went silent. Sean fell asleep for part of the time, but for the better part he gazed out the window at the serene waterway separating Vancouver Island from mainland British Columbia. *Just stunning*, he thought. This is what life was meant to be like—drinking in beauty such as this.

Bart finally broke the silence. "You awake now?"

Sean nodded. "Wish I wasn't—but, yeah, I'm fresh as a daisy. I needed that little nap."

"Well, you're also dealing with a three-hour time difference between Washington and Victoria, so that kind of takes a toll."

"Yeah, I'll certainly feel that tonight. I'll be wanting to go to sleep three hours earlier."

Bart opened his window a crack. "Mind if I smoke?"

"No, you go right ahead." Sean rolled his window down as well. "In fact, give me one, too."

"I thought you quit."

"I did. But, give me one anyway."

They both smoked in silence for a few minutes. Then Bart broke the peace again. "We'll be going to a few restaurants first. Flash Colin Wentworth's photo around and see if anyone remembers him dining with anyone. Then, we'll head to the property, which is just a few miles south of Campbell River. Very isolated area—no neighbors to speak of. Colin had several acres."

"Are the two buildings still sealed up?"

"No, free and clear now. And cleaning crews have been there already—property is going up for sale in a few days. Wentworth and his wife, Katy, had relatives back in England."

"Okay, so we'll be left alone to look around."

"Yes, and everything was left in the state that it was in."

"Good."

With one hand on the wheel, Bart took his glasses off, blew on them, and polished the lenses against his shirt. Then he turned his head toward Sean. "What was the deal with this Colin Wentworth?"

Sean sighed. "Well, you know as much as I do. The Brits say he was MI5, however I don't believe that for a second. What's he been doing here in Canada for the last twenty years? They said he retired five years ago, but if he was operating here for the British for the fifteen years prior to that, he was clearly MI6, *not* MI5."

"The Brits didn't show us much professional courtesy, did they?"

"Clearly not—their agent was operating right under our noses, doing God knows what."

"'Why were those letters sent to him?"

Sean shook his head. "Don't know. Worries me."

Bart was silent for a couple of minutes. "Sean, who wrote the letters?"

"Can't tell you that."

"Okay. Can you at least tell me why they're so important?"

"No, I can't let you in, Bart. And, trust me, you don't want to know."

Bart slowed down as he prepared to turn off the highway onto a secondary road. "Sean, I'm in the loop on a lot of sensitive stuff, you know that. I'm sure it wouldn't shock me."

Sean laughed. "Oh, yes it would, my friend. It shocks me, and I unfortunately know all about it." He made an upward motion with his hand. "In fact, I'm in it up to my neck. I try not to think about it too much. Except that I have to deal with it day in and day out. It haunts me."

"You mean the letters?"

"No, what the letters pertain to."

"Oh."

"Leave it alone, Bart. Okay?"

"Okay, buddy. Right now, we're going to drop in on the first restaurant in the area. This one is about twenty miles south of Colin's property. Then we'll work our way up to the other ones closer to his house."

"Good. Do you have your pad?"

Bart reached into the backseat and grabbed a large tablet. "Got it. And the skills acquired back in my days as an NYPD sketch artist are still with me. In fact, I think I'm even better now."

Sean chuckled. "Good. We're gonna need those skills. I'm counting on you—but no pressure."

An hour later, they were about ten miles further north, and had put four restaurant and bar visits behind them. No luck at any of them. They'd flashed Colin's photograph around, but no one recognized him. He had clearly kept a low profile.

There was only one restaurant to go—actually more of a pub. A place called Finnegan's, which was the closest one to Colin's house, just under ten miles. If they struck out there, they would have to head north of Colin's house and canvas whatever restaurants were in that vicinity.

Once inside, they headed straight for the front bar. Sean flashed his RCMP badge and then held out Colin's photo. "Have you ever seen this man?"

The bartender, who was also the owner, laughed loudly. "Sure, Inspector, but I guess I won't be seeing him anymore, will I?"

Sean was encouraged. "You must have heard about his death?"

"Of course."

"We're investigating. Can you tell us when you saw him last?"

The bartender laughed again. "What's to investigate? He killed himself, didn't he?"

Sean nodded. "Yes, but we still always try to fill in the blanks—what led to his death, how he was feeling beforehand. Things like that."

The guy grunted. "Seems like a fucking waste of time to me."

Sean was starting to lose his patience. "I'm not here to debate RCMP policies with you. Just answer my question, please. When did you last see him?"

"Christ, I don't know. Can't give you the exact date. He used to drop in here quite a bit. We chatted together a lot—a nice old Brit." The bartender scratched his head. "But, the last time I saw him was probably just a few days before I heard they'd died. Came in by himself—didn't have Katy with him, which was unusual. But, he joined some friends over there in that booth." He pointed to a corner near the back of the bar.

Sean was getting excited now. "Describe them to me."

"Well, they stood out because they were strangers. We know all the regulars here, but a lot of tourists drop in for a beer and a bite during the summer. These two seemed to want to be on their own though—took the back booth, even though the place was almost empty. And I remember her more than him—brunette, the most perfect green eyes I'd ever seen, and a body to die for. A hot babe. Married though—noticed the wedding ring. And him, well, he stood out a bit, too—kind of good looking, around early fifties maybe, well dressed, thick mop of brown hair."

Bart opened his sketch pad. "Could you help me draw renditions of each of them?"

"Renditions? Ooh—big word! You mean a sketch, huh? Sure, buddy. Never done that before, and it's a slow day, so it should be fun."

Sean held up his hand. "Before we do that, tell me about their encounter with Colin."

The bartender cracked open a beer and took a swig. "Well, it was kinda strange. After they'd had drinks and ordered food, Colin came rushing in from the rain. Nodded just a quick hello to me, and then went right over and sat down in their booth. He had a big envelope with him."

"Did they seem friendly to each other?"

"Yeah, seemed to know each other. Chatted for a bit. Then me being the snoop I am, I noticed Colin open the big brown envelope and pull out a smaller white envelope. He handed it to the guy, and then Colin just rushed out again. Didn't even say goodbye to me. A bit weird."

Sean nodded. "You've done really well, sir. Now, I want you to work with my constable here and come up with a couple of sketches for us. Okay?"

"Okee-dokee, Inspector."

*****

An hour later, they pulled into the long driveway leading to Colin's estate. Bart stopped at the spot where the one agent was shot on the road. Before they got out, Sean held out his hand. "Let me see those sketches again."

Bart passed them over. "Do you think you recognize them?"

"Not her. Maybe him. Vaguely familiar. Don't know where from, but I think I've seen him before. Wondering how they all knew each other, too, but Colin apparently rented out his house during the summer, so maybe they were tenants here?"

Sean put the sketches on the dashboard and opened the car door. "Okay, show me where the body was."

Bart pointed. "Right in that grass patch there."

Sean knelt down and examined the area. Then walked around the perimeter, staring down the whole time. He looked up. "Pretty clean. He used our agent's gun, didn't he?"

"Yep."

Sean walked back to the car. "Okay, let's look inside the buildings."

Bart drove down to the main cottage. "This is where Colin and the one agent were found."

They got out and walked up to the front door. Bart produced a little instrument from his pocket and picked the lock. Once inside, he pointed out where the bodies had been found. Sean walked around and looked in every nook and cranny. Opened drawers, looked in the fridge, lifted up the mattresses and carpets.

"Clean. Let's go check the cabin out."

They walked along the dirt path to the cute cabin and Bart picked that lock with ease, too. Once inside, Sean used his keen eyes to survey the scene. His powers of observation were notorious within the rank and file of the CIA.

He walked all around the little cabin, checked all the cabinets, the fridge, the stove, under the mattresses, inside the toilet tank. Then he went into the tiny office in the back.

Lying on the floor was a power cord. He called out to Bart in the other room. "Did you guys take a laptop when you were here?"

Bart walked into the office. "No, we didn't take anything."

"Okay, our guy took the computer—left the power cord behind."

Sean walked around the office, examining little post-it notes that were stuck to the wall. Then he saw the calendar. The month of September was displayed.

"That's strange. If the killings took place in August, why would September be showing already?"

He took the calendar off the wall, and flipped back one page. The previous month was July, and there were torn shards between the two months.

"Bart, someone ripped off the page for the month of August."

Suddenly, Sean noticed something else. Impressions on the September page.

"There are slight indents on this page. For things that were written in on the page that was torn off, the impressions have come through onto September."

Sean pulled the diamond assessing loupe out of his pocket, and bent over the calendar with his right eye against the lens. He scanned the entire month and could just make out the faint impressions for various appointments: *Poker night; Doctor; Dentist; Lion's Club; Chamber of Commerce.*

He studied the bottom of the calendar carefully. Down around the latter days in the month, there was something. He rubbed his tired eyes, and then stared through the lens once again. The longer he stared, the clearer the words got.

It was faint, but the impressions were there: *Bradley Crawford! Wow!*

Sean looked up and smiled at Bart. He now knew why the sketch had looked so familiar.

Chapter 12

Brad took one last look in the mirror before heading out. Kristy had indeed been right. He needed a haircut badly. But, so what—he was semi-retired now; the sense of urgency just wasn't there anymore. And neither was the urgency to shave. He had a three-day growth going, and wasn't the least bit concerned.

He chuckled to himself. This retirement thing was great in so many ways. No schedules or meetings to attend. No deadlines. And, he could grow his beard and hair as long as he goddamned wanted to.

But—he longed to break another story. A big story. Like the ones that had earned him his two Pulitzers. He remembered those exhilarating days—they were as clear in his mind as if they were just last week. He missed that feeling—being up at the podium, being recognized by his peers. Knowing that his bravery and perseverance had broken open the truth.

Brad reached into his closet and pulled out a crimson-colored tie. It went well with the blue suit he was wearing today. He stood in front of the mirror again and slid the knot of the tie up to his Adam's apple. Then pulled down his collar and took a good hard look. Yeah, he still looked okay, especially in a suit and tie. But, he didn't have the occasion to dress up all that often anymore. It was nice once in a while—brought back memories of his working days.

He slid his hands through his thick brown hair and scratched at his beard.

"Well, don't you look like the dude today?"

He turned around and smiled at his pretty wife. "Thanks, Kristy. Yeah, still holding my own, I guess, despite my advanced age."

She wrapped her arms around his waist and gave him a squeeze.

"You still look handsome to me, just as handsome as the day we got married. And you're only fifty—that's hardly advanced."

Brad gently kissed her lips. "You have to say things like that to me—that's what a wife's supposed to do."

She grinned. "True. Just don't ever piss me off—you'll hear what I really think."

Brad smacked her on the bum. "Gotta go. Having lunch with that guy I told you about."

He slipped into his suit jacket and walked out to the foyer. "I should be back before three o'clock. Having lunch at the Library Bar at the Royal York."

"With that Israeli guy you were telling me about?"

Brad nodded. "Ziv Dayan. Worked with Israeli Intelligence for a couple of decades. Retired here in Canada about ten years ago."

"Is he scary?"

"No, not at all. A great guy. We worked together on a few stories in the past, and he became a good friend. But, I haven't seen him in years. It'll be good to catch up with him."

Kristy smiled knowingly. "You're not a 'catch up' kind of guy, dear. You want his help, don't you?"

Brad laughed. "Yeah, I do. Luckily, my friends know me almost as well as you do. They're not under any illusions that I'm one to waste time on meaningless little reunions. Despicable, aren't I?"

Kristy kissed him on the cheek. "Yes, you are. But, also loveable. Which is what makes you such a great journalist. People gravitate to you and trust you. And you're not afraid to ask for help—you're fearless that way."

Brad pinched her cheek. "See you later. I'll meet you in bed for a little afternoon delight when I get back."

"Deal."

*****

Seated at their reserved table, Brad watched as Ziv sauntered through the dining room. It had been about five years since they'd seen each other, but from what Brad could tell he hadn't changed a bit. Tall, dark, a "don't fuck with me" look about him – and he still moved like a cat. Even though he'd noticed Brad as soon as he entered the restaurant and gave him a little wave of recognition, he still allowed his eyes to wander from side to side, as if looking for some unseen enemy. Brad guessed that Mossad agents probably did that instinctively.

Ziv had worked for the Mossad as a field agent and cryptologist. He had a bachelor's degree in English language, and a master's in linguistics. Brad knew a few details about some of the assignments Ziv had been attached to, and shuddered when he remembered what the guy had had to deal with. He'd lived a life of danger and survived it. Survived to retire to the relatively safe country of Canada.

Brad stood and they embraced each other. Old friends of convenience. He pointed at the two cold beers sitting invitingly on cardboard coasters. "I took the liberty of ordering a couple of Molson Canadians. I assume you're accustomed now to drinking our Canadian beer?"

Ziv grunted. "I still prefer Israeli beer."

"Israel actually has its own beer?"

"Of course! I know you Canadians think you make the best beer in the world, but Israeli beer beats yours by a country mile. Try Maccabee and Goldstar sometime, and you'll know I speak the truth."

They sat down, raised their glasses and toasted. Brad chuckled. "Okay, cheers to Israeli beer! And, by the way, old buddy, you're a Canadian now, too, so try to show some patriotism towards our suds."

"Yeah, finally got my citizenship last year. A nice feeling. And, I do love it here, but I will always be an Israeli first and foremost."

"Do you miss it?"

Ziv shook his head. "No, not at all. Hard to miss living in fear all the time. Wondering when the rockets will come flying again. The constant fear of bombardment from the Palestinians and of course from Iran sitting in the shadows, wears you down. That's how Israelis live—and it's not just the fear. On top of that, the cost of living there is so high; it's very tough for a family or someone like me in retirement to make ends meet."

"Do you miss the work?"

Ziv quickly nodded. "Yeah, I do miss that. I miss the intrigue. Not the fieldwork—was getting too old for that. But, the puzzle-solving, the cryptic stuff—I thrived on it."

"But, I heard through the grapevine that you still have your hand in."

"I'm just a private consultant now. Done some jobs for the RCMP and CSIS. Been offered work by the CIA, but I've turned those jobs down. I hate those bastards—wouldn't lift a finger to help them."

Brad laughed. "Well, you'll love the job I have for you then."

Ziv frowned. "Over the phone you mentioned you were in possession of some letters? What's that all about?"

"They were written by a CIA hit man—rather infamous. Died in prison in 2011 of natural causes. All twenty letters were sent to a Richard Sterling in Coventry, England. Don't know who that is—can't trace him. But, I think some of these letters are cryptic—I think he was trying to say something, but disguising what he was saying just well enough to get the letters past prison security."

"Okay, spill the beans. What was his name?"

Brad whispered. "Hal Winters."

Ziv suddenly leaned forward and rested his elbows on the table, his hands clasped together at his chin. He whispered back. "You're fucking kidding me, right?"

Brad shook his head slowly. "No, I'm not. He was convicted of mass murder—ten people shot dead in the Mall of America on September 15, 2001. Four days after 9/11. He was seen wearing an airline captain's uniform before the shootout began. Sent to a federal prison in Georgia for the rest of his life—a life that only lasted ten more years."

Ziv whispered again. "I know all about the legend of Hal Winters. We ran in some of the same circles, as you can appreciate. I never met him; only knew him by reputation. All of us who worked in Intelligence knew the major players. He was probably well aware of my name, too."

Brad leaned forward and lowered his voice. "Can you help?"

"Knowing your subject matter, my answer would be an immediate yes. And I can tell you also that I was well aware of that Mall of

America incident, and never believed for a second that Hal Winters would have shot innocent shoppers. That's just nonsense—he was too much in control of himself, and a trained assassin of the highest order. He never shot wildly, and from what I heard he also never missed a target he wanted to hit. So—something caused him to confess to that slaughter. What that was is the big mystery."

Brad picked up his menu and scanned it. "What's your price?"

Ziv laughed. "Now that I know what your subject matter is, I won't charge you a thing."

Brad frowned. "What?"

"No fee at all. But, I do have one condition—my name on the byline of your story right alongside yours. I want equal credit. We'll be partners. You've won two Pulitzer prizes—that's something I want more than anything else in the world. Hitching my wagon to you gives me an honest shot at it. If your instincts tell you that this has a story behind it, then I trust those instincts. So—that's my offer. Can you handle me as a partner?"

Brad smiled and held out his hand. "I can't think of anyone else I'd rather partner with. We have a deal."

Chapter 13

Leslie Fields slipped on her high-heeled shoes, took one last look in the full-length mirror, and then headed purposefully out the door. Today was a day that was pre-planned. First, some shopping for her darling nieces—twins—and their birthday was approaching fast.

Then she had to drop in to the Canada Immigration office to file for renewal of her permanent residency. The required five years was up, so she had to beg, borrow, and steal to make sure she was allowed to stay in Canada. Well, it wasn't that bad—not like most Americans had to face. Her employer had already filed a special exemption on her behalf, and there was no doubt that the exemption would be approved.

Most people had to have a spouse vouch for them, but the law did allow for special circumstances if an employer found it impossible to replace the talents of their employee with those of a domestic Canadian.

And Leslie's talents were hard to replicate.

She was an aerospace engineer, seconded to the Canadian aerospace industry as a consultant. Canada wanted her…and needed her. They worked closely with NASA on joint projects, and Leslie had been instrumental in the refinement of the Canadarm, which had been a fixture of the space shuttle program right up until it was disbanded. Now, her consultancy work was focused on helping Canadian corporations partner with American interests in the exploding private aerospace industry. Britain's Richard Branson was soaring ahead of preferred innovators on the "proper" side of the Atlantic, and Leslie's job was to make sure he had some competition.

At least, that was her official job. With her talents, she did a lot of other things, too, and all together, her employment challenges kept her life as hectic as a life could be.

Leslie strolled along Front Street in downtown Toronto, then turned onto Yonge Street. She loved Toronto. Such a clean city and so much safer than her native Baltimore. She could never have strolled down the streets of Baltimore without having one hand in her purse, clutched tightly to a can of mace.

Leslie was forty years old now, but looked no more than thirty. Dirty blonde hair that seemed to get "dirtier" the more she washed it. Makeup was a rare thing for Leslie—she didn't like how it made her face feel, and she felt phony when she wore it. She preferred just to be herself, and luckily her looks allowed her to. She was tall, around five feet eight inches, and she had a nice figure. But, she worked at it, and knew that she had no choice, being in her forties now. The older she got, the more she noticed how much harder it was to lose weight.

But, gyms weren't her thing. She just worked out in the extra bedroom of her downtown condo. Much more comfortable and she didn't have to deal with the jerks who saw gyms as an opportunity to pick up women. She hated how the gym culture had evolved over the years—it seemed now that it was simply a place to be seen. You couldn't just work out in torn T-shirts and ratty old shorts. No—had to be designer stuff now, otherwise the lingering looks would linger too long. And the not so subtle pointing and whispered catty remarks.

Leslie wasn't "for show."

She strolled into a children's wear shop called Dainty Darlings. The outfits displayed in the window looked like just what she was hunting for. Cute, girly, and as feminine as could be. Leslie thought little girls should indeed look like little girls, not tomboys.

The young saleswoman helped her go through several selections until she finally decided on two party dresses. And not the same either. The twins didn't like looking like twins—they insisted on looking different from each other. Leslie was proud of them—they were turning eight, but were already asserting their individualities.

The sales clerk gift-wrapped the dresses, and Leslie wrote down the address in Baltimore to send them to. She took two birthday cards out of her purse and wrote out special loving notes to each of them, making sure to say very different things. She knew the girls would look at each other's cards and scrutinize them carefully to make sure that the notes were individual. They had been accustomed their entire lives to being treated like carbon copies, and their revolt was in full swing now. Leslie chuckled—such smart and suspicious little ladies.

After the shopping was over, Leslie took the subway north and got off at Queen Street. She walked for a bit, then popped into the immigration office. The official had the forms waiting for her, having been prepped in advance by her employer. She took five minutes to sign them, swear out an avadavat, and then she was gone.

Okay, two things out of the way. One more to go today.

She glanced at her watch. Plenty of time.

Leslie hopped onto the subway again and went south back to Front Street. From there, she walked west to University Avenue, and after a two block walk north she saw the sign for the restaurant she was looking for.

She loved this spot—one of her favorite places in the entire city. Rogues Gallery was a legendary restaurant and bar, frequented by some of the city's highest rollers. Leslie had been coming to this place for about three years, at least once a month. A place popular for power lunches and, on this day, Friday, she knew she'd see some familiar faces. Friday was the popular day for the regulars.

She'd reserved a specific table—not the table she usually dined at, but today this was the table she had to have. She wanted a view today. It was just one of those days.

Her phone rang. She looked at the screen and smiled. *Impatient man.*

"I'm almost there. Hold your horses." She hung up and sighed. *Should be an interesting day.*

Leslie pulled open the front door and walked into the foyer, almost breaking one of her heels on a raised floor tile. She motioned to the maître d' and pointed at the floor. "That almost made me take a face plant. You need to fix it."

He looked down and then clasped his hands together in apology. "Yes, Ms. Fields. I'll take care of that." He motioned to a corner table near the window. "Your table is ready."

He led the way and pulled out her chair. She sat down gracefully, facing away from the window. "Thank you, Marcel. I'll have a glass of Merlot—whatever you have open is fine—while I look at your glorious menu."

"Certainly, Ms. Fields. Do you wish to try something different? We have a delicious cheese soufflé as a lunch special today."

She looked up and smiled. "Maybe. Let me look at everything first and I'll let you know. But, right now, I just want that wine!"

Marcel bowed and rushed off to the bar area.

Leslie opened the large menu and then took a quick peek over the top. She surveyed the faces throughout her section of the restaurant. Some of the usual suspects. She glanced to her left at the man with the dark complexion sitting at the table right next to her. *Handsome.*

Suddenly, there was another man—standing right in front of her.

In a quiet but angry voice, he demanded, "What are you doing here?"

Leslie placed her menu down on the table. "I'm here to have lunch. By myself."

The man leaned over and rested his large palms on the table. "This is *my* place. You promised me you'd never come here again."

Leslie stared up at him, her lips trembling. "I—promised—no—such thing.'"

"Yes, you did. You're disrespecting me."

"Gerry, calm down. You're...scaring me."

Leslie glanced around and noticed that several people were looking in her direction, including the handsome stranger sitting at the next table.

She stood. "You're making a scene. Please leave."

Suddenly, she was on the floor. The smack across her face had come hard and fast, so fast she hadn't even seen it. One of the chairs had toppled over on her journey to the floor, and now Gerry was standing over her, fists clenched.

"I'll teach you to disrespect me, you bitch!"

The dark stranger at the next table was on his feet in a flash.

His right fist lashed out at Gerry's forehead before he had a chance to duck. He staggered backwards several steps, then recovered and rushed forward at the stranger.

Gerry met an Oxford sole in the face, followed by a quick left fist to the groin. He went down hard.

Leslie watched as the stranger grabbed her dazed attacker by the necktie and yanked him to his feet. He glanced down at her. "Do you want to call the police, ma'am?"

She struggled to a kneeling position and rubbed the right side of her face. She could feel a bruise starting to form already. "No, that won't be necessary. It will only make things worse."

The stranger nodded, then pulled Gerry by the necktie to the front door. "Leave, buddy, before I hit you again."

Gerry glared at Leslie one last time, then staggered through the door and out onto the street.

The tall, dark, handsome stranger came back to Leslie's table and picked up the fallen chair. She sat down and looked up at him. Leslie could feel an involuntary smile enveloping her face.

"I don't know how to thank you. Please—sit."

The man sat down and gently brushed his fingers against her right cheek. "We'll ask the waiter to get some ice for that."

Leslie grimaced. "I think it's going to hurt for a while."

The man smiled at her. "Yes, it will, but it's just a souvenir of war. Sometimes those are good reminders of the people we should avoid. What was that all about?"

Leslie looked down, feeling embarrassed. "My ex. We split a few months ago, and I guess it's still kind of raw for him."

"Your decision to split?"

She nodded.

"Has he ever done this before?"

She shook her head.

"You should get a restraining order."

The maître d' arrived with the glass of Merlot. The stranger addressed him, while pointing at Leslie's cheek. "We need a small bag of ice."

He bowed. "Certainly, right away. I'm so sorry that happened, Ms. Fields."

Leslie gave a little wave of her hand. "Just one of those things, Marcel. Not your fault. Luckily, I had a knight in shining armor here."

Marcel grinned. "Well, you picked the right day and the right table. That one next to you is his every Friday."

She gazed into her new friend's jet-black eyes. In a brief moment of frivolity, she thought how mesmerizing they were.

Leslie held out her hand. "I'm Leslie Fields. Who are you, my convenient hero?"

The man smiled and gently shook her hand. "My name's kinda funny. Ziv. Ziv Dayan."

Chapter 14

"Do you trust him?"

Brad gave Kristy's hand a little squeeze. "Yes, I really do, hon."

"But, you're going to share the byline with him. You've never done that before with anyone."

They were hand in hand, walking south along Yonge Street towards their Harbour Square condominium complex. It was a nice day for a walk—sunny and warm, with a certain buzz in the air. Just one of those days when everyone seemed to be smiling.

Including Brad. He now had a partner in this mystery, a mystery that had captured his imagination. And a partner who could be of tremendous help to him. Ziv Dayan was just one of those special people—dependable and amazingly clever. And he had skills that Brad needed.

"I know, I know. I've always worked alone. But, this time I need someone. Ziv brings some skills to the table that I don't have. And he has contacts and an inside knowledge of the intelligence community. I don't have a clue about that stuff—it's way over my head. Sometimes you have to give up independence to get to the end result. And that's what I think I have to do on this project."

"What's his share of the action?"

"I've agreed to give him an equal share of whatever price the story brings—and equal billing for any prizes that might come my way."

Kristy stopped to look in a shop window, pulling Brad along with her. She pointed. "Oh, look at that suit, Brad. You'd look devilishly handsome in that."

He laughed. "I have more than enough suits, Kristy. And I don't even need them that much anymore."

She leaned in and kissed him on the cheek. "You'll need a new one for your third Pulitzer. Let's get you fitted for it."

"Not today, dear one. I have to catch a plane." Brad glanced at his watch. "And I need to get my ass in gear. Want to get out to the airport before rush hour traffic."

"Okay, well, when you get back I'm going to drag you into that store. Deal?"

"Deal. But, right now, let's pick up the pace. No more window-shopping."

Kristy pursed her lips into a pretend sulk. "You're no fun."

"Yes, I am. And I'll be even more fun after you get to walk down the red carpet with me again for yet one more prize."

She patted him on the bum. "True. You're usually pretty horny after you win something!"

"Yep, I sure am! And I have one of those feelings again—that this is a story that will be an important one."

"Well, after what we went through on Vancouver Island, I would certainly agree with you. But, I'm afraid for you. People kill for reasons, important reasons. And the CIA, for God's sake—and Colin was probably MI6. And now you're partnering with this Ziv guy, who was Mossad. Doesn't this all seem a little unreal? Like, what chance do you have?"

"Well, all of that's true, but it also means this is probably going to be an earth-shattering story, whatever the hell it is. And I want to be the one to tell it."

Kristy wrapped her arm around his waist. "You've been in danger before with the stories you've written. And I know danger is something that won't stop you. You're kind of fearless that way. And how you took charge and protected us on Vancouver Island was just you. I'm used to you and I love the way you are. But, I'm also terrified of losing you one day."

He ruffled her soft brown hair. "Don't worry, Kristy. I'll be careful. And hey, now I have a Mossad agent in my corner. They don't come any tougher than that. And, remember, no one knows we were at that cabin that night. There's no evidence connecting us. We're free and clear."

Brad smiled to himself as they walked. He loved his wife. They were two peas in a pod. She had been so supportive in everything he had attempted in his career, yet was successful in her own right as well. Kristy had a well-earned reputation as one of the best editors in the media and literature business. She had a master's degree in English and a string of bestselling books behind her name as the editor of record. Novelists lined up to get Kristy's expertise—having her as their editor pretty much guaranteed that publishers would give their books a hard look. Brad had also used her as the editor for every single article he'd ever written. There was no one he trusted more.

Despite her education and expertise, Kristy was a paradox. And probably not too different from most editors. She personified the old adage: "Those who can, do; those who can't, teach." Kristy would be the first to admit that she wasn't able to put pen to paper and actually compose articles, or tell stories. She didn't have that kind of imagination, or the required lack of inhibition. She couldn't think outside of the box that way—couldn't summon up the ability to create characters or scenarios. And while Brad had not as of yet written a novel, it was something he wanted to do one day. And he knew that, unlike Kristy, he was made that way. He had an intense sense of curiosity that was sometimes insatiable. He was able to decipher mysteries, and at times, just imagine mysteries.

But he also knew that while he could create, he wasn't the best at writing. He needed someone like Kristy to add structure to what he did. Sometimes, the rough drafts of his articles rambled and lacked cohesion. But Kristy would only need a few hours to straighten them out for him, make them flow, make them pounce. When she was finished, his articles were powerful. The ideas and investigatory work were all his, but Kristy helped refine them and make them resonate.

So, when he did finally get around to writing that best-selling novel one day, which he would, Kristy would be his editor. He wouldn't trust it to anyone else.

They were in the elevator riding up to their thirty-eighth floor apartment, when Kristy suddenly wrapped her arms around his neck and kissed him hard on the lips. Then she pulled her head back and stared into his eyes. "I don't like it when you go away. Please be careful."

Brad kissed her back. "How scary can this trip be, hon? I'm meeting with a movie star."

*****

He gazed out the window of the jet as it winged its way south, heading toward the land of plenty. The land of dreams, both broken and realized. Some made it, but countless others never even came close—wasting away instead as waiters, strippers, and valet attendants.

Hollywood.

But Brad wasn't going to Hollywood itself. Instead, he'd be visiting the playground of the rich and famous.

Malibu.

A week ago, he had contacted Brock Winters' agent and asked for an appointment. Most people wouldn't have had a hope in hell of getting an audience with a famous movie star, but the name Bradley Crawford carried a lot of weight.

As the respected Pulitzer Prize winning journalist that he was, most celebrities were honored to be chosen for an interview. He never had any trouble opening doors. Fame had that one advantage—along with the best tables at restaurants and the predictable upgrades to first class on airlines and penthouse suites at hotels. Pretentiousness at its most obvious, but Brad was always glad to accept the attention. He'd be crazy not to.

The puzzle that was Hal Winters had to include the man's son. A son whose career had skyrocketed in spite of Hal's arrest for the mass murders back in 2001. Not much publicity had been thrown in Brock's direction. Only a few of the mainstream news outlets made the connection between the mass murderer and his famous son. It was surprising, but true. And Brock seldom drew attention to his infamous dad. When he granted interviews, he generally kept his personal life a secret. And no one pried too much either, perhaps due to Brock's famous temper. Plenty of paparazzi had been beaten senseless by the actor, only to be paid off later for agreeing not to press charges.

The types of movies Brock chose to star in seemed to support his persona. Generally, he played an action hero—or a psychotic killer. From one extreme to the other. And those roles came after he'd languished for years as a dim-witted waiter in a sitcom.

Then, within two years of Hal's arrest back in 2001, Brock had starred as the leading man in *Killer of Men*. Brad thought that was an odd role for the son of an infamous hit man. It was almost as if it was tongue in cheek. Giving his dad the finger? Or giving the authorities the finger? And, after that movie, he'd played an FBI agent, a basketball star, a New York police officer, an anti-terrorism specialist, a fireman, a demented rapist, a serial killer. The list went on—all action type roles, and ironic choices, considering who his father was.

From what Brad could determine, Brock lived alone in a beach house in iconic Malibu. He had been married and divorced three times with no kids complicating his life. He had been rumored to have been in and out of rehab over the years for substance abuse. But, nothing confirmed, and if he had been in rehab it was probably some kind of very private facility.

Brock Winters was rumored to have a net worth of 200 million, and was solidly on the A-list of Hollywood actors. All of that achieved in basically the last thirteen years. Ever since his dad had been locked away for life for the mass murders of ten people. Brad thought that was odd.

The plane landed on time at LAX, and Brad weaved his way through customs and immigration with his trusty duffle bag in hand. He wasn't planning to stay long—one night at the most. His appointment with Brock was for today—cocktails on his deck overlooking the mighty Pacific.

He grabbed a cab outside the terminal and gave the driver the address. However, the cabbie didn't need details—he knew exactly where Brock Winters lived, along with every other celebrity. He was proud to disclose who Brock's neighbors were: De Niro on the north side and Diaz on the south. Brock was in good company.

The taxi fought its way out of the greater Los Angeles area and headed along the Pacific Coast Highway, officially known as State Route 1. The driver estimated it would take about an hour due to traffic.

The latest census showed that about 14,000 people lived in Malibu, which was nothing more than a twenty-one-mile-long strip of prime Pacific coastline. Even though it was really no better than just a beach community, it was incorporated as an actual city in 1991. Most residents lived within a mile of the highway, but some resided a mile or so from the beach nestled in narrow canyons and along the foothills of the Santa Monica Mountains. The area possessed beautiful beaches made famous in numerous movies: *Surfrider, Zuma, Topanga,* and *Point Dume.*

Contrary to the perceptions of most people, the Malibu area never really got all that hot—average temperatures throughout the year hovered around seventy degrees, and it rarely got hotter than eighty. But, it was dry—with the exception of the powerful storms that would sweep in once in a while, residents would rarely see rain. Particularly the last few years with the drought that had engulfed almost the entire state of California. Houses in the foothills and built within the canyon walls had suffered horrible grass and forest fires within the last two decades. And mudslides had also become quite common—bringing the flimsy homes down upon each other—only to be rebuilt by owners with deep pockets, who would merely await the next disaster. Such was life in Malibu—there was a price for paradise and its wealthy residents were willing to pay it.

Those who lived right on the beach had different challenges to deal with. High tides and ferocious ocean storms put the rather ugly-looking homes in constant peril. They were all built on stilt-like foundations to help weather the high waters. These beach homes were on tiny lots with very little privacy between neighbors. And while they had incredibly beautiful views and beachfront, the homes looked hilarious—like matchstick shacks sitting precariously on flimsy stilts. But, in reality, they were the most expensive shacks money could buy.

Malibu, like Florida's Key West, was a state of mind. It didn't matter what it cost, it was just the place to be. It didn't matter how tacky it all was, or how silly it all looked, it was the place to be for those who could afford it.

The taxi slowed down and turned off Highway 1 onto a narrow driveway.

Brock's house.

Looked normal from the back, but Brad knew that on the beach side it would be supported by the mandatory stilts.

This was Zuma Beach. The ancient haunt of Frankie Avalon and Annette Funicello. Now the haunt of Winters, De Niro, and Diaz. And countless others who could afford the price of admission, reportedly to be around five million for the smallest matchstick home.

Brad paid the driver, then strolled up the small walk to the front door. Although, in this community, it was hard to decide which was the front or the back. He knocked on the innocuous door and waited.

Expecting a servant to answer, he was surprised when the star himself swung it open. A beer in hand, Brock motioned him in. No hello. No greeting of any sort.

Brock Winters walked towards the deck area of the house, and Brad followed. He glanced around as he walked—not at all what he expected. The furnishings were nondescript, "beachy" type, nothing fancy. The house was expansive though—big rooms all with magnificent views of the ocean. As they walked through the living room, he saw a buxom blonde lazing on the couch, seemingly stoned. Her head bobbed as Brad passed—she gave him a glance through glazed eyes and then just as quickly closed them shut again.

Brock slid open the sliding door to the deck and motioned Brad to follow. He walked over to a small fridge, leaned his head back and drained the rest of the beer in his hand. He opened the fridge and pulled out two more cans, tossing one to Brad and cracking open the other one for himself.

Then he plopped down in a chaise lounge and motioned again with his hand for Brad to sit in the one opposite. So far, the man hadn't spoken a word.

Brad was surprised how different he looked from the characters he played on the big screen. Sure, he was tall—well over six feet— with long blonde locks and a scruffy beard. He looked the action hero type, but not half as magnetic as he looked in theatres. There was a handsomeness about him, but not half as handsome as the photos Brad had seen of his dad.

Brock was dressed in a striped bathing suit and white T-shirt. The mandatory flip-flops completed the image down below, while a red bandana around his forehead finished him off up top. He looked like a beach bum, which was probably all he was when he wasn't working on a film. His build was powerful though—broad shoulders, barrel chest, and muscular arms. Brad could tell he worked out; it was probably essential with the kinds of roles he played.

Then he spoke. In a soft, drawling voice that belied his appearance and reputation.

"So, my agent tells me you're doing a story on my father?"

Brad nodded. "Yes."

"Why?"

Brad shifted back into the chaise lounge and took a swig of his beer. "Because, I think there's a story there. A story that relates to government secrecy and a life of licensed crime. I'll be blunt. Your dad was a killer. And licensed by our government to be that killer."

"The press would disagree with you. As far as they're concerned, he was a hit man for the mob, and finally, in his last act, a mass murderer of innocents."

"Yes, but I don't agree with that. Do you?"

Brock took a long swig of his beer. Then he stared at Brad for a good ten seconds. "You have a stellar reputation. That's the only reason I agreed to see you. Can I really trust you to be fair?"

"All you have is my word—but you already know what I've done in my career, I'm sure. I always go for the truth, whatever that truth is—good or bad. I can't promise that I'll paint your dad in the way that you want, but I can promise that when I'm finished it will be the truth. And if I'm not certain of the facts, there won't be a story at all."

"Fair enough. My dad is not the way he's been portrayed. My dad is a patriot, and everything he's done in his life has been at the behest of the government of the United States of America. He's a soldier, trained and indoctrinated the way they wanted him to be. But, he's held onto his humanity."

Brad leaned forward in his chair. "Did you keep in close touch with your dad over the years?"

Brock stretched his massive arms outward and then clasped his hands behind his head. "He left us when I was seven. My mother was a bitch, a whore, and a drunk. He had to leave. But he always kept in touch with my brothers and me. He was the only one I ever looked up to in my entire life." Brock's eyes started tearing up. "He gave me more security and confidence than my mother ever did, even though I only saw him a few weeks a year."

"Did your dad tell you what he did for a living—or did you hear that only from the press and other sources?"

He raised his voice. "The press are bullshit! They say and print what they're told. My dad was railroaded. He served his country bravely, and they hung him out to dry. I know what he did and who his bosses were. He worked for the CIA, not the mob. And he didn't kill all those people in the Mall of America—he shot the two officers who had fired upon him. He didn't shoot the other eight innocent victims. The Feds did that. To frame him. To make him a monster."

Brad thought that Brock was starting to sound like a little boy at this moment. Which was an amazing realization—this big famous movie star was a little boy defending his dad. A dad whom he was clearly proud of—proud to the core.

"How do you know these things?"

Brock's eyes started twitching, and he looked down at his lap. Started squeezing his beer can. "I just know."

"What would you like the world to know about your dad?"

"Just what I said. He's a patriot. The things he's done to protect this country are beyond what anyone could imagine. He's not a monster. He's my father."

Brad felt his mouth suddenly go dry. His antenna was up. He took a needed swig of beer, and then stood. "Brock, you talk about your dad in the present tense. He died in 2011."

Brock rolled sideways off the chaise lounge and walked over to the sliding door. "Time for you to go. We'll talk again sometime. Nice to have met you."

Chapter 15

July 16, 2011...He rolled out of bed and stretched. Walked over to his puny little sink and splashed water on his face. Then he brushed and flossed his teeth. Some of the meatloaf from last night's meal came flying out onto the aluminum mirror. He ripped off some toilet paper, wet it, and wiped off the mirror.

Then gazed at his image. It was different seeing his face reflected back from a metallic surface—didn't look half as good as he remembered. But, of course, they couldn't let him have a glass mirror. That would be taking far too great a risk with a trained killer like him.

He tried to convince himself that it was the metal surface that was causing his face to age—that he'd look better reflected in glass. But he knew deep down inside that wasn't the case at all. He'd been in this cage at the Atlanta Federal Penitentiary now for almost ten years. It was taking its toll. Hal Winters was starting to look like an old man.

He was turning sixty in a couple of days. He wondered if they'd sing Happy Birthday to him in the dining room, bring him a cake, and let him blow out some candles. They didn't do that for everyone—it seemed to be a selective thing with the guards. If they liked you, you got perks. If they didn't like you, they had ways of making sure you got the message. And ignoring your birthday was just one of those ways. A simple thing, but hurtful as hell when there was no one in your life who seemed to care anymore. With Hal, he'd only had two birthdays celebrated in all the time he'd been here.

He chuckled to himself. Funny, in all the years prior to being incarcerated, he'd never cared about his birthday—hadn't really cared about anyone else's either. Hal had just never made time for things like that. He regretted that now. Mind you, he'd been away a lot, too, so he'd missed the birthdays of his three boys almost every year. And his wife, Anne, well he'd tried to be attentive, but that had also been difficult. He had just never been one to show his emotions all that well—had never been a huggy/kissy kind of guy. Didn't really know how. Hadn't seen affection when he was growing up as a kid, and didn't relate to it all that well when he had his own family.

He moved out when his sons were twelve, ten, and seven. His two eldest vowed to hate him forever and followed through on that vow. But his youngest, Brock, was different. He respected the tough love Hal dished out, and seemed to want more of it even after Hal had moved out. Hal had never been abusive—he'd just been absent. He couldn't remember ever spanking his kids, but they certainly knew when he was angry. It showed in his face and in his voice.

Anne was probably the one hurt most by who Hal was. He recalled that when they were dating, things were different. They'd laughed a lot together, and she understood him. She knew that affection didn't come naturally to him, so she tried her hardest to make up for that. Anne had enough affection for both of them.

But after they were married, his job gradually became more and more demanding. And by the time they'd had their first child, it was almost as if she was a single mother. He was home long enough to get her pregnant and then he was gone again—sometimes for weeks at a time. They started arguing when he'd arrive back from a trip, and they didn't stop arguing until he left again. And he was distant from her during his brief visits home. Moody, pensive, reflective.

No surprise—putting bullets in peoples' heads just had that kind of effect.

And he had to suck it up himself—there was no one he could talk to, no one to confide in. He couldn't tell his family that he worked for the CIA, and he certainly couldn't tell them he was their top assassin. So, when he killed people, the images and the guilt stayed in his head. There was no one to console him and tell him they deserved to die. He had to convince himself of that—but most of the time, he didn't know why those people had to die anyway. He was just doing a job, no questions asked.

Eventually, Anne's mind started its gradual deterioration. The loneliness, the social isolation, and low self-worth, all began taking their toll. She started drinking and whoring around. And when she infected him with gonorrhea, Hal moved out. He didn't hate her for it—he actually blamed himself. But he knew that she'd sunk almost as low as she could go, and he wasn't going to go down the rest of the way with her.

He left the kids with her. That was the paradox. And that was, as Hal knew now, the selfish side of Hal Winters. He was too selfish to even see that selfishness in himself at the time. He should have fought to have the boys removed from the home—but where would they go? Who would look after them? He couldn't take care of them, not with his job, and he wasn't prepared to change occupations. At that point in his life, it was in his blood.

From what he'd heard, Anne straightened herself out somewhat after the divorce, and the boys turned out okay despite everything. Well, okay was a relative term. Maybe his sons would have been exceptional if they hadn't been from such a dysfunctional family. Brock was certainly a phenomenal success, if success was measured by money and fame. But he knew that Brock was a bitter man. He wished that wasn't true, but it was—and Hal bore the guilt for that. Brock adored his dad, and Hal didn't have a clue as to why. In contrast, the other two boys wanted nothing to do with their father.

And Hal still loved Anne. He didn't understand that either. Maybe it was just guilt once again, and the fact that he had nothing left to look forward to in his life. All he could do was look back and wonder how things might have been different.

At this age in his life, he should be lounging on a beach in the Caribbean, or golfing with his boys, having candlelit dinners with Anne, playing ball with his grandchildren. Normal everyday joys. Instead, all he could reflect upon was the mess he'd left behind. And, of course, the bullet holes he'd put in the heads of dozens of people, sometimes from several hundred yards away. Impersonal murders, almost like a video game.

This wasn't the retirement he would have envisioned when he first joined the military as a young man. Assigned to the Air Force almost immediately, they told him that by the time they were finished with him he would be one of the most skilled pilots in the world. Able to fly virtually anything, even a hot air balloon or a zeppelin if it came down to that. They told him that they had a need for versatile pilots.

Following through on their promises, it wasn't long before Hal's skills were in great demand.

But then one day some very grim men told him that there were other skills he needed to learn. Killing skills, sniper skills, covert skills. So, his training continued.

Yes, indeed, when they were finished with him, Hal Winters was not only the most skilled pilot in the world, but also one of the most skilled killers ever to walk the face of the Earth.

And then those same grim men told the young Hal Winters that he was being reassigned. Out of the Air Force and into the underground world of the CIA—specifically, the elite ultra-secretive Special Activities Division. Otherwise known as SAD.

He was too naïve to realize he would never be able to retire from such a job.

Hal rubbed the metallic mirror one more time and smiled. His teeth still looked good at least. The dental care in the pen was pretty darn excellent. Better than he'd ever had out in the real world.

He walked over to the open toilet and took a long leak. Then he moved to the center of his tiny cell and dropped to the floor. In less than two minutes, he pumped out a hundred push-ups. Then he flipped himself over on his back and muscled up fifty sit-ups. Jumped to his feet and commenced his karate routine, almost balletic in its performance. Slow, sure, and deadly.

After he finished his routine, he reached under the bed and pulled out two long one inch thick boards from a stack he kept underneath. The guards were good enough to keep him supplied. Helped work out his frustration, which was good for the guards, too. No one wanted someone like Hal Winters to be frustrated. He rested the boards on top of each other supported by two cement blocks that the guards had also supplied to him.

Then Hal stared at the boards—actually stared right through them. He moved both hands in a tight arc, and tensed his stomach muscles. His glare was intense and his focus was almost self-hypnotic.

Then he screamed, well, not exactly a scream—more comparable to the snarl of a mountain lion. Simultaneous with the scream, both hands moved in a blur—one inward toward his chest and the other one knifing down onto the wooden planks.

Then Hal took a deep breath and looked down at the broken planks lying on the floor. He'd stopped counting broken boards a long time ago—the last he remembered it was 7,000.

Some of the other prisoners counted sheep.

He glanced at his watch. Almost time for his outing in the yard. He was up to two hours a day now; one first thing in the morning and one later in the afternoon. After his fresh air break, he'd have breakfast in the dining room. He enjoyed his outdoor time—it was nice to socialize with some of the other prisoners and play some hoops. It cut into the boredom, the incredible isolation.

He got along with most of the men. He was infamous, of course, for the mass murders in the Mall of America. And the word that the CIA had planted in the prison was that he'd been a Mafia hit man before he went crazy that day in the mall. So, no one seemed to know that he'd worked for the government. He was thankful that the CIA had kept their promise to keep him safe. He enjoyed playing the role of mob enforcer—put him in the higher echelon of the prison population.

He heard the jangle of keys as the guard approached. He backed away from the door as he unlocked it.

"Good morning, Hal. Sleep well?"

"Oh, just peachy, Bill. What's for breakfast this morning?"

Bill motioned for Hal to head out into the corridor. "Bacon and scrambled eggs. You'll love it. Build up an appetite outside first."

"Yeah, I will. The usual crowd out there this morning?"

Bill followed closely behind as Hal moved towards the heavy metal door exiting to the yard. "A few new ones today. They checked in a couple of days ago. Seem like good guys."

"Okay, always nice to meet new people." Hal turned back around before heading outside. "Hey, Bill, I want you to know that I appreciate you very much. Nice of you to drop off some new boards for me the other day. I had to go several days without, and I hate getting rusty."

Bill chuckled. "My pleasure, Hal. You're my favorite prisoner. But, you just gotta promise never to use those hands on me, okay?"

Hal laughed. "Don't worry. That'll never happen." Then he winked, a twinkle in his eye. "I've never worked for free. Someone would have to pay me a princely sum to do you."

Bill gave Hal a gentle shove out the door. "That's not funny, Hal. Get outside before I shit my drawers!"

Hal gave him a thumbs up and headed out into the yard. He looked around. Not much activity this morning. No one was shooting baskets. And there were just four other guys huddled off in a corner, chatting. He didn't recognize any of them.

No guards were out, but that wasn't unusual. They usually stayed inside behind a watch window.

Hal just shrugged and walked over to the basketball court. Picked up the ball and threw a perfect hoop. Ran forward and picked up the bounce, then executed a perfect lay-up.

It came from behind. A smash to the back of his head that felt like a brick. Hal fell to his knees, but his instincts told him to go into a roll. Which he did—just barely escaping an object that had been destined for the top of his head.

He was looking up now and through his blurry eyes he could see four figures—the new guys. Each held bricks in their hands. Hal went into a sweep with his legs, taking down two of the brick holders. He jumped to his feet and quickly brought his heel down on the knee of one and the forehead of the other. To the sounds of their screams of agony, Hal turned and ran for the safety of the door back into his familiar corridor.

He looked around as he ran. Still no guards.

He was only twenty feet from the door when he was tackled from behind. There were only two guys now, but two were enough.

Hal went down with one of the guys' arms locked around his

waist. Before he could react, he was hit again. He knew it was another brick—no fist except his could make that kind of impact. He felt himself being flipped onto his back—he tried to resist but the darkness was coming. He could feel it enveloping him quickly, so much so that the pounding of bricks against his face and head didn't even register.

Finally, mercifully, the darkness won.

*****

The light stung his eyeballs as he peered through the narrow slits of his swollen lids. His head pounded like a hundred jackhammers, and he could tell it was wrapped with something. He tried to move his hands, but they were strapped down. He couldn't tell where he was, but from what little he could see it looked antiseptic. A hospital room of some kind.

Hal suddenly remembered. The yard. The new guys. Bricks. He winced at the memory.

A nurse was standing over him now. She gently rubbed his shoulder. "Don't move, Mr. Winters. We're taking good care of you."

Hal moved his lips, but the words were hard to come by. "Wh-Where?"

"Shh. You're in a private wing of the prison hospital. You're safe here."

"How...long?"

"You've been here for a couple of days. In and out of consciousness. You've had a concussion, but you're going to be fine."

Suddenly, the door opened and a man in a suit appeared. He spoke with authority. "Nurse, could you leave us alone for a few moments, please?"

She gave Hal one more pat on the arm and left the room. The visitor pulled up a stool and sat down close enough to the bed for Hal to get a good look through the narrow slits of his eyes. He was a good-looking sort; not as handsome as Hal, but pretty darn close. "Who are...you?"

"Your new best friend. You almost lost your life a couple of days ago, Hal. If it wasn't for that guard friend of yours, Bill, you'd be dead."

"Who?"

"Well, those prisoners were just carrying out an order. We think the hit was ordered from outside the prison, and we also think there was some help from the inside. Someone wanted you dead."

Hal winced. "Why?"

The visitor shook his head. "Don't know. Perhaps someone found out you were CIA? Anyone's guess. The main thing is that you're alive and we intend to keep you that way."

"I'm...a...target...now."

The visitor reached down and opened a briefcase that was sitting on the floor. He pulled out a pile of papers. "These are copies of all of the letters you've written in the ten years you've been here." He shook his head. "You've been a bad boy, Hal. Dropping little clues— very clever. The guards here did a piss-poor job of screening your letters. We have to get the originals back, which we will. Not all of them—just the ones that worry us. The original letters are dangerous. Needless to say, you won't be allowed to write any more."

Hal managed a muted chuckle. "I'll be...dead...anyway."

The visitor nodded his head. "Yes, you will be. Today you will die. And per your written wishes, you'll be immediately cremated without a service. The urn with your remains will be delivered to your family."

Hal gasped.

The visitor smiled. "Of course, that will be the charade. You know that we at the CIA are great at charades—and staged theater. You'll be officially dead, which will save your life. I presume you will hold up your end of the agreement and ensure that the tape you have secreted away will not be released. I don't know who you have it hidden with, but we will allow you a chance to make private contact with that person, be it family or someone else. Whoever you want to be told that you're still alive, we will allow you the ability to get in touch with them. Your secret, we don't have to know. Above all, we do not want that tape released."

"Where?"

"You can't stay in this prison, of course. I'm going to move you someplace very secure, and you'll be among people who will not be a threat to you. There won't be any hardened criminals. You'll actually be far less confined than you are here."

Hal blinked several times, trying desperately to get some fluid into his eye sockets. The visitor clued in quickly, and reached over to the side table. He unscrewed the cap on some eye drops and squeezed two drops into each eye. "Better?"

Hal gave a slight nod.

"Hal, let me say this to you—just between you and me. I know you've been dealt a bad hand. I know you're not who you were framed to be. You're not a mass murderer, and you don't deserve to be here. But you know how these things work. I know what it is that you know, and you have to be silenced for that. But I'll make it my personal mission that you're treated as humanely as possible. And the place I'm going to send you to is about as secure and as humane as any prison could possibly be. Okay?"

Hal nodded, then moved his mouth open and closed. The visitor picked a plastic bottle off the table and squirted some water in between Hal's open lips.

"Something you wanted to say, Hal?"

"Yes.... Who...the hell...are you?"

The visitor's handsome face broke out into a genuine smile. "I'm the Director of the CIA's Special Activities Division—where you used to work. My name's Sean Russell. And it's indeed an honor to meet you, Hal Winters."

Chapter 16

The meeting was on the third floor of CIA headquarters in Langley, Virginia. Sean Russell waited patiently in the foyer, sipping a cup of coffee.

Waiting to be summoned.

He had no idea what the topic of this meeting was, but it had to be important for it to be scheduled for first thing in the morning.

He shuffled through the generous selection of magazines, settling on one highlighting home improvement projects. Sean owned a country home on a few acres just outside McLean, only about twenty minutes from the office. A lovely drive along empty rural roads; a pleasant way to start and end each day. His house was about forty years old now and was in need of some major updating—a project he'd been putting off for years, waiting for a time when his work schedule wasn't so hectic.

But Sean realized that he'd just been making excuses to himself. He knew in his heart that his schedule would never be relaxed, so he might as well just get on with it. And it might be good therapy. Take his mind off the crap he had to deal with. He was pretty good with his hands, so most of the work he could do himself. Which would save a considerable amount of money. But with how much he'd squirreled away over the years that was the least of his concerns. More important that he just have an outlet for his nervous frustration, and a busy project to occupy his mind would do that for him. Something—anything—other than CIA business.

The door to the cavernous office opened, and Jarod McKenzie poked his head out. "Come on in, Sean. I'm ready for you."

Sean dropped the magazine onto the table, making a mental note to steal it on his way back to his own office. He stood and followed

Jarod in through the open door. "Okay, I guess I'm ready, too. Unusual for you to want to meet first thing in the morning. Must be a special occasion."

Jarod motioned for Sean to take a seat in the living room area of the office, a nicely adorned corner with leather chairs and ornate table lamps. Very relaxing—and no doubt intended to be very deceiving.

Jarod was the director of the National Clandestine Service, an umbrella unit of the CIA that oversaw all covert activities, including Sean's SAD division. Jarod was Sean's direct superior. A casual kind of guy, very confident, but known for being ruthless. Sean had a good relationship with Jarod and up until now hadn't seen the ruthless side that he was famous for, other than the normal everyday ruthlessness of anyone who worked for the CIA.

Jarod poured both of them black coffees, then sat down in the chair opposite Sean. "How are you doing with the retrieval of those letters Winters wrote?"

Sean took a sip of his coffee. "We're making some progress. I know who has them now. But he lives in Canada, which complicates things a bit. And he's a famous journalist, which complicates things even more. I think he's looking for a big scoop here. Next steps are underway, and I'll keep you posted."

Jarod crossed his legs. "Good. Time is of the essence, as you can appreciate. And yes, the fact that he's a journalist does make matters worse. If he only had just photocopies of the letters it wouldn't be as much of a concern. But the fact that they're originals is very dangerous indeed. Copies have no credibility as to authenticity. But, originals—they're a different story entirely."

Sean nodded. "Agreed."

Jarod clasped his hands behind his head. "And the facility in Colorado? Are things running smoothly there?"

"Yes. The experiment seems to be unfolding nicely for us. It's been a few years now, of course. There has been some attrition, which is only natural, but the conditions there are constantly being improved and refined. And the test group seem to have resigned themselves to their situation. Psychologically, we've had some challenges, but that was expected. And the psychological stresses are just part of the experiment anyway, so no real surprise in that regard."

"Good. You seem to have that well in hand." Jarod paused and poured himself another full cup from the pot sitting on the coffee table. "Today we have another problem to deal with. You're well aware of the uproar caused by this Senate report on enhanced interrogation methods we inflicted on suspected terrorists?"

"Yes. But, let's call it what it was—torture."

"Sure, we'll call it what it was. It was indeed torture. But the Senate and House leaders were well aware of it. We briefed them way back in 2002 on this stuff. Now it's become political and they're all pretending that they didn't have a clue. Typical politicians. We're being thrown under the bus, as usual. Everyone wants results, but they always wash their hands of what we have to do to get them those results. They're slime."

Sean shifted uncomfortably in his chair. "We did violate the Geneva Convention. We did it knowingly, and it was only a matter of time before it became political. And now since we've shown that we don't care about the Geneva Convention, our own military personnel will be subjected to horrific torture whenever they're captured. We reap what we sow."

"True. But, they were just fucking Arabs, for God's sake. I mean, who really gives a shit?"

Sean kept silent, not knowing how to respond.

Jarod continued. "I don't know how all this is going to shake out. But we have to cover our tracks. As you know, most of the torture took place in prisons we set up in Poland, Iraq, and Croatia. We're in the process of closing those facilities down and destroying records. Just to make sure this doesn't get any worse."

"Well, that should help contain the problem."

"Yeah, it will. But, we have another problem. We have a prison right here in the United States—in fact, it's only a few miles from here. We've had some people suspected of being members of sleeper cells contained there for years. They've been subjected to the same torture tactics that the Senate made a big deal of. We're now in a very difficult position. We can't just let them roam the streets of America, allow them to talk. They have to get the hell out of here—or disappear. If the public finds out that we've been torturing people right here on U.S. soil, well, I don't have to tell you what that will do to the CIA."

Sean's mouth felt like sandpaper. He was in the loop on most things, but he had no idea that an illegal prison existed right here on U.S. soil. "What do you want from me?"

Jarod walked over to his desk, opened a drawer, and pulled out a thin file. He tossed it to Sean. "Review this. It contains the names of all of the Muslims we've imprisoned here. We've decided that instead of making them disappear, it's best that we simply transport them out of the country, and then put them on the no fly list. Take away their passports, and revoke citizenships for any who are actual U.S. citizens—and there are a few of those. Drop them on some desert in Iraq and let them find their way to wherever they want to be."

"Have any of the prisoners in this—prison—actually died while in our care?"

Jarod nodded. "Yeah, that's part of the problem we face. The remaining prisoners know about the deaths. At least when they're back in the Middle East, they can only talk to the Arab press, and no one pays attention to that crap. There might be stuff that will find its way onto social media eventually, but we can fight back at that just the way we have with the fringe news outlets. Easy to discredit any news coming out of the Middle East. We thought about just killing the remaining prisoners before this Senate report came out, but we can't do that now. Too much of a spotlight on us, and I worry that one of our own may become a whistleblower. If we just spirit them out of the country, that's at least humane enough that no one here will feel compelled to talk about it."

Sean felt his stomach turning on him—acid that always found its way upward when he had to think about things like this. He forced himself to ask the next question while fighting a choking sensation in his throat. "How many died?"

"About a dozen. Several from waterboarding, but we had a few that developed severe bloodstream infections from our drilling into the roots of their teeth. Usually effective tactics to get information, but sometimes fatal. We also had a couple who died from anal penetration—the objects we used ruptured their bowels. Not intended consequences for sure, but you can see why we don't want any of the remaining prisoners walking our streets. Some of these deaths were witnessed, which of course is another technique we use, as you know. Being forced to watch does get results. Oh, and we had several heart attacks also—those occurred while they were being interrogated. Sometimes the stress is just too much."

Sean suddenly started choking. The stinging acid had risen in a virtual fountain and was now sitting lodged in his throat. He rushed behind Jarod's desk, and leaned over the garbage can. Within a couple of seconds, he was vomiting, the morning's breakfast of bacon and eggs now wallowing at the bottom of the can.

He pulled a tissue out of the box on Jarod's desk and wiped his mouth. Breathing heavily, he walked back to the couch. Jarod hadn't made a move during the ordeal and was now staring at Sean with a curious look on his face. "What was that all about? Are you okay?"

Sean nodded. "Yeah, just some acid reflux. Probably...too much coffee...this morning."

"Alright then. Here, have some water." Jarod poured a tall glass for Sean, who quickly downed it in one gulp. "Okay, carrying on. I want you to take charge of the exodus of these scum. They belong in the Middle East, not here. Organize it all from start to finish, including the destruction of passports and revocation of citizenships. And I've arranged for a military transport to be at your disposal once you're ready to ship 'em out."

Sean poured some more water. "How many are left?"

"About a hundred, give or take."

"Where is this prison exactly?"

Jarod pointed at the folder on the coffee table. "Everything you need to know is in that little file."

Sean grabbed the folder, stood up and walked toward the door. Then he stopped and turned back to face Jarod. "Tell me, did we get any useful information from any of these people?"

Jarod shook his head. "Not really. But they were probably trained to withstand torture. Or the leads we were given were false. We'll never know. A few of them gave us phony information, probably just to get the torture to stop. In any event, the way I look at it, if they weren't already part of sleeper cells, they would have been eventually. It's just the way these goat-fuckers are created."

Sean made his way to the elevator, thinking to himself that he had finally seen the ruthless side Jarod McKenzie was famous for. In fact, ruthless wasn't even the right word. Heartless was probably closer to the truth. Sean felt like he needed a shower, badly.

*****

He was sitting in his kitchen, the room that would probably be the first recipient of his renovation project. The pinched home improvement magazine was the first thing he wanted to read, but Sean resisted the temptation. He knew he had to leaf through the secret prisoner file first.

He opened the file and began scanning. The address of the prison was paper-clipped onto the inside of the folder. He could picture the approximate location—it was a large warehouse well off a major north/south highway running through the center of Virginia. Sean wondered what the conditions were like inside and how well guarded it was. Knowing the CIA, he knew the living quarters were probably deplorable, and it would be patrolled to the hilt by uniformed CIA officers.

He then started scanning the names. There were several with lines drawn through them; presumably those were the dead ones. He recognized quite a few Persian names, and recalled back to when he and Jannat were together. She had taught him quite a bit about Iran.

Up until 1919, no Persian citizen had a last name. Just first names, with either prefixes or suffixes to help identify them from another person with the same first name. But the population finally reached a point that last names were needed. Then, in 1935, Persia became known as Iran, a noticeable change to the world, although, in effect it was really just the Persian version of the country's name. But when the name changed, a lot of the rich history of Persia disappeared in the blink of an eye. The Persian language had many similarities to Arabic, and Farsi was the dialect of the language that distinguished it from Arabic. In Iran, ninety-nine percent of the population was Muslim, and a full fifty percent still spoke Persian instead of Arabic. It was still spoken in six countries throughout the Arab world, whereas pure Arabic was spoken in twenty-five countries. Those from Persian heritage were stubborn, naturally so, in holding onto their language as the last vestige of their rich history.

Sean continued scanning the list, which was organized alphabetically by last name. He suddenly got the urge for a stiff drink. He got up and poured himself a scotch neat, took a quick sip, and sat down again. With the glass in hand, he finally reached the S section of the listing.

The glass slipped from his hand, the precious liquid splashing onto the table and into his lap. He didn't notice the cool wet shock to his crotch. How could he? His eyes were transfixed on one name. And the acid once again began rising into his throat.

Her name was there, callously written in sloppy handwriting.

An image popped into his head—a tall, classy lady with green eyes, long black hair, and an exotic face that would melt an iceberg. Her smile flashed across his eyes, and her kiss caressed his lips. The image changed. Now there were tears rolling down her cheeks as she packed her pretty little suitcase. The night he'd thrown her under the bus for his career.

Jannat Shirazi.

Chapter 17

"So, whaddaya think?"

Ziv stretched his legs and blew out a long breath. "Hal was a very shrewd man. And the prison guards obviously weren't too bright—either that or he just managed to charm them into being easy on him. The letters are indeed somewhat cryptic, and you would think the prison screening would have caught them before letting the U.S. Postal Service have them."

Brad got up from his chair and walked to the railing of his balcony. He shielded his eyes and looked out towards the islands.

"I love it way up here. It feels safe and totally isolated from the world. But, for me, at least I can hop on the elevator and head down to civilization again. Hard to imagine how Hal Winters must have felt. The only connection to the outside world he had was the occasional letter—and maybe the occasional visit with someone, most likely only that one son, Brock."

"Yeah, but he probably adjusted after a period of time. Got used to the isolation—took pleasure in the simple things, like going out in the prison yard for an hour or so."

Brad turned to Ziv and winced. "And that's what got him killed."

"Really? Was it a hit?"

"Sounds like it. July 16, 2011. He was attacked—unprovoked—by several new arrivals. Beaten to a pulp. The official record says that he died of natural causes—which is technically true, I guess, because it took two days before he succumbed to his injuries. But, the prison warden must have wanted to sugar-coat what happened to him."

Ziv shook his head. "Bad enough he was framed for that mall slaughter, but then he had to die like that."

Brad nodded. "The story goes that someone inside the prison found out he was CIA, and not the Mafia hit man of his cover story. At that point, he was dead meat."

"He was close with that movie star son, wasn't he? What's his name again? I'm not up on American movies."

"Brock. And, yes, they were close. I told you I flew down to L.A. to interview him—I was surprised at how emotional he was about his father. And, strangely, he talked about him a couple of times in the present tense, as if he were still alive. In denial, I guess, or he just can't let him go."

"I do recall now seeing a couple of Brock's movies—wasn't particularly impressed. Hard to believe he made it so big. Or—maybe not so hard to believe?"

Brad sat down on the bottom edge of his lounger. "What do you mean by that?"

Ziv smiled. "Forgive me. It's just the retired secret agent in me talking. But, humor me—Hal pled guilty to mass murder, that by all accounts in the alternative press were murders he didn't commit. And witness statements that were apparently buried seem to support his innocence.

"He was dressed in a pilot's uniform a few days after 9/11. Weird— what was that all about? He then gets sent to a medium security federal penitentiary, but he was supposed to be this mad dog mass murderer. Those types go to maximum security prisons, not medium security. And you mentioned that shortly after Hal went to prison, his son's career took off like a rocket."

"Payoff for pleading guilty and shutting the hell up?"

Ziv nodded his head slowly. "Does make you wonder, doesn't it? Quid pro quo? None of this quite adds up. And then, we have these letters…"

Brad walked over to a table near the sliding patio door and poured two glasses of lemonade. He handed one to Ziv and then raised his glass in a toast. They clinked, and Brad chimed, "To solving a mystery."

Ziv took a sip. "God, that's good. A relief on a hot day like this." He gulped some more and then put the glass down. "As I said, he was shrewd. These letters you showed me do have some things that jump out. And out of the twenty letters, I agree with you that only four of them are relevant. The others seem to be just letters."

Brad swatted at a mosquito, cursing as he did. "Damn little bastards! Okay, what jumps out at you, Ziv?"

"Well, I agree with some of the key words that you pulled out of the first two letters. They seem out of place, and one word in particular is an odd choice for someone to use in a letter. In the fifth letter, you noticed that he used the word *nonce*. In the context he used it, it's correct—the phrase was "I'm doing fine for the nonce." The word nonce can mean *for the time being*, but it can also mean *code*.

"So, I find that strange—he was an articulate man, for sure, but who in hell would say I'm doing fine for the *nonce*? In normal conversation, you would say, for now, or for the time being. But, a person would almost never use the word, nonce. That's just weird. So, was he trying to say that the letter was in code?"

Brad was jotting some notes down on a pad of paper as Ziv was talking. "Yeah, I thought that was an odd choice of word, too—along with quite a few other words and phrases. What do you think of all of those other ones I wrote down?"

"They're strange—yes. But, let me take them home with me and run them through a software program I have. It'll speed things up for us a lot."

Brad folded his arms across his chest. "I really don't want them out of my sight, but I don't want to take photos of them with my phone either. Don't like the idea of them being on an electronic device. And I can't make copies for you because my Canon's on the fritz." He scratched his head while pondering Ziv's request. "Okay, just promise me you'll protect them with your life. I don't want to tell you what Kristy and I had to go through to get them."

Ziv looked at Brad suspiciously. "We're supposed to be partners. Shouldn't you tell me?"

"Not right now—maybe later. I'm afraid I'll scare you off."

"Okay—promise?"

"Promise."

"Remember who I am, Brad, old buddy. Not very much scares me anymore—except women, of course!" Ziv laughed as he took another sip of his lemonade. "There is something I can tell you right off the top of my head about those four key letters though—without the help of the software."

Brad perked up. "What?"

"Okay, the dates of the letters are significant. And since those four letters are the only ones that seem to be trying to tell a story, I think the dates he chose as to when to write them were deliberate."

Brad poised his pen over his pad. "Shoot."

"The first letter was dated December 7, 2001. That was Pearl Harbor, 1941. The second letter—which was actually his fifth—was on July 2, 2006. That was the date of the purported Roswell, New Mexico UFO crash back in 1947. And the third letter you picked out, which was Hal's ninth, was dated September 11, 2008. That day needs no explanation.

"The fourth letter you identified, Hal's seventeenth example of penmanship, was dated July 7, 2010. That was the date back in 2005 when the London terrorist bombings occurred—three subway trains and one double-decker bus were bombed, killing fifty-six people and injuring 700."

Brad looked up from his notes, and began flicking the end of his pen. "All significant dates in history."

"Much more than that, Brad. Each of those dates in history is tainted by conspiracy theories as being *false flag* inside jobs, with the one exception being Roswell—and that one is theorized as being a cover-up. So, if we're to attach any significance to why Hal Winters chose those dates, we might think that he's trying to draw attention to a cover-up or false flag of some sort."

Brad whistled. "Wow, that just gave me the shivers."

Ziv chuckled. "That's the journalist in you. But it's far too coincidental, in my opinion, that those dates were chosen. Of course, he could just be trying to say that his conviction was a farce, a cover-up. It could just relate to his case rather than something more sinister.

"But, I keep coming back in my mind to the fact that he pled guilty to something he probably didn't do, was sent to a medium security prison despite being a convicted mass murderer, and his son Brock's career began a meteoric rise right after Hal was convicted. And—on the day of the mass murders in the Mall of America, Hal was dressed in a pilot's outfit when he entered the store. The detective in me says that these things have meaning."

Brad reached down and picked up the pile of twenty letters, stuffed them back into a thin briefcase, and handed the case to Ziv.

"Okay, I entrust these to you. Get outta here and start figuring out the rest of the story. You're not going to get onto my byline by sitting here drinking lemonade."

Ziv took the case and walked back inside to the living room area of the apartment. Brad followed behind and slid the patio doors shut.

As Ziv headed toward the hallway, Brad called after him. "Hey, what's that about you being afraid of women? I don't recall you ever having a fear of the opposite sex before."

Ziv turned around and laughed. "Oh, I was just kidding. Actually, though, there is a new lady in my life and I do kinda find it scary how much I'm into her. She's sort of won me over, so to speak, and I'm a bit anxious about allowing myself to fall too hard. But, what's that saying? 'Better to have loved and lost than never to have loved at all?'"

"I'm glad for you, Ziv. You haven't really allowed anyone into your life since Isabelle died. That was a long time ago. This woman must be pretty special. I'd like to meet her. What's her name?"

"She is special, Brad—very special. And we met in the most unusual way. Almost like fate intervened. Her name's Leslie. Leslie Fields."

Chapter 18

It was a warehouse just like any other warehouse. A massive one-storey steel on steel structure, with a large parking area. It was just, well, a warehouse. But there were a few differences to the discerning eye.

Most people driving by this building wouldn't notice or pay any real attention to the differences, but to Sean they were obvious. Probably because he knew what kind of cargo was being stored inside.

People. Living, breathing people.

The warehouse was located just off the main Virginia north/south highway, only about twenty miles north of the Langley area. Little did Sean know that Jannat had been living in a prison for the last five years just a half hour drive from where he worked.

As he approached, he took note of the unique characteristics of this warehouse. First, there wasn't a single window. Second, the entire property was surrounded by metallic fencing at least eight feet high, topped with curls of barbed wire. That alone was a dead giveaway. Third, there were no signs indicating that the building was any kind of business establishment. There was one sign, though—and it read: "No trespassing. Violators will be prosecuted." Another dead giveaway.

And the final difference was the gate, which was attached to a guard hut. As Sean approached in his car, he could see that there was one guard in attendance inside the hut. He pulled up and waited for the guard to emerge. The man was uniformed, and adorned with a holster and sidearm. Sean recognized the uniform as typical of the CIA's security force. Most people weren't aware that the CIA had its own uniformed officers, as does the Secret Service. Their jobs consisted solely of providing security and support for plain-clothed field agents.

Sean rolled down his window as the guard approached. He had a clipboard in one hand, with the other one poised above the mouth of his holster.

Sean flashed his credentials, which the guard immediately compared against a sheet on the clipboard. He then smiled and said, "Okay, Director, you're free to come and go as you please. Consider us at your service."

Sean smiled back. "Thanks, Officer. Much appreciated. I'll be arranging for the liquidation of this place."

The guard nodded. "I understand. My orders are that you have full carte blanche. I heard that you'll be in charge of emptying this place out. Sooner the better. This is a boring assignment. Looking forward to getting posted somewhere else."

Sean nodded his head in the direction of the warehouse building. "Don't blame you at all. It looks pretty bleak."

"It is. God speed to you."

Sean raised his right hand in salute, and the guard returned the gesture. He turned on his heel and went back into the hut. Reached under the desk and pressed a button. The metal gate slowly slid open and Sean drove forward into the parking lot, choosing a spot in the front row closest to the building.

He climbed out of his car and walked forlornly up to the shiny metal door, a door as cold and antiseptic as what lay beyond it. Pressed his thumb against the buzzer button and waited. He felt his breathing getting labored, not looking forward to what he would be witnessing behind the unforgiving walls of this prison.

The military flight to the Middle East was scheduled to leave in a week's time, taking most of these poor souls with it. Souls who would have absolutely no official identities. Sean, in line with his orders, had already arranged for all of their papers to be destroyed—incinerated like garbage. Passports for the few that were American citizens had also been revoked, and all of their records whitewashed, as if they had never existed in the first place.

Well, almost all. All except one.

The military transport would be landing at an Iraqi air force base at Fallujah. What the Revolutionary Guard would do with them after that was anyone's guess. But no one would care. The only thing that mattered was that they would no longer be on U.S. soil, no longer able to talk about what they had witnessed and been subjected to. And the "warehouse" would be cleaned and vacated as if nothing had ever transpired there.

The door swung open and Sean was greeted by another uniformed guard. He showed his credentials once again and was led into a grim reception area. He took a seat and waited.

Within a few minutes, he heard footsteps coming in his direction from a long hallway. A tall bespectacled man walked up to him and held out his hand.

"Hello, Director Russell. I'm Doctor Fitzpatrick. Call me John. I'm the managing director here."

Sean stood and shook his hand. He put on the sternest and most heartless CIA expression he could muster. "Hi. Call me Sean. Thanks for your time today. I want a tour, a final look-see before we get all of this scum out of the country."

The doctor chuckled. "Make sure we do it under the cover of darkness. Can't have any nosy journalists getting wind of this."

"We will. Next Wednesday night, we'll take them out of your custody. Buses will pull up at the front gate. You can load them in and we'll take it from there."

"What will happen to them over there?"

Sean grimaced. "Do you care?"

"No, not really. Just professional curiosity."

"Don't worry about it. Not your concern."

Sean pulled a sheaf of papers out of his pocket. "This is a list of the prisoners. I want to do a head count. Can you take me on a tour?"

"No problem. Follow me."

The doctor led the way back down the long hallway. As they moved their way along, Sean noticed there were several empty rooms with windows facing into the hall. He saw tables and chairs in some, others empty except for ropes and chains hanging from the ceilings. One room was padded with rubber from floor to ceiling. Each of the rooms were distinguished by one feature—large blood stains spattered onto the floors and walls.

Fitzpatrick noticed the direction of Sean's eyes. "Kind of a mess, eh? Those were our interrogation rooms. I assume you've arranged for a cleaning crew to come in?"

Sean nodded. "Yep. The entire building will be sanitized. By the time we're finished it'll look like a vacant IKEA."

"Good. Okay, the next hallway will take us along all the residents' rooms. We house them four to a room. All the rooms have one-way glass that we can peek through, and you'll notice placards on the outside of each, listing the names of the residents. All fucking Arab names, of course, so they all kinda look the same. But you should be able to use these cards to do your head count. We won't go into any of the rooms, but you can look in through the windows."

They stopped at the first room they came to. Sean gazed in through the window. It was equipped with two sets of bunk beds and a chemical toilet up against the wall. There was a pail of water that Sean guessed functioned as the sink. Two women were lying on the two upper bunks, while two shirtless men were stretched out on the lower bunks.

"You mix the sexes in this place?"

Fitzpatrick laughed. "Part of our interrogatory practice. Denigrates them, takes away their dignity."

"Do you try to keep married couples together?"

"No, quite the opposite. If we know they're married, we separate them—make the wives live with other men. Again, part of the strategy. After they're raped a few times by strange camel-fuckers, they become very pliant and anxious to tell us anything we want to hear."

Sean's stomach began erupting on him a bit. "Once they've told you what you want to hear, what do you do with them?"

"We reward them with a few days of privacy in single dorm rooms. Then we throw them back in again. It works real well—actually saved us from having to torture some of them ourselves. As you know, their dignity is everything. When we strip that away from them, they have nothing left to fight for."

"Lovely. What tricks do you use on the men?"

"Generally broom handles."

"I see."

They moved further down the corridor. One room after another, the same grim scene in each. Sean was checking all of the names on the placards carefully. So far, he hadn't seen Jannat's.

He checked each name off, one by one. After two more corridors, Fitzpatrick announced they were finished.

Sean re-counted his checkmarks. "I get 103 people. There are supposed to be 107. And one of those names has particular intelligence interest to us." He looked up from his list and glared at the doctor. "Where are the missing four?"

Fitzpatrick looked at the list. "Oh, those four. I forgot about them. Follow me."

He flashed his card against a magnetic reader on the wall, and Sean heard the click of a door unlocking. The doctor swung it open and led the way down another hallway. There were several nurses milling about. All of them smiled politely as they passed.

Fitzpatrick motioned with his hand, directing Sean to follow him through another door. This room was a huge ward, with dozens of empty hospital beds. Empty except for three.

"This is the infirmary. Those three Muslims have been here for quite some time. They can't possibly make the trip to Iraq. Too difficult for us to make them comfortable, and they'd need care and restraints along the way."

"What do you intend to do with them?"

The doctor shuffled his feet. "We plan to euthanize them. Same stuff vets use. Painless and quick."

The acid was rising fast now. Sean coughed and fought it back down. At the same time, it felt like his blood was boiling up inside of him. He wanted so much to just rip this doctor's head off, right then and there. But—he had to play his role. Just a little while longer.

"That's unacceptable. No one else is to die here. I thought we made that clear."

Fitzpatrick's eyes flared. "It's just three. Well, four including one other one. We can easily dispose of the bodies."

"You're not hearing me. No one else is to die on U.S. soil."

"Well, they won't make it there alive without medical help."

Sean rammed his index finger into the man's chest. "That's why you're going with them. You and three of your nurses. You will make sure they get to Iraq alive, and that they get immediate medical help when they arrive there."

"They can't possibly ride on buses from here to the airport."

"I'll send ambulances in addition to the buses."

"I can't fly. I have a fear of flying."

Sean's temper was starting to get the better of him. "Too fucking bad for you. I'm sure some of these people had a fear of broom handles as well, and perhaps even a few were scared of waterboarding. Suck it up, Doctor. You're going and I'm not going to argue with you about it anymore."

The man nodded. "Well, they're not in good shape. One has lung cancer, two have pneumonia, and there's a fourth one who's catatonic."

Sean shoved his list in front of Fitzpatrick's face, and pounded his index finger against one name on the page. "This Shirazi woman. We have a special interest in her, due to the historic significance of her Persian name. It's well connected in Iran, and we think her connections may be deeper than we know. I don't see a woman in this ward. Where is she?"

The doctor scowled. "She's the fourth one. Follow me. In a separate room. That bitch is the catatonic one—more trouble than she's worth. And if she has any special intelligence interest, we certainly haven't found it. She hasn't uttered a word in three years."

Fitzpatrick stomped on down to the end of the ward, with Sean following close behind. "What do you mean, catatonic?"

"Doesn't relate, goes into sudden tantrums, won't talk or even look any of us in the eye. For a few months after the incident, she actually suffered from 'locked-in syndrome.' We managed to go down the rabbit hole and bring her out of that, but she hasn't advanced beyond catatonic. At least now she can eat, drink, and wipe her own ass. When she was 'locked-in' we had to do all of that shit for her."

Sean grabbed the doctor by the back of his jacket and wrenched him to a stop. He spun him around to face him. "She's an important intelligence asset to us. What incident are you referring to that drove her into 'locked-in syndrome'?"

Fitzpatrick looked shocked at being handled so roughly. "We didn't know she was a special asset to you guys. You should have told us!"

"It's only come to our attention in the last few days. Again, what incident drove her under?"

"Three years ago, we made her watch while we interrogated her husband. We did some—ugly—things to him. Unfortunately, he didn't survive. She watched him die."

Sean spun the doctor around again and shoved him forward. "Go on. Take me to her. Now!"

The doctor turned his head back to face Sean. "I don't like being treated this way. You have no right to—"

Sean clenched Fitzpatrick's skinny little throat in his fist and squeezed—squeezed until the evil man's face turned red and his eyeballs began to bulge.

"I could kill you in seconds, you pitiful excuse for a doctor. Don't fuck with me. And you'd better not miss that plane next week or I'll come looking for you. Now, lead me to Jannat Shirazi."

Sean released his hand and Fitzpatrick struggled to catch his breath. But he said not a word. Just motioned with his hand and led Sean through a door into another room. Then he pointed.

"There she is. She's all yours, what's left of her."

Sean tried his best to hide the tears that instantly welled up in his eyes. Jannat was sitting on her bed, chin resting on bent knees, arms tightly encircling them. She was rocking from side to side, moaning. Her long black hair was greasy and lifeless and the skin on her arms was flaked and torn. Jannat's once beautiful face was haggard and scratched. Her figure was just a ghost of what it had once been. Sean guessed that she weighed no more than ninety pounds.

He hadn't seen her in eighteen years, so he was prepared for the fact that she would look different. But he hadn't expected this, not in his worst nightmares. And that's what this was—a nightmare. An image flashed through his brain, from the horror movie, The Ring. Jannat reminded him of the horrific-looking girl who crawled out of the well.

This was the woman he had loved with every fibre of his being. He had cast her aside for his career, but he had also made the conscious decision back then to let her go so that the CIA interrogators wouldn't get their hands on her.

In a weird twist of fate, they had gotten her anyway.

Sean walked to the foot of the bed and knelt down on the floor so as to be at eye level with her. He whispered her name over and over again.

It was like he wasn't even there. She stared off into space with a wild look in her once ravishing green eyes. Eyes that now looked like insanity—and death.

Sean got to his feet and turned to face Fitzpatrick. He wasn't thinking rationally now. But he was indeed thinking like a human being, and for that he was thankful. He didn't know whether or not he was doing the right thing, but he knew he had to do something.

"Prepare Jannat Shirazi for travel. I'm taking her with me."

Chapter 19

Leslie Fields took a quick glance at her Rolex. Oops—running a bit late.

She had to pick up the pace.

Ziv lived in a condo on Queen Street West, which was just a short subway ride north from her apartment on King. Well, she could walk it just as easy, but tonight she'd have her overnight bag with her, so it was more convenient to just hop the train.

She ruffled through her dresser drawer—the bottom drawer where she kept the special stuff. Out came the leathers—well, really just leather singular. It was a onesy, with a zipper at the back which slid down right to the bottom of her ass. Impossible to get zipped up all by herself, but Ziv would help. She'd arrive at his condo half-zipped and he could take his time finishing her off.

Once he finished zipping her up, she'd order him into the bedroom to wait patiently for her, flat on his back. Oh, yes, he'd be nicely surprised tonight, but she knew full well he was up for it. He just didn't know she knew, or how she knew.

She reached into the bottom of the drawer and pulled out her leather Cat Woman mask. Even though the onesy was tight, black, and sexy as hell, she knew the mask would be his favorite. She just knew. Something about being a predator, and since he'd been a predator on the streets of the world for most of his career, being the prey for a night would be a fantasy unlike any other for him.

She knew Ziv had a lot of fantasies. He'd just been afraid to talk about them with her so far. So, tonight would be the moment of truth. When the utter glee on his face would give him away. Cat Woman would make him as hard as a rock.

Sometimes the simplest things had the most powerful effect. The human brain was unpredictable, and of course well known for being the most erotic sex organ. Nothing happened if it didn't happen in the brain first. Why some people had such powerful fantasies, Leslie had no idea. She was willing to play the game, of course, no harm in that. But, she didn't really understand it.

Perhaps something that happened in childhood, some shock or something extremely erotic and impactful? Images from childhood were the most powerful, and they generally molded the way people thought for the rest of their lives.

Leslie sat on the edge of her bed and stared at the Cat Woman mask. She smiled, thinking how excited Ziv would get when she slipped it on.

Then her smile turned upside down when she recalled the night he'd poured his heart out to her about his late wife, Isabelle.

A car bomb in Paris meant for Ziv. But, Isabelle beat him to the car, anxious to tour the city on the first vacation they'd taken in years.

In fact, as a couple, they hadn't left Israel for at least five years. Ziv had traveled many times, of course, in his role as a Mossad agent, but Isabelle had never accompanied him. So, all of their vacations had tended to be in Israel, for security reasons.

But they got careless once and went to Paris. Isabelle and their rented car blew into a million unrecognizable pieces when she turned on the ignition. Ziv had been crossing the street, intending to hop into the passenger side when it happened.

Isabelle had wanted to drive that day.

The blast blew him off his feet and rendered him unconscious, suspended in a medically induced coma for several days. When he awoke to the news that the love of his life was gone, taken instead of him, he vowed that he would kill the animals if it was the last thing he did.

And he did.

With the help of the Mossad, he tracked them down in Lebanon a year later. One of them died instantly from a concussion grenade installed under his mattress. The other killer died while Ziv watched from a phone booth across the street. One call was all it took for the telephone to become a deadly weapon.

That was twenty years ago, and he hadn't allowed himself a serious relationship since. Leslie felt honored to be the one. Yet, she had to be careful not to allow herself to get too close. Close meant complications, and she didn't want too many of those in her life.

She smiled when she thought of what a paradox Ziv was. He was strong, handsome and confident. And very intelligent—he had to be, just to survive in the job that he'd done for most of his adult life. One of the most well-trained intelligence operatives on the planet, which could probably be said of anyone who'd worked for Mossad.

But, the paradox of Ziv was, in a nutshell, a man who was trained to be in control in his job—but, from a sexual standpoint, he was apparently more than willing to completely give up control. In fact, after tonight when she opened up his secret, he would be begging her forever to be the one in control. And, probably at times, to even make it hurt. Leslie just knew these things.

As far as she was concerned, that was okay. It made everything so much easier.

She went into her bedroom and squeezed her body into the skin-tight leather suit. Left the back unzipped from the bottom of her ass. Then, she stuffed a change of clothes into the overnight bag, along with the mask, four sections of rope, a ball equipped with a thick elastic band, and an ominous looking bull-clamp. Then she pulled up the handle on her case, and wheeled it towards the door. Last but not least, she donned a long, stylish London Fog trench coat to cover up the erotic suit and her exposed ass. Couldn't have scummy men getting excited on the subway. That wouldn't do, because despite the way she was dressed, Leslie was a classy lady.

One last look in the hallway mirror before she made her exit. She smiled at her reflection. As usual, not much makeup. She liked it that way. Because she was looking at the real Leslie Fields. And, with the real Leslie Fields, she honestly didn't think there were many men who could resist when she put her mind to it.

After all, the mind was indeed the most powerful sex organ.

*****

Ziv was pacing back and forth, excited as hell. He could feel his heart pumping hard, which was what always happened whenever he'd been on assignment for Mossad.

Missions that took him around the world, sometimes dangerous, sometimes benign. But, it was the chase that got him—the clues that took him from point *A* to point *B*. The satisfaction of getting to point B.

And it felt as if, right now, he was close—very close. To point *B*.

Tonight was doubly exciting—the clues in the letters were starting to form a pattern in his mind. And, as a bonus, Leslie was coming over in about an hour. That alone always got his heart pumping.

Ziv took one final look at his notes. He had to phone Brad before he burst. Picked up the phone and dialed.

"Hello?"

"Hi Brad. It's me. We need to talk."

"Want me to come over?"

"No. I have a date tonight, but I wanted to talk to you now. Didn't want to put it off. I'm pumped at what I've found out. And you will be, too."

"Should we talk about this over the phone?"

Ziv hesitated for a second. "I think we're safe. No one knows what we're doing."

"Okay, then. Give it to me."

Ziv shuffled his papers. "Well, first off, I put all the notes through that program I told you about, along with all of the data that we have about Hal's arrest, the dates, his family information, etc. A definite pattern starts to form."

"We already discussed the dates of those four particular letters—how they seemed significant."

"Yeah, the program picked that up right away too—how those four dates correspond with famous dates of possible false flags or cover-ups. And the word nonce was used twice, which seems to be an attempt by Hal to pound away at the fact that he's writing in code. But, there are also two phrases in one of the letters that are interesting. One is *two different directions*, and the other is *on the wings of a dream.*"

"What's so intriguing about those?"

"They're both titles of songs by the late singer, John Denver."

"He mentioned another John Denver song, too, when he was writing about his wife, Anne— *Annie's Song.* He talked about how that song reminded him of her."

Ziv was tapping his pen furiously on the desk.

"Yes, Brad. I think all three of those references to John Denver were very significant. And not only is Denver a city in Colorado, but John Denver also lived in Colorado—and was a pilot. Which was actually how he died."

"Okay, I'm trying to follow you."

"Let's keep in mind that Hal Winters was definitely trying to say something, create a pattern, but he had to do it cryptically. Otherwise, the letters would never have been allowed to leave the prison. He had to get them past the prison screening filters. And he succeeded. So, we have to try to think like him here, and then tie in some other key facts."

"Carry on."

"Right. Some of those key words you pulled out of the letters are intriguing: *mirages, tricks of the brain, eyes are playing tricks, seeing things that just aren't there.* He also wrote about being given a bad deck of cards, and that one of the guards bought him a new one. And remember again those three John Denver songs that he squeezed into his letters: *Two Different Directions, On the Wings of a Dream,* and *Annie's Song.*"

"I'm trying to follow you, Ziv. It's pretty muddled right now, but I'm keeping up."

"Okay, here's where it gets even more interesting. The ninth letter—the one you said was the one that Colin gave to you—was dated September 11. In that letter, he states that he just weighed himself and was shocked to see that his weight had dropped to 175 pounds. And then he goes on to ask this Richard Sterling guy to send a birthday card to his eldest son, Logan, as his birthday was coming up on 17/5. So, May 17 of the following year. But, the kicker here is that in America, they would show that date as 5/17, not 17/5 like you Canadians would show it."

"Hey, you're a Canadian now, too."

"True, but I still think of myself as Israeli, and in Israel we would also show it as 5/17. But, Hal, being American, went against the grain and showed it as 17/5."

"So, he asked that a card be sent to his son, and he went to a lot of trouble to use the number 175 twice; once for his weight and once for the birth date."

"Exactly. But, get this. What's really interesting, in addition to the number 175, is that his eldest son's name is Garret not Logan. And his other two sons are named Heath, and, of course, Brock, who you've already met. And none of them have a birthday in May."

"That's strange."

"Yes, it is. He went out of his way to squeeze into his letter the number 175 and the word Logan.

"I did some digging. The newspapers all said Hal was dressed in a pilot's uniform that day that he walked into the Mall of America. But they never said what airline's uniform it was. There's video footage of him in the open mall area before he changed out of his clothes. I managed to get a look at it through my contacts back in Tel Aviv. Don't ask. Anyway, the uniform was United Airlines, and it was a captain's uniform."

"Jesus!"

"Yes, and let's remember that this was just four days after 9/11. Two United Airlines and two American Airlines planes were hijacked that day. And then there Hal is, four days later, dressed in a United Airlines captain's uniform in Minneapolis. I'm scratching my head over that. Coincidence?"

"He's trying to tell us something from the grave with these letters, Ziv. I don't think there's any coincidence here at all."

"No, me neither. And my nifty little computer program doesn't think so either. I've plugged everything into the program and it spit out a summary. We used this software at Mossad for years—I think they have a newer, better version now. But this thing still works pretty good. Mind you, bear with it—the summary isn't necessarily logical. We have to attach our own logic to it. It just takes all the facts and comes to some conclusions, even if they're illogical. I'll read the summary to you:

> Subject Hal Winters, a trusted black ops agent, skilled pilot. Refers to deceptions and mirages. Was involved in trickery. Dates of letters correspond with historical deception dates. Consistent with use of number 175, wrong birth date of son and deliberately incorrect name of son. Seen wearing United Airlines uniform close to 9/11 terrorist attacks. Incorrect name of son, Logan, refers to Logan Airport, Boston. United Airlines flight 175 departed from Logan Airport before being hijacked and crashed into south tower of WTC. Consistent reference by Winters to John Denver songs is deliberate message. Evidence points to subject matter being airline flight. Subject Winters was a pilot, John Denver was a pilot. Subject Winters was dressed in United Airlines captain's uniform and references flight 175 and Logan in his communications. Focuses messages on John Denver songs with no apparent linkage as to why. Conclusions: Subject Hal Winters was the pilot of United Airlines flight 175. Key message intention is Denver International Airport. Existing data on said facility consistent with deception messages from subject Winters.

Ziv heard a gasp at the other end of the line. "Brad, are you there? You okay?"

"What the fuck, Ziv? This is crazy!"

"I know, I know!"

"Do you really trust that program? Geez—this makes no logical sense at all. Flight 175 crashed on September 11 into the south tower. And Hal Winters was arrested four days later, way off in Minneapolis."

"I warned you. It's computer-speak. We have to mull this over and attach our own logic to it. It merely assembles all the information and assimilates it in a fashion that would take our brains forever to process.

Then it comes up with calculated conclusions—not necessarily logical, but calculated."

"I can't believe the Mossad relied on this too often. How can we make sense out of it?"

"Well, all I'll tell you is this: the program was accurate ninety percent of the time. So, I think we need to sleep on this and talk some more tomorrow. Deal?"

"Good plan. But, I don't think I'll be able to sleep too much after hearing all this. My brain is just spinning now. Here's a crazy thought— if this is indeed accurate, what the fuck does this tell us? Where does this take us?"

"I know, I know. My brain's spinning, too. Let's just put it out of our heads for now, and we'll hash it out tomorrow."

"Okay. Thanks for this, Ziv—I think."

Ziv hung up the phone and poured himself a glass of Merlot. He glanced at his watch. Well, at least he knew that he would have a wonderful distraction in just a few minutes. Something to help him forget the craziness of the Mossad program conclusions.

He shut off the computer, bundled the twenty letters up into a neat little pile and carried them over to his open wall safe. Stuffed them inside, closed the heavy door, and spun the dial. Nice and safe now.

Tomorrow, he and Brad would debate the findings.

Tomorrow was another day.

And tonight was tonight.

He jumped with excitement at the sound of the doorbell. He walked—no, ran—to the door and opened it wide. There she was, his intoxicating new love.

Leslie sashayed through the door, pulling her trusty little suitcase behind her. She let go of the handle and wrapped both arms around Ziv's neck. "Well, my favorite secret agent, do you think you can handle a rocket scientist tonight?"

He kissed her. "You know it. Great to see you, Les. Just finished up my work, so I'm all yours for as long as you want me."

"You know I want you. But, first I want a glass of wine, and I can see that you already have a bottle open. So—pour."

Ziv laughed. Leslie closed the door behind her and pulled her case into the bathroom. "I'll change later. Right now, let's toast to something—anything."

Ziv reached for her coat. "Don't you at least want to take off your jacket?"

"No, my dear. I have a surprise underneath, and even more in my suitcase. So, you can fantasize about that for a few minutes while we toast."

They sat together in the living room and clinked their wine glasses. Ziv leaned forward and kissed her neck. "I'm intrigued. But I'll put my curiosity on hold for a few minutes. So, what shall we toast to?"

"Well, how about that project you're working on?"

"Sure. As good a toast as any."

They clinked their glasses again.

"How's it going, by the way? You haven't told me much about it, but from your intensity over it, it must be kind of exciting."

"It's going okay."

"Secret agent stuff?"

"Ha, ha. You know I retired from that."

"Yeah, but you mentioned you still do some consulting."

"A wee bit here and there. Nothing earth-shattering. Why don't we toast instead to what you're doing?"

Leslie laughed. "Trying to change the subject, huh? Okay, well, I'm working on a new advanced telescope that's going to be installed on the International Space Station. The most powerful telescope ever invented, and it should give us earlier warnings of near-earth objects. See, now? I'm not secretive at all. Not like you."

"No, you're not. But I won't tell anyone about your telescope, don't worry. I don't think anyone would give a shit, anyway. But, how do I know it's not some secret weapon being installed up there?"

"Now, that would be silly, Ziv, since we share the ISS with the Russians."

"Oops—forgot about that. Okay, good answer. I think I've had too much wine. Why don't we stop talking and have some fun before I make the mistake of pouring another glass?"

Leslie flashed him her sexiest smile—a smile that Ziv knew always preceded a sexy romp in bed. She grabbed the empty wine bottle and took it into the kitchen.

"Okay, I'm going into the bathroom. Why don't you get ready, then come in and join me? I'll actually need your help for one part of the surprise."

Ziv's heart felt like it was trying to leap out of his chest. And his jeans suddenly felt far too tight. "Deal. Call me when you're ready."

He ran into the bedroom, then into his ensuite bathroom. Quickly ran the electric shaver across his face and splashed on some cologne. Then he heard an authoritative summon; a tone in her voice that he'd never heard before.

He ran back to the other bathroom and cautiously opened the door. There she was, clad in tight leather from her neck to her toes. Her shapely ass was exposed, and her face was shrouded in a mask. She looked more authentic than the movie version of Cat Woman.

He stammered. "Wh-what's this?"

She took hold of his hand and guided it down to the zipper at the base of her ass. "Shut up and just zip me."

Ziv was shocked. But, nicely shocked.

How did she know? Have I given her clues?

He was eager to obey her command, but before he did he couldn't resist slipping his hand between the crack of her exposed bum. He slid it in as far as it would go.

Leslie whirled around and slapped him across the face. "You'll have to wait. Zip me up. Now! And then go to your room and lay on your back!"

He fumbled nervously with the zipper and managed to get it all the way up to the base of her neck. Then he quickly headed back to his bedroom. Laid on his back and waited.

She was there in seconds, standing at the foot of his bed, resplendent in black from head to toe. And that mask—it did things to him.

She had her case with her and opened it up. Said not a word, but went straight to her work. She pulled four sections of rope out of the bag. "I'm going to restrain you. Because you've been such a bad boy."

Ziv could feel his body shivering with excitement. She ripped open his shirt, popping the buttons off in the process. Then yanked off his jeans, underwear and socks.

Next were the restraints. She tied his feet to the footboard—tight, but not tight enough to cut off circulation.

Then she slithered her leathered body on top of him and sat on his chest. Pulled his arms back over his head and tied his hands to the headboard. Again, not too tight, but tight enough. He knew he wasn't going to escape from this, but he didn't care either.

Leslie reached down into her bag and pulled out an odd looking ball. "Open your mouth, you naughty boy!"

He obeyed. She shoved the ball in between his teeth as far as it would go, and pulled an elastic attachment up and around the back of his head. He couldn't move, talk, or even scream now. But, Ziv didn't care. This was a game she wanted to play with him tonight, and one that he wanted to play, too. He trusted her.

She started licking his neck, and then quickly moved her tongue down to his chest. Continued on down to his navel, and then her mouth pounced on his penis. She bit it gently at first, but then got more aggressive. Her teeth were scraping hard against the head of his penis and he moaned. Her hand reached down into her bag and pulled out the bull-clamp. She attached it to his left nipple while her teeth continued scraping hard against his penis.

Ziv shook his head from side to side. He wasn't liking this too much at all. She took the cue immediately and popped the clamp off.

His penis had already started retracting with the discomfort, so she went to work with her hands. In a few seconds it was hard again and she slid her crotch up on top. Ziv's eyes were like saucers as he watched her gyrate. And he discovered something wonderful about the skin-tight black suit. It had a gaping hole in the crotch, that she accentuated by spreading her legs outward. Suddenly, he loved this Cat Woman even more. He could fuck her with the entire leather outfit still intact. He loved the feel of leather.

He entered her smoothly and they began to rock together. Ziv gazed up lovingly at the masked face. Seeing those exotic eyes gleaming through the slits made his penis even harder. He had the feeling that the orgasm that was on its way was going to be the biggest blast he'd ever had.

She closed her eyes and rocked harder now—frantically. He could hear her heavy breathing as well as his own. With his mouth constrained by the ball, he was finding it hard to get enough air just through his nose alone. Made the sensation even more exciting, almost dangerous.

He was starting to feel lightheaded. She was rocking now just as if she were riding a stallion. For a weird second, Ziv wondered if she'd ever owned a horse. Slapped his thighs as she rode, bent his penis to extremes—stretching it to limits it had never experienced before. It was exhilarating.

All of a sudden his eyes were distracted by movement through the open bedroom door.

Out in the hallway!

The front door had opened and two dark figures were entering; slowly, quietly, hunched over in commando fashion.

Why is that door open? I always lock it!

He started moaning as loudly as he could to warn Leslie, but her eyes were closed, her moans were louder than his, and she wasn't paying any attention to him at all.

They entered the bedroom quietly, each brandishing pistols. Dressed in black, including balaclavas covering their faces.

One leaned across the bed and pistol-whipped Leslie across the side of her head. She flew off the bed and crashed to the floor. The intruder then walked around the bed and put the barrel of the gun up against the back of her head. The other stranger shoved his gun into Ziv's forehead while at the same time holding one finger up in front of his mouth.

"*Shh.* I'm going to take this ball out of your mouth. Don't yell out or my friend will kill her. Understand?"

Ziv nodded his head. He noticed the man had a British accent.

The man pulled the elastic off the back of Ziv's head and popped the ball out of his mouth.

"We'll be quick. Give me the combination to your safe."

Ziv swallowed hard and drank in a deep breath of air.

"Now! If you don't tell me the combo, my friend will kill Cat Woman over there. And then you'll be next."

Ziv didn't have a choice. If his hands and feet were free he could do something about this. But—he was a captive audience and completely helpless. A feeling he wasn't accustomed to at all.

He whispered, "Okay. Don't hurt her. We're cool here. It's 35-14-27."

The man shoved the ball back into Ziv's mouth and walked out to the living room. Ziv heard the spinning of the dial and the sound of the safe door cracking open.

Within seconds, he was back in the bedroom with the pile of Hal Winters' letters under his arm. His friend pulled the gun away from Leslie's head, and her shoulders sagged with relief. She hadn't said a word since they'd entered the apartment, but her eyes behind the mask reflected sheer abject terror.

The leader was all business. Quick and focused. He nodded to his friend. "Okay, let's go."

They both shoved the pistols into holsters on their hips, saluted Ziv mockingly, and left the apartment without another word.

Ziv thought to himself that these guys had known exactly what they wanted. Slick and professional. No mess, no unnecessary violence.

They were professionals, just like him. This was exactly how he would have done it.

And—at least one of them was British.

Chapter 20

Sean was driving in a daze. On auto-pilot; seeing but not absorbing the scenery around him. He was aware of the road ahead and the other cars in front and behind, but he wasn't paying careful attention the way a driver should. Luckily, it was only about a half hour drive to his house.

He glanced over his shoulder. Jannat was lying still across the backseat, covered in a blanket. Doctor Fitzpatrick had assembled her meagre belongings, and threw them into a large plastic bag for Sean to take along with him.

Before leaving the prison with Jannat, Sean had cornered the doctor in the man's office and warned him about saying anything to anyone about the fact that Jannat was not going to be on the plane to Iraq. He told him to amend the records to show that she had boarded the plane. No one at the Air Force base would bother to do a head count before loading the plane. The pilots were under orders to just take their human cargo to Fallujah, and that was it. And the doctor and three nurses would be on board to ensure all went well.

Fitzpatrick had at first seemed puzzled when Sean ordered him to keep his mouth shut. But the reason he gave him was that Jannat Shirazi's existence on U.S. soil was to be classified, as she was an extremely valuable asset. Only a handful of people knew she was remaining behind, and Sean said he couldn't tell the doctor who those people were.

So, if Fitzpatrick said something to anyone, he would have no way of knowing if that person was in a need to know position. Eventually, he seemed to buy the argument.

Sean recalled his parting question—"What are you folks going to do with her?"

He'd answered in a way that he knew would shut the man up.

"We're going to brainwash her and turn her out. She'll be ours by the time we're through with her. Once we get her out of this catatonic state, we'll meld her back into Muslim society, into one of the most active terrorist cells in D.C. Jannat Shirazi will become a plant for us, because she has the Persian connections to be credible. We'll own her."

The doctor had nodded in agreement. "Makes sense. I wish I'd known. Would have delivered her to you in a better state."

Sean was about eighty percent confident that the doctor would keep his mouth shut. That was important, because he needed time to figure out what to do. And he also needed to keep Jannat safe and bring her back to life.

When he drove out through the security gate, the guard just waved him on. He didn't seem to notice that there was someone curled up on the backseat. The dark tinted windows of Sean's Cadillac CTS shielded her nicely.

Now, what to do? He was glad he'd spirited her out of there. God knows what would happen to those poor people when they arrived in Iraq. Most would probably never be heard of again, especially since they'd arrive there with no identification at all. They would no doubt be considered expendable, especially the Iranians. There was no love lost between Iraq and Iran. Sean shuddered thinking that Jannat could have been part of that exodus.

He shook his head. *What am I doing? Have I lost my mind?*

He thought back eighteen years, to that horrible memory of when he chose his career over the love of his life.

How could I have done such a thing?

He knew in his heart that if he'd just told the CIA to shove that job up their ass, Jannat wouldn't be in the sad state that she was in right now. If only he'd had the courage to do that. His life had been empty since that moment, consumed with subterfuge, killings, deceptions, and betrayals.

What kind of person am I? Who does that?

Well, now he'd finally made the choice he should have made almost two decades ago. He'd chosen humanity, and he wasn't accustomed to making a choice like that. There hadn't been much humanity in his occupation. But now he was in a real pickle. He had taken responsibility for a life that was in ruins.

Am I ready for this?

His misery had been building for a few years now; second-guessing everything. He'd been the loyal soldier, but his heart just wasn't in it anymore. What he did now, he did out of a misguided sense of duty and obligation. He obeyed orders. That was all. There was no longer any enthusiasm or excitement with his assignments. Most of them just made him feel sick.

He thought about the project in Colorado that he'd overseen, and how inhumane that was. How sick. It was all on his head.

And in his gut. At the time he first learned about the plan—which had been conceived by the others who came before him—it had made logical sense in a strange, perverted way to him. He inherited the project from its diabolical creators. But it didn't make sense anymore. Now, it was just sick. And it made him sick to think about it.

And the abject atrocity of 9/11; the deception pulled over the eyes of the world. A secret he and so many others had a hand in protecting and propagating.

The hatred he and so many others had fostered against the Middle East, against Muslims as a race and a culture. The genie was out of the bottle now, and there was probably no way it could be stuffed back in. People were convinced now that Muslims were evil and that those twisted savages were determined to kill them; steal their freedoms and their way of life. Hatred that was considered to be necessary to get support for endless wars, and confiscation of sovereign resources.

Absolute hogwash—the only ones committed to stealing freedoms were their own elected governments. But propaganda was a powerful thing. Most people believed what they were told, especially when it emanated from sources they'd been taught to trust.

The mainstream media—the most effective weapon ever devised—and one that Hitler himself had perfected so many decades before.

Ironically, Hitler has taught us a lot.

Now here Sean was, basically a fugitive with a prisoner in his custody. He would probably spend the rest of his life in a military prison if he were caught. But that wasn't his biggest concern right now, whereas it would have been two decades ago. Right now, his biggest concern was for the life and well-being of the lovely person lying on his backseat.

Sean's mind was wandering—remembering back to their times together. Times he remembered, ironically, as the happiest of his life. Ironic because he'd found a way to justify casting her aside so easily, just like a sack of garbage. He shuddered as he thought about what he'd done.

The dinners they'd shared together, the hysterical laughs, the movies they'd debated, amusement parks they'd visited. Her gentle kisses, her ravishing smile, her passionate love-making.

Her gentle caress. Her touch.

Suddenly, he felt her touch. It was real, like it used to be. Lovely, soft fingers sliding along his bare forearm, coming to a rest on his shoulder.

"Are we safe yet?"

Sean whirled his head around and there she was. Sitting forward away from the backseat, hand resting on his shoulder. He stared into her tired green eyes and wondered if he was dreaming.

She cocked her head and gazed back. "You haven't changed very much, Sean."

He put his eyes back on the road ahead. All of a sudden, his heart was pounding and his throat was screaming for water. No, he wasn't dreaming. Not at all.

He concentrated on a spot a quarter of a mile away—a pull-out. Sean guided the Cadillac into a gentle turn and an even gentler stop. He didn't want this dream to end, and he was terrified that sudden movements would destroy the moment.

Once the car was stopped, Sean unfastened his belt and swiveled around in his seat. She was still sitting forward, drinking in his stare. He couldn't find the words—shock had taken over.

Then she broke the silence again. "I'm going to get into the front seat with you."

Jannat pushed the seatback forward and opened the passenger door of the sleek coupe. Slowly, she stepped outside and then back in again. Now she was sitting right beside him, facing him. She pushed her hair back behind her ears with both hands and continued to stare.

Sean finally found the ability to speak. "How? What?"

"I've been faking it for three years, Sean. First the locked-in syndrome, and then the catatonia. I had to—to survive."

"I don't…know…what to say."

"Don't say anything if you don't want to. Just listen. They killed my husband. Then I was raped continuously by other prisoners. And by the guards. And by that doctor. He was actually the worst. I was his slave virtually every night. Once I realized I was probably going to die, I decided to fake it.

"I became a nurse, Sean. After you and I parted. A psychiatric nurse. I knew all the symptoms, knew how to fool them. I used that knowledge to get myself out of a bad situation, give myself a chance to retain my sanity. But it still didn't end. That doctor raped me even when he thought I was locked-in. But at least it was just him and not all the others. He did it secretly, after lights out. He couldn't take a chance on the other staff finding out. Sick enough to rape someone, but most of those animals would still draw the line at raping a disabled person. So, he'd sneak in late at night. And of course, I had to still pretend. Had to lie there and take it. I wanted to just kill him."

Sean was crying now. He couldn't stop it. The tears were pouring down his cheeks. Jannat reached over with one hand and wiped them away. Just the way she used to.

"I'm so—sorry—Jannat. For all that. For everything."

"Shh…don't apologize. There's no point now. What's done is done. I'm alive, and that's all that matters. Because of you. You saved me. And I'm so thankful for that."

Sean held her bony hand. "You were so brave. I don't know if I could have done what you did, endure what you did."

"No, I don't think you could have either. No man could imagine what that is like. And no Christian could imagine what it's like to be hated so much—just for being who we are."

Sean lowered his eyes and shook his head in disgust.

"I always suspected you were CIA, Sean. I guess now I know for sure."

Sean reached his right hand toward her and caressed her sunken cheek. "I never stopped loving you, Jannat."

She gently wiped away some more of his tears. Then she whispered, "Yes, you did, Sean."

Chapter 21

Ziv sat alone in the waiting room of the Toronto General Hospital. He'd been lingering for an hour already, and the antiseptic smells were getting to him.

He didn't care much for the noises of sickness and injury either—the monotonous beeping of monitors, clanking of trays, rubber wheels of hospital beds running along the shiny tile floors, and the moans and anguished cries of patients.

He felt an overwhelming urge to race out to his car and drive as far away as possible. Hospitals always affected him this way. He'd spent far too much time in them during his brutal career, waiting on severely injured colleagues; comrades in arms who were either close to death or fearful that they were.

It was the psychological effect of hospital environments that impacted Ziv more than anything else. It wasn't that he feared death—in his job, he was never able to afford that luxury.

Death had always been so close that he probably became numb to it after a while. It was more just the loss of control, the fact that a bunch of people in white coats were in charge of your fate. And in a place which was intimidating by its very nature.

He crossed his legs and absentmindedly picked up a magazine. It was one called *Living and Loving*, with the headline article being, "Seven Ways to Spice up Your Love Life." He quickly dropped it back into the rack without opening it.

That's the last thing I need to read about tonight!

He thought back to just a couple of hours earlier. A time when the evening was going about as splendidly as an evening could. He and Leslie together, in a way that seemed at the time as if it had been pulled

153

right out of his dreams.

Then everything turned on a dime. The intruders, the threats, Leslie being pistol-whipped; then seeing the bad guys leave the apartment with the letters.

Letters that were priceless because they were originals. Letters that weaved a trail, told a story, a mystery he and Brad had just started piecing together. A ticket to ride. A ticket to a possible Pulitzer prize. The third for Brad, and the first for Ziv.

And now here he was at a hospital, worried out of his mind about Leslie.

Back at the apartment, after the intruders had left, she'd pulled herself off the floor and begun untying Ziv's restraints. She was shaky, mumbling incoherently, swaying from side to side. Blood was streaming out of a wound on the left side of her head.

Once Leslie succeeded in getting Ziv untied, she just lay down on the bed and started sobbing. Ziv tried to coax her to her feet, but that didn't work too well. She reluctantly stood but then sagged backwards onto the bed again.

He ran into the kitchen and phoned an ambulance. Then grabbed some bandages out of a drawer and dashed back into the bedroom again. She'd dozed off in just that short period of time.

He bandaged her head quickly, pulled her up into a sitting position and then slapped her face, hard. Leslie's beautiful and normally expressive eyes opened once again, but stared blankly back at him. It seemed as if she barely recognized him. And he barely recognized her without the mischievous twinkle that normally danced in her eyes.

When the paramedics arrived, they didn't waste any time. Made no attempts to try to get her to walk, because they recognized as well that she was on the verge of unconsciousness. Bundled her up on a stretcher, did everything to keep her awake, and whisked her off to the hospital. Ziv followed in his car.

Now he was waiting. And, much as he tried, he couldn't prevent his brain from taking a painful walk down memory lane, back twenty years to when his Isabelle had been blown to smithereens in Paris.

A bomb that had been meant for him.

Plenty of people had died around Ziv over the years, some who deserved to die and some who didn't. But, except for Isabelle, he hadn't loved any of them. Their deaths had been only clinical to Ziv. But he'd loved Isabelle with every fibre of his being. Her death was the only one that hadn't been clinical—it had been utterly heartbreaking. And for two decades he'd gone along thinking he'd never recover from it.

Until he met Leslie Fields. Maybe it was the way he met her, saving her from that thug at the restaurant. Her being vulnerable and overwhelmingly feminine. A real lady, and beautiful like his Isabelle had been. He'd been in the right place at the right time to save her. Almost like fate. Meant to be. And they'd bonded almost instantly.

Now here she was in a hospital, hurt because of him. Reminding him of how Isabelle had been killed—because of him.

Ziv's mind was really wandering now. Thinking back to how Isabelle's death had changed everything. He hadn't felt affection for any woman since her death, until he met Leslie. But, between Isabelle and Leslie, his sex life had just been a long one-night stand. Meaningless encounters, animalistic in nature. No tenderness or affection from either side.

And he hadn't wanted any.

Then he gradually allowed himself to fall into sadomasochism, forcing it to get rougher and rougher. He hunted for women who were just raw sexual animals, not the type he could ever take home to Mother. Isabelle had been the type Mom would have loved. With Isabelle gone, he'd had no desire to even come close to replicating her.

After a few years of meaningless one-night stands, he started getting weary of it all, and even frantic about his strange behavior. Was this the way the rest of his life was going to be? So, he relented and went to see a shrink. One that Mossad had on confidential retainer, just for their agents. Mainly for the stress from fieldwork, but also just for any old problem they might encounter from time to time.

Ziv recalled the shrink and his conclusions vividly:

"Agent Dayan, it's interesting that you never fooled around on Isabelle. Nor did you ever have the desire for sadomasochism when you were together."

Ziv's eyes had been aimed at the floor. He shook his head slowly. "No."

"Your sex life with Isabelle was always consumed with feelings, I gather? Loving feelings?"

Ziv raised his eyes and stared through the heavy lenses of the psychologist's glasses. "Yes, it was always intense that way."

The doctor jotted down some notes on a piece of paper.

"That experience will happen again for you. Believe it or not, you're still in shock from Isabelle's death. You're reluctant to allow yourself an intense, loving relationship again, because of the fear of being reminded of how you felt about Isabelle."

Ziv looked at the doctor curiously, and cocked his head in concentration.

The doctor continued. "You're subliminally pushing yourself to the opposite extreme. Picking women to be with who are the exact opposite of the woman you were in love with. You're just going for sex of the rawest, most unemotional kind, just to satisfy the sexual need as opposed to the loving need. You don't want to be in love again, and you're not looking for that type of woman for that very reason."

Ziv nodded.

"In addition, you're also punishing yourself—blaming yourself for what happened to the love of your life. We need to work on getting you to forgive yourself. And, once you do, the type of women you seek right now and the kind of sex you seek, might suddenly become abhorrent to you. You'll be able to love again, look at a woman as more than just a raw sex object or an instrument of punishment. Do you follow me?"

Ziv's eyes were wide with awareness. "Yes, Doctor, I do indeed follow you."

"And I don't want you feeling bad about what you're doing either. There is a reason for it—you're not sick or twisted in any way. In fact, sexual games can be a lot of fun and even healthy, if they're being done for the right reasons and with the right person in a loving, trusting relationship.

"In your case, doing them with tramps who will do them with

any man, and asking them to do things with you that are meant as punishment—or just to avoid being reminded of Isabelle—are the wrong reasons. In the long run, those reasons could be harmful to your ability to have a meaningful relationship again.

"I'll be brutal—sinking that low with women like that after the lovely woman you were married to, is sinking your own self-worth right down along with them. You deserve better. There are a lot of people who are capable of having sex just for the sake of sex. But, I don't think you're one of them. Which is why you're ashamed of yourself and came in to see me.

"So, that was the first step to recovery. You've been acting out of character ever since Isabelle's death. And you need to give yourself permission to be in love again. Isabelle would want that—if she loved you the way I perceive that she did—she would want that."

Ziv was shaken out of his daydream by the sound of a baby crying in the waiting room. He looked around—the room had filled up even more since he'd drifted off in deep thought.

The doctor had been right. When he met Leslie, he was shaken out of his false persona. He started feeling like himself again. Looked at women in a different light. Got excited picking out gifts for Leslie, got a warm feeling inside when he sent her flowers. Felt his heart beat fast every time he heard her voice over the phone. Enjoyed the feeling of butterflies in his stomach whenever he saw her. Bought new clothes, wanted to look nice for her.

Kissed her tenderly whenever he got the chance. He couldn't deny the affection and respect he felt for her. Their love-making, much to his surprise, had been wonderful right from the beginning. He'd had no need for the games or animal roughness. It had been tender and loving right from the start. And almost as intense as he remembered with Isabelle.

He was returning to his old self again. And to his surprise, he didn't feel guilty. Didn't feel like he was betraying what he had with Isabelle. And his self-worth, with Leslie, had taken a steep curve upward. It felt right. And he felt no desire at all to be with those other types of women. And no desire to be punished. He felt good about himself again.

But, how had she known?

When he saw her dressed in leather, it did get a rise out of him. Not just because she looked darn sexy, but the memories of that kind of sex were still in his mind. He couldn't just turn away from it that easily. So he went along. And he remembered the doctor's words of advice—that it would be okay and even healthy with the right person. And Leslie was the right person.

But when she started hurting him, that's when things started to change. He liked her looking that way, dressing that way, acting that way—but the hurting part seemed foreign now. Instinctively, he didn't want that kind of sex with Leslie. It started reminding him of the tramps he'd been with, and that memory cranked him downward into an abyss he didn't want to be reminded of with Leslie. He didn't want to think of her that way.

But, how had she known?

He must have said the odd thing from time to time in their conversations to make her think that he would be titillated by that kind of sex. He must have. There's no other way she could have known.

"Mr. Dayan?"

Ziv looked up. A man in a white coat was standing in front of him. Ziv felt a knot form in his stomach. He didn't like white coats.

"Yes?"

"Hi. I'm Doctor Brooks. The nurse pointed you out to me. You can visit with Ms. Fields now. She's awake and doing fine. We're going to keep her overnight though. She has indeed suffered a concussion, just a moderate one—but serious enough to warrant observation for a few hours."

"Will she be okay?"

The doctor smiled. "She'll be fine. There won't be any continuing side effects. I commend you for having the good sense to keep her awake after she fell and hit her head. It could have been worse if she'd fallen into a deep sleep. Could have been comatose. But, she'll be fine, thanks to you."

Thanks to me, she's suffered a concussion. Thanks to me she's here to begin with...

Ziv clasped his hands together. "Oh, Doctor Brooks, I'm so relieved. Thanks for all you've done."

He nodded. "Follow me."

Ziv hadn't reported her injury as an assault—simply said that she'd fallen and hit her head on the edge of the bed. He didn't want the police involved, considering what the thieves had stolen. Would have added too many complications, ones he just wasn't prepared to deal with. Before the paramedics arrived at his apartment, he'd asked Leslie to stick with that same story. He hoped that she'd remembered to do that.

The doctor turned on his heel and walked quickly down the hall. He stopped in front of room 207 and gestured with his hand. "She's in the second bed on the right. Take all the time you need."

Ziv pushed open the door and noticed that the room was fully occupied. Six beds, three on each side. Each with curtains hanging from surround rods. He walked quietly down to the second bed on the right and peeked around the curtain.

There she was, sitting up in bed, sipping some juice. Her head wound had been redressed, and the color had returned to her face. Leslie's patented twinkle had returned to her eyes, and she flashed it as soon as she saw him.

He walked over to the side of her bed, leaned over and kissed her cheek. She cupped his face in her hands and softly kissed his lips.

Ziv whispered. "How are you feeling?"

She whispered back. "They're taking good care of me. Thanks for getting me here. It could have been worse, if not for you."

He grinned. "Sorry for slapping you—but you deserved it!"

She laughed, and choked a bit on her juice.

"The doctor said you could leave tomorrow. I'll come pick you up in the morning." Then he whispered, "I hope you remembered to tell them you hit your head on the bed."

Leslie looked down at the glass in her hand, nodded, and started playing with the straw. "Ziv, what was that all about?"

He just looked at her. Didn't know how to answer.

She glanced up. "What were those documents they stole?"

Ziv's throat went suddenly dry. "Just something I was working on."

"That project you alluded to, that you wouldn't tell me about?"

He nodded.

"What are you into, Ziv? Tell me."

"I can't."

Leslie held onto his hand and started crying. "I'm scared to be with you. You're keeping secrets from me, and those secrets must be dangerous. Don't do this."

"It will be over with soon."

She brought her hands up to cover her crying eyes. "Please leave, Ziv. I'm afraid to be with you."

"I'll be here to pick you up tomorrow."

"No. Don't. I'll find my own way home. We need a break for a while."

Ziv leaned over the bed and kissed the top of her head. Then he left the room without looking back.

As he walked down the hospital corridor, a painful image flashed in front of his eyes. Isabelle's smiling face behind the wheel of the rental car, gesturing for him to hurry up and get in.

Then the concussion knocking him off his feet. Seeing the outline of her head just before the vicious fireball of the explosion swallowed her up forever.

The moment he lost her.

And now he'd lost another.

Ziv Dayan's next task was to tell one of his dearest friends that his third Pulitzer Prize was now probably nothing more than just an impossible fantasy.

Chapter 22

Kristy walked into the dining room from the kitchen and poured Ziv another cup of coffee. Yet, it was probably the last thing he needed at that moment. Brad noticed that he'd been jittery the moment he walked in the door.

And no wonder, with the news he had to deliver.

He reached across the table and squeezed Ziv's shoulder. "It's okay, bud. The main thing is that you're okay. And it sounds like Leslie is coming around nicely, too."

He nodded, and took a sip of his black coffee. Then a grim look came over his face, and he stared into Brad's eyes. "You trusted me with those letters. And now they're gone. And Leslie's out of my life now, too. Not a good week, to say the least."

"Leslie will come around—she's just in shock. And you couldn't help what happened. You had them in the safe. Someone discovered that you had them. This has been kind of dangerous from the beginning. I never did tell you what happened back at that cabin on Vancouver Island. What Kristy and I had to go through."

"Tell me."

Brad took a deep breath, and then exhaled slowly. "I killed our landlord in self-defence. A CIA agent broke in, used Colin as a shield. I had to shoot both of them. The guy coerced those letters out of Colin, killed his wife to scare him into complying. Then he must have discovered that one of the letters was missing so he dragged Colin over to our cabin to get it. And on our escape out of the place, I had to shoot another guy out by the main road."

"Jesus!"

"The news outlets simply reported it all as a murder/suicide. No mention at all of the two bad guys who were killed. And they described Colin as having been with British Intelligence, MI5. But, he'd been in Canada already for many years before he supposedly retired, so I suspect he was MI6, not MI5. Which kind of adds a new dimension to this."

Ziv nodded slowly. "MI6 has agents placed everywhere around the world, just like the CIA and Mossad. We friendly countries do spy on each other, but most people don't realize that. The objective of foreign intelligence services is to find out as much as possible about their enemies—but also to find out even more about their friends. It's called gaining an advantage, and using it. Not too much different than industrial espionage."

Kristy sat down across the table from the two men. "Ziv, if Colin was indeed MI6, what would he have been doing with those letters? And why did he sneak one to Brad before all hell broke loose?"

"I don't know, Kristy. That's a real puzzle. Someone sent them to him. For a specific reason. We don't know who that was or why that was. We know Hal Winters had written the letters to a Richard Sterling in Coventry, England. By the tone of the letters, they seem to have been close friends. So—we have two British connections here: Colin Wentworth in Canada and Richard Sterling in England. I would hazard a guess that Sterling was also MI6 or at least MI5—or perhaps was just a front for who Winters was really writing the letters to. Maybe Sterling didn't even exist?"

Brad jumped in. "I tried to trace this Richard Sterling guy—there are loads of them in England, but none that I could trace to Coventry. And I went back in the records as far as I could."

"It's possible that name was just a blind, Brad, the more I think about it. Or he was killed and the records erased. What matters is that those letters somehow were either stolen or sent from this Richard Sterling to someone else, who then sent them along to Colin Wentworth. You said that you found a large envelope in the garbage in Colin's office with the return address being a post office box in McLean, Virginia. You're probably right thinking that the letters were mailed to him in that envelope. And, no coincidence that's the town where the CIA is headquartered. Used to be called Langley, but now the whole area there is known as McLean."

Kristy tapped her finger on the table. "But, why did Colin try to drag Brad into it by giving him one of the letters?"

Ziv leaned back in his chair and scratched the back of his head. "I think the man panicked. Living in an isolated area—which is an uncomfortable feeling for an intelligence agent—and perhaps got a tip that they were closing in. And by "they" I mean the CIA. Perhaps someone tipped Colin off that they'd traced where the letters went and they were coming for him? He might have wanted Brad to be his ace-in-the-hole, a bargaining chip?"

Brad nodded. "That makes some sense. He picked me because I'm a journalist—at the very least, he knew I might do something with a letter from a prolific killer. But then, when the CIA guy just shot Colin's wife in cold blood, he got scared. He knew he couldn't really bargain with the guy. That's when he led him to me."

"And then you killed them both."

Brad grimaced. "Thanks for the reminder, Ziv."

Ziv chuckled. "You're welcome. But, it would be helpful if we knew who sent the letters to Colin."

Brad suddenly snapped his fingers. "Well, you just mentioned a big clue a second ago—that damn envelope!"

He dashed over to his desk and pulled the large brown envelope from the bottom drawer. "Yep, McLean, Virginia is the return address, and, as you said, that's where the CIA is based."

Ziv smiled. "Sometimes the obvious is sitting right in front of us—in this case, an envelope."

Brad tried his best to hide the sheepish look he knew had come over his face. "I think I'm getting rusty. Forgot all about that damn envelope until you mentioned it."

Ziv waved his hand. "Hey, join the club, I'd forgotten about it too. And, look at me—forgetting to lock my apartment door. I might as well have just invited the bad guys in for tea."

Brad started pacing the kitchen. "So, if the letters went to Colin from McLean—Langley—that means someone from the CIA sent them to him. And then the CIA goes there to kill him? To get the letters back? Doesn't make sense. Tells me that someone went rogue—someone without the authority to do so sent those letters to Colin. Perhaps a whistleblower?"

Ziv leaned his elbows on the table and clasped his hands together. "Either that or someone at the CIA sold his soul. Was paid off. There aren't many people working there with a conscience, so I kinda doubt that it was a whistleblower."

"You don't like them too much, do you? No professional courtesy between Mossad and CIA?"

"Not much. Been screwed over far too often."

"I'm sure you Israelis weren't angels, either."

Chuckling, Ziv muttered under his breath, "No, we weren't."

"So, this is turning into one tangled web. Winters writes these letters to Sterling in England, they then end up in the CIA's hands back at Langley. Then someone from there sends them back to a Brit again, this time in Canada. Then the damn letters end up in my hands. I turn them over to you, and they get stolen again. This is bizarre!"

Ziv lowered his voice in reply. "Just to tangle things up even further, one of the guys who stole them from me spoke with a British accent."

"You didn't see any signs of tampering with the lock on your door?"

"No, I either left it unlocked or they had a key. It's not the kind of lock you can pick."

"Did you tell anyone about what we've been working on?"

"No. No one at all."

"Not even Leslie?"

"No, most definitely not. She was curious, and she knew I was Mossad and still worked as a consultant, but I never told her anything about what we were doing."

Brad nodded. "Someone found out that you had the letters. Somehow—they found out."

"Phone taps? Surveillance of you and me meeting together? And maybe there was some evidence from that cabin on Vancouver Island that identified you as being there?"

Brad shook his head. "No, I cleaned it pretty good. Even ripped off a page of his calendar that had my name on it."

Ziv rubbed his chin. Then he got up and pulled Kristy's calendar off the hook on the kitchen wall. He flipped up one of the pages and then shoved it over to Brad. "Look carefully. You can see the imprints from the overlying page. Just barely, but you can see them. With a magnifier, it would be very easy."

"Shit!"

"Yep. Should have taken the whole calendar with you."

Brad folded his arms across his chest, and squeezed them together tightly. "I might not have gotten off as scot-free as I thought, eh? Someone may have known that I had those letters, but was cagey enough to make me think I was as free as a bird so I wouldn't dive underground?"

"Exactly."

"And if they knew I had them, they could have easily discovered that you and I were collaborating. Could have seen us together, listened in on phone calls."

"Starting to look that way."

Kristy had been listening carefully to the two of them, and was now starting to breathe hard. Brad reached out and gently rubbed her hand. "We're safe here, Kristy. The security is far better than what Ziv has in his building."

Ziv laughed. "That's for sure. We have one security guard, who's drunk most evenings. I live in a slum compared to you guys. He has a laptop computer on his desk supposedly tied into the security monitors, but most of the time he's looking at porn."

A buried memory suddenly popped into Brad's head. "Christ, I'm either developing early dementia or the shock of killing three people jumbled my memory. I took something else from that cabin—Colin's laptop! When we got back I just stuffed it away in my bedroom closet."

"Go get it."

"It's password-locked."

"Doesn't matter. I'll get into it. Give it to me—I'll take it with me.

Won't take me long, I can assure you."

*****

Sean's heart just wasn't in it—the towering piles of paper on his desk, along with a few top-secret files. They were all begging for his attention, but all he could think of was Jannat.

He'd gotten her nicely settled in at his home, in one of the guest bedrooms. She was comfortable, calm, and most importantly, safe. For now, at least.

But, she was just a ghost of what he'd remembered. There were hints of the stunning beauty that Jannat had once been, but they were just that—hints. Her sweetness was still there, her shy nature—but the affection towards him had completely disappeared. Sure, she was thankful for what he had done, had hugged him several times already; even kissed him gently on the cheek once. But that was the extent of it. No deep conversations, no softness, no reminiscing. She seemed cold and distant, and that was a major departure from the special person she'd been a couple of decades ago, especially with him.

He shook his head, admonishing himself. What did he expect? He'd thrown her out of his life. When he was driving her back in the car, he professed that he'd always loved her, but she'd bluntly told him that wasn't true. In hindsight, he regretted saying it. It sounded phony now, insincere.

She was right—how could he have loved her yet done what he had to her? Or, maybe his definition of love at that time was just different from what it was now? Or his disgust for the life he'd led was causing him to re-examine everything, and regret what he'd given up?

Once Sean had gotten her tucked into bed, he'd called a doctor friend—someone he'd known a long time who was discreet and could be trusted. He came over to Sean's house and did a complete physical examination. Recommended some tests at the hospital; just the usual routine blood tests to check for things like iron, and other possible deficiencies. In the meantime, he recommended a nurse—again someone discreet—and Sean agreed. She was at his house now, and would be there as long as Jannat needed her.

The doctor's most urgent recommendation was that Jannat get

nourishment—fast. Luckily, the nurse was also a registered dietician, so she'd take care of Jannat's nutritional needs on a priority basis.

Sean felt good about all this. It seemed that what Jannat needed most right now was rest, nutrition, and a safe environment. And Sean would give her all that. The doctor was confident she'd bounce back fast.

His heart ached. Seeing her that way. Knowing the way she'd been abused. No wonder she seemed so detached. It wasn't just Sean she was detached from, it was probably society and the world at large. And no doubt experiencing a monumental dose of cynicism towards human beings in general, particularly non-Muslims. She had been raped continuously for five years. By even those who were in charge of the prison, supposedly in charge of her safety. Even the doctor himself.

Sean bit his lower lip.

I want her back.

But he caught himself with that thought—did he really want her back? Or did he just want redemption? Was he being selfish and callous again like he'd been eighteen years ago? Back then, he had deemed Jannat expendable for the sake of his career. Was she now just his ladder to redemption? Because he was now ashamed of who he was, what he'd done, and what he'd missed out on? Was he saving Jannat to try to save himself?

Sean didn't know the answers to these questions. But, he was glad that he was at least asking them of himself. He thought that was a good sign.

Suddenly, the phone rang, jarring him out of his thoughts.

"Russell, here."

"I have what you want."

It was a voice he recognized, and it was the call he'd been waiting for. "Good. Any complications?"

"No. It was a snap. All twenty of them in my trusty hands as we speak."

"Okay. Well done. I'm going to get on a plane and fly up there. How's tomorrow for a meet?"

"That would be fine. But, you'll need to wire 100 million to a Cayman bank account first."

Sean leaped out of his chair. "What the fuck are you talking about?"

"Ransom, Sean. Ransom."

"Perhaps we have a bad connection. I thought I heard you say ransom."

"That's what I said. No bad connection here."

Sean could feel his heart starting to pound in his chest. "Your assignment was to get them back for us. You've done that. Don't play games with me."

"I'm a free agent. The Brits are willing to pay me fifty million. But, since the U.S. has much more at stake here, I would guess that you'd be willing to pay double that."

"The British have no stake in those letters. It would be treasonous if you did that."

"Don't threaten me, Sean Russell, agent extraordinaire. And don't think I'm stupid either. America has been blackmailing the British government—and many others—for decades. They're finally fighting back—at least the Brits are. They're weary of being dragged into every fabricated war that you clowns dream up. And the United Kingdom is going bankrupt in the process, putting extreme pressure on the elected leaders to break their ties with you. Let you flounder on your own.

"Which creates a free market for explosive stuff like these letters, and for people like me. The British are sick and tired of America extorting them over salacious Royal Family behaviours. You've been holding all the cards for far too long. They will no longer tolerate your threats to humiliate them and destroy the image and symbolism of Royalty. With these letters, they will finally have the goods on you—and threaten you with something far worse. Can you imagine, Sean, how the world will react to the secrets of 9/11 being exposed, let alone the secrets of Denver? Coincidentally, the Queen actually owns property near Denver. A cute little coincidence, huh?"

As was becoming all too common lately, Sean felt the acid rising from his stomach. "Those letters alone are not enough to cause a crisis. They're subjective, cryptic, and open to interpretation. The Brits can't blackmail us with those. They can cause us a lot of trouble, for sure, but they're not a slam-dunk."

"Good point, Sean. But, those letters together with a certain tape recording of the entire cockpit adventure of Hal Winters and his co-pilot on Flight 175, will be enough to collapse and shame America in the eyes of the world. You remember that flight, don't you, Sean? The one that the entire planet thinks crashed into the South tower of the World Trade Center?"

Sean was finding it hard to breathe. "What...do the British... intend to do with all this information if they get...get their hands on it?"

"I don't know. I would expect, though, that it'll be used much like the nuclear threat has always been used. MAD—Mutually Assured Destruction. I would guess that they want to level the playing field; quid pro quo, so to speak. You don't show yours, and they won't show theirs. They want to be free of your non-stop extortion. They want to be free of your foreign adventures. Get my drift?"

"Yes, I get your drift. Loud and clear. I'll have to think about this. Give me a few days. The CIA can't get its hands on that kind of money all that easily. And this is way over my pay grade. I need to consult."

"Go consult, Sean. That's what you guys do real well, isn't it? Aside from killing and kidnapping people, of course. You absolutely excel at those little skills."

Sean took a needed sip of water. "Where can I reach you?"

"You can't. I'll reach out to you."

Chapter 23

August 9, 2013...The hustle and bustle of mealtime was always a highlight of the day. Of course, it was all relative. There weren't many highlights to compare with, but eating was still such a powerful social event, even in this place, that it was something wonderful to look forward to.

Hal Winters opened the door of his windowless room and walked into the outer corridor. The sound of the dinner bell was incessant—it would go on like this for five full minutes. Monotonous gongs that were three seconds apart. Summoning the masses. But only the masses in his section of the compound. There were other dining rooms elsewhere, in other sections that he'd visited only on "social" nights.

Dinner was being served, and you had to be seated within fifteen minutes of the gong making its first annoying sound. And it was a good mile's walk to the dining room. That's why most of them had bicycles.

Hal's was parked right outside his door. No need to lock it—if someone stole it, they wouldn't get very far. And if for some reason the bike did disappear, they would just give Hal a new one. No one had to go very long without getting what they needed here. A new hairbrush, shaver, more comfortable bed—didn't matter. If you needed it, you got it.

This was the damnedest prison he'd ever seen.

Hal pulled up his pant legs to give him more mobility, climbed onto his bike, and headed on down to the dining room. Other prisoners were already on their way; he caught up to one of his best friends and rode alongside him.

"Hey, Keith, how ya doin' today?"

Keith turned his head away from the road, and smiled. "Hal, haven't seen you all week. They got you in those simulators again?"

"Yeah, keeping myself up to date."

"Well, they want you sharp to teach those new young pilots everything you know. I'll bet a lot of things have changed since back when you used to fly all the time."

Hal nodded. "Seems to be a new thing every month or so, but it's no sweat. When you spend your life doing this, it's like riding a bike. Easy to keep up."

Keith put on the brakes quickly to avoid a young lady who swerved in front of him. "Hey, watch out!"

Hal laughed. "Calm down, Keith. Still safer than getting hit by a car."

"True, true—but after a while, things start becoming the new normal. The hierarchy of danger simply adjusts with the environment, doesn't it?"

"It does at that."

"Well, Hal, at least you get to go out into the big wide world still. Pays off to have a skill like yours. I wish I was specialized at something that was in huge demand."

Hal shrugged while he calmly turned left onto the intersecting road ahead. "It's no treat, Keith. It just makes me long to be free again. When I'm out, it's still just another prison. I'm in the cockpit either flying in supplies, or teaching new pilots after their simulator sessions. It's really just an extension of this bizarre place."

Keith lowered his voice. "I'll bet you get the urge once in a while to just fly off into the wide blue yonder, huh?"

"Sure, get it every time. Then I turn my head and look behind me at the heavily armed guards—armed with knives for when we're above 10,000 feet, and guns for when we're below that ceiling. And then I just shake my head and force myself back to reality again."

"Yeah, when I think of it, it's probably actually worse for you. You've only been in this place for two years, and you still get teased by seeing the outdoors once in a while. Most of us have been here a lot longer than that, and haven't seen the sun since we came in."

Hal glanced up and looked at the ceiling of the tunnel they were riding through. Then at the solid concrete walls surrounding them. "It is ominous, isn't it? In a certain way that's just so hard to believe. It's surreal. As you know, I came here from a prison. So, this is one hell of an improvement. But the rest of you—you came from the real world, came from honest backgrounds. Being imprisoned was foreign to most of you. At least I was used to it, and this is like fucking freedom compared to where I was."

Keith didn't reply. Hal glanced across at him and could see tears running down his cheeks. "Hey, hey, let's pull over for a second."

Keith nodded in agreement, and they both guided their bikes into a shallow pull-out. Hal rested his big hand on Keith's back and started rubbing it. "It's okay, bud. Sorry if I upset you. Maybe we shouldn't talk about freedom and all that shit. We'll never have it again, so no point getting ourselves all upset."

Hal could see that his friend was having a hard time. Keith was a big guy, but a guy with a heart of gold. Very emotional, cried easily. Didn't before, but since last year it had become a daily occurrence. He was about forty years old now, Hal figured, and he was one of the ones who was brought here in 2001.

His girlfriend, Janice, who he'd been flying with twelve years ago when they got nabbed, died last year of a kidney ailment. They did all they could—the hospitals in this massive dungeon were amazing, and so were the doctors and nurses. All of them prisoners in their own right.

The care was very good, and the facilities were state of the art. But, not good enough for Janice. Keith had begged the authorities to let her leave, to take her away to a facility in the outside world where she might have a better chance. But, they refused. And she died.

Keith hadn't been the same since. He'd lost a lot of weight, and his skin color was a sickly gray. That of course had the potential of happening to everyone down here, just due to the fact that they were never outside. The authorities did provide artificial lighting centers throughout the gargantuan complex, as well as tanning beds, blue light relaxation areas, and artificial beaches with swimming lagoons. But, at least half of the people were too depressed most of the time to take advantage of those things. Keith was one of those people. Hal understood.

Keith rubbed his eyes and turned his head towards Hal. "Do you ever get claustrophobic? Like, does it ever just make you panic once in a while if you really think about where we are?"

Hal shook his head. "No, maybe my pilot training has a lot to do with it. Being in confined spaces for a good part of my career got me desensitized. But I can understand what you mean, though. It affects a lot of people in here. That's why they have the shrinks. Take advantage of that service—they might be able to help you. And, of course, they're just like you—prisoners too, so they'll empathize with you."

"Yeah, I should. Since Janice died I haven't done much to help myself."

Hal looked up at the ceiling. "It's normal to feel claustrophobic down here. When you think that we have at least fifty feet of terra firma sitting above our heads, it's a normal reaction."

Keith laughed. "You're not really helping me too much, Hal old buddy!"

Hal chuckled. "Sorry—I'm such an insensitive prick, huh? Well, look at it this way. There are three more levels beneath us. Those folks down there must really feel it when they think about how deep they are!"

"True, true—could be worse. That's how I'll have to look at it."

Hal mounted his bike. "Shall we get going? We're gonna miss dinner if we don't get our asses in gear."

Keith slid back onto his seat. "Okay. Race you?"

"No, you won the last two times. I can't take any more humiliation."

Keith made a mocking face. "Something tells me you've been letting me win. I've watched you in the gym, buddy. No one here can keep up with you, not even the young guys. You're just trying to make me feel good by letting me have the odd pathetic victory."

"You're right. Aren't I a treasure?"

Keith smiled, and under his breath he muttered, "Yes, you are."

"What?"

"Nothing—let's ride."

They picked up the pace and rounded the last corner. They could see the dining room straight ahead, with its crystal chandeliers illuminating the elegant interior. "Funny, huh? A classy restaurant and none of us have any classy stuff to wear."

Hal nodded. "Just part of the illusion. To make us feel special three times a day, and to try to convince us that it's not too bad down here. But, let's face it—they really don't care if we, as human beings, are happy or not. We're just the canaries in the coal mine. We're the ones all this is being tested on. We'd better enjoy whatever parts of it we can, because it's gonna get real crowded in here eventually if we don't start dying off."

A frown came over Keith's face. "I try not to think about that. I heard rumours that a new dorm level is being built adjacent to this one. No connection to this one, same depth, but totally separate. And quite austere."

"Yep, after this experiment is over, a lot of us will be moving over, I think. That may be several years from now, or sooner. We just won't know. It all depends upon what's going on up above. But, the elite are coming, no doubt about that. That's what all this is for—it's certainly not for you and me. We're just being forced to test drive it for them, get the kinks out, let them see how people adapt—and how they don't."

They started to slow their bikes down as they approached the dining room's bicycle garage. A lot of people were starting to linger near the front entrance, waiting for their turns to be seated.

Keith whispered. "People like you would probably be allowed to stay here, right? You know, those of you with special skills—pilots, doctors, dentists, engineers."

"Yeah, probably. But, I'll be too old. That's why they're working me so hard as an instructor. And letting me fly out once in a while under their supervision—they want my utmost cooperation, so they just stimulate me to be happy—and hopeful. But I'll be expendable once enough pilots are trained in all of the aircraft types they have in this facility. They'll want the younger ones, not people like me. So, I'll probably be over in the new dorm with you."

"I'm being selfish here, but I hope you do come with the rest of us."

They parked their bikes in the racks and started heading over to the dining room entranceway. "Keith, it's okay to be selfish. At this point in our lives, considering where we are, we might as well be. There's nothing else. Hey, speaking of selfish, wanna come with me to the brothel tonight? I'm heading over there after dinner."

Keith swallowed hard. "You must be trying hard to make me forget Janice. You've never asked me to go there with you before. I don't even know exactly where it is."

Hal grinned. "Well, it's about time you do come with me. It'll be fun. We have to hop the monorail—it's about ten miles westward. The station is only about a mile from here, so we can just leave our bikes there and jump on the train. The girls are pretty good—they've got some great talent, with new ones coming in all the time."

"What else is down that way?"

"Several nightclubs. Music's pretty loud all along that strip, but it'll be fun. Come with me."

Keith pulled out his wallet. "How many credits for a cheap fuck?"

Hal laughed. "It's dirt cheap. Twenty credits is all you need for a BJ, and only fifty for a fuck. And two for hard liquor shots. If you haven't got enough, I'll spot you."

Keith shook his plastic transparent card, and the number 200 lit up in red. "No, I've got plenty. Sure, I'll go with you."

Hal slapped him on the back. "Good! Don't worry, I'll take care of you. I won't let some dirt bag drag you off. Only the best for you. Hey, at least down here you don't have to worry about picking up the clap. Those girls are being tested all the time."

They walked up to the entrance, and Keith scanned the menu hanging on the side of the concierge podium. "Look at this. We have a choice tonight of duck a l'orange, striploin steak, or spaghetti Bolognese. Not bad!"

"Yeah, and at least all the meals are free. We can blow all our credits on booze and whores!"

A young lady, no more than eighteen or so, clad in a blue and white striped uniform, greeted them at the door. "Follow me. I have a nice table for the two of you."

Hal figured the uniforms they made the girls wear in this place were striped on purpose—to subtly remind them all that they were still really just prisoners. The illusion only went so far.

They took their seats and a waitress came up to them almost immediately to take their orders. Hal chose the duck and Keith went for the steak.

Keith leaned his elbows on the table. "This is nice. You and I haven't eaten together for quite a while."

"Yes, it is nice, Keith. Let's do it more often. Sometimes you just skip meals completely. I've knocked on your door many times and you've politely told me to get lost."

"I know, I know. I get so down and it takes some effort to snap out of it."

"I understand."

Hal glanced around the dining room. It was pretty full. He looked fondly at the tables that were occupied by families. He wished he had that kind of comfort down here, but it also made him feel a little sick to his stomach thinking that this place was their existence, their life—the only life they'd know. Even though there were schools down here, what were these kids being trained for? What life could they look forward to? He knew that there were all levels of grades being taught, even right up to the community college level. He heard rumors that university level courses would be offered soon, as some of the kids were reaching that age. But, very selective university courses. Skills that would be needed in a dungeon environment. Lawyers would be deemed useless, as would business executives. University degrees would be focused on medicine, pharmacy, geology, hydrology, and engineering. Community college courses would focus on skilled trades such as plumbers and electricians.

And those lucky graduates would be able to stay in this section of the complex and not be forced to move to the new dorm. Hal wondered if the parents of those kids would be so lucky. He doubted it. Apartheid would exist down here, probably even to a worse extent than it ever did in South Africa.

"Hal, I'll bet you get extra credits for the work you do here."

"Yeah, that's the way it works. If you have a skill they need, you get some perks."

"I was a chartered accountant up there in the real world. No need for that down here. Instead, I get paid a pittance of credits sweeping floors and cleaning the public washrooms. Compared to the six figure salary I made in my previous life."

Hal grimaced. "You can't look at it that way. It'll drive you crazy. Forget about your previous life. At the very least, everyone here is put to work. It's far better than a prison environment where only a chosen few get to do something useful. Just think how miserable you'd be if you didn't have anything to do. Maybe see if you can enroll in a course—learn a skilled trade? Would increase your value to them, earn more credits, and you might be able to avoid moving to the dorm when it's finished."

Keith scratched his chin thoughtfully as he pondered Hal's suggestion. "That's not a bad idea. I'll give it some thought. I guess setting new life goals is probably a good way to survive."

"It may be the only way."

Keith leaned forward and lowered his voice to a whisper. "Have you ever considered trying to escape from here?"

Hal lowered his eyes, and went silent for a few seconds. Then he whispered back.

"Yes, it's all I think about. I have an advantage that most in here don't have. I'm a pilot who can fly anything. Every day, I hop the monorail and head down to work at the far end of the complex. It's only a fifteen-minute walk, but I like to ride the train and read the local newspaper, hoping to read something that might give me an opening, an idea.

"Two monstrous metal doors slide open that let me into the hangar. That's where the simulators are, and an unbelievable fleet of aircraft. Including the three planes that were detoured here on 9/11.

As you know, I flew one of them, United 175, and you and Janice were brought here on Flight 11. Those planes are still there, immaculately maintained, and now over-painted in a sickly military green.

"I have dreams of flying out of here in that plane, 175; the one I flew twelve fucking years ago. That's my fantasy. And it would be my victory. But—it's just a dream, Keith. It's impossible. I'm good, but I'm not that good. This place may seem like a country club at times, but it's a fortress. I'm given some latitude, but not that much.

"Keith, that dream keeps me alive, though. And that's what I think you need—get yourself trained in something specialized, so you can have some kind of dream, too. I'm an old man now, but you still have a lot of life left in you. Use it."

Keith raised his glass of water. "Let's toast. And if your dream ever comes true, take me with you?"

They clinked glasses. "I will, buddy. So, what are we toasting to?"

"To Emerald City."

Hal laughed. "Yeah, ironic that these clowns actually call this place Emerald City. The arrogance of them is unbelievable. Talk about shoving it down our throats and having a good chuckle over it."

Keith clenched his fingers together until they turned white. "That local newspaper you read every day—*The Emerald City Clarion*. What a joke. And the joke's on us. They actually think we want to read the daily news about what happens down here?"

Hal lowered his voice even further. "If this is indeed Emerald City, I want to meet the wizard. And when I do, I'm going to choke the life out of him with my bare hands."

Chapter 24

They can run, but they can't hide.

That's the phrase that ran through Sean's head as he went to work.

No one's going to blackmail me.

He picked up the phone and summoned his chief systems engineer. The man's name was Jim Diamond, and he was indeed a diamond—a diamond in the rough. No social graces, never looked anyone in the eye, probably autistic in the extreme. But there was nothing he couldn't crack, no trail he couldn't uncover.

Within minutes, Jim was sitting in Sean's office. As was typical, he immediately sat down in the guest chair, looked down at something invisible on his shoes, and fidgeted with his hands.

Without looking up, he asked, "What can I do for you, Sean?"

"I have a mystery for you to solve for me. I suspect there was an altercation of some sort in Toronto, Canada, involving a man named Ziv Dayan. He's a retired Mossad agent. He had something that I wanted. It's been taken from him. I want to know how."

Jim folded his hands across his chest. "So, police reports, hospitals, the usual?"

"Yeah, whatever you can find."

Jim got up from his chair and headed for the door. Without turning around, he said, "Be back to you in a few minutes."

Sean knew that it wouldn't take long. And while he wasn't overly optimistic that Jim would find anything, he hoped that he would at least be able to give him a place to start.

It concerned him that the blackmailer had the letters, but even worse that the recording that Hal Winters made in the cockpit of flight 175 had now finally seen the light of day. He had always assumed that

Hal had sent it to his son, Brock. He knew that Brock had paid his clerk half a million dollars to steal the letters from the CIA vault and send them to Colin Wentworth on Vancouver Island. But the tape had always just been a threat. Something Hal had bargained with, threatened them with—to keep himself alive.

And the CIA had no alternative but to succumb to the threat. That tape, along with the letters, would have been explosive.

So, Sean had arranged for Hal to be incarcerated in a medium security prison in Georgia, with all the freedoms any prisoner could desire. And Sean had used his considerable clout to get Brock's movie career moving upward like a rocket. All it took were a few threats and some selective blackmail to make that happen. Roles started coming to Brock without him even having to audition. Brock was probably as surprised as anyone. He never knew that his dad had leveraged threats to make that happen. Hal made it clear to Sean that Brock could never know that his success had anything to do with his father.

Sean smiled when he remembered that. The most prolific assassin the CIA had ever produced had a heart of gold. He didn't even come close to fitting the stereotype that most people would imagine of a cold-blooded killer.

The most important conditions he had imposed upon the CIA for his silence, were the safety of his family, and the success of Brock in Hollywood. Sure, he'd wanted to stay alive, too, but Sean had the impression that that was the least important of his conditions.

Now, since 2011, Hal had been in a different facility entirely. An experimental facility that was fabulously attentive, while at the same time inhumane as hell. The premise for why a few thousand people were incarcerated there for the rest of their lives was barbaric, to say the least.

And Sean had full rein of the place. No decision about that facility could be made without his approval. It was an assignment he resented, and it made him feel sick every time he visited there. All those people; no hope, no future for any of them.

Emerald City.

And not a single one of them had done anything wrong to justify being imprisoned there. Well, except Hal Winters of course, but all the killings he'd committed were either done at the behest of the CIA or in defense of his own person, such as that day at the Mall of America. He certainly wasn't a mass murderer. He'd killed two agents that day in self-defence. That was it. The FBI had killed the other eight, just for the sake of framing Hal. Lives that were deemed expendable once Hal yelled out threatening that his death would expose the truth about Flight 175.

Sean had gotten to know Hal quite well in the last few years. Since Hal's transfer to Emerald City after his near-death experience at the Georgia prison, they'd chatted many times over coffee during Sean's visits. Sean made sure Hal's pilot experience was put to good use. He ordered the flight training facility to use Hal as the chief instructor. There was no one more qualified, and it kept Hal reasonably happy. And Sean wanted him happy. He also used him for flights in and out of the facility. The fewer pilots who knew what went on there, the better. So, Hal was a good choice.

Supplies were needed from time to time, and new residents were being brought in monthly. Just a handful here, a handful there. Usually handpicked. Sometimes just taken right off the streets. A few had been car-jacked. Some disappeared while hiking in the mountains. Others "died" in avalanches.

Occasionally, sailboats and yachts had disappeared without a trace. A few children had been taken from their beds at night—Emerald City didn't have enough kids, so they needed more. Perpetuation was important, even if they wouldn't be with their own parents. There were enough adults in Emerald City who would willingly adopt them, just for the comfort of raising children.

Of course, there were also a few public beheadings, and deaths by fire, that were allowed to be splashed all over the mass media. Fresh horror from the Middle East. Muslim extremists terrifying the world over and over again. Executions by ISIS—another creation of the CIA. Theatrics that even Hollywood and Brock Winters would have been proud of. After being "beheaded," these rather specialized candidates were immediately transferred to Emerald City. Hal had handled a couple of those flights, too.

Those public killings accomplished two key things for the CIA. They created new specialized candidates for Emerald City, while at the same time infuriating the so-called civilized world, uniting them against Muslims. This supported the agenda of America in waging war in the Middle East, securing oil supplies for American oil companies, and ultimately toppling the Assad regime in Syria. All long-term objectives of U.S. foreign policy.

There was one rather high-profile flight that Hal Winters had made on behalf of the CIA. This particular long-range military transport left the hangar at Emerald City in daylight with Hal at the controls, ably assisted by an Air Force major as first officer. Sitting behind them in the cockpit were two armed CIA agents, making sure that Hal didn't pull anything funny.

It refueled at Eielson Air Force Base in Fairbanks, Alaska, and then continued on towards its destination under the cover of darkness.

It was March 10, 2014, two days after a jumbo jet disappeared over the Indian Ocean with 239 passengers and crew. Those passengers originated from fifteen countries, and some of them possessed skills that would be needed at Emerald City. Desperately needed.

Hal skilfully piloted the military transport all the way from Alaska to a mysterious island that most people knew very little about. An island by the name of Diego Garcia, right smack in the middle of the Indian Ocean.

Diego Garcia was a British territory, but leased by the United States in 1970 as a top-secret military installation. Very little information was available to the general public about this tiny little island, despite the fact that American tax dollars generously funded the mysterious activities that took place there.

While Diego Garcia was nothing more than seventeen square miles of coral and sand, it was one of the most valuable pieces of real estate in the entire world. Strategically important as a refueling center for the various wars that had been fought in the Middle East, as well as a central command for drone warfare. And Sean was sure that much more than those functions were performed there. Judging by the rumors, he'd heard of a secret prison for suspected terrorists and political enemies.

It was so far out in the middle of nowhere, it was accountable to no one.

After America had consummated the lease of the island from the British, they kicked out 1,500 native residents, known as Chagossians. Peaceful people whose ancestors had occupied the island for countless centuries. Simple farmers and fishermen.

They were told that they no longer had the right to live in their homes. It was now a military base, which was deemed much more important. These helpless folks had no choice—they were all shipped out and dropped onto the Mauritius and Seychelles island chains. In those new lands, they were viewed as intruders, and never accepted. There was no way the locals would allow the new arrivals to hone in on their livelihoods. So, they were relegated to urban slums.

The Chagossians were proud, industrious people who were told that no one wanted them. Anywhere.

About 850 of the original exiled group were still alive today, and 4,300 more had been born in exile. The group actually retained legal counsel at one time and sued the British government, whose jurisdiction it was, since they leased the island to the United States. But under pressure from America, the claims were summarily dismissed by the British courts after several futile attempts.

The only salvation the Chagossians ever received was a brave documentary made by an Australian filmmaker in 2004, called *Stealing a Nation*. A powerful film which, not surprisingly, received only limited exposure in the U.S. and Britain. No one remembers it today.

So, Hal obediently navigated the mammoth military plane onto the runway at Diego Garcia in the middle of the night and proceeded to one of the hangars. It was a quick turnaround. The plane was refueled, and 227 passengers were loaded onboard. No luggage, no carry-on bags. Just 227 bedraggled and confused passengers.

Sean knew that twelve people wouldn't be making the journey back to Emerald City. They were the crew from the phantom airliner that disappeared in the middle of the Indian Ocean. People not deemed to be of any value at Emerald City. Instead, they found their destiny at the bottom of the sea.

But, the passengers? Now, they were a different story entirely. Particularly two dozen brilliant engineers.

Sean had met with Hal Winters a few days after he'd returned from Diego Garcia with his terrified and confused human cargo. Of course, Hal and the other residents at Emerald City never got to see the news about what went on in the outside world. The only news they got was what went on in their underground compound. So, Hal had no idea that an airliner had disappeared into thin air just a few days before.

The two of them were having coffee together in Hal's room. Sean asked him how the mission had gone and briefed him on his next outing.

Hal stretched his long frame out along the bed, and propped his head up with his fist. Sean remembered the conversation as if it were yesterday.

"What was that all about? All those people in the middle of nowhere?"

"Hal, you know I can't tell you that."

"What's that fucking island used for? I'd heard rumors about that place over the years, but my God, I never imagined it to be as sophisticated an operation as what I saw."

"Forget what you saw, Hal. There's nothing you can do about it anyway."

"Obviously not. But, I'm just curious."

"It's top secret. Even I haven't got a clue."

"You know what I saw there, don't you?"

"I can probably hazard a guess."

"A jumbo jet, with red and blue markings. And the words and logo of Malaysia Airlines painted on the airframe."

Sean nodded and didn't reply.

"Did you fuckers steal another plane?"

Sean just stared straight into Hal's eyes and tried hard not to blink.

Hal swung his legs from the bed onto the floor and rested his arms on his knees. He stared right back.

"I've gotten to know you, Sean, and I have to admit I kinda like you. Even though you're my captor, I kinda like you. And I'm a good judge of people. I appreciate what you've done for me, and living here is a hell of lot better than back there in that Georgia prison cell. But for God's sake, what are you people doing? How can you live with this? This experiment is about as heartless and brutal as it gets, and that's quite something for someone like me to say."

Sean didn't know how to respond. What Hal said was as if his own conscience was talking to him. He couldn't disagree, but couldn't bring himself to agree either. So, all he said was, "I've come to like you, too, Hal."

Sean's thoughts were interrupted by the return of Jim Diamond. He shuffled into the office and sat down in the same guest chair, head down, staring at a piece of paper in his hand.

"Boy, that was sure fast, Jim. What do you have for me?"

"Ziv Dayan and a lady friend checked into Emergency at the Toronto General Hospital last Friday. Her name is Leslie Fields and she suffered a concussion; stayed overnight for observation."

"Police report?"

"No official report. An officer on station at the hospital questioned Mr. Dayan, who responded that she'd fallen and hit her head on the side of the bed. The officer filed an unofficial report stating that he suspected the injury might have been sustained through some sadomasochistic ritual."

"Why did he think that?"

"She checked into the hospital wearing some leather outfit, skin tight, neck to ankles."

"I see."

"A few more things. The first phone call Mr. Dayan made on his mobile upon leaving the hospital was to a Bradley Crawford. And the first phone call Ms. Fields received upon leaving the hospital was from a man named Simon Worthington, a British citizen living at Bloor Square in Toronto. You should know also that two days after leaving the hospital, Ms. Fields moved out of her King Street apartment. New residence unknown."

Sean smiled. "Anything else?"

"No, that's it."

"Okay. As usual, I appreciate your efficiency."

Jim nodded and hurriedly left the office without another word.

Sean punched the intercom button on his phone. His secretary answered after the first buzz. "Cheryl, get me on the next flight to Toronto."

Chapter 25

"It has to be one of the strangest places in the world, Brad." Ziv walked into the expansive living room of Brad's penthouse apartment, and flopped down on the L-shaped couch.

"What place are you talking about?"

"Denver International Airport."

"So you're convinced that this story leads there?"

"Well, that's what my little Mossad program told us. You'll recall it kicked out a summary of the four letters and it emphasized several key points: Hal Winters was the pilot of United Flight 175 on 9/11; the letters pertained to an airline flight; and the key element of the letters led to Denver International Airport. All the clues in the letters tied into those three main points."

"We don't even have the letters anymore. Our story has lost all of its verifiable evidence."

"Maybe, maybe not. At least we might know now where the letters were pointing. It's a lead."

"True. But, we need more than just conjecture."

Ziv waved his hand in the air, dismissing Brad's comment. "We've come this far. I think we need to go a bit further."

"Okay, let's say I buy that. And, as you know, I'm not one to give up easily on anything. We've stumbled onto something pretty serious, with all that's happened. But we need something more to go on than just some lame conspiracy theory. We need to be realistic here. Otherwise, we're just pissing into the wind."

Ziv nodded. "Got any scotch?"

Brad laughed. "Yeah, I do. That might make any theory sound plausible, eh?"

He disappeared into the kitchen and came back with two tumblers in his hand, each half-full of the amber liquid. Brad raised his glass.

"Cheers! Oh, how's Leslie's recovery going?"

Ziv took a long sip. "Don't know. It's a little strange. Both her landline and mobile numbers are out of service. And I phoned her landlord, who told me that she moved out."

"Hmm…that is strange. She must have been really terrified that night. Maybe she decided you're too big a risk for her?"

"Maybe. But my antenna's up. Something doesn't add up. One thing about Leslie—she didn't strike me as someone who would be afraid of anything. Full of confidence—not one to run from a problem. Know what I mean?"

"So, what are you saying?"

"Nothing, nothing at all. Yet. As I said, my antenna's up."

Brad stretched out his long legs and rested his feet on the coffee table. "I'm glad Kristy's out shopping—she never lets me do this when she's here. So, why is Denver Airport so strange? I've never been there, so enlighten me."

Ziv leaned forward. "Before I do that, I need to tell you about Colin Wentworth's computer."

"Did you hack into it?"

"Yeah, I did. There wasn't much on there. He seemed to be in the habit of erasing his search history every week or so, and deleting emails on a regular basis as well. But there were a couple of interesting ones that he didn't delete, maybe because he intended to still maintain contact with that person."

"Who?"

"Brock Winters."

"What?"

"Yep. The two of them were in contact about those letters. At least I'm pretty sure it was about the letters. They were both careful in how they said things, but about a couple of weeks before you arrived at Colin's place on Vancouver Island, Brock sent a message saying, "Package is on the way.""

Brad scratched his head, puzzled. "But the package of letters was sent from someone at CIA headquarters. It didn't come from Brock."

"You're right, but I think Brock had a contact in there, and he directed that person to send them to Colin. There were a couple of other emails before that one, where Brock used the words, 'I know where they are,' and 'The media won't care, so you do with them what you will.'"

"Wow, this is quite the revelation. Did Colin ever reply?"

"The trained agent that he was, he only used words like 'confirmed,' 'agreed,' and 'affirmative.'"

Brad stood up and started pacing his living room. "So, we have a famous movie star who adored his father, despite the man's assassin background. And he believed that he was wrongly imprisoned—in fact, framed for the mass murders. And judging by alternative media reports, he might have been right. But, why was he framed? That's the question.

"And somehow Brock found out those letters were in the CIA's possession—somehow they retrieved them from this so-called Richard Sterling in Coventry, England. Brock wanted revenge on his dad's behalf. He decided to throw caution to the wind and get those letters into the hands of someone who might know what to do with them. He clearly didn't trust going to the press."

"His father was probably in touch with him right up until the day he died."

"If he died."

"True, you got the impression talking to Brock that he was still alive, didn't you?"

"Just a slip of the tongue on Brock's part—talked about him in the present tense. Kinda got me thinking. Imagination on overdrive, maybe, but this whole thing is so weird, anything's possible."

"Maybe Hal gave Brock hints about who he'd been writing to? And maybe he talked in some kind of code in phone conversations from prison—a code they both understood?"

Brad nodded. "I think that makes sense. They were indeed close. And Brock seemed like one bitter young man to me. But, let's go back a bit here—your program spit out a summary that said Hal Winters was the pilot of United 175 on 9/11. What the hell is that all about? The whole world saw flight 175 smash into the south tower of the World Trade Center. If we believe your program to be correct, then what on earth did we all see? And is the program telling us instead that flight 175 landed at Denver International? I'm getting a headache thinking about this."

Ziv got up from the couch and walked over to the panoramic window overlooking Lake Ontario. He gazed out at the sailboats. "Hal mentioned something about mirages in one of his letters. Said something about seeing things that didn't exist."

Brad stared at Ziv in silence for a few seconds, then gasped. "You think—no, it couldn't be—could it?"

"Hate to break it to you, Brad, but with today's technology, anything's possible. I'll share more with you later about that. It's incredible, and horrifying to consider, but…let's take this one step at a time."

"Agree. Tell me about Denver."

"I will. But, first, have you ever heard about the Svalbard Global Seed Vault?"

"Yeah, kind of a Noah's Ark for crops, right?"

Ziv nodded. "It's in Norway, on the island of Spitsbergen, in the remote Arctic Archipelago. Only about 800 miles from the North Pole. It's a seed vault, storing frozen "spare" copies of seeds from around the world. It's a global effort, supported by virtually every major country. Governments fund it, as well as charitable foundations such as the Bill & Melinda Gates Organization.

"The vault is located 400 feet inside a sandstone mountain—and heavily secured by automated systems because there are no permanent staff on site. This mountainous island was considered ideal because there is virtually no seismic activity there, and it's shrouded in permafrost, which acts as a natural freezer. But even that isn't left to chance—massive refrigeration units are located in the vault to make sure it never thaws. As well, it's over 400 feet above sea level, which guarantees that it'll stay dry even if the polar ice caps melt.

"The place officially opened in 2008, and as of now there are approximately 1.5 million different seed samples stored there. It has the capacity for about 4.5 million. Tens of thousands of new spare copies are added each year. It is thought that any seeds stored there can survive virtually any catastrophe, and the vault can keep them preserved for hundreds, if not thousands, of years. Ready and waiting for whatever's left of the human race to crawl out of its hiding places and start to thrive and propagate once again."

"An Armageddon obsession."

Ziv cocked his head. "Just good planning. Yep, if Armageddon happens in whatever form it takes, civilization will have a seed bank to draw from. That's the entire objective behind the Svalbard Vault."

"Okay, so how does this tie in with Denver?"

"I've done some digging—there's a lot of speculative stuff on the Internet, but I was able to find out some classified musings from a contact I have at the Israeli embassy in New York. It is indeed probably the strangest place in the world, Brad. The thing was built in 1995, even though Denver already had a perfectly good airport that served its purposes just fine. That was the first puzzle that got people scratching their heads. The old airport was closed when the new one was built, yet the new one has fewer gates and runways than the old one had. What it does have, however, is a lot more acreage. The place is monstrous—occupies 53 square miles and is now the largest airport in the entire United States, and second largest in the world.

"Some areas that it was built on were lowered, and others were raised—all told, they moved 110 million cubic yards of earth around, about a third of what had to be moved when the fucking Panama Canal was built. The airport has an amazing array of fibre optic cable, 5,300 miles all told—longer than the Nile River. Plus another 11,000 miles of copper cable communications network. Unheard of for just an airport.

"Five large bunker-type buildings were built during the early stages of construction, there for everyone to see. Then one day they were gone—officials explained that they made mistakes in the building of those structures, so they decided to just bury them. Usually buildings are simply demolished, not buried. But, these were buried. Leaves me scratching my head.

"Like the Svalbard Vault, this airport is well above sea level—5,300 feet to be exact, which is why Denver is nicknamed the Mile High City. It will survive any likely cataclysm involving water, and of course the Rocky Mountains will act as a barrier between Denver and the Pacific Ocean anyway. So, like Svalbard, it's perfectly positioned to survive disasters.

"Making this place weirder than any other airport in the world, to the naked eye at least, is the grotesque artwork that exists in the terminals. It's not hidden—it's there for every man, woman, and child who transits through there to see. It's unfathomable to me that such art would be on display in such a public area. There are pictures on the Internet—take a look when you have a few moments. You'll get the chills—and maybe some nightmares."

Brad was scribbling furiously on his notepad. "Tell me about some of these pieces, Ziv."

"Picture a large green soldier wearing an eagle symbol on his hat, with a bayonet-tipped gun in one hand and a large curved sword in the other. Underneath the soldier are scenes of poverty and distress—a woman clutching a baby and children sleeping in ruins. There's a statue of an open suitcase, but inside the suitcase is a horned demon with its head in its claws. There's another mural with an African woman in native garb, a Native American Indian, and a little blonde girl with the Star of David on her chest and a Bible in her hands. Each of these figures lays dead in open coffins. Then there's a burning city with children sleeping on piles of bricks and a line of mourning women carrying dead babies. Standing above them is a huge soldier wearing a gas mask and brandishing a sword and a machine gun."

Brad looked up. "Christ, that's absolutely bizarre! All of that out in the open, in an airport terminal, there for all travelers to see?"

"Yep. And that's just a small part of it. You'll see all the images online. Some have been painted over, apparently because they were even more gruesome. It all just gives me the chills, and I don't understand how any of this would have been allowed in the first place. It's sick."

"I'm speechless. I think I need to see it in person."

"Apparently, there are weird low and high frequency sounds that emanate into the airport as well, making travelers dizzy and sick to their stomachs. And there are countless air vents jutting out of the barren land that surround the airport, areas that are surrounded by barbed wire fencing."

Brad poured himself another scotch. "And Hal Winters' letters are pointing in the direction of this macabre airport."

"Yes, but brace yourself for more. As I said, I had some chats with my Mossad contact at the embassy in New York. He talked to me in confidence about what he'd heard through the rumor mill. He's certain that the higher-ups in Mossad know everything, but he's only picked up snippets. He says there's an entire fucking city underneath the Denver airport, and that it stretches for miles in every direction, and several stories down. It even has a cute little nickname within intelligence circles—Emerald City. Every comfort imaginable is down there—sewage treatment, heating, air conditioning, swimming pools, leisure centers, beaches and synthetic lakes, hospitals, schools, restaurants, nightclubs, roadways, trains. And contrary to the water shortages America is suffering through, this underground city has its own private aquifer deep beneath the surface. Water has been diverted from some of the country's major aquifers into this private source, a supply of fresh water that is forecast to have a lifespan of several hundred years."

Brad whistled. "If true, it's astonishing! Ironic also that America is drying up with their never-ending drought. Maybe this place explains the relatively sudden and massive water level depletion in California and Nevada? They're letting America wither away so they can have an endless water supply in case Armageddon happens."

Brad paused, then lowered his voice to a growl. "And we can easily guess who's going to be living down there, can't we?"

Ziv laughed. "I think it's easier to guess who won't be living down there."

Chapter 26

She bore into him with her scintillating green eyes. Eyes that were starting to regain their life, their vitality. He took both her hands in his and spoke softly.

"I have to go away for a few days. But the nurse will be staying here with you—you won't be alone at nighttime."

Jannat squeezed his hands—just slightly, but enough for Sean to be encouraged.

"Don't worry about me, Sean. I'll be okay."

He eagerly soaked up the image. She'd been with him only a week, and already the recovery was noticeable. Her skin was showing signs of effervescence again and the dry flakiness had disappeared. But what was most obvious was the weight she'd put on. The nurse told him that twenty pounds had been gained already and Sean wasn't surprised. Her face was full, and while she was eighteen years older than when he'd last seen her, she was starting to resemble the exotic, ravishing beauty he'd fallen in love with.

Jannat stood up and walked from the living room into the kitchen. "Would you like some coffee before you go?"

"No, I've had my three cups already. If I have any more I'll be doing the "purple polka" on the way to the airport, and there's no place to pull off."

Jannat chuckled. "That's one thing that hasn't changed about you—your love of coffee."

Her back was to him now, which somehow made it easier for him to say what he'd been longing to say. "I've changed in other ways, too, Jannat."

She turned around to face him, full coffee cup in hand. "You're still doing what you do, Sean."

"I…yes…but—"

"No buts about it, Sean. You're still doing it. Today, you're going somewhere. I don't know where, but I'm guessing it's just the same old story, the same old business you've always been involved in."

"It's just a job—that's all it is to me now."

Jannat leaned up against the kitchen counter. "Let me guess—directly or indirectly it has to do with Muslims, am I right?"

He slowly nodded.

"Something to do with the evil we're being branded with."

Sean looked down at the floor.

"You can't answer me. Around the world, you and your types have succeeded in blaming us for every horror imaginable. And we both know that you and your types have created those horrors yourselves and lied to the world about them. Just so you can control our world. Steal what we have. Destroy our religious beliefs. Incite hate. Humiliate our culture, demean us into shame. It never ends, does it? What, or who, is going to stop you?"

Sean walked over to her and rested both hands on her shoulders. "It will end one day. It has to."

She shook her shoulders, knocking his hands clear. "You've made me your personal mission. You're trying to make up for throwing me away years ago, and then you just turn around and inflict more horror and lies upon my people. Because it's your job. How can you live with yourself, Sean?"

Sean turned away from her. In a whisper, he replied, "I don't know if I can anymore, Jannat."

He felt her arms wrapping around his waist from behind. She squeezed gently and whispered, "Then you have to reclaim your soul. Bring these people to justice. Be a whistleblower. I'll testify for you, as to what happened in that illegal prison. What you people did to us. End this, Sean."

Sean whirled around and hugged her. Tears were streaming down his cheeks. "I don't know if I'm brave enough."

Jannat leaned her head back and stared into his eyes. "I can't tell you how to feel. Or what to do. But there must be some good people somewhere who have the courage to bring an end to this. There has to be someone. God help us all if there isn't."

Her green eyes were studying him, glinting in the morning light streaming through the kitchen window. He could see the hurt, see her horrific memories reflecting back at him. And knowing that he'd played a role in bringing those horrors down on Jannat and millions of others like her, gnawed at his heart.

He kissed her forehead. "I have to go. A plane to catch. We'll talk again when I get back."

Jannat flashed a thin smile. "Yes, Sean. We'll talk." She brushed her fingers up against his cheek. "I know you're a good man. But, you're conflicted—you're in too deep. It's not fair for me to cause you more conflict than you already have. I'm sorry. I'll be forever in your debt for saving my life. Know that. When I'm well again, I'll be on my way—just like eighteen years ago."

*****

The flight to Toronto was smooth. September was a good time of the year to fly. The summer storms were over, and the skies were generally clear and calm as autumn gradually began to make its presence known.

Sean charmed his way through immigration and continued on into the outer concourse area, where he immediately saw a guy holding a sign with his name on it. Dressed like a chauffeur, he motioned Sean towards the parking area. They walked without saying a word to each other until they reached a black Lincoln.

The chauffeur handed Sean the keys, along with a badge and a little plastic folder containing identification. "You're a detective with the Toronto Police Service. Name's Chad Roworth." The chauffeur then slipped a holster and gun from his waist and handed it to Sean. "It's already loaded. When you're finished, you can leave these things at the usual drop-off."

Sean nodded. He fastened the badge to the front of his belt, and clipped the holster to the left side of his waist.

The chauffeur disappeared without another word.

Sean drove the Lincoln out of the covered parking area, and weaved his way through the maze of roads that led out of the Pearson airport complex. He knew his way around Toronto fairly well, having been here many times in the past. Took the exit onto the 401 eastbound and merged into the heavy traffic.

As he drove along at a snail's pace, he thought about his conversation with Jannat. She was right, he was conflicted. He'd been doing this for so long now, it was a part of his being. It was his life. But lately, even before Jannat had come back into his life, he'd been having serious pangs of conscience. Voices in his head telling him that everything was so wrong, so twisted. Those voices came so often now that it was starting to get scary. Was he going crazy? Or was his conscience just that tormented? Sean was feeling a sense of impending doom—that something was going to happen.

When he'd seen her again after all these years it was in a way that he never imagined he would. A living skeleton, barely existing, in a CIA prison only half an hour from his house. Suddenly, it became personal—everything he'd done was rammed home, deep into his soul. He'd saved her—but he was ashamed that he'd had to.

Sean took the exit onto Avenue Road and headed southbound. Towards the Bloor/Yonge area, where the apartment complex known as Bloor Square was situated. Where a British man named Simon Worthington lived.

Suddenly, Sean's breath became laboured. He was finding it hard to breathe, almost like an asthma attack. But Sean didn't suffer from asthma.

Feeling a sense of panic, he quickly pulled into a shopping center lot and parked the car. Then he lowered his head down against the steering wheel, wrapped his arms around the sides of his head, and drank in the deepest breaths he could imagine. At the same time, he started to cry.

He pictured Jannat's sweet face, her green eyes pleading for some kind of justice, some example of righteousness. What she had endured was beyond belief, and the knowledge of that was tearing Sean's soul to pieces. He could feel it deep down inside. Images were running through his head.

He pictured poor Jannat watching her husband being tortured to death. Could see the tears streaming down her face as they callously dragged his body out of the interrogation room, and then just threw her back into her cell again with other men. No time to mourn, no one to comfort her. And then, raped by other prisoners that very same night after watching her husband die. Just for good measure, raped once again by the doctor himself that night in his examination room.

Then, poor, sweet Jannat, the trained psychiatric nurse, faking the symptoms of locked-in syndrome, to give herself some chance of survival. But even that didn't end the brutal inhumanity of it all. The sick and twisted CIA doctor simply continued the nightly rapes, while she lay motionless in the hospital ward trying desperately to pretend that she was detached, locked away from the world around her and all its external stimuli.

But she still felt everything—not just the pain, but the absolute degradation as well.

Those poor people were treated worse than animals. And why? Because they were Muslims. Sean knew that the systematic drum-beating into the minds of normal, everyday people had accomplished exactly what the CIA had wanted to accomplish. Muslims were feared and hated everywhere now, all to further the geo-political agenda of the West. The *intended* consequence was that there was universal support now for perpetual war in the Middle East. The *unintended* consequence was that an irreversible culture of hate had been created under false pretences, resulting in unmanageable refugee migrations, and racist violence on home soil. And, just like toothpaste, it couldn't be shoved back into the tube. It was going to get worse.

Jannat was right. Someone had to be brave enough to do something. To try to right the wrongs. Set the record straight. Expose the lies.

Sean leaned his head back against the headrest. The tears were still streaming down his cheeks, along his neck, soaking the collar of his white shirt. But he was breathing easier now.

The brainwashing he'd received every year since joining the Agency had worn off, had lost its effect. Sean knew why. This had become personal. What he had been a part of was now eating away at him. He pictured those poor souls living under the Denver airport, pictured the hapless Muslims that had now been shipped to Iraq without identification, most of them psychologically scarred for the rest of their no doubt short lives.

He felt the pain of these people, felt their humanity. His career, and his life, were finished. He'd lost himself long ago, and it was too late now to resurrect.

And then he felt Jannat. Could feel her fingers gently stroking his cheek. Apologizing to him for creating conflict in his mind.

Imagine that—apologizing to me!

He'd cast her aside like garbage almost two decades ago, and then participated willingly in manipulating the world with lies and subterfuge. He'd lost count of how many people he'd killed to further the agenda of the U.S. foreign intelligence service. How he'd looked the other way when people had been tortured, sometimes to death.

He was forced to face the fact that the only woman he'd ever loved had been subjected to the same brutality that he'd willingly participated in during his entire fucking career.

And the ultimate disgusting act of inhumanity was the imprisonment of thousands of innocent people in an underground city, as mere guinea pigs. Being used to test living conditions. To ensure that all would be well for society's political and money elite to hide their sorry asses from a cataclysm should it ever happen.

Sean shook his head from side to side.

I'm a fucking coward. I've sunk as low as any human being can sink.

He rubbed his fists against his cheeks, wiping away the moisture. Then he reached his right hand down to the left side of his waist and pulled the pistol out of its holster.

Sean Russell tilted his head back, cocked the hammer of the gun, and rammed the barrel between his teeth up into the roof of his mouth.

Forgive me, Jannat. Forgive me, God.

Chapter 27

"Yep, she was a pro, Brad. She took me hook, line, and sinker."

The cab turned from Front Street onto University Avenue, one of downtown Toronto's most majestic streets. It headed north a couple of blocks until Ziv signalled for the driver to slow down.

"There it is. Rogue's Gallery. Just pull up in front."

Brad paid the driver and the two men stepped out onto the wide sidewalk.

"So this is where she first reeled you in, huh?"

"Yeah, the whole thing was obviously staged. I was sucked in beautifully."

Brad took off his sunglasses and studied the building. "Looks like quite the high-end place." He pointed. "You were sitting at that table in the window?"

Ziv nodded. "And she'd reserved the table right beside me. I always sat at that window table, but I'd never seen her there before until that day. I remember the maître d' mentioning that she usually sat at a different table. He knew her by name, too, so she was a regular, like me."

"So, she'd done her homework. She knew in advance who you were, what your skills were. Must have been confident that you wouldn't just sit there and let some guy beat her up."

"Right. The perfect way to meet me, without it looking obvious. She must have had an inkling that I'd be suspicious if she was openly friendly towards me. I would have been wary of that."

"It was perfect, wasn't it? Very smart. The way it worked, you were the one who made the move on her by swooping in as her knight in shining armor."

Ziv unbuttoned his jacket. It was a nice warm September day, and the sun was making the temperature soar by the minute. "I was such a sucker, Brad. My guard was completely down. If I had been in Beirut instead of Toronto, I would have suspected everyone in the restaurant. But, Toronto?

"And she's brilliant—she must have already known that you had the letters, and knew that we'd met and joined up. We were either bugged, or under surveillance. She calculated that I was the best route to you, to get her pretty little hands on those letters. I mean, you're happily married—you're not exactly going to be easy prey for a beautiful woman. Would be tougher to start an affair with you than to start a romance with me."

Brad shook his head. "Hey, wouldn't be the first time a femme fatale lured a guy into a web. But she definitely out-spied you, Ziv."

Ziv chuckled. "You got that right. And she did it not only once, but twice! Stuck to the same formula, too—arranging it so that she got hit both times, drawing on my chivalry and deflecting any possible suspicion. And making sure that I was tied to the bed the second time, so I wouldn't be able to fight back. Just brilliant—gotta give her credit, at least."

Brad checked his watch. "I've still got some time, but not too long. Let's go in and see what we can find out."

Ziv led the way into the restaurant, and was greeted right away by Marcel, the same maître d' who'd been on duty the day he met Leslie.

Marcel gave a slight bow. "Hello, Mr. Dayan. So good to see you again—it's been a long time."

"Yes, it has, Marcel. Been busy." He gestured to Brad. "This is my good friend, Bradley Crawford."

"Oh, such a pleasure to meet you, Mr. Crawford. I recognized you right away when you came in the door. I've read many of your stories and columns. Particularly liked the one in Investigative Reports magazine about the Mexican border tunnels. You should come here more often—a lot of news people dine here."

Brad shook his hand. "Thank you, Marcel. Looks like a lovely restaurant. I'll bring my wife here for a nice romantic dinner sometime."

Marcel pulled a notebook out of his pocket. "What's your wife's name? I try to record all of our customers, and when you come in next time it would be nice for me to address her by name."

Brad was impressed. This was one very personable and organized maître d'. "That would be nice. Her name is Kristy, with a K. Do you actually write down the names of every guest in that little book?"

Marcel's face beamed with pride. "Why, yes, I certainly do. I'm not just the maître d', I'm also the owner. I take pride in knowing all of my customers."

Brad nudged his friend. "Isn't that interesting, Ziv?"

Ziv took the cue. "Marcel, have you seen Ms. Fields again since that day I had that fight with her ex-boyfriend?"

"No, she hasn't been back in. That was certainly a terrible day. First, she tripped on a broken tile coming in the front door, then that man hit her. It was so brave of you to have stopped him, but I did wonder what happened to the two of you."

"Well, we became…friends. But, I'm afraid something may have happened to her. She seems to have disappeared. Was hoping you could help."

Marcel blustered. "Oh…dear. That's t-terrible. I hope she's okay. Such a lovely lady."

"Did you know her ex-boyfriend?"

"You mean that man who hit her? I don't think he was ever her boyfriend. He came in once in a while by himself, and I saw them having lunch only one time together. A couple of weeks before that day he hit her."

Ziv rested his hands on the reception counter and leaned forward. "Do you know his full name, Marcel? When he made his appearance, I recall she called him Gerry. Did you write it in your little book?"

Marcel smiled. "Well, of course I did!" He started leafing through the pages.

"How do you organize that book so you know who's who?"

A sly little smile came over Marcel's pudgy face. "I use word association—things that I notice about people, then I categorize. Like for Ms. Fields, I wrote her name under the Classy Lady category. For you, I wrote your name under Tall, Dark and Handsome." Marcel blushed. "I'm sorry."

Ziv put his hand on the little man's shoulder. "That's okay, Marcel. So, how did you classify that man?"

"I didn't like his accent, so I wrote his name under Snotty Brit."

Ziv turned toward Brad. "Geez, I forgot the guy had a British accent. Just like the guy in my apartment!"

Marcel frowned. "What's that?"

Ziv waved his hand. "Nothing, Marcel. Would you be so kind as to tell me his name?"

Marcel looked at him for a few moments, then gazed back down at his little book. "I guess since you're trying to find Ms. Fields, it would be okay. Well, she may have called him Gerry, but his name was actually Simon Worthington. Maybe Gerry was a nickname?"

Brad stepped forward. "Has he been in here again since that day of the fight?"

"No, but I think he would have been too embarrassed to ever come back."

"Do you have a phone number for him in your book?"

"No, I don't keep information like that."

Ziv reached out and shook Marcel's sweaty hand. "Thanks, Marcel. We appreciate it."

"Are you not staying for lunch? You can have your old table."

"No time for lunch today. See you next time."

They left the restaurant and strolled north along University Avenue until they reached King Street. Then they turned right and continued walking in silence until they reached a multi-story apartment building. Ziv pointed up.

"That was her apartment, on the eighth floor. See that balcony with the silver barbecue? That was where we used to sit and drink martinis at midnight."

"You checked with her landlord?"

"Yeah, he said she paid her lease up and just moved out. The unit was furnished, so she didn't have to worry about a moving truck or anything like that. And she didn't leave a forwarding address."

"What about her employer?"

Ziv shook his head. "I have no idea who she worked for up here in Canada. She was an aerospace engineer, had done contract work with NASA for years. Then got assigned to work with a Canadian space research company.

"She wouldn't tell me who—said it was classified work. Probably defence related. But, she did say she was working on an advanced telescope for the ISS. I phoned the two largest aerospace companies based here in Toronto: Space Systems Inc. and Orbital Logistics Ltd. They wouldn't confirm or deny that they had her under employ. Phoned NASA and got the same answer from them. Got my contacts to do a search through databases—no record of her."

"She's good, no doubt about it."

Ziv looked up at the balcony again. "I've been retired too long, Brad. Old and rusty now. I'd forgotten completely that the thug in the restaurant had a British accent—just like one of the two guys who broke into my apartment. In addition to Colin Wentworth and Richard Sterling, we now have a third British connection, this Mr. Simon Worthington."

Brad rubbed Ziv's shoulder. "Well, you may be getting rusty, but you're not that old yet. If it makes you feel any better, I think Marcel back there was itching to suck your dick."

Ziv coughed. "Gee, thanks for that. Glad to hear I'm not losing my charm."

They both laughed, and then continued walking east along King Street.

"I'll get my guys going on a search for Worthington—see if we can pick anything up on him."

Brad took off his jacket and slung it across his shoulder. "Do you think Leslie is still here? If she's CIA, then her job is done. The letters are back in their hands, and probably once again safely stored away down in Langley by now."

Ziv nodded. "Could be. If she is CIA, you'd be right. But the British connection confuses me. What was Simon Worthington's role in all this? Remember, the CIA probably stole those letters originally from Richard Sterling in Coventry—and then killed him.

"So, a Brit had them first. Then they were stolen from the CIA by someone Brock Winters probably paid off, then sent off to another Brit, Colin Wentworth on Vancouver Island. Which is where you came in. Then you gave them to me, and they were stolen by another Brit, probably this Simon Worthington.

"So, it seems that there's a game of ping pong going on between the Americans and the British. Leslie's an American, but her partner in crime here is British. So, the question is, was Leslie CIA or freelance? Were she and Worthington MI6 maybe? Or, just Worthington? Was Leslie playing both sides of the fence?"

"So, maybe the letters aren't back in CIA hands—yet."

"Maybe not."

Brad stopped to throw some change into a hat for a homeless guy sitting on the sidewalk. Ziv dropped a few quarters in the hat as well.

"Ziv, where was she from? What city in the States?"

"Baltimore, Maryland. That was her home town."

Suddenly, Ziv slapped himself on the side of the head. "Shit! I really am getting rusty! We may have a connection. C'mon, follow me."

They were approaching Yonge Street and Brad was having a tough time keeping up to Ziv's long strides. He was clearly a man on a mission now. Brad grabbed him by the sleeve of his coat, and dragged him to a stop.

"Where are we going? What's this connection?"

Ziv pointed towards Yonge Street. "Right over there. That little store on the corner, Dainty Darlings. Leslie dragged me in there once, to show me the outfits she had sent her nieces for their birthday.

"Twins, they turned eight a couple of months ago—Brenda and Heidi. Surprised I remember those names. They live in Baltimore, and she bragged about them all the time. I could tell she adored them. Anyway, the store sent the dresses to them, so they probably still have the address in their files."

"Sounds like a good lead. Let's check it out."

They waited for the light to change and then crossed the street. Ziv buttoned up his jacket.

"Put your coat back on, Brad. We need to look respectable. And let me do the talking—I'm gonna do some creative bullshitting."

Once in the store, Ziv walked over to a rack of dresses for eight to ten year olds. He pretended to browse until the sales clerk came over.

Brad flashed her a friendly smile. She was a pretty lady, about thirtyish. Impeccably dressed.

"Can I help you, gentlemen?"

Ziv looked up and smiled with feigned relief. "Oh, yes, please. I'm trying to pick out a couple of dresses for my fiancé's nieces. They're twins. She bought outfits from you a couple of months or so ago, for their birthday. But, they've just been chosen to perform at a school concert, and we want to send them new dresses for that occasion. And, while they may be twins, the dresses have to be different. Know what I mean?"

She laughed. "Yes, that individuality thing. I don't blame them. How old are they?"

"Eight."

"Well, if I were an eight-year-old, I'd be thrilled to wear one of these dresses." She pulled two off the rack and held them up.

"They look very nice." Ziv turned to Brad. "What do you think?"

Brad shrugged. "I'm not the right guy to ask, but I'm sure Leslie would approve."

"Gee, I sure hope so. Would hate to make a mistake."

Ziv turned back to the sales clerk. "My fiancé, Leslie, had to leave suddenly for Europe and she called me from the airport, asking me if I'd do this." He chuckled. "She says she trusts my judgement, but I'd rather put myself in your hands. If you say these dresses are right, then we have a sale."

The clerk beamed. "Alright, then. Follow me to the counter."

She scanned the barcodes and Ziv paid with his VISA card.

"Would you like a box for these?"

"Oh, forgot to tell you—we'll need you to ship them for us. I'll pay the shipping charges with cash."

"No problem. Where would you like me to send them?"

"Well, you must have that on file. You sent them last time for us."

"Okay. Name?"

"Check under my fiancé's name, Leslie Fields."

The clerk input the name into her computer. "Here we are. Sure, we can send them. And don't worry about the shipping charges. These dresses will be going on sale in a few days anyway, so the difference will cover it."

Ziv smiled. "Aw, that's so nice of you. Could you just swing your monitor my way for a second? The girls said their names were misspelt last time, so I want to make sure they're right."

"Oh, sure." She swiveled the monitor around and Ziv scanned the address quickly, locking the information into his brain.

"No, the names are spelt correctly. Thanks so much for your help. It's been wonderful."

"You're so welcome." Suddenly, she squinted her eyes at Brad. "Don't I know you? From a magazine or something?"

Brad laughed. "Yeah, you probably do. I was on the covers of *People*, and *Forbes* a couple of years ago."

She pointed. "That was it. Probably saw you on *People*. *Forbes* is a bit too heavy for me. What's your name?"

"Bradley Crawford."

"Oh, yes—you won some awards. Can I have your autograph?"

She thrust a pen and paper at him and Brad obliged.

Once out on the sidewalk again, Ziv said, "207 Lundy Lane, Baltimore, Maryland. Remember that in case I forget, which I seem to be doing a lot of lately."

Brad patted him on the back. "Got it, don't worry. And well done by the way!"

Ziv squeezed Brad's shoulder. "If this story develops for us, that girl will be darn glad she got your autograph!"

"That's a big 'if.' We'll keep our fingers crossed that we get some good luck. So, what's your next move, Ziv?"

"Baltimore is lovely this time of the year."

Chapter 28

Hal changed his shirt. Wanted to wear something a little bit different tonight for dinner. The last few nights he'd just worn sports jerseys from three of his favorite teams: Red Sox, Yankees, and Cardinals. But tonight he wanted to wear a shirt with a collar, and one that actually had buttons for a change.

It wasn't like this was "the last supper," But, it was darn close.

He looked at the calendar hanging on the wall. It was September and he'd been in this underground city for over four years now. He didn't have to cross off the dates, because the Emerald City Clarion was kind enough to tell him in bold print what day it was every single morning.

He opened his door, walked out into the tunnel roadway, and climbed onto his bike. At least there was no worry about weather down here, he thought. Every day was a good day for a bike ride.

Fifteen minutes later, he arrived at the restaurant. Well, the "dining establishment" as they all liked to call it. The pretty hostess greeted him and ushered him towards a table in the corner. Hal sat down and the hostess withdrew the napkin from the water glass, and with a flourish laid it on his lap.

He looked around before studying the menu—saw his good friend, Keith, sitting with another couple a few tables over. Keith was waving to him, trying to get his attention. Hal smiled, got up and walked over.

"Hal, haven't talked to you in a couple of days. There's one empty seat here—join us?"

"No, I feel like being alone tonight. But I do want to talk to you later. I'll knock on your door, okay?"

"Sure. Hey, I got my graduation certificate today. I'm now a journeyman electrician. And I have you to thank—I think it was two years ago now when you told me I should get training in something. My accountant's degree is pretty useless down here. So, thanks for the push."

"Congratulations, Keith. I was glad when you told me you enrolled—that certificate will set you up much better down here."

"Yeah—I'm almost as important as you now!"

Hal laughed and punched him playfully on the shoulder. "Well, let's not get carried away now, Keith."

"Hey, have you met Joan and Matt?"

Hal held out his hand. "No, I don't believe I have. Name's Hal Winters—pleased to meet you."

Matt nodded and smiled politely. But, Joan gushed, "Oh, you're that CIA guy; you piloted one of the 9/11 jets here. I'll bet you have lots of stories to tell!"

"Well, Joan, I do indeed have lots of stories, but none I want to tell."

Matt jumped in, his voice condescending. "So, I guess a few dozen people can blame you for being down here, huh?"

Hal placed his hands on the table and leaned in close to Matt. "You and I just met for the very first time, yet you have the nerve to say something like that to me? I'll make you a promise, Matt, providing that you make me one, too. If you promise never to say anything like that to me or behind my back again, I promise to let you live. Deal?"

Matt's mouth opened wide and stayed that way. Hal smiled and made a slight bow to Joan, who winked at him in return. Then he turned and walked calmly back to his table.

Keith followed. "Hal, I apologize for that. He's just an arrogant prick—a Wall Street lawyer in his old life. No one likes him."

"That's okay, Keith. I don't care if he likes me or not. All I care about is that he shuts his pie-hole."

"I think he got the message. So, what do you want to talk to me about later?"

"Later, Keith. Go be with your friends."

"Okay, I'll see you later then. Oh, I saw you down at the tennis courts this afternoon—that young guy didn't stand a chance with you. You've still got the moves, Hal."

"I just got lucky—I think he has a father complex. Didn't have the heart to go for my jugular."

"You're always way too modest. Ciao!"

Hal sat down at his table again and looked at the menu. Then his eyes drifted up and he studied some of the other groups of people. He recognized several passengers from his flight, and a couple of the flight attendants. One in particular—the most senior one that had been on United 175 that day. Her name was Kathy, and she'd been in her early thirties back on September 11, 2001. Now, fourteen years later, she was solidly in her forties, and, sadly, hadn't aged well at all. She saw him looking, and waved. Then she got up and walked over to his table.

"Hi, Captain Winters. Good to see you. I think we usually eat at different times, because I only see you in here a couple of times a week. We should have dinner together sometime."

Hal smiled and stood. "Kathy, I wish you wouldn't keep calling me Captain Winters. My name's Hal."

"Force of habit, I guess, a sign of respect. I hope you're not offended."

"No, of course not. But, Kathy, you know full well that I was just a "pretend captain" that day. So, you don't need to show me that respect."

"You deserve it. You tried to stop it—tried to save us all. Got us all out of the plane before you even thought of leaving yourself. Told us to run. I've never forgotten that. In my mind, you weren't a pretend captain at all. You were the real deal."

Hal nodded. "Well, thank you, Kathy. I appreciate that. But, will you please promise to call me Hal from now on?"

"Okay, Hal. Oh, that sounds strange." She giggled. Then she leaned in and kissed his cheek. "You're my favorite person in here, Hal. And so many people think the same as me. You've gone out of your way to give guidance and reassurance to everyone you come in contact with. Without you, I don't think a lot of people would have lasted this long."

Hal kissed her back. "Thank you for that. You've made my day, Kathy."

She flashed him one last smile, a lingering one, and then walked back to her table.

Hal let out a long sigh, and sat down again. The waitress came by and he ordered a salmon filet, along with rice and broccoli. Some apple pie for dessert, washed down with coffee.

He enjoyed the meal. In fact, he usually enjoyed the meals in Emerald City. But the environment, and the knowledge of where he was, usually dampened his appetite. And the administrators here knew that's the way it would be with most people, so part of the experiment was to deliver meals that were high on the scale of gourmet most of the time. But sometimes, the meals really fell down. And it would be like that for a week or so—then, all of a sudden, the quality would improve again. Like night and day.

Hal knew what they were doing—they were transforming mealtimes into a psychological experiment. They studied the moods and attitudes of people when the meals were poor, then recorded how everyone's outlook changed when the meals improved again. At every meal, there were attendants in white coats walking around with clipboards, listening in as they passed by the tables, jotting little notes down on their pads.

Hal knew exactly what they were doing.

And they also made sure that people didn't see armed guards walking around. He knew they were positioned elsewhere, ready to be summoned at a moment's notice. Emerald City indeed had its own police force, and even a fire department. The residents couldn't aspire to those jobs though—they were off limits for obvious reasons. Only military types held those jobs.

But they went to great lengths to try to make the residents feel like they weren't really prisoners. Again, part of the experiment.

And that was their weakness.

Hal thought about his family. He missed them, especially Brock. Once he'd been moved from the penitentiary in Georgia, to Emerald

City in Denver, he was allowed a phone call that same day. Sean Russell wanted him to make that call, to make sure that whoever it was who had the recording from the cockpit of United 175 that Hal had mailed off on 9/11, knew that Hal was alive and well. That he hadn't died in prison, even though the official story said that he had.

That call was made to Brock. Because Brock was the one who had the mini-cassette. In a safe place. At least he thought it was a safe place.

In a phone call Hal made to Brock a couple of months ago, Brock confessed, in coded terms, that the tape was missing—stolen from a safe at his office. And he'd neglected to make a copy of the recording. Hal tried not to show concern over the phone, because if someone had been listening in they might guess that he no longer had any leverage to keep himself alive.

Hal and Brock had a code between them. They mastered it when Brock was just a child. Back then, it had just been for fun. But they used it over and over again in their conversations, so much so that Anne and the two other boys actually joined in on conversations that were absolute farces. Hal and Brock were talking about one thing, and the other three were talking about something else entirely. It was sort of funny, but also sort of sad.

So, Hal used that code to tell Brock where the letters he'd written to Richard Sterling had ended up. Hal knew—from an MI6 visitor he'd had at the Georgia prison—that Richard had been killed and the letters were in a CIA vault.

Hal also told Brock, again in code, who to send the letters to once he was able to get them out of there. Another MI6 contact, Colin Wentworth, a name given to him by his visitor at the Georgia prison.

Neither Hal nor Brock had any idea who had stolen the mini-cassette, but, at the very least, if they got the letters into the right hands they could help the British in exposing what had really happened on 9/11. That had been Richard Sterling's role until he got killed. And then, after that, Colin Wentworth's role. But he died, too. And Hal had no idea who had the letters now.

His leverage had dried up. If those letters fell into the wrong hands, the hands that also had the mini-cassette, then Hal's life was in danger, as were his family's lives—particularly Brock's. Hal didn't really care about his own life anymore, but he did care about his family. And he cared about the poor people in here.

And, strangely enough, considering that he was a killer by profession, Hal Winters cared about justice.

He had the feeling though, that as long as Sean Russell was in charge of this facility, he and his family were safe. He liked Sean a lot. Sean had saved him by transferring him out of Georgia. And he trusted him—for some reason that he couldn't put his finger on—he trusted him. Maybe it was Stockholm Syndrome at work, but in the four years he had known Sean, they had sort of become friends, in a strange kind of way. Maybe it was just mutual respect. He had the feeling that Sean liked him, too.

Hal left the dining room, climbed onto his bike and wheeled himself back to his room. Once there, he checked his watch. Only 9:00. He set his alarm clock, and then drifted off to sleep. A restful sleep, borne from a wonderful meal.

At exactly 11:00 the alarm went off. He got up, splashed some water on his face, opened his door and walked down the tunnel. He knew where he was going.

About 100 yards down the deserted tunnel, he turned right onto the pavement of another tunnel. Deserted as well.

Well, at least devoid of people. It wasn't completely empty. There was machinery parked in this tunnel, important machinery.

Hal had walked this tunnel every night for the past week, always at the same time. He wanted to be certain that guards didn't patrol here at this late time of the night. And every night, it had been the same story—empty and quiet.

They were so confident that no one could escape from this underground monstrosity, that patrols were deemed unnecessary. The idiots in charge also wanted to convey some kind of comfy, cozy, homey feeling. Delusional to the nth degree.

Just all part of the experiment. Hal resented very much being a guinea pig.

He walked down this second tunnel for about fifty yards until he arrived at the spot. An important spot. He looked up and stared at the four foot by four foot square vent in the ceiling. His 20/20 vision could tell that there were no fasteners—it just lifted upwards into the ventilation duct. The only problem was that the ceiling in this tunnel was about fifteen feet high. But that was only a small problem. Like every problem Hal had faced during his life, there was always at least one solution. In this case, there was only one, and it was parked another thirty yards down the tunnel. Parked in the same spot every night.

He walked down to the slick little front-end loader, orange in color, and rich in features. One of those features was the option to be able to operate it with or without a driver. Hal reached across the front seat and lifted up the lid of a container integral to the console. There it was—a tiny little remote control. That's all he would need.

That and the loader's hydraulic lift that could telescope thirteen feet into the air.

Hal walked out of the secondary tunnel, and then back along the main tunnel. He went past his own room, choosing instead one several doors down. He knocked lightly.

Keith opened up and Hal slipped in, closing the door behind him.

He motioned for Keith to sit down, then he leaned over and turned on Keith's little radio. Jazz music, just in case there were bugs in the rooms. Hal was pretty sure there weren't, but he wasn't taking any chances.

Because tomorrow night's dinner was his "last supper."

Keith frowned. "So, what's up? You look serious."

"Remember two years ago you asked me to take you with me if I escaped?"

Keith leaned forward, eyes squinting. "Yes."

"Do you remember that movie, *The Great Escape*?"

"Sure."

"Well, tomorrow night I'm going to be Steve McQueen, and you're going to be Richard Attenborough."

Keith gasped. "Are you serious?"

"Dead serious."

"How?"

"You'll have to trust me."

"I do."

"It might be dangerous."

"I don't care. I'm with you. What about all the others?"

"We'll never get out if we try to take more people with us. We'll get them help once we're out, and then blow this abomination wide open for the whole world to see. Tomorrow night, 11:00, come to my room."

"Jesus!"

"No, just Hal. You'll only see Jesus if we're unlucky."

Chapter 29

The cold steel of the gun barrel was completely unforgiving against the roof of his mouth. Poised menacingly—willing and ready to blow his skull into a thousand pieces.

Sean shivered, as that gruesome image flashed across his brain.

As he held the gun in place, index finger twitching against the trigger, his life passed in front of his eyes exactly the way spiritualists always said it would.

The things he was thankful for, and those he wasn't.

He saw his parents, sitting at the end of the table at Christmas time, smiling, laughing, and proud as punch.

Graduation day—his law degree. Could see his own face now, beaming from ear to ear, his image adorned in a black gown and cap.

His first car—a Chevy Chevelle, still his favorite car out of all that he'd owned. Probably because he could barely afford it at the time, so it had meant more to him. Now, he could pretty much afford anything, so a new car never felt all that special anymore.

He saw the first time he had sex, watched it unfold in his mind in living breathing Technicolor. In the back seat of his Chevelle—breathless, frantic, totally unemotional. He'd been set up with a tramp by his best friend—told him she'd be an easy lay. And what the hell, he had to have his first lay someday, so why work for it? He could even remember how he felt afterwards—how he was just so anxious to get her out of his car. Didn't want her to linger. Didn't want to remember any longer than necessary that he'd wasted his first fuck on someone who would do it with anyone.

Then entire countries flashed in his mind, places he'd been. He could see streets and dark alleys, men begging for their lives only to have their anguished cries ignored.

Bullet holes in foreheads, smashed knee caps, faces held underwater until the decrease in thrashing indicated the inevitable and ominous death threshold.

Sitting on a rooftop with a sniper rifle cradled in his arms, pulling the trigger on a human being 300 yards away, so far away that it wasn't even personal. It was just a video game.

Then he saw Jannat—she crossed his brain's line of vision, blocking out everything else. Her long black hair, mesmerizing green eyes, and the figure of a supermodel. That smile that was not only addicting, but incredibly knowing. It was like she could see right into his soul.

With the cold steel of the gun still invading the sanctuary of his mouth, he heard her voice. That soft intonation that she owned—that voice that no other came close to. The voice that always stirred his heart.

Something about her head resting on his lap had always consumed him with a comforting feeling that was beyond compare—just a simple thing like that. He hadn't experienced that feeling with her for almost two decades, but it was still as vivid as yesterday. Her little giggles every time he said something silly. Her shoulders quivered whenever she laughed, while at the same time cute little dimples magically appeared, framing her luscious mouth.

His brain recalled one of the last things she said to him before he left the house to board the plane to Toronto: *"There must be some good people somewhere who have the courage to bring an end to this. There has to be someone. God help us all if there isn't."*

Sean felt a pounding sensation in his brain. And phrases started forming in his consciousness: *I am a good person. I have always been courageous. I am that someone.*

The next thing he became vaguely aware of was that his index finger had stopped twitching. But, for some reason, the finger stayed where it was—it wasn't ready to retreat, even though part of his brain was telling it to.

He commanded his hand to pull the gun from his mouth—but

it wouldn't move. Then he tried forcing his eyelids to open, but they remained frozen shut. And once again his index finger began its ominous twitching against the trigger.

Suddenly, he heard her scream. It was a silent scream, but it reached his ears anyway. He could see her mouth open, but she was restraining herself from making even the slightest sound. She knew her life depended on it.

But Sean's brain still heard the scream nonetheless, from deep within her wonderful heart and soul. She was lying on a bed, her strength of will forcing her limbs to be still, to not betray her. While a man in a white coat, a coat that normally represented comfort and caring, was pounding his body into hers. Grunting, groaning, humping and moaning, while Jannat lay as still as a board.

With her mouth wide open, silently screaming. Hoping and praying that someone, anyone, would help her. But, night after night, help never came.

The screams got louder—but they sounded different now to Sean's ears. They weren't silent anymore.

And they weren't Jannat's screams.

His eyelids flickered open. At first, things were a blur, but gradually his eyes began to focus clearly through the windshield. And what he saw stirred the fires of rage in his belly.

This time, his hand responded to the command from his brain. He pulled the gun out of his mouth and slipped it back into the holster.

Sean opened the car door and jumped out. Slamming the door behind him, he sprinted to the other end of the parking lot.

He counted three of them—against an elderly couple lying on the pavement. The thugs seemed to be in their mid-twenties; white, two with shaved heads and wearing leather jackets. They were laughing as they took turns kicking the old couple. The woman was screaming as loud as her advanced age would allow, while the old man was trying desperately to cover her body with his. Groceries lay strewn all over the ground, and the side panel door to a Chrysler minivan was in the open position.

Sean could see that the old couple were of Middle Eastern descent, and their faces were completely smeared in blood. But, that didn't stop the thugs. They kept laughing and kicking to their hearts' content.

Sean was only a few feet away now, but too late to stop one guy from rearing his leg back and leveling a football kick at the man's head. The kick was so powerful that it lifted the poor man's body clear into the air, rolling him off the woman.

The same guy now had a clear shot at the woman, and he brought his leg back again preparing to give her the same cruel treatment.

Sean caught the guy's foot in mid-air and, with both hands working in unison, twisted the foot with one hand while holding the lower leg stationary with the other. He'd done this move many times before, but never with as much ferocity as he did right now. The foot almost twisted clear off in his hand as he heard the snapping sound of multiple bones in the ankle.

The man screamed in agony while Sean still had a hold of his leg. With both hands still grasping tightly, Sean started moving in a tight circle, swinging the guy around. At first, the guy was hopping on his one good leg, but then the circle got so tight and fast that he went airborne, falling downward briefly as he lost his footing, scraping his chin hard against the ground.

But, the speed of the circle increased rapidly and the man rose in the air, body perfectly parallel to the ground. Sean's feet moved like Muhammad Ali, dancing deftly within the tight circle until he finally decided it was time to let go.

When he did, the body of the thug went sailing through the air, smashing face first into the front grill of a beat-up pickup truck which Sean assumed belonged to them.

Both of the other men just stared at their friend as he crumpled helplessly to the ground. Then one of them clenched his fists and moved towards Sean.

"C'mon, see if you can fucking do that to me, man!"

The fire in Sean's belly was roaring—so much so that the acid he usually felt when he was under stress wasn't making its appearance this time. For just an instant, Sean thought that was interesting. Maybe he just hadn't had enough fire in his belly lately, not enough passion.

Maybe the lack of those things was what always caused the acid to percolate.

He took a step towards the second creep, and said mockingly, "No, I won't do that to you, *man*."

"Ha, ha—didn't think so. I gonna make you pay for what you done, asshole!"

Sean suddenly ran at the man, with both his hands up in front, palms forward. He looked shocked as Sean closed in. He didn't expect that he'd be rushed like a linebacker. He focused his eyes on Sean's hands, puzzled as to what they were going to do. Then Sean went down, sliding towards him on his bum as if he were sliding into home plate. Both feet went up in the air at the last second and took direct aim at the man's knees.

Sean heard, as well as felt, the double snap, and the thug wobbled and toppled like a wooden marionette that had lost its strings. He shrieked in pain and shock as his eyes took in the state of his legs— two useless lower limbs that now bent in the opposite direction of where they had bent just seconds before.

There was one guy left. Sean stood up and moved towards him, but the coward raised his hands in the air. "Hey, I surrender, man!" He looked down at Sean's waist. "I can see your badge! You can't touch me, you're a cop! I'm surrendering!"

Sean sneered. "Just like you're pretending to be a human being, I'm pretending to be a cop."

His skilled hands moved fast, both of them pounding into the man's face, and then just for good measure, Sean brought his knee up into his groin. He doubled over and collapsed to the ground, sobbing.

Sean grabbed him by the lapels of his leather jacket, and dragged him over to the pickup truck. He opened the door, and climbed inside, still holding onto the man's jacket with one hand. The thug was groggy and not offering one ounce of resistance. Sean reached his right hand out through the open driver's side window, and grasped onto a fistful of hair, yanking his head in towards him. Then he shut the door with his left hand.

Switching hands, he turned the keys that were hanging in the ignition, and roughly pulled the thug's head in through the open window with his left hand.

Then Sean pressed the power window button, which caused the window to rise automatically until it met with resistance. The punk struggled, but now Sean had both hands free as the window rose on its own.

One fist clenched around an ear, the other with a tuft of hair, the guy wasn't going anywhere. The window rose, crushing into his throat and raising his head towards the upper rim of the window frame. Then it stopped, with the man's head trapped in its path.

He started choking.

"Aw, too tight for you? Okay, I'll lower it a tiny bit." And Sean did, and the choking stopped. But, the head was stuck solid.

"Your friends won't be able to go anywhere in the state they're in, and neither will you now. Actually, you're the lucky one. No permanent damage. Well, except for this."

Sean then slammed his open palm into the thug's nose. He didn't scream, because the window was too tight to allow him to do that. He just gasped, as the blood began streaming down over his mouth and chin.

Sean turned off the car and climbed out on the passenger side. A small crowd was gathering now, and he pulled the badge off his belt buckle and flashed it high for all to see.

"Police. This is a crime scene. Does anyone have a phone? Mine got busted in the scuffle."

A lady nodded and held her phone out to him.

"Thanks, ma'am. But, would you please just phone 911 for me? I have another emergency I have to get to. Ask for four ambulances, too, please."

She nodded nervously and dialed. Sean jogged over to the old couple who were now sitting up on the pavement. Through their bloodied eyes, they looked up at him in gratitude. The man's shirt was torn on the sleeve, so Sean ripped it off and used it to dab the blood away from the eyes of both of them.

"Ambulances are on their way. I hope you'll both be okay."

The man spoke in a whisper. "You're the police. Aren't you staying?"

Sean smiled kindly at both of them. "No, I have to go. Another emergency to attend to."

The woman was busy adjusting her hijab, which had fallen down to her neck. She positioned it back up over her head again and then reached out suddenly and grasped Sean's wrist. Being that she was Muslim, Sean knew that she wouldn't normally be allowed to touch another man like that. For a brief second, her husband's face bore a look of shock. But, then he smiled, looked at her and nodded.

She spoke softly, with a strong accent. "You are a kind man. And you are a brave man. We cannot ever in this lifetime thank you enough."

Sean stood. "I really have to hurry away now. You can thank me by not giving a good description of me to the police when they arrive."

They both looked puzzled for a moment, but then a shadow of understanding seemed to come over the expression in their eyes. He didn't know how they could have understood anything about the favor he'd just asked of them, but in some strange way he thought they did.

The old couple smiled and nodded.

Before running back to his car, Sean said one last thing.

"Please be well—and be happy. Believe it or not, I have you to thank—much more than you have me to thank." Sean bowed. "So, my thanks are extended to you—in this lifetime and in any others that may come our way."

Chapter 30

Hal glanced around to make sure no one was watching, then he carefully slid the steak knife onto his lap. Wrapped it up in the cloth napkin and slid it into his back pocket. He was pretty sure the waitress wouldn't notice that a knife was missing when she cleared the table, and if she did she probably wouldn't say anything anyway. After all, she was a prisoner, too.

He was just having soup and salad tonight. Didn't want a heavy dinner weighing him down or making him drowsy. Not tonight.

The soup was good—potato and leek. He slurped away while casting his eyes around the dining room.

Several tables over, Keith was having dinner with a young lady. She was around thirty, buxom and shapely. Hal remembered her—one of the girls from the bordello. Patsy? He'd been with her twice. Kind of a sweetie, not the typical whore.

Which she wasn't, of course. Hal remembered her telling him that before she came to Emerald City, she'd been a waitress. She and three other girls were snatched off a street in San Francisco late at night after they'd finished work. All three of them real lookers, perfect candidates for the underground bordello. Thrown into a van and drugged. When they woke up, they were already in their new quarters.

Hal liked her. She'd been a good fuck, and was a good conversationalist. But that was where it ended for him.

Patsy had seemed lonely, and he tried his best to make her feel better about her new lease on life. Tried to get her to just accept it and make the best of it that she could. And also urged her, just like he'd urged Keith, to get educated in something so she could eventually crawl out of the sleazy bordello.

He remembered that she'd been living in a kind of dream existence—not accepting that this was permanent. She seemed to think that one day soon the cavalry would come roaring in and save them.

Hal told her in no uncertain terms that the cavalry was already here. That her captors were the cavalry. She didn't seem to grasp that, or at least wouldn't allow herself to grasp that.

Not until Hal told her about his own role on 9/11.

She'd only arrived in Emerald City in 2010, so just like others who had been brought there in the years after the Twin Towers disaster, she was well familiar with that news event. The ones who had been there prior to 9/11 only knew about it by listening to the more recent arrivals—since there was no outside news allowed inside the underground dungeon.

So, Patsy had truly believed the official story that nineteen Muslim hijackers had taken over four jumbo jetliners with measly box cutters.

She truly believed, just like the rest of the world did, that two planes had smashed into the Twin Towers, that a third one had crashed into the Pentagon, and that a fourth had been taken over by passengers and nosedived into a field in Pennsylvania.

She believed all that crap until Hal burst her little bubble, telling her that he had been the pilot of United 175 and that it was sitting right at their fingertips, parked in the underground hanger of Emerald City. He remembered the look in her eyes, the look of absolute shock and disbelief.

Yes, she was one of the many who couldn't grasp that their government could have done such a horrific thing to its own people.

To reinforce his argument, Hal introduced her to several of the flight attendants and passengers from his flight. They told her the same story. At that point, Patsy became a believer. She stopped living in a panacea, thinking naively that the cavalry was coming.

While Hal was not in the habit of deliberately hurting people's feelings, he did believe in tough love. That the only way people could survive and fight for themselves was if they knew the truth, be that truth good or bad. Everyone he came in contact with in Emerald City needed help in some way—and he did his level best to help them all.

Not because he had any particular missionary zeal, but more because he cared about people being able to make the best of their situations. Despite the fact that he'd snuffed out more souls than he could remember, he did care about people. The good people. The innocent people.

He could be ruthless when he had to be, but he could also be caring when the situation demanded it. And he'd been through scarier times in his life than most innocents could ever dream of in their worst nightmares. So, he was better equipped than most.

Keith glanced over in Hal's direction and waved. Hal waved back, smiling inside. It was kinda cute seeing the two of them dining together. Only in Emerald City would a man have no qualms about being seen out in public with a hooker.

Everything was different down here. The morals weren't puritan, nor were they loose or fake either. People just understood that their lives were doomed and that sexual comfort was no longer a back-alley pastime like it was up above in the real world.

Life was just far too short now and far too hopeless for making judgements on others. The camaraderie was also more sincere because the desperation and isolation were real issues. Everyone just threw away the book here. There were no hopes, no dreams, and there wasn't a chance in hell they would ever get out. Efforts to improve themselves were made only out of the need to survive, not for any personal satisfaction. Ambition had been sucked out of every single one of them.

Except for Hal Winters. No one person, or one thing, could suck the ambition out of Hal. Mainly because he wasn't afraid of one single fucking thing, and never had been. Well, not entirely true—he was afraid for his family and their safety. Particularly Brock.

He finished his salad, and waved over at Keith one last time before leaving the restaurant. He climbed onto his bike and thought to himself that after tonight he wouldn't be riding this thing again. And he was going to miss it. Well, he would just have to get himself one once he was topside again. Maybe Brock would buy him a bike as a welcome out gift.

He thought to himself how nice it would be if Brock invited him to live at his beach house in Malibu. That would be a great way to wind down the remaining years of his life, living with the son he loved more than life itself.

They'd always had a bond—almost like the one twins reportedly had. They talked to each other in code, dreamt of each other, even communicated sometimes through their dreams. They'd even discovered that on many occasions they'd had the exact same dream on the exact same night.

As he cycled back to his room, Hal shook his head sadly, thinking that if their bond had been that strong despite him being absent a large part of the time during Brock's formative years, how strong could it have been if he'd been there—truly been there?

Once back in his room, he set the alarm for 11:00. Keith should be knocking on his door around that time, but Hal wanted to make sure he didn't sleep through the knock. Although he doubted that, because he was excited tonight.

He felt the juices of adrenaline surging through his body, just the way they used to whenever he was stalking a victim—waiting to slit a throat or blow out some brain matter. He took the steak knife out of his back pocket and laid it on the mattress. Then covered it with his leg as he stretched out for a badly needed nap.

*****

"What do you mean you're in love with her?"

Keith winced. "It's true, Hal. We've been seeing a lot of each other. I can't leave without her."

Hal took a threatening step toward him. "Are you sure you're not confusing love with lust? For Christ's sake, you've been fucking her in an underground city, along with dozens of other guys. I've even fucked her. Are you nuts?"

"I'm sorry, Hal, but I'm putting my foot down. She's coming with us."

Hal turned his attention to Patsy. She was standing just inside the closed door to Hal's room. They'd arrived right on cue at 11:00 and

Hal couldn't believe his eyes when Keith entered with her in tow.

"Are you in love with him?"

She looked scared. Her mouth was trembling and her arms were folded across her chest. She looked down at the floor. "Yes," she mumbled.

Hal lunged at her and shoved her up against the wall. He wrapped his right hand around her skinny throat and squeezed. Keith started to protest, but Hal extended his left arm out towards him in a threatening gesture, his index and third fingers poised to strike. Keith wisely shut his mouth as quickly as he'd opened it.

Hal glared into Patsy's eyes. "I'll ask you only once. Your eyes will tell me the truth. Have you told anyone else about this?"

Her pupils were dilated and sweat was glistening on her forehead. She shook her head. Hal squeezed harder. She shook her head again. He studied her eyes carefully, in a way that he'd been trained to do.

Then he released his grip. "I believe you. I can't leave you behind now that you know what we're going to do. My friend here has forced my hand."

He lowered his voice to a menacing whisper and rammed his finger into Patsy's chest. "But, believe this—if you do anything to jeopardize our escape, I'll kill you quicker than you can undo your bra."

She gave several quick and nervous nods of her head. Then she whispered, "Thanks, Hal. Keith and I just want to be together."

Hal sneered at her. "That's real sweet. I always wanted to be the Pope, too, but you can see how that dream turned out."

Keith put his hand on Hal's shoulder. "Thanks, Hal. I appreciate this."

Hal pushed his hand away. "You didn't give me much choice, buddy. So, don't patronize me. You had no right to tell her about this—no right at all. I took you into my confidence. This was my plan—you were the lucky one I chose to get out with me."

"I know, I know—it was wrong."

"Fuck off. I said don't patronize me. You're just lucky she's still breathing."

Hal reached down to the bed and picked up the steak knife, still wrapped in the napkin. He stuffed it into his back pocket.

Keith asked, "What's that?"

"Just a little something to slit your throats with."

Hal put his hand on the doorknob. Before opening the door, he whispered, "Now, follow me. We're going to walk down this tunnel and then turn into another tunnel. Walk slowly, with no real purpose. You two lovebirds can stroll hand-in-hand and whisper sweet nothings. Make it look like we're just out for a moonlight walk—without the moon, of course."

They made it to the second tunnel in less than ten minutes. Once they were under the grate for the ceiling air vent, Hal raised his hand, signalling the other two to stop. "Lean up against that wall and start kissing. Make it look real." He pointed down the tunnel. "I'm just gonna walk down there and drive that machine back."

Within a couple of minutes, Hal was back with the loader. He took the remote out of the console and pressed the button for the extension lift, holding it until it reached its full height. It came to a stop just a foot or two below the air vent. He pressed the button again and brought the lift back down.

Keith and Patsy looked up, astonishment on their faces. Keith let out a low whistle. "That's how we're getting out of here?"

"Yep. Keith, you're first. Get up on this lift. Once you reach the grate, push up on it quietly and slide it into the ventilation duct. Then crawl into the duct."

"But—"

Hal growled. "No buts. You can't back out now. Get up there."

Keith climbed onto the lift, and Hal pressed the button once again. When he reached the ceiling, Keith followed his orders. He slipped the grate into the duct and then hoisted himself inside.

Hal lowered the lift again. "Patsy, your turn."

He helped her up onto the lift and then raised it to the ceiling. Keith helped her climb inside the duct.

Now it was Hal's turn. He lowered the lift, crawled on and raised it back up to the ceiling. Keith and Patsy slid back deeper into the shaft to make room for Hal. Once inside, he looked down through the opening and pressed the remote, lowering the lift back down.

Then he shifted his thumb to a circle on the unit, similar to the directionals on a television remote. He pressed the Forward arrow and the little machine started to move down the tunnel. Hal steered it along the wall and back into the exact same spot it had started from.

Lastly, he lowered the grate back into place. There were no signs left behind as to what they had just done, or how they had done it.

Keith whispered. "It's pitch black in here."

Hal held up the remote. "Has a built-in flashlight." Hal pressed another button on the remote, illuminating the ductwork ahead of them. Then he reached into his pocket and pulled out a lighter. He flicked it and held it aloft. The flame leaned back towards him. "Okay, this way. Let's go. Crawl carefully and quietly."

Patsy spoke in a high-pitched whisper. "How will this lead us out?"

"It's an air ventilation system. It has to draw air in, so this ductwork will lead to one or more vertical shafts. We just have to find one of them."

Hal led the way through the narrow duct. There was only about a foot clearance around his body, making the space feel very claustrophobic. He pushed that thought out of his head. He'd crawled through many tunnels in his life, and this was just one more. But it was a more important tunnel than all the others he'd dragged himself through. This one led to freedom.

They crawled for about ten minutes until they came to an intersecting duct, connecting from his left. He held the lighter up again and the flame flickered away from the connecting duct. "We have to hang a left. Let's go."

Another ten minutes passed, but it seemed like an hour. Keith was right on Hal's heel, and pulling up the rear was Patsy. They were all breathing heavily now, not from lack of air, but from the exertion and stress of crawling along through such a tight space.

Then he saw it. Just up ahead, a vertical shaft connecting to the tunnel they were crawling in. Hal picked up his pace. Once underneath the shaft he held up the lighter. The flame flickered downward, almost extinguishing itself.

"This is it!"

He turned his head to face his comrades. "We're going up now. Won't be easy. Shove your back up against the wall of the shaft, and then pull your legs up into a tuck. Bring your feet up against the opposite wall to push your back upwards. Then keep doing it, step by step. You'll be walking upwards. I'll go first. Watch me. Okay?"

Hal had done this sort of thing many times before, so it was easy for him despite the fact that he was a lot older than the other two. He pushed himself upwards, foot by painstaking foot.

Once he'd gone about twenty feet up, he shone the remote. He could see that he was about halfway. There was a grate at the top, just like the one they'd come through back in the tunnel. He shone the flashlight down.

"Okay, Patsy, you come next. In case you slip. Keith will be able to catch you."

She eased herself into the shaft, and began mimicking what she'd seen Hal doing. He was surprised at how well she was coping. But she was also shorter than he and Keith, so it was much easier for her to tuck her body into a tight ball.

When she reached him, Keith followed.

Once they were all at the halfway point, Hal continued upwards and whispered instructions for them to match him move for move.

He was within five feet of the top now. The fresh air was heaven-sent, rushing down towards them in a refreshingly intoxicating caress. Hal looked up through the grate and saw stars. Freedom was only a few feet away.

Suddenly, Patsy gasped. Hal looked down. Both of her hands were grasping her lower leg and she was struggling with it. She looked up at Hal with tears in her eyes. "I'm stuck!"

He shone the remote down. Her foot was stuck through an open joint in the metal ductwork. She must have pushed too hard with her foot at that point, and the metal separated. Then her foot just slipped right through. It had gone through right past her ankle, and the metal was tearing into her skin. Blood was streaming along her lower leg.

Keith cursed and started pulling on the sheets of metal, trying to pry them apart. They wouldn't budge.

Patsy was sobbing now. "Help me. It hurts."

Keith looked up past Patsy, into Hal's eyes. "Hal?"

Hal raised his head and looked up longingly at the grate. Freedom was only seconds away.

Then he turned his attention back to Patsy. He stroked her head gently. "Shh—don't cry. I'll get your foot free."

Keith shifted his position in the shaft to inch a little bit closer to Patsy. "What are you going to do, Hal?"

"Quiet, please. A few moments of silence is all I need."

Then he allowed himself to slip into a zone—a zone very few people understood. He leaned his body at an odd angle down towards Patsy, and began moving his hands in a tight circle.

He closed his eyes and began to meditate. It only took about a minute to hypnotize himself. Then he opened his eyes again and, instead of the sheet metal, all his brain saw now were imagined wooden boards. His eyes were able to look through those boards, past them to a point on the other side. Then he tightened the muscles in his abdomen and summoned that incredible strength up through his body and down into his arms. He imagined that energy, could see it, feel it.

He brought his left hand in towards his stomach while his right hand shot out like a lightning bolt into and through the metal ductwork at a point just above Patsy's ankle. Then he calmly peeled the shattered metal back and away from Patsy's foot just as easily as if it were the plastic lid on a jar of mustard.

Her foot was free. She looked up at him, eyes registering the shock that words couldn't possibly express.

All Keith could do was exclaim, "Jesus!"

Hal reached into his back pocket and took out the knife. He unwrapped the cloth napkin and then tied it tightly around Patsy's ankle.

"Have you ever had a tetanus shot?"

Patsy shook her head. "No."

"When you're on the outside, that's one of the first things you're gonna have to do."

She nodded.

"Okay, out we go."

Hal pushed himself up until he was at the grate, and then shoved up on it. It wouldn't budge!

He shone the remote up over the grate, and around to each outside corner. Sure enough, the corners were fastened down with nuts.

Damn!

He reached his hand up and through the opening at one of the corners. His big hand could only come within an inch of the nut.

He glanced down at Patsy. "We need you, dear. You have the smallest hands. You'll have to squeeze through this grate and unscrew these nuts." Hal looked past her at Keith. "Push her up alongside me, and support her feet while she works."

No one said a word. Patsy manoeuvered her body into position between Hal's legs, and Keith pushed on her feet. She made a slight squealing sound from the pressure Keith was exerting on her injured foot, but she didn't miss a beat. Slid her tiny hand up through one of the corner openings and began to twist on the nut.

It took a few seconds, but then it began to budge. "It's turning!"

It was a slow process, but her little hand was doing its important work. One by one, each nut came off.

"Now, push up on the grate, Patsy, and slide it off to the side. Quietly."

She did, and Hal placed his hands on her bum, giving it a firm shove. She rolled off onto the grass. Hal followed, and then Keith pulled himself out.

They all just sat in the grass for a few minutes, catching their breaths. Keith and Patsy gazed up at the sky in wonder—neither of them had seen it in several years. It was as if they were blind people who had just regained their sight.

Hal, of course, got to see the outside world every week or so, with the flights he had to make. But, for him, the feeling of freedom itself was what he was experiencing right now, and he felt drunk from the rush. His heart was pumping hard, and he could sense the hint of a smile cross his face.

This is it. We're out!

But, reality was now setting in. They weren't free yet.

He leaned forward on his elbows and whispered to his friends. "We're not home free yet." He pointed. "Look over there. Barbed wire fencing. We're gonna have to bend the tops upwards and then down towards the opposite side of the fence. Be prepared to bleed. But, we have no choice. That's the way out."

They struggled to their feet, legs cramped from being in the shaft for so long.

Suddenly they weren't alone!

"Stop where you are! Hands in the air!"

They whirled around. Standing just ten feet away was a soldier with a rifle trained at them, the barrel moving in a slow arc from one to the other.

Keith and Patsy slowly raised their hands. Hal raised his left hand, but snuck his right hand into his back pocket, grasping the steak knife by its blade.

"Both hands, buddy!"

Hal nodded. "Sure. No problem here."

He brought his right hand out of his pocket and suddenly thrust it outwards, in a move that was so fast it would have been just a blur to the soldier. Far too fast for him to react.

The knife blade glistened in the moonlight as it streaked through the air. With uncanny accuracy, it found its mark, embedding itself deep into the soldier's throat. He gasped and dropped his rifle, thrusting both hands up to his neck before collapsing to the ground.

Hal rushed over to the soldier. He was still alive. Gurgling noises were seeping from his throat. His hands had circled the knife, clearly reluctant to withdraw it, so they were instead locked in a desperate and futile struggle to just stop the bleeding.

Hal intervened and swiftly yanked the knife out of his throat and then promptly rammed it back down again, this time into the soldier's heart. A massive sigh passed across the sentry's dying lips.

Keith and Patsy just stood there in shock, hands to their mouths.

Hal picked up the rifle and started running. "C'mon! No time to mourn!"

They ran to the barbed wire fence and without hesitation began to climb. Hal threw the rifle over to the ground on the other side.

"Push up and then down on the barbed wire. Once we have a few strands out of the way, we can ease ourselves over."

But, it was not to be. This time there were two.

"Get down from that fence, or we'll shoot you where you stand!"

*****

Brock Winters was sleeping the way he usually did. Not too deeply, probably not even close to being in his REM stage.

Sometimes he wondered if he ever really reached that deepest point of sleep. He never felt refreshed when he awakened; it was almost like he hadn't been asleep at all.

The soothing sound of the waves lapping against the shorefront of his Malibu beach house was always at the forefront of whatever sleep he did get. It seemed as if he could always hear those waves, and he increased the odds of hearing them by leaving the sliding door of his bedroom open every night.

He knew he was asleep, though. Because he could hear his own snoring. That didn't happen with too many people, but it sure did with him.

But out of the darkness something else was going on in his brain while he slept tonight. It wasn't a dream. It wasn't a nightmare. It wasn't even a movie script. It was—an awareness.

Suddenly, Brock's eyes popped open and he lurched up in bed as if being pulled by some unseen force.

Only one thought was at the forefront of his consciousness.

Dad!

Chapter 31

Brock's long blonde locks were plastered across his eyes. He swept the wet stringy hair up along the top of his head with a massive mitt of a hand. And his face was soaked with sweat too. He lifted up one corner of the silk sheet adorning his round orgy bed and soaked up the moisture.

There was a stirring beside him, accompanied by a slurred moan.

"Co...ver me...up."

He looked down at the pillow next to him, at the brunette head partially covered by outstretched arms. He tried desperately to remember her name. Brock lifted the corner of the sheet higher and took a look underneath.

Sure enough, she was naked—no surprise there—and she had the tattoo of a serpent snaking along the length of her shapely back.

Hard to believe I don't remember that!

He threw the sheet back down and slid it up higher to cover her bare arms.

"Thank...you."

"You're welcome. What's your name again?"

"I...don't...remember." Then she sighed, and almost immediately began snoring—actually it was more like snorting.

Brock slid out of bed and headed for the bathroom. On his way, he noticed a small strip of tinfoil on his dresser covered with a leftover dusting of white powder. Now he remembered—and he wished he hadn't.

It was always the same old, same old, night after night. Some trashy little bimbo with a name that really didn't matter—not even to her. A night of drinking and snorting, followed by totally forgettable sex.

What was the point of sex if you couldn't remember it? Or worse, if you didn't want to remember it?

In a few hours, whatever the fuck her name was would wake up, want to snort again—maybe even drink some hard stuff. Then be all over him trying to seduce him into bed again. And all he'd want to do now that he was awake and sober, was get her out of the house so he could forget that she'd even been there.

Then a night or two later it would begin again. Another meaningless encounter with another brain-dead bimbo.

Brock sighed, pulled up the toilet seat, and took a pee.

He stared down into the toilet bowl.

Yep, there it was again. Traces of blood. I'll have to get that checked.

He thought about putting on some clothes, then decided against it. He walked naked out into the living room.

Oops—another one!

This one was blonde and lying on the floor, her head resting on one of the pillows from the couch. He walked around the furniture to get a better look at her face. When he saw it he winced.

Sure hope I didn't fuck that...

Brock quietly slid open the patio door and walked out onto his deck. The sky was still pitch black except for the moon and the stars. He didn't know what time it was, but the moon was high in the sky. He closed his eyes and thrust his face forward into the nice warm breeze. Nothing like the breezes coming in off the ocean—very little compared to this. The feeling of that soothing salt air on his face, and the sound of the waves rippling onto the sand twelve feet beneath his feet.

He looked to his left—the lights were still on in Cameron Diaz' house. Must be a party. He looked to his right—Robert De Niro's house was dark except for a dim light in the upstairs bedroom. He knew De Niro was an avid reader and also suffered from insomnia. He guessed what he must be doing. And he was pretty sure there weren't any bubble-headed bimbos sleeping at his place. De Niro didn't stoop that low.

So, why do I? Don't I deserve better, too?

His long blonde hair was blowing around and annoying him. Brock reached down to a little glass table and picked up his signature red bandana. Slipped it over his head and across his forehead.

There, that's better.

Then he stretched out on the chaise lounge and drank in the night air.

And he thought about his dad.

Something had awakened him tonight—it wasn't a dream, and it certainly wasn't the tramp sleeping next to him. It was just a feeling.

Something had caused him to sweat profusely—either what he'd been thinking about, or the after-effects of the cocaine. And, of course, cocaine always made his brain race even when he was asleep. It could have just been that. Or the cocaine might have made him more aware, more sensitive.

But he woke up thinking his dad was in trouble, and it was strange also that over the last few nights Brock had felt tension. He'd sensed that something was up, something was going on pertaining to his dad. He couldn't discern what it was, but he sensed that Hal had been concentrating hard on something, planning something. And then tonight, the feeling that something had gone wrong—terribly wrong.

The last time he'd talked to his father was a month ago, told him in code that the letters were gone once again. And God only knew where this time. And a month before that he'd told Hal that the tape recording had been stolen from the safe in his office. The same people who had killed Wentworth to get the letters probably had the tape now, too.

Brock wasn't sure where his dad was now, but he had an idea. He knew that he'd been moved from the Georgia prison after his death had been faked. But, since then, Hal had been very careful, even in code. Told him that he was being well looked after and the conditions in the new place were far better than Georgia. But the only hint he'd given to Brock—at least Brock thought it was a hint—was in telling him to buy a John Denver CD for his mother. That she had always loved that singer and that her favourite was *Annie's Song*.

Well, Brock did just that, and was told by his mom in no uncertain terms that she hated John Denver's music and had never even heard the tune *Annie's Song* before. Brock thought at first that she'd just been saying that due to the resentment she still felt towards Hal, even after all these years. Which, in Brock's mind, told him that she still loved him.

But, after that surprise, Brock put two and two together. The tape recording from September 11, 2001, of the cockpit conversations and the chatter from the military air traffic control, made it clear that the plane Hal was piloting ended up in Denver. And that they'd pulled along runway 13A until they saw the ground open up. Leading to a tunnel to—somewhere.

That's when the recording ended, and that's when his dad had made a run for it. Only to be caught later in Minneapolis, but not before he'd already mailed the tape recording to Brock.

Brock rubbed his tired eyes and went back into the living room. Took a giant step over the ugly slut on the floor, and walked across the massive room to a side table. Opened the drawer and pulled out a business card.

Then Brock picked up his cell phone. He quickly changed his mind and grabbed the cordless handset to the landline instead. He glanced at his watch—wasn't sure what time it was in Toronto right now, but it was probably still nighttime just like in L.A. But Brock didn't care—this was important.

He dialed the number on the card. After three rings, a groggy voiced answered.

"Hello?"

"Is this Bradley Crawford?"

"Yes, who's this?"

"Brock Winters."

There were a few moments of silence at the other end, then a suddenly more wide-awake voice. "Brock? What's up?"

"When you visited me in Malibu, you suspected that my dad was still alive."

"Yes, I did."

"Well, you're right. He is. We've talked many times since his "death" in 2011."

"So, his death was faked. Where is he?"

"I'm not supposed to know, but I suspect somewhere in Denver."

"That's interesting. For various reasons that I won't go into right now, I think you're right about the Denver thing."

"I had a tape recording, Brad. It's been stolen. Also, there were letters that my dad sent to a guy in England that the CIA ended up getting their hands on. I got them away from the CIA, and had them sent to someone in Canada, but then that guy was killed and the letters went missing again."

Brock took a deep breath, and then exhaled slowly. "I feel like I've failed my father miserably. And I fear that he's in trouble. Just a feeling I have, but my feelings are usually pretty accurate. That's why I'm calling you. I'm prepared to tell you everything I can recall from the tape recording that might help you with your story. And let the chips fall where they may."

"Who was the recording of?"

"My dad, his co-pilot, and verbal instructions from the tower."

"What flight was that?"

"United 175. My dad was the captain that day. That plane and flights 11 and 77 were diverted to Denver on 9/11. It was all on the recording. How my dad reacted, what the tower was saying, and what his co-pilot was saying. Those three planes plus the one that crashed in Pennsylvania, were just test planes in a military hijacking exercise. They were never hijacked—that was all bullshit. The military substituted them with fake blips on the radar screens."

"Brock, should I fly down there or do you want to come here?"

"I'll fly to Toronto. Brad, I don't know what it was that hit those fucking towers and the Pentagon, but it sure wasn't those three planes. They all went to Denver. And the tape recording was what was keeping my father alive. If the wrong people have that recording, his days are numbered. He's lost his leverage."

Chapter 32

It was a wet afternoon at 207 Lundy Lane, Baltimore, Maryland. The rain was pouring down in sheets, misery brought upon the city by a fast-moving system from the Atlantic.

Ziv was parked just down the street from the house, in a borrowed minivan that was of questionable origin. Sitting in the passenger seat beside him was an old colleague from Mossad, retired now just like Ziv. He lived in Baltimore, so this was an easy gig for him.

The van had been provided by his friend, and Ziv was confident that this van along with probably many others similar to it, went through many different iterations in the course of a normal week.

They'd been parked on the street for a few hours already, watching the house. No sign of Leslie Fields yet, but this, unfortunately, was his only lead. Since she disappeared without a trace from Toronto, Ziv figured this would be the logical place for her to go. It was the home of her sister and she adored her twin nieces.

He was convinced beyond a doubt that Leslie had set him up for the theft of the letters from his apartment. And, of course, he was also convinced that she'd set him up the day she met him at the restaurant, too. Both incidents were far too coincidental, and Ziv didn't believe in coincidences.

She was as sly as a fox, and she was either working for the CIA or Britain's MI6.

There was also another possibility that occurred to him—she could be a lone wolf looking to score from the highest bidder. It wouldn't be the first time a contract agent had gone rogue for personal gain. Judging by the tug of war over these letters that seemed to have transpired between the CIA and MI6, anything was possible. Both agencies seemed to want the incriminating letters at any cost.

He was jarred out of his thinking by the ring of his mobile.

"Hello?"

"Ziv, it's Brad. Where are you?"

"I'm in rainy Baltimore, bored to death, sitting in a car down the street from Leslie's sister's house."

"No sign of her yet?"

"Nothing. This is the third day in a row now. I'll give it one more, then just give up and fly back to Toronto."

"Got some news for you. Brock Winters called me—he's flying here the day after tomorrow. There's a tape recording, Ziv. Of Hal Winters, his co-pilot, and their communications with the ground. In the cockpit of Flight 175 on 9/11."

"Well, isn't that interesting—"

"Yeah, but unfortunately it was stolen from him—he has no idea who has it. He's also admitted to me that his dad is indeed alive, but doesn't know where he is now. He suspects somewhere in Denver due to clues his dad mentioned over the phone.

"And, of course, from the tape recording as well—the conversation between the two pilots confirms that their plane indeed landed in Denver."

Ziv whistled. "Christ, this story gets better even *without* the letters!"

"Brock's flying to Toronto to offer whatever help he can in our investigation. He's afraid for his dad now. Has a bad feeling that he can't explain. And now that both the tape recording and letters are missing, he's afraid Hal has lost his leverage. Time's running out for him."

"Okay, so now I'm looking for a cassette tape as well as a pile of letters. Two needles in a haystack instead of just one."

Ziv heard Brad chuckle at the other end. "Daunting, isn't it? Okay, we'll talk when you get back. Good luck."

"Thanks. I'll need it."

The man sitting beside Ziv in the minivan lit a cigarette and popped the window open. "So, who was that?"

"My partner back in Canada. Bringing me up to date on some

stuff."

"Sounds like the two of you have hooked into quite the story. But I'm glad my role is limited. Don't tell me any more than you have to."

Ziv smiled at his old friend. "Don't worry, Mort—all I need you for is this surveillance stuff. And any help I might need if I see her."

"Good. I don't hurt women though, Ziv—just so you know."

"No one's gonna get hurt, don't worry."

Suddenly, Mort pointed through the windshield. "Hey, a sign of life. Look!"

Ziv tried to focus, then turned on the ignition and hit the windshield wiper stick. The view became clear—and he saw her. Walking out the front door of the modest bungalow, with a green garbage bag in her hand. Down the steps toward the garbage can at the curb.

Leslie Fields.

Ziv's heart skipped a beat as he watched his ex-lover. The dirty blonde hair, perfect figure, beautiful face, walking with the elegance and poise of someone who could have easily been a model in her younger years.

He shifted the van into drive and began edging forward, trying to time his arrival at the curb simultaneous with her arrival.

"Mort, grab her when I stop. Throw her into the back, and cover her with that old blanket that's back there. Hold her down until I find a safe place to park this thing."

Mort nodded. "No problem." He glanced over his shoulders in both directions. "Coast is clear. Let's be quick."

Ziv brought the van up to the curb just as Leslie was lifting the lid off the garbage can. She looked up, a puzzled look in her pretty eyes. Mort yanked open the door and lunged at her. She screamed and started struggling, kicking her feet out and swinging her arms.

Mort got her in a bear hug with one massive arm, trapping her arms at her side. With his free hand, he pulled open the sliding door of the van and threw her inside. Then he climbed in after her and slid the door shut behind him.

The van was on the move again—Ziv sped down to the end of the block and turned left. He'd seen an empty parking lot when he was cruising around the other day—one of many that were now desolate due to the ongoing demise of shopping malls. A perfect place for an interrogation.

Ziv parked at the far end of the lot, a spot as quiet and isolated as he could hope for. He stepped out of the van and walked around to the other side, slid open the door and crawled onto the floor in the rear.

Mort was holding her down with the blanket over her face. He had his hands full—she was still struggling and making muffled sounds of distress. Ziv knew she hadn't seen him yet, so she'd be shocked to her core as soon as he yanked the blanket off her face.

He motioned Mort to move out of the way, and then he sat on Leslie's torso. Mort held her feet down.

Ziv peeled back the blanket.

She stared up at him with eyes that defied description. They were beyond terrified.

Drool covered her mouth and chin. Her lips moved and at first there were no words. But then they came. Slow and shaky. "Please, please don't hurt me. I have money. You can have it."

She doesn't recognize me!

"Leslie?"

She stammered. "Oh God—is that who you want?"

Ziv nodded, and slid off her stomach. He could see the slight differences now, in her expressions as well as in her voice. He'd made a grave mistake.

"We're twins."

Ziv rubbed his forehead, and then leaned over and helped her into a sitting position.

"I'm so sorry. What's your name?"

She was regaining her composure; a look of calm was coming over her face. "Monica. Please don't hurt me because of something she's done."

Ziv shook his head. "We wouldn't have hurt you. And we wouldn't have hurt Leslie either. I just want something back that she stole from me."

Suddenly, Monica started to cry. "Please take me home. My little girls are there all alone."

Ziv turned to Mort. "You drive. I'll chat with Monica."

He reached into a holder on the back of the front seat and took out a bottle of water.

"Here, take a sip."

She grabbed it eagerly and drained almost half the bottle. Then she looked into his eyes. "Thank you, sir. Thank you for taking me home. I don't know what she took from you, but I'm sick of this."

"Sick of what?"

Monica took another sip. "She's always putting me into difficult situations. I feel like I'm always in danger just by being her sister. Even worse that I'm her twin."

"You are pretty identical."

She nodded. "Last week, a man from the Treasury department came by my office, and asked me if I was Leslie. After I finally convinced him I wasn't, he wanted to know where Leslie was. I told him she's been gone for a while and that I didn't know where. I don't think he believed me. I saw cars parked on our street for several days afterwards, and then this week I noticed your van."

"I'm not with Treasury."

"Okay, well about five nights ago my house was broken into. I was visiting my ex-husband with the girls. Came back and the house was a mess. Reported it to the police, but they've done nothing. No fingerprints that they could find."

Ziv reached out and gently squeezed her hand. "I'm so sorry that I've added to your fear. Please don't worry—you won't see me again."

"I believe you. You seem sincere, despite the fact that you just kidnapped me!" She laughed. She had a more infectious laugh than Leslie did, and Ziv couldn't help but laugh along with her.

"I gather you two don't get along too well?"

"I let her stay here when she's in the area. And she's my sister, so I love her for that reason and that reason alone. But she scares me. I know that she's an engineer with NASA, but something tells me she's involved in things that are illegal, too. It scares me.

"We had a big shouting match before she left this time, and I told her that I don't want her visiting us anymore. I'm more scared for the girls than for me. And that shouting match was even before the Treasury guy and the break-in happened. And now here you are, throwing me into a van. She's a hazard. I want her out of my life for good."

"I understand."

She looked straight into Ziv's eyes and stared at them for a few moments without blinking. "Can you tell me what it is she does? What her secrets are?"

Ziv shook his head. "I don't know, Monica. All I know is that she stole something very valuable from me. I tracked her down here. Just wanted to get it back."

"Well, you can have it back. What is it?"

"I can't really say. I'll know it when I see it."

"So, you both have secrets."

"Yes, but the difference between us is that she steals her secrets from the people who trust her."

Monica frowned. "That doesn't surprise me in the least. Twins are supposed to be close, but we've never been. She's lied her way through life, even back when we were kids. I love her, but I also hate her. Hate that she exposes me and my girls to whatever it is she has her fingers in."

Mort pulled into Monica's driveway. "Okay, ma'am, you're home safe and sound."

Ziv slid the door open and gestured to Monica. "You're free to go, Monica. Again, I'm so sorry to have scared you."

She slid her bum along the floor of the van until she was sitting at the edge of the door. Then she turned back to face Ziv.

"I feel that I can trust you, despite what just happened. And I want this to end—if there's something in the house that is yours, I want you to take it. And maybe you can let the others who are looking for it know that you have it? So they'll leave me alone?"

Monica slid down off the edge of the door and headed towards her front walkway. Ziv followed her.

"I appreciate that. I'll take a quick look and be on my way."

He turned to Mort. "Keep the engine running. I won't be long."

Monica opened the front door and Ziv followed her inside. A cute little house, decorated in very feminine colors. It was easy to tell that this was a girls only house.

She turned to him and whispered. "What's your name?"

"Ziv."

"What?"

"Ziv. A weird name, I know. Israeli."

She smirked. "Well, maybe that explains a few things…"

Two little girls came running out of the kitchen. "Mommy, where did you go? We were worried. You took out the garbage and then you were gone!"·

Monica knelt down and swept the girls up in her arms. "I'm sorry. I went for a little drive with this old friend of mine. Meet Ziv. And Ziv, this is Brenda, and this one on the right here is Heidi."

Ziv squatted and turned on the charm. "You're both adorable— and boy, I don't think I could ever tell you apart. The men will be fighting over you two someday when you're a lot older, but I don't think they'll know who it is they're fighting over."

Both girls giggled. Then Heidi shouted, "Just like our mommy and Aunt Leslie when they were growing up. Mommy's told us all the stories."

"Yeah, I'll bet they have a lot of stories to tell you girls."

"How do you know my mommy, Mr. Ziv?" Heidi giggled again. "That's a funny name."

"I met your mommy a long time ago. I know your Aunt Leslie, too—we worked together."

Brenda jumped in. "Oh, are you a rocket scientist, too?"

Ziv figured he might just as well play along. "Kind of. Was training to be an astronaut for a time, too."

"Wow!"

Monica motioned to Ziv to follow her down the hall. "Girls, Mr. Ziv just wants to look for something that Aunt Leslie has—something she forgot to give back to him."

Heidi giggled. "Aunt Leslie does that to me all the time, too. Takes things like my candy and stuff, and never gives it back."

Brenda ran ahead of them, into a room that looked like it functioned as an office. "Maybe Mr. Ziv can help us look through Aunt Leslie's telescope later? Since he was an astronaut, he probably knows everything!"

Monica led Ziv into a back bedroom. "Here, everything's all back in its place now after the break-in. This is Leslie's room. I have no idea if they took anything or not, but go through all the drawers and closets and see if what you want is here."

Ziv spent the next ten minutes looking into every drawer, closet, nook and cranny.

Even lifted the mattress up to see if the letters might have been spread out between that and the box spring. Nothing.

He turned to Monica, who'd been standing watch in the doorway.

"Thanks so much, Monica. Either she never had it here to begin with, or the thieves took it. I'll be on my way."

"Okay—well, I hope it's not here any longer. And when she finally drifts back here again from wherever she is, I'm kicking her out for good. I'm done with being scared. I don't know what she's into, but it terrifies me that she's exposed us to it."

Ziv nodded and started walking down the hallway.

Suddenly, he heard the pitter-patter of little feet behind him. Brenda slipped her little hand in his.

"Mr. Ziv, before you go, could you please teach us how to use Aunt Leslie's telescope? Pretty please?"

He looked at Monica and she nodded her approval.

"Okay, be glad to, Heidi."

"No, I'm Brenda!"

He rubbed the top of her blonde head. "Sorry, Brenda."

She pulled him by the hand to the back office. He saw the telescope set up on a tripod in front of the window. It was a large diameter lens, with an offset eyepiece.

Brenda was rubbing her hands together with excitement. "Oh, boy!"

Heidi came over and stood beside Ziv. "We've tried to use it before ourselves, but it doesn't seem to work. It's all dark when we look through. Aunt Leslie kept promising to show us, but she never did."

Ziv reached up and removed the rubber cap from the lens. "Well, Heidi, no wonder you can't see anything. You have to take this off first."

"We did that. Still can't see nothing."

Monica corrected her right away. "Heidi, the proper way to say that is still can't see *anything*."

Heidi pouted. "Okay, Mommy."

Ziv adjusted the eyepiece and took a peek through. *That's strange— it's still dark.*

He rubbed his eyes and tried again. Nothing.

He walked around to the front of the telescope and unscrewed the outer lens, revealing a two-inch deep cavity behind it. He looked inside.

There was something blocking the inner lens.

Ziv reached his hand inside and pulled off two strands of tape that were holding the object against the inner lens. Then he pulled it out.

A mini-cassette.

Chapter 33

Sean parked the Lincoln on a side street, just off Avenue Road. He got out and began to walk—it wasn't far. He'd been to this place before.

A diamond importer as far as the general public was concerned—a place where you could buy one hell of a nice engagement ring at a wholesale price. But, in reality, it was a front for a CIA forged documents office. Whatever an agent needed could be obtained at this little shop.

It was only about a ten-minute walk from where Sean had parked, but that was plenty of time for Sean's quick brain to reflect back on what had just transpired. He had been a finger-twitch away from blowing his brains out. Yet, he was stopped—saved, redeemed—whatever the fuck it was. Regardless, he'd stopped himself—or something spiritual had intervened. Sean had never considered himself a religious man. In fact, he didn't know if he really believed in anything. But that helpless Muslim couple being beaten senseless was a life saver for him. Was it a coincidence? Or something far more mysterious? Something that was meant to happen, at that place, at that point in time? Fate?

What were the odds of that happening in that very parking lot, at the very moment when Sean was just about ready to pull the trigger? And for it to happen to him—someone who was so conflicted about the things he'd been involved in. The abandonment of the love of his life two decades ago. The eventual rescue of her from a fate worse than death. And the demonization of Muslims that he'd participated in through lies, deceptions, false flags, and other nefarious means.

There were still things he was meant to do. He knew that without a doubt now. Something he couldn't explain had intervened to save him from himself, and he couldn't deny it. It wasn't a coincidence at all. And his conscience had come to life, had finally overcome all of the patriotic brainwashing. His brain had cut through the bullshit and reconciled that things were just wrong, very wrong indeed. And he'd played a role in all that was wrong.

But, he could now play a role in all that should be made right.

Maybe his soul was already doomed, but Sean didn't care about that since he didn't believe in the afterlife anyway. He only believed in the here and now, and at this point in time the here and now stunk to high heaven.

He crossed the street and walked half a block north on Avenue Road, then opened the front door to Schmidt's Precious Stones. There was no Mr. or Mrs. Schmidt, and never had been, but it sounded authentic at least.

Sean walked to the front counter. There were no jewels on display in the shop—only several viewing and buying tables, each equipped with hold-up alarm buttons underneath. Several CCTV cameras were mounted in the ceiling and Sean knew that the entire shop was alarmed—through the walls, floors, and even the roof.

An attractive young lady walked towards him from the back of the shop.

"Yes, sir, can I help you?"

Sean smiled and spoke the code sentence. "I'm to take delivery of a large shipment of diamonds from South Africa."

She nodded and motioned for Sean to follow her—led him through a door which opened into a hallway. They walked past several other doors until they came to a dead end. She reached up and pulled open the casing to an electrical box. Inside were a dozen circuit breakers—she closed and opened three specific breakers in rapid succession.

Suddenly, the wall creaked and opened inward. Sean nodded his thanks to the girl and walked in, shutting the wall behind him.

It was a massive room and about as high tech as could be imagined. Half a dozen technicians were pounding away at their keyboards, while two complete walls looked as if they were made of glass with side-by-side mounted large screen monitors. Each monitor had a different live scene being displayed, probably from every corner of the Earth. Sean paid no attention to any of the staff as he walked through, and neither did any of them pay attention to him. These were the CIA geeks—the analysts, the watchers, the autistic savants. Dealing with people was not their forte—but they were geniuses at dealing with both significant and insignificant details.

He knocked on the door of a private office and entered without waiting for an invitation. A skinny bespectacled man jumped up from behind his desk and held out his hand as Sean approached.

Sean nodded politely, and shook his hand. "Hello, Henry."

"Good to see you again, Sean. Been a while."

"Yes, it has. Do you have what I need?"

Without fanfare or time wasted on pleasantries, Henry reached into his top desk drawer and withdrew a document.

"Here you are." Henry looked down at the sheet. "An official search warrant for the apartment of Mr. Simon Worthington, Suite 521, Four Bloor Square, Toronto, Ontario."

Sean took the warrant out of his hand and studied it. "Looks good, Henry. I see it's signed by a Judge Charles Dillman. You checked, I assume? He is indeed a sitting judge?"

"Of course, Sean. This document is beyond reproach." Henry chuckled a rare chuckle. "And the signature is probably more authentic than even Judge Dillman himself could sign."

Sean smiled. "Alright then, I'll take your word for it. Give me a large brown envelope, Henry."

Henry handed him the envelope, which even had the official stamp of the Ontario Provincial Courts in the upper left corner.

"I'm impressed, as usual, Henry. I'll be on my way."

Sean turned and walked toward the blank wall that he'd come through just moments earlier. Henry called after him.

"Put in a good word for us down in Langley, please? Sometimes we feel kind of forgotten way up here."

Before pushing the red button, which released the lock on the fake wall, Sean turned and smiled. "We couldn't do what we do without guys like you, Henry. I will indeed sing your praises."

Henry's face beamed with pride, and he bowed slightly. As Sean gripped the handle that pulled the wall open towards him, he noticed that the rest of the geek squad still had their heads down, staring at their terminals or typing on their keyboards. It was as if they hadn't even noticed he'd been there—and in all likelihood they probably hadn't.

*****

Bloor Square was a prestigious condominium complex located near the corner of Yonge and Bloor streets. One of the most vibrant districts of the dynamic city of Toronto, close to high-end shopping, office towers, entertainment, and of course the iconic subway system. It was probably the most ideal of all downtown spots, if you absolutely had to live in the inner city itself.

The British citizen, who went by the name of Simon Worthington, had chosen well. Sean suspected Worthington was MI6, though his analysts had so far been unable to find a trace of him in British records. But it was coincidental that he was the first person to call Leslie Fields when she left the hospital.

It fit nicely. Leslie had clearly set up Ziv Dayan, and either she or Worthington had possession of the letters—and the tape recording from Hal Winters' cockpit as well. A recording that had been made fourteen years ago and now had probably been converted by Leslie to a more modern format. But conversions didn't hold weight. Originals were what mattered. Same as the letters—copies could never be leveraged by anyone. But the originals, now those were a different story entirely.

He had to get the originals back—of the letters and of the cassette recording.

Leslie was a sneaky little bitch—always had been, always would be. That was one of the reasons Sean had hired her in the first place. Brilliant, seductive, and as deceptive as any person could be. She was good at what she did.

Sean had put her under contract with the CIA ten years ago. Her education in the aerospace field had put her into regular contact with the Russians, the Chinese, and, of course, the British. Which was probably how she met Mr. Simon Worthington. She was no doubt fucking his brains out and getting ready to deceive him just like she'd deceived Ziv Dayan. Worthington most likely thought he was an equal partner with Leslie—foolish boy.

The two of them had obviously concocted final farewells to their structured little lives—decided to become double agents. Probably planned to escape to some sandy little atoll somewhere and live the rest of their lives in blissful peace, far from the long arms of their respective countries.

By extorting fifty million from the Brits, or preferably a hundred million from the Yanks. Hell, with that kind of money they could buy their own atoll.

No doubt, one of those countries would pay. The Brits definitely wanted the letters and the recording to blackmail the U.S. government into leaving them the fuck alone. And the Americans wanted those items back just to keep the terrible secrets of 9/11 and the Denver Airport from exploding onto the public consciousness. If those secrets became public, it would be a game-changer. Not only in how it would horrify the world as to what America had done, but it would also shock the planet into seeing what an absolute lie the last twenty years had been.

The enemies of the U.S. were just creations, cartoon figures, designed brilliantly to justify the confiscation of oil resources and the continuance of a war without end.

There would always be an Al Qaeda, an ISIS, an Al Nusra, or a Boko Haram. And when those name brands became boring or tedious, new brands would mysteriously rise up, created out of thin air.

Because it was just so fucking easy to do, and the brain-dead public was just too busy taking selfies to even notice.

Millions of innocent lives had been lost because of those lies. And untold hate had been fabricated against almost two billion people. It had reached the tipping point now—the genie was out of the bottle and it would be very hard to get it back in. Unless the real facts became known, once and for all. The hate fervor was so out of control now that the world was on the verge of a religious war. The CIA had surely never wanted or expected it to go this far, but it had. And it seemed as if no one knew what to do about it, how to pull back from it.

But Sean knew what to do about it.

He walked into the front foyer of the Bloor Square complex and rapped on the glass to get the attention of the security guard seated at a desk in the lobby. He put down his newspaper, an irritated look on his face. The little rent-a-cop shook his head, basically telling Sean to go fuck himself.

Sean pulled the fake police badge off his belt and held it up to the glass; rapping on it again—harder this time.

This time, the guard jumped to his feet without hesitation. He ran over to the door, unlocked it and opened it wide.

"I'm so sorry. I didn't know you were the police. Come in, come in. How can I help you? We law enforcement officers have to stick together."

Sean suppressed a chuckle and handed the little man his ID folder. "I'm Detective Chad Roworth of the Toronto Police."

The guard looked over the ID and handed it back to him. Sean clipped the badge back onto his belt and then handed him the brown envelope. "This is a warrant for a search of premises. I need to search the apartment right now."

The nervous Pinkerton guard glanced over the warrant and handed it back to Sean. "Okay, I support this. Can you tell me what it's about?"

"Only what the warrant states—suspected stolen property."

"Right. Would you like me to come up with you as backup?"

Sean couldn't help but smirk. The little guy was trying so hard to be relevant; and probably hadn't seen any action in his entire life. This was his big chance.

"No, your best help to me would be to stay down here. Do you know if Mr. Worthington is in the apartment right now?"

"He's not. Everyone in the building has to sign in and out with me. He left this morning quite early, and hasn't come back yet."

"Good. I'll need a master key."

The guard hurried back to his desk and Sean followed. He pulled a key out of the top drawer. "Here you go."

"Great. Now, if Mr. Worthington comes back, I want you to sign him in as normal, and then ring the apartment phone—two rings and then hang up. Got that?"

"Yes. Roger that."

Sean felt the same smirk returning. "Be cool if he comes back. Do not say a word about any of this. He could be dangerous, so this is very important for your safety and mine. And if you give any kind of warning to him or tell anyone else about my visit, I will arrest you for obstruction of justice."

The man's hands were shaking now. His voice quivered. "Oh d-don't worry about m-me."

"Alright then."

Sean walked over to the bank of elevators, confident that the hapless little Pinkerton man wouldn't be any trouble at all.

He got out on the fifth floor and walked down the hall to apartment 521. He knocked on the door and listened carefully for any sound of movement inside. Rapped one more time just to make sure, waited a minute, and then inserted the key.

Once inside, he moved fast. Checked every possible hiding place. It was a typical one-bedroom apartment, with an office as well. Quite expansive, and expensively furnished. When he looked inside the closet, he wasn't the least bit surprised to see women's clothing. Even the notorious leather outfit that his analyst told him Leslie had worn to the hospital the night the letters were stolen from Ziv Dayan. Sean chuckled at the image that jumped into his head. Yes, indeedy, Leslie would look damn hot in this costume.

Once Sean checked the office, he struck pay dirt. There was a floor safe. He knelt down and began fiddling with the combination lock—put his ear up close to the cylinder and turned the dial. No luck—he needed his stethoscope to do this properly. And the safe was far too heavy to carry out.

Suddenly the phone rang. Twice.

Sean dashed over to the door and positioned himself so that it

255

would swing in towards him when it opened. He held his breath and waited.

Simon Worthington—or at least Sean guessed it was Simon—made his entrance, humming a little tune. He shut the door behind him and before he could take another step Sean chopped him on the back of the neck. With a surprised grunt, he went down, smashing his face against the floor.

Sean knelt down and flipped him over. "Simon Worthington, I presume?"

He was a good-looking man, blonde hair, blue eyes, square-jawed. And his eyes bore the shock of someone who might have just seen a ghost.

"I want those letters back, Simon. You're going to tell me the combination to your safe."

Worthington shook his head, and then took a swing at Sean's head with his right hand. Sean caught it before it connected. His left hand thrust upward and made an attempt to scratch at Sean's eyes. That was deflected by Sean's forearm.

Sean jumped to his feet. "I see we're going to have a problem here." He brought a foot down onto Worthington's throat and pressed hard with his heel. The Brit started choking, but managed to get both hands around Sean's foot. He lifted up and twisted. Sean lost his balance and fell back against the wall.

Simon was fast. He was on his feet now and reached a hand underneath his jacket. Out came a pistol. Before he had the chance to aim it, Sean ducked sideways and lashed out with his foot kicking the gun from Worthington's hand.

But the Brit didn't hesitate for a second—he rushed Sean with his head down, wrapping his arms around his waist. Sean went down with Worthington on top. Now his hands were on Sean's throat, squeezing hard. Sean pounded the palms of both of his hands against the Brit's ears and he heard a gasp as the pressure resonated inside his head. But, Worthington didn't let go.

Sean managed to get his knee into position and rammed it into the man's crotch. So hard that it forced him up and over Sean's head, landing with a thud behind him. But he was up again in a millisecond. Sean jumped to his feet as well and sent himself into a spin, delivering a vicious kick to the side of Worthington's head. He went down hard, smashing the other side of his head into an end table.

Sean knew he had him now. As the man was moaning, stretched out on the floor, Sean bent over and grabbed his right hand. He bent the wrist backward until he heard the telltale snap. Worthington screamed.

But Sean wasn't finished—he didn't want to take any more chances with this guy, so he performed the same procedure on his left hand. Another scream, followed by a sobbing moan.

Sean stared down at him. "Are you ready to tell me the combination to the safe?"

No answer, just a steady moan.

Sean was losing his patience now. The screams had probably been heard by other tenants, so he needed to get out fast.

He walked over to the balcony door and slid it open. Then he went back and grabbed Worthington by the lapels of his jacket and dragged him outside. Propping him up against the railing, he stared into his eyes. "We're only on the fifth floor, but that's still sixty long feet—if I drop you, you'll become a mushy pancake when you hit the hard cement of the parking lot. Is that what you want?"

The man just stared back, silent.

"Okay, have it your way." He lifted the limp-wristed Simon Worthington up until the upper half of his body was hanging over the railing.

Suddenly, reality set in. Breathless, Worthington exclaimed, "No, don't! I'll tell you!"

Sean pulled him back down and threw him inside the apartment again. "Okay, tell me. Now! I'm losing my patience with you."

"It's twenty—seventeen—five."

Sean ran over to the safe in the office and spun the dial. Then he opened the door; the first thing he saw was a pile of papers. He pulled them out and glanced at them. Sure enough, they were the Hal Winters' letters. He counted them—all twenty intact. Sean checked inside the safe again. A bit of cash, a Rolex watch and a woman's diamond ring.

He walked back into the living room and stood over Simon Worthington.

"Where's the cassette tape?"

The man looked up, a pained expression in his eyes. "I don't have it."

"Is it with Leslie?"

A look of surprise in his eyes now. Surprise that he knew who his partner was, Sean guessed.

"Leslie had it hidden. But, she found out that the Israeli guy took it."

"Where's Leslie now?"

"Out of the country. Belize."

"Tell her to stay there. If she ever comes back to America or Canada, trust me, I'll know about it. She'll be killed. And I suggest you join her there, Simon Worthington, right after you get metal rods implanted into those pathetic wrists."

Chapter 34

He'd never been in this section of Emerald City before. Because he'd never been a bad boy until now.

It reminded him of the prison in Georgia. Same tiny room, none of the luxuries that he'd been used to over the last four years. Dingy, dark, depressing.

This was his punishment for trying to escape the delusion that was Emerald City. And, Hal supposed, for killing that unlucky soldier as well, although the guards seemed to be more concerned with his attempt at escape than with the grisly death of one of their own.

It had been several days now—Hal had lost count how many. He had no idea where Keith and Patsy were. This prison section was quite extensive. After they were captured, they were loaded onto a special train that was destined to make only one stop.

It didn't stop at the normal little stations along the way where Hal saw, through the tinted glass window, hordes of people he knew, all waiting patiently for the next regular train. None of them had any idea that this particular steel-wheeled monster was a prison train to hell. And probably all of them wondered why it hadn't stopped for them.

No, this train was an express to the prison, which by Hal's estimate was about thirty miles along one of the tunnels that intersected with the main route.

One of the toughest things Hal had adjusting to was the quality of the meals. He'd become accustomed to mainly gourmet food in Emerald City's main restaurant. Now he was eating crap. Some porridge shit in the morning, bread and butter with watery soup for lunch, and Swiss steak or chicken mush with mashed vegetables at dinner—which Hal was convinced all came straight out of a Purina can.

But, that wasn't the worst of it. No, the worst was the tedious but useless mental torture they had been trying to inflict on him ever since literally throwing him into this prison wing.

He knew he was still too important for them to kill.

First off, he figured his time in this prison would be relatively short, because he was desperately needed to continue the flight training. They were a long way from finished.

Secondly, he figured that whoever had stolen the cassette tape from Brock's office hadn't yet communicated that fact to the administrators at Emerald City. With Hal's intelligence background, he guessed that the only explanation for that anomaly was that someone was using it for extortion. The main reason he was still alive was the existence of that cassette tape. Sure, the letters were damaging as well, but not as damaging as that cassette.

The third reason why Hal was convinced he hadn't been killed yet was his leadership position amongst the general population on his floor of Emerald City. He knew he was admired and respected, despite the fact that most people in there knew he'd been a CIA assassin. Down in Emerald City, that sort of thing just didn't really matter much to people—labels and judgements just seemed to disappear.

In fact, his notoriety had probably garnered even more respect in Emerald City than it generally would topside. Ironic. The administrators liked the influence Hal had on the residents—he calmed them down, instilled hope, made them laugh, and gave them ambition. This made managing the facility much easier for them.

So, it was paradoxical that Hal Winters had actually become an asset to them—not just in the flight training he provided, but also as an important cog in the wheel of their twisted little psy-ops experiment.

So, they wanted him cooperative, degraded, and humbled. They didn't want him to attempt another escape, and they couldn't take the chance that he could incite others to try. They had to break him—break his spirit, destroy his confidence, and strip away his adventurous nature. Make him play the game. And stay alive to finish the tasks that they wanted him to finish.

In a lot of ways, Hal knew he was invaluable to them. But only in a form that they would be comfortable with. The old Hal had to go. And a new Hal had to emerge.

But the old Hal wasn't going to cooperate.

He chuckled to himself as he recalled their attempts over the last few days to break his spirit. It was a pattern he'd been used to in his long career with the CIA. Techniques he himself had used in efforts to mind-fuck prisoners; to break them like wild horses.

This Emerald City prison was full of baddies. Ironic that it was a prison within a prison. The plush quarters he'd been living in were just an illusion—still a prison, but a fairyland kind of existence. But, just like any city topside, Emerald City had its share of crime: murders, rapes, robberies, assaults. It wasn't any different in that respect than any other society. That's why the underground city had a police force and a prison. The only difference from cities above ground was that there was no court system. Martial law prevailed. If they said you were guilty of something, you were guilty.

So, on his first day after being captured, they deliberately threw him into a cell that already contained three scruffy pieces of scum. Once inside the cell, he was overcome by the sickening smell of body odour, compounded with the pungent aroma of something else—Hal knew instinctively what that other smell was, and it made his stomach turn.

Double bunk beds framed the cell, and Hal immediately climbed up onto one of the top bunks, because the three scum were occupying the others.

He was promptly told by a skinny guy who was lounging in torn jeans and a T-shirt, that that was his bunk. Hal nodded respectfully and climbed down. He then proceeded to the top bunk on the other side of the cell. A fat beer-bellied slob told him that was his bunk. Hal climbed down again and sat on one of the lower beds. That one was apparently taken, too, he was told—as was the last remaining bed on the other side of the cell.

So, four beds and four inmates, but not one bed available for Hal. He smiled knowingly, which probably irritated them even more than just his mere presence.

"So, where do you chaps propose that I sleep?"

A guy with tattoos covering virtually every inch of his upper body and wearing only a pair of jeans, quickly unzipped and eased his pants down exposing his penis. He pointed to his crotch. "Right here, buddy. Make yourself comfortable."

Hal ignored the comment and sat down on the floor. He glanced at each of them one by one, sizing them up. He knew this was going to be the first session in the administrators' psy-ops exercise with him. He wasn't surprised at all. In fact, during his ride in the prison train he knew this would be coming.

He watched warily as the fat slob got to his feet. Under the jeans were tight little bikini briefs and a sweatshirt that wasn't near long enough to cover up his hairy belly button. In a mock attempt at being seductive, he wiggled his grotesque ass and flashed a toothless grin.

All three were licking their lips and making grunting noises as they walked towards him.

Hal stayed on the floor and held up his hand in the stop sign.

"Guys, we can do this the easy way or the hard way."

Tattoo man started laughing. "You're kidding, right, buddy? That's the exact line I was going to use on you!"

"Well, isn't that a coincidence, huh?"

"Stand up against the wall, face in. We're going to give you a ride you'll never forget."

All three started laughing. Kind of a sick mixture of laughing and grunting. Hal saw that the penises of Fat man and Tattoo man were now erect, and Skinny guy had a distinctive bulge in the crotch of his jeans.

Hal grinned. "I'm not standing up. You'll have to come down here and romance me. I like being pursued."

Fat man grinned back. "Well, this is interesting. What do you like?"

"I like a little foreplay first—to get me in the mood. You know, kiss me a little—that kind of thing. Make it passionate."

Fat guy smiled and got down on his knees. He stuck out his tongue and started crawling towards Hal, wiggling his ass as he did—while his two ugly friends giggled like little girls.

Hal instantly transformed his mind into the zone. Took himself out of the horrifying reality of the moment, and sent his brain off into a different place.

In Hal's zone, the slob's tongue was now going to be just a nice piece of filet steak.

He opened his mouth and the threatening tongue entered with ease. Hal could feel it swirling around against the tip of his own tongue, and against the posterior of his teeth. He raised his hands and place them firmly against the back of the man's head, giving the appearance of a passionate embrace.

The giggling in the background continued.

And it continued even as Hal summoned the strength from his abdomen and concentrated on allowing it to surge into the roots of his front teeth. He held the slob's head firmly as he felt the energy arrive. Then he clamped down hard with his teeth and, as he did, he grasped the man's head even tighter, pulling it against his with a vice grip that was now unbreakable.

The man started shaking his head like a dog with a toy, trying desperately to free his tongue from the grasp of Hal's teeth. This made Hal's job even easier—he released his hands and the man's head yanked backwards pulling the tongue free, but not before leaving more than half of it dangling from Hal's teeth.

The thug fell onto his haunches, screaming in pain. But, the screams sounded strange—without a tongue any sound emanating from a mouth sounded strange. He tried to form words, but they wouldn't come.

Hal spit the disgusting organ out of his mouth and swung one foot upwards, smashing it into the ugly face of the shocked thug. He fell backwards and rolled over onto his side, his hands up to his mouth trying to stem the flow of blood that was streaming out. Guttural sounds filled the prison cell, reminiscent of a mutilated animal.

The giggling from the other two scum had stopped now, replaced instead by absolute silence. They stood as stiff as boards with their hands over their mouths, experiencing vicariously what their friend was going through.

But the silence didn't last long. Tattoo man was the first to speak.

"You're gonna get your ass kicked now, man." He smashed a fist into his open palm, and Hal could see that the man's erection was still intact—in fact it seemed even more erect than before.

Hal got up from the floor and assumed a stance. "C'mon, painted man—make love to me like your friend did. Show me what you got, you ugly mother-fucker."

The man lunged at Hal. At the same time, Skinny man advanced from Hal's left. Hal instantly summoned his abdomen once again, and it obeyed. With incredible force, both of Hal's fists lashed out in two different directions. Directly into the foreheads of each man. Both went down, and Skinny guy immediately scurried off into a corner.

Tattoo man took the hardest punch—he lay on the floor with his eyes closed, wincing in pain. Remarkably, his penis was still erect. Hal ignored the harmless guy in the corner and grabbed Tattoo man under the arms. He roughly yanked him up to a semi-standing position and dragged him over to the back frame of one of the bunk beds. Shoving him up against the frame he grabbed the man's still erect penis and squeezed it into the opening of the hinge that connected the upper bunk to the lower bunk. The guy was wavering on his feet, but Hal only needed to let him go for a second.

Both of Hal's hands moved in a tight circle, then he lashed down with his right hand so fast that it was a blur even to Hal. The edge of his hand slammed the erect penis violently against the lower edge of the hinge.

With the force Hal's hand exerted, the metal hinge performed like a surgical knife. The severed penis smacked down to the floor and actually did a little bounce before it came to a macabre rest.

Tattoo man toppled over, holding his crotch and sobbing. His head came to rest on the massive belly of Fat man.

Hal turned his attention to Skinny guy. The man was still cowering in the corner, panic written all over his face. He raised his hands into the air. "It's okay, man! I'll leave you alone!"

Hal laughed. "Oh, you will, will you?"

He decided to ignore the man. He was no threat, and Hal had delivered the message that he'd wanted to be sent.

Except that the people he wanted to send the message to hadn't received it yet. He walked over to the cell bars and began banging on them, yelling at the top of his lungs.

"Medical help needed! Quickly!

*****

The two days after the incident in the cell comprised the next stages of the psy-ops against Hal Winters.

First of all, he was moved to his own private cell once the three would-be rapists were hauled away. The paramedics had been summoned, but Hal thought it was strange that they hadn't shown any inclination to protect the severed tongue and penis in ice. They simply plopped them into a garbage bag and tied it up.

Hal didn't give a shit whether or not they re-attached them, but he was curious as to why they hadn't followed the normal procedure that would have been followed up in the real world. He concluded that it probably just wasn't worth their bother. They were non-contributing members of the new society.

If keeping people like that required time, effort and expertise, then Emerald City probably preferred that they simply be dead. Which gave Hal a pretty solid hint as to the imminent fate of at least two of the men; the mutilated ones.

He was glad to once again have the privacy of his own cell. He immediately started concentrating on getting his mind in the right zone to handle what he knew would be coming next.

Their plan to break his spirit and dignity with the gang-bang hadn't worked the way they thought it would. Hal was a bit surprised that they'd even tried that. His skills should have been well-known, and they should have also known that those three men would not have been a difficult matter for Hal. Emerald City had clearly underestimated Hal Winters. Perhaps because of his age?

He could have easily killed them if he'd wanted to, but that wouldn't have sent the brutal message that he'd wanted to send. Killing them would have been too clean. He wanted them to see the mess, see the indignity of what they'd caused him to do. Hear the moans and groans from the victims. Be convinced that he wasn't fucking around.

One thing he was certain of—they wouldn't attempt to torture him. That tactic only worked when information was needed. It did nothing to break spirits. It only created resentment and rage. Since there was no information to glean from Hal, there was no point in torture. It would achieve nothing.

So, after the failed gang-bang attempt, he knew they'd take a softer approach. Mind games, try to get into his head. Change the way he thought about things, about how he thought about himself.

Perhaps even attempt to destroy the intense concentration Hal had mastered—that same concentration that permitted him to summon super-human strength into specific spots in his body.

But they would fail at that, too.

Hal Winters was a machine, created by the same masters who were now in charge of his fate. They didn't seem to realize what they had created when they molded people like Hal to do their bidding. He was Doctor Frankenstein's monster, and the only way to destroy him was to kill him.

For now, at least, Hal was fairly confident that wasn't going to happen.

Instead they tried what Hal knew they'd try.

For the two days after the attempted rape, they confined him to a laboratory. One that was equipped with surround sound speakers, wall to wall screens, and one-way glass. He was barraged with sounds, voices, and monotonous sentences being repeated over and over again.

Propaganda preachings about duties, obligations, subservience, obedience. And the screens on the walls displayed swirling graphics, never-ending sequences of the same abstract objects, occasionally interspersed with pornographic images just to see if he was still awake.

They'd wired him from head to toe—sensors delivering crucial data to computers outside the laboratory room. No doubt monitored continuously by technicians watching for any signs of mental submission.

He wasn't allowed to eat anything over the two days. Water was all he was permitted to drink, and the constant noise prevented him from getting any sleep. But Hal had been ready for this, and none of it fazed him in the least.

At the end of the two days, the speakers were shut down and the images on the screens disappeared. Into the laboratory walked two men in white coats—Hal guessed these were the psychologists overseeing the virtual lobotomy.

They sat down across the table from him, and one did the talking while the other jotted down notes on a pad of paper.

In a soft voice, the lead doctor asked, "How are you feeling, Hal?"

"Just peachy. Thanks for asking. Nice to know you care."

The doctor nodded. He was careful not to show any expression.

"Tell us what you're feeling after this experience. Just say whatever comes into your head."

"Okay. Fuck off."

"It's natural to have that kind of reaction to what you've been through. Tell me some more."

"Fuck off some more."

"No, Hal. I want you to tell me how you feel—the thoughts that are going through your head about your experience."

Hal chuckled. "I'd really enjoy a hamburger right now. And I also think we need to just cut the crap. Do you have any idea who you just tried to brain-fuck?"

"Yes, we do, Hal."

"I don't think you do. Let me educate you so you don't waste any more time here. The U.S. government has trained me to go without food or sleep for up to ten straight days, without any ill effects. I have the ability to not hear whatever it is I do not wish to hear. So, while my ears may be open, I can close them at will.

"Your non-stop barrage of propaganda over the last two days was just noise with no identifiable messages. Only the din of noise was heard by me, except for the approximate twenty minutes it took me to zone it all out. Well, okay, I cheated on myself a bit. Once in a while, I'd tune in again just to give myself a laugh or two.

"I also have the ability to not see what I do not wish to see. My eyes may appear to be open, but as you well know, the eyes are merely a function of the brain. I can shut off the signals from the eyes to the brain, thereby blocking out whatever is right in front of me.

"Your silly little graphics on the screens didn't register with me one fucking bit. Because I didn't even see them."

He chuckled. "But I must confess that I did turn my eyes back on for a bit, just to watch your lovely porn."

Hal placed his hands on the table and began opening and closing his fists.

"And I'm surprised you don't seem to be aware that I was trained in all of this, even to the point where I can defeat a lie detector test. You have indeed wasted your time with me."

Hal noticed that there was suddenly the faint hint of expression on both men's faces. Looks of consternation and embarrassment, along with a good dose of frustration.

The lead doctor broke the silence. "Hal, we know you're probably just playing games with us. Trying to counteract what you've had to endure. Let's go back to the beginning of our meeting. What are you feeling right now?"

Hal smiled. "Do you really want to know what I'm feeling?"

The doctor smiled and nodded.

"If you don't agree to get me a hamburger with lettuce, tomato and onions, I feel like I'm going to have to rip both of your heads off with my bare hands. And I think you know by now that would be mere child's play for me.

"So, let me turn that question back at you, Doctor—what are you feeling right now?"

Chapter 35

Bradley Crawford never could have imagined that a phone call on a lazy Sunday afternoon would lead him to eventually thinking long and hard about the famous and long-dead physicist, Sir Isaac Newton.

But, it would.

It was a voice he'd never heard before—a deep baritone, but articulate and pleasant. Non-threatening in how he spoke, and Brad's instincts told him that this was a man he needed to meet. Even though he was a stranger and the subject matter of the phone call was somewhat sinister.

And when the phone rang, he knew as soon as he heard it that this was the phone call that would change everything. He knew in his gut. Maybe one of those psychic moments that everyone experienced once in a while.

He was stretched out on the couch looking at his notes pertaining to the Hal Winters' letters when the phone shattered his concentration. And he knew. He just knew.

He jumped from the couch and ran to his office.

"Hello?"

"Is this Bradley Crawford. The journalist, Bradley Crawford?"

"Yes, it is. Who's this?"

"I can't tell you that. Not yet, anyway. I have something you lost."

Brad could feel his heartbeat pulsing in his neck. "What's that?"

"A bunch of letters."

"Okay."

"I want to meet you."

"Are you the one who stole them?"

"I know that they were stolen from your friend, Ziv Dayan. I stole them back again."

"Do you want money?"

"Absolutely not. I want to talk to you about the letters. And I know Ziv has a very important cassette tape. I want to hear that tape."

"Is this a horse trade? Cassette for the letters?"

"No. In fact, the tape is more damning than the letters. But, together, they're devastating."

Brad's hands were getting sweaty. "I need to know your name."

"Not over the phone. You can trust me. Correction, you'll *have* to trust me if you want your story."

Brad's mouth was getting drier by the second. "Do you want to come here?"

"No. Go down to your front lobby security desk. There's a sealed envelope waiting for you. Inside will be the place and time. Bring your friend."

The man hung up.

Brad raced out into the hall and took the elevator down to the lobby. Sure enough, there was an envelope with his name on it.

He ripped it open when he was back up in his apartment. Inside was a single sheet of paper, with the words: *3400 Kingston Road, Scarborough. Tuesday, 10:00 p.m.*

Brad stared at the sheet. Did he dare? Was the story worth the chance?

He thought back to how this all started months ago on Vancouver Island. How he and Kristy had escaped within an inch of losing their lives. And how he'd killed three people, all because of what those letters represented.

How could he even consider meeting a stranger who had popped up out of nowhere? It could be a trap. To get the cassette tape? Or to kill him and Ziv to silence them?

When Ziv had returned from Baltimore, the first thing they did was play the tape that Ziv had retrieved from Leslie's telescope. The tape that Brock Winters had hidden away in his safe for years, until Leslie had somehow found out about it and arranged to steal it from him.

The tape that basically turned the story of 9/11 upside down.

In fact, the tape was so powerful that the letters really weren't all that important anymore. So why was he even considering meeting with this man?

Well, for one, he obviously knew who Brad was and he knew where he lived. So, the best defence being an offence, it seemed to Brad that he had no choice but to meet him now. How could he just ignore the phone call and wait? Wait for the man to show up one day, or take Kristy hostage to make Brad meet with him? He was obviously serious or he wouldn't have gotten in touch with him.

Brad being a journalist was another reason why he was leaning in favour of meeting with this stranger. This story was compelling, made even more so after he'd listened to the tape recording. If the recording was real—and tests would have to be done to prove or disprove that— then the historical record was about to be changed.

And a diabolical deception was about to be exposed. A story so powerful that every human being on the planet would be clutching their chests in utter shock and disbelief. Yes, as a journalist, this was a story he wanted to tell.

And the last reason Brad wanted to meet with him was just due to a feeling he had. A feeling that this man was sincere and could be trusted. Something in his voice. A sense of urgency and passion? He detected some anger in the man's voice too, but not threatening anger, and not anger directed at Brad. It was almost like it was anger borne out of frustration. Just something in the tone of his voice. Brad was good at sensing the feelings of others, and he concluded in his mind that this man wasn't a threat.

Or, Brad considered, he was just being naïve and gullible because he wanted to get those letters back, and he wanted desperately to break this story wide open. And, at this point, he didn't have enough facts to do it with. He needed more. Needed corroboration. From somewhere. From someone.

Some of that corroboration would come from Brock Winters. But even that was hearsay. He knew his father was alive, but couldn't prove it. He could testify that the tape recording was what his father had mailed to him back in 2001, but he couldn't prove that it was his father's voice on the recording or that the tape hadn't been tampered with. Not yet anyway. Not until the tests were done.

But, even then, there was no beginning to this story and there was no end—the tape itself only gave a brief moment in time during the story. It didn't tell the story itself.

And the letters were a desperate attempt by Hal Winters to leave breadcrumbs for people to follow—at least for people who were smart enough to follow them. The standard journalistic principles of "Who, What, When, Where and Why" hadn't been addressed yet. The "How" may have been partially answered so far, but certainly not proven.

There were still far too many loose ends. The story could be written, but at this point he would have to fill in the blanks with conjecture. Which meant that the story just wouldn't fly. It would just be one more outrageous conspiracy theory that no one could prove.

After the stranger hung up, Brad phoned Ziv. Just a quick conversation. They agreed to meet down in a coffee shop on Front Street.

Brad packed up his laptop, kissed the puzzled Kristy goodbye and headed out.

He didn't tell her that in a couple of days he was planning to meet a complete stranger at an insecure location. She wouldn't be able to handle that, especially after Vancouver Island.

Lately, she'd done her best to avoid asking him about the story. She knew what he was like. A dog with a bone. He couldn't get the implications of the story out of his head and hadn't even attempted to tell her what he and Ziv had heard on the tape recording. He knew it would terrify her. So, until this thing was over, he would keep her in the dark. Not nice, but necessary.

And she knew it, too—she'd seen it before. When he got caught up in the Mexican border story, his life was threatened several times. And again, when the scandal with the mayor was uncovered. That was the worst—political threats were ominous because politicians, until removed from office, had the power to carry out almost any act they wanted to.

So, Brad protected her as much as he could—he knew how frantic she could get and sometimes it was just better that she didn't know. She was involved at the horrifying beginning of this letters ordeal, but now that it was picking up steam and the implications were becoming clear, Brad felt more at ease if she was in the dark.

And Kristy knew. She played along. She knew that Brad was protecting her. It didn't eliminate her concern, but at least her concern was more just what her imagination dreamed up than the brutal reality of what was coming to light.

Brad walked to a booth at the back of the coffee shop. Ziv was already there, eating a cheese Danish.

"Hey, bud. What's so urgent today? It's Sunday."

Brad sat down and immediately pulled his laptop out of its case. "I got a phone call from some guy. He says he has the letters—stole them back."

Ziv leaned across the table. "Who is this guy?"

"Don't know. Wouldn't tell me over the phone. He wants to meet with us, and he knows you have the cassette tape."

Ziv shook his head. "I don't like the sound of this, Brad."

Brad clicked on the Google Earth icon on his laptop, and then keyed in the location that the stranger had given him. It configured itself, giving him a bird's eye view. Brad zoomed in and then went to a street level view.

Brad swung the computer around. "Here's where he wants to meet us. Tuesday night, 10:00."

Ziv studied the image. "It looks like a ramshackle old warehouse. And Kingston Road is kind of a seedy area, too. I don't like it. We're not going."

Brad looked up. "Ziv, I can't explain it, but I got a good feeling from this guy. Something about him—didn't make me uneasy at all. There was nothing threatening about him."

"That's just a voice over the phone, Brad. You can't tell anything from that."

"I know, I know—but my gut feel tells me to go."

Ziv shook his head again. "No, we're not going. Tell him to meet us at my place or your place."

"I already phoned the number back. No answer. Phoned Bell and tried to get a name. No luck. Must be one of those disposable phones."

"That alone should tell you something. No, we can't do this."

Brad stared at Ziv for a full minute. "I'm going alone, then."

"You're crazy. After what you went through on Vancouver Island, I would think you'd be a little more careful. It could be an ambush."

"I'm going to take that chance. I want this story, Ziv."

The retired Mossad agent leaned back in his seat and folded his arms across his chest. Brad could almost see the wheels turning in his head.

Suddenly, Ziv whispered. "Okay, then. I'm going with you. Hopefully this character is just like the deep throat guy from the Watergate scandal. But we're not taking the cassette with us. That may be our only bargaining chip to stay alive. And I'll be armed, too, just in case."

Brad sighed with relief. "Thank God! I was only bluffing—I wouldn't have gone alone."

Ziv laughed. "Sneaky bugger."

"I'm excited about this. There's something about this guy. I want to find out what it is."

"I'm guessing he's CIA, Brad. After Vancouver Island, you should know you can't trust these pricks."

"Our story is going nowhere if we don't take some chances. With how much we know so far, can you in all honesty say you're willing to walk away from this?"

Ziv rubbed his forehead and frowned. "No, especially after listening to that recording. I have more questions than answers now. The fact that all four of those planes that were supposedly hijacked were just "test" planes. That they never crashed into the towers or the Pentagon at all. That they instead landed in Denver—well, three of them did. One crashed into a field in Pennsylvania."

Ziv paused, and then slapped the palm of his hand down on the table. "So, what the fuck hit the Towers and the Pentagon? We were all glued to the TV and clearly saw a plane hit that South Tower, for fuck's sake! The whole world saw that!"

"Boggles the mind, doesn't it?"

"And that opening in the ground that Hal and his co-pilot mention in the recording—the one leading to some kind of tunnel. What the hell was that all about? It ties in with the weird stuff we discovered about the Denver airport, doesn't it? Just one more weird thing."

"Everything points to Denver. Hal Winters alludes to Denver in the coded phrases he inserted in his letters. The recording tells us clearly that Hal's plane landed there, and most likely the other two "hijacked" planes as well. And Brock told me that Hal is still alive, but he doesn't know where he is."

Ziv winced as he took a sip of his hot coffee. "Speaking of Brock, I thought you said he'd be here in Toronto by now."

"He phoned me yesterday. Got delayed with a public relations thing he had to do for his latest movie. So, he's flying up here on Thursday. In his own plane. Brock's a pilot just like his dad. Two peas in a pod, those two."

"Okay, well, that's pretty good timing, then. If we have any luck with this stranger and we get out alive, we'll be able to share more with Brock when he gets here."

"We'll get out alive, Ziv. I have a good feeling about this."

Ziv reached his hand across the table and poked his index finger into Brad's chest. "If we don't get out alive, I'll never ever forgive you and I won't ever work on a story with you again."

Brad laughed at his friend. Then he turned his head and looked out the window. Watched the shoppers strolling along, bags in hand, smiles on their faces, enjoying the nice warm autumn weather.

They looked so simple, so content—and so naive. None of them with even the slightest inkling about what he and Ziv knew. Brad felt a sense of privilege for that—his curious brain and unusual occupation brought him into a totally different realm of reality than the majority of the population.

But, just for a quick moment, he thought that perhaps that was more of a curse than a privilege. Was it better to know? Or better not to know? Would his life be happier if he hadn't discovered all of the horrible things he'd investigated during his career? Was it better to be naïve and in the dark? That naïve and dark place where he was keeping his very own wife?

His mind was swirling now; so much to think about, so much to do.

But Bradley Crawford had no way of knowing that in a couple of days' time his brain would be infiltrated by something else, something he never could have predicted.

A certain law in physics that had stood the test of time for centuries, and had become the basis for the design and integrity of virtually every invention known to man.

Sir Isaac Newton's Third Law of Motion.

Chapter 36

Brad's first look at the building made him regret his decision. Maybe Ziv was right—maybe this was a trap.

It was 9:45 p.m. and already dark. He parked his Audi Q5 in the empty parking lot and glanced at his friend sitting next to him. Ziv's face reflected the apprehension that Brad felt.

"What do you think?"

"I think we should turn around and get the fuck out of here."

"Starting to think the same myself. Should have listened to you."

"Not too late, bud. Let's go."

Brad nodded and shifted the car into Drive. He'd just begun his U-turn to get out of the parking lot when suddenly Ziv grabbed his arm. "Wait! Look!"

The dilapidated warehouse had been in total darkness when they'd pulled up. Now there was a dim light flashing on and off through one of the tiny windows. A light that seemed to be intended for them.

Brad stopped the car. "He's signalling us."

Ziv reached down to his waist and pulled the Glock out of its holster. He glanced at Brad. "Okay, I'm game if you are. But, I'm keeping this gun in hand until we know it's safe."

Brad took a deep breath. "We've come this far, we might as well see it through."

"Is your life insurance paid up?"

Brad laughed nervously. "Yeah. In fact, double indemnity if I get shot."

They got out of the car and cautiously made their way up to the front door of the warehouse. The light inside stopped flashing.

Brad noticed that while the walls of the building looked to be missing a few bricks, and the roof was sagging in parts, the door itself was solid steel and appeared relatively new. He shifted his eyes to Ziv, who nodded reassurance while he held the Glock at the ready.

He whispered. "Turn the handle, then step back against the wall. I'll go in first."

Brad twisted the handle and pushed the door slightly open. Then he jumped back. Ziv gave the door a heavy kick and dropped to his knee with the gun trained through the semi-dark chasm. Brad noticed that there was a dim light farther back inside the building; its glow barely noticeable through the doorway.

Ziv slowly rose to his feet, then stepped carefully across the threshold, gun waving steadily from side to side. He whispered to Brad. "Stay here until I call you."

He disappeared into the building. Brad held his breath as he waited anxiously to hear Ziv's voice again. But instead of his voice he heard a grunt, then the sound of something metallic hitting the floor.

Footsteps coming towards him from inside.

"Come on in, Bradley Crawford. Ziv and I are just getting a little intimate here."

He peeked his head around the corner. There was Ziv—a tight grimace across his face, arms pinned behind his back. Behind him stood a tall, broad-shouldered man. He had a ruggedly handsome face, with eyes that were steady and unwavering. He smiled pleasantly at Brad.

In a voice that could have belonged to a broadcaster, he said, "I'd love to shake your hand, but you can see mine are kinda busy right now."

Brad stared back at him and didn't return the smile. "Let him go. We don't have the cassette, so there's nothing to give you."

"Come on in and close the door behind you. We'll talk."

The man backed up, still with a firm hold on Ziv's arms. His right foot found Ziv's errant pistol on the ground, and gave it a good kick off into a corner of the room.

Brad entered cautiously and shut the door. He looked around, expecting to see others. But the man was alone.

The warehouse belied its appearance from the outside. Several pallets were stacked neatly at one end, and there were shelving units arranged efficiently throughout the expanse. A table with four chairs was in the middle of the huge space. He noticed a Starbucks cup and several tins of cola.

The man walked backwards, pulling Ziv with him. When he got to the table he kicked one of the chairs out and eased Ziv down into a sitting position.

His hands were free now and he gestured at Brad.

"Come. Sit down. Neither of you have anything to fear from me. I had to disarm your friend here just in case his trigger finger slipped."

Ziv rubbed the feeling back into his right shoulder, and jerked his head towards the table, signalling Brad to join them. "It's okay, Brad. If he wanted to kill us we'd be dead by now."

Brad walked slowly over to the table, sat down, and cracked open a can of cola. His throat was as dry as sandpaper. He tilted his head and sucked back at least half of the contents.

Then he spoke to the stranger. "Okay, here we are. What do you want with us?"

The stranger sat down as well. "I wanted to hear that tape, but since you don't have it, that plan is scuttled. So, I guess we'll just have a chat instead."

Ziv shifted his chair to face the stranger. "Who are you?"

"My name's Sean Russell. I'm the Director of the Special Activities Division at the CIA."

Ziv nodded. "One of the SAD boys."

"Yep. That's a good acronym, isn't it? And I know who you are. Ziv Dayan, ex-Mossad, assigned during your career mostly to Europe and the Middle East. Now retired here in beautiful and peaceful Canada."

Sean turned his attention back to Brad. "And you're the famous Bradley Crawford, two-time Pulitzer Prize winner. No doubt trying to earn another one."

Brad nodded. "You must be the one whose men almost killed my wife and me on Vancouver Island."

"That would be me, yes. They got a little exuberant."

"An understatement."

The rugged man looked down at his hands and frowned. He clenched his fists and looked up again, straight into Brad's eyes.

Then he spoke, in a voice that was even more baritone than what Brad had heard so far.

"I want to help you guys with your story."

Brad stared back, unblinking. "Why on earth would you want to do that?"

"Because everything is wrong. And I have to try to make it right."

Ziv leaned forward, resting his elbows on the table. "How can you possibly expect us to trust you?"

Sean reached into the inside pocket of his jacket. Ziv flinched.

"No, it's okay, it's okay." Sean held up a little machine. "This is a recorder. You can tape our conversation. A low tech tool that still does a perfectly adequate job. I was hoping to use it to listen to that little cassette you have."

He slid it across the table to Brad. "Here, Mr. Reporter. You can do the honors."

Brad opened the recorder and noticed a cassette was already in place. Then he clicked it to Record and pushed the machine into the middle of the table.

"Okay, as we say in the biz, we're on the record now. Why do you really want to help us?"

Sean sighed. "Aside from disillusionment, I have a personal reason which I don't want to get into right now. It's not important. Suffice to say, it involves a loved one. And I think it took what happened to her to be the final straw in a career I've become ashamed of. Call it *redemption*, whatever. I need to be a whistleblower. It's the only way I can stop myself from dying."

Ziv jumped in. "What do you mean by that?"

"You were in the business a long time, too, Ziv. You're well aware of the brainwashing that goes into making us who we are. The personal issue I referred to snapped me out of it—perhaps it made me human again. I don't want to do this anymore."

"Your career will be finished. And you may go to prison. America has never looked too kindly on whistleblowers. Have you reconciled that in your mind?"

Sean nodded. "I have. And it doesn't matter to me anymore. Whatever happens, happens. That's a chance I'm prepared to take. I'm actually a lawyer by profession—maybe if I'm not disbarred, I can practice the law instead of breaking it."

Brad cracked his knuckles. He could feel the adrenaline surging through his veins. "Is Hal Winters still alive?"

"Yes."

"Is he a prisoner in some underground city under the Denver airport?"

"You've done your research. Yes. He's been there since we faked his death back in 2011. He tried to escape recently. I'll be seeing him again soon. Right now, he's in lockdown, but I'll get that changed. Otherwise, he's fine—we've actually become quite close over the years."

"Close? That's a joke, right? You're free and he's not."

"Freedom is a relative term, Brad. In reality, I'm not much freer than Hal is. And, despite the violent life he's lived, I think his conscience is actually clearer than mine."

"What the fuck is Denver all about? We know from the tape recording in the cockpit that Hal's plane landed there. And then he took off and ran for his life. Did the other planes also land in Denver on 9/11?"

Sean nodded. "Three of them did. But United 93 was shot down over Pennsylvania."

"What? I thought the passengers overcame the hijackers and it crashed to the ground. They made a movie about it—immortalized the passengers as heroes!"

"There were no hijackers on any of the planes. And Flight 93 was shot down by two Sidewinder missiles fired from an F15 fighter jet. Flight 93 took off too late, and it threw the whole exercise into disarray. The passengers were on the air phones, hearing stories from the ground about the towers being hit. They panicked, thought they were being hijacked, too. So—it was shot down."

Brad and Ziv shook their heads.

"I know, I know—but that's the least of it. There's a lot more to tell and you'll be shaking your heads a lot harder by the time I'm finished."

Ziv opened a can of cola and gazed around at the building they were in.

"Who owns this place?"

"We do."

"By we you mean the CIA?"

"Yep."

"Why? This is Canada."

"We need places like this from to time. Fronts that perform a covert function. You know what I'm talking about. Israel does the same thing."

Ziv nodded and took a long sip.

Brad stood and started pacing around the table. "What the fuck hit those towers and the Pentagon, Sean? We all saw the video footage of United flight 175 hitting the South Tower, live on TV for fuck's sake! Yet, while all that was happening, Hal Winters was piloting the real flight 175 to Denver?"

"Missiles hit the two towers, and the Pentagon as well. Fired from naval vessels out in the Atlantic. Precision missiles. And designed to fragment outwards on impact with the face of the buildings. To cause the carvings that looked like wing impacts. Those involved in the charade were handsomely rewarded—they were patriotic to a point, but money made them even more patriotic."

Brad gasped. "The only clear video of impact was the one that hit the South Tower—supposedly Hal's plane. We all saw a plane, for fuck's sake! There are tons of video shots of the thing."

"You saw a hologram, Brad."

"What?"

"Holograms are the most innovative military tools ever developed. And not just by our military. The Chinese and the Russians have perfected them, too. In fact, google it. A few years ago, the Chinese caused quite the stir when an entire city with gleaming skyscrapers popped up on the other side of a river in Shanghai. You can easily see it, ghostly on the horizon—people walking across the bridge were stunned. They captured it on video. Then it disappeared as quickly as it appeared.

"And then we had fun with the Iraqi people a decade or so ago. Tried to fuck with their heads by displaying a giant hologram of Mohammed floating in the sky over Baghdad. They really thought it was the Second Coming."

Ziv reached into his pocket and pulled out a pack of cigarettes. "Can I smoke in this shithole?"

Sean chuckled. "Sure. Give me one, too."

Brad was still pacing. "If that was a hologram, it was moving through the air at a speed that the government estimated at 560 miles per hour. Can these holograms actually do that?"

"Oh, yes. They sure can. Because the three-dimensional hologram was actually being projected from the missile. Very advanced technique. As the missile rockets through the air, the projection is emitted from the missile itself and shrouds it by displaying what we want you to see. It can display anything we program it to display—a plane, helicopter, even a flying submarine if we wanted to be silly."

Brad muttered under his breath, "Jesus Christ—the world was sure duped."

"Yes, it was. But—there were several mistakes made in the process. If you take a good look at the video of 175 hitting the South Tower, you'll see that the image of the plane is very dark, almost black. Which is contrary to the gray/blue color of a real United Airlines 767.

"In addition, if you look at the video shots that are on the Internet—the ones with a vantage point looking up at the plane hitting the tower—take a close look at the belly. There's a cylindrical object that is clearly visible. No passenger jet has a cylinder on its belly. The hologram wasn't configured properly to completely cover the missile. You can see the fucking missile outline, but most people haven't paid much attention to this.

"So, they got the color of the hologram wrong when they programmed it, and they didn't configure the hologram properly to completely shroud the missile.

"In addition, there's another aspect of the plane argument that falls flat—again, very few people except pilots and engineers have picked up on this either. A commercial jet is not designed to fly at speeds like that so close to sea level. It was reported as flying at 560 miles per hour. And, of course, the missile which you couldn't see, was flying at that speed. They're designed to fly at that and much higher speeds at any height whatsoever.

"But, the airframe of a commercial jet would break up into pieces at that speed that close to the ground. The air is far too dense. Commercial jets are designed to fly at speeds over 500 miles per hour only when they're up around 30,000 feet where the air is thin. Until they climb to that height, they're flying at about half that speed. They can gradually increase the speed as they climb, though. For example, at 18,000 feet, the air loses about half of its density. So, the jet can probably fly at about 350 miles per hour at that height, but can't safely reach 500 miles per hour until over 30,000."

Ziv stood up and started pacing with Brad. "Sean, I can't believe they've gotten away with this. So much is wrong with it, it's mindboggling."

Sean nodded. "There's a famous line—from a John Travolta movie called *Swordfish*. The release of that movie was actually delayed because of 9/11, as some aspects of it were reminiscent. The line was, *'What the eyes see, the mind believes.'* So, what they pulled off capitalizes on this basic fact of human nature.

"Even though the plane hologram was almost black, no one seems to question that the color wasn't the United Airlines color scheme.

"Even though the hologram has a cylindrical object coming out of its belly, no one questions the fact that passenger jets don't have such shapes on their underside.

"Even though people are told that commercial jets can't possibly fly that fast so low to the ground, people saw a plane flying that fast and that's all that matters. All logic goes out the window.

"And the planners of 9/11 were smart—they know human nature and they played on it. Knowing full well that no plan is perfect, they knew that the gullible aspects of human nature would make it work despite the imperfections. They knew that people would believe their eyes, and would believe what they were told."

"Surreal."

Sean continued. "That's not all. Everyone saw perfect theater that day—the footage of flight 175 cutting into the South Tower like a knife through butter. Once again, *'What the eyes see, the mind believes.'* What people saw was a virtual impossibility.

"The wings and nose are the weakest parts of a plane's body. Made of aluminum, they are incredibly weak. If you've ever sat in a wing seat on an airplane, you've probably seen words painted on the wing: *Do not stand here*. The reason for that warning is that it could simply snap just from a person walking on it. Yet, on 9/11, we saw the plane and its wings carve holes in the South Tower and completely disappear inside of it. In reality, the nose and airframe would have crumpled and the wings would have simply snapped off."

Brad stopped his pacing. "But it hit the building with such force!"

"No, the missile hit the building with such force, and a missile is designed to penetrate and explode—that's how they're constructed. So, the explosion and penetration was caused by the missile, but the error in the hologram was that it was shown going through the building. Again, the planners were fearful of cutting off the projection of the hologram too soon because the shape of the missile would have been seen. So, they allowed the hologram to actually show the plane image penetrating the building. They kept the hologram projecting too long.

"There's a famous principle in physics, brought forth by Sir Isaac Newton centuries ago, and proven true time and time again since then. It's one of the most basic principles of physics, known as The Third Law of Motion. The law states: For every action, there is an equal and opposite reaction.

"Think of it this way—when you walk across a floor, you're pushing against the floor and it pushes back against you. The tires of a car push against the road while the road pushes back against the tires. All forces are interactions between bodies of mass—there is no such thing as a unidirectional force or a force that acts on only one body.

The action and reaction are simultaneous and it doesn't matter which is the action and which is the reaction.

"In the case of the Twin Towers, everyone believes what they saw. A plane traveling very fast smacks into a tall building. Naturally, they assume that it's possible for the plane to carve a path right through it, because that's what they saw and that's what they were told.

"But, Newton's Third Law of Motion tells a different story. It doesn't matter which object was moving at the time—doesn't matter whether it was the tower or the plane. The action causes an equal and opposite reaction. Therefore, since it's equal between the two objects, picture the South Tower moving at 560 miles an hour instead of the jet moving at that speed. Picture instead the jet standing still, and the tower slamming into it at that speed. What do you think would happen?"

Ziv scratched the back of his head and replied in a soft voice. "The plane would crumple like a tin can."

"Exactly. Because, basically, the plane is just an aluminum can to begin with. But, the twin towers were constructed of very thick structural steel columns. For a jet to be able to cut into that tower, knowing that you can't even safely stand on one of the damn wings, is physically impossible.

"And with Newton's law, it doesn't matter which object was moving. The reaction is equal and opposite. So, basically, a structural steel tower hit an aluminum plane at 560 miles per hour, instead of the other way around. It would have simply crumpled like that pop can you're drinking out of. But the hologram showed it cutting through the building as smooth as a knife through butter.

"It was the ultimate deception based on very bad science. And they got away with it. It was a mirage and people bought it—hook, line, and sinker.

"Sir Isaac Newton is probably rolling over in his grave."

Chapter 37

Brad popped the recorder open and checked the cassette. He was relieved to see that only half of the capacity had been used so far. He didn't want to miss any of this—it was beyond his wildest imagination.

While all of it horrified him, it also excited him more than any story ever had before. He salivated at the chance to break this story, to tell the world what had really happened on that fateful day fourteen years ago.

The journalist inside him was intrigued. But he couldn't help but catch himself at the same time. Stories were one thing, but a globe-shattering revelation like this carried with it a certain responsibility.

Did he dare break this story? Was he ready for the fallout? How would the world look after a story like this came out?

But if he didn't tell it, how many more 9/11s would the world have to face? If they got away with it this time, would they be empowered to do it again—and again—and again? What was worse? Sparing the world from the despicable and murderous deception that had been foisted upon them—or breaking it wide open and letting the chips fall where they may? And letting the wounds heal, and perhaps creating an environment where more responsible and decent governments would rule in the future?

He knew he was facing a journalist's worst moral dilemma: having to make the decision to either tell the story—or bury it. He recalled debating this hypothetical dilemma when he was studying journalism in university.

And even back then, at a school of higher learning, there was no clear answer. It was left to students to examine their conscience if it ever happened, and to just follow where their conscience led them.

Brad was confident he would know the right thing to do when the time came. Right now, he would concentrate on just getting all the facts and taking advantage of this incredible opportunity that had fallen into his lap.

He considered the aspect of fate, and what role it might have played in this story so far. Was it fate that a famous investigative journalist such as himself happened to be staying at a cottage on Vancouver Island around the very time that these letters were in the possession of his landlord?

Did fate intervene again to allow him and Kristy to escape with the letters? And had fate brought Sean Russell virtually to his doorstep, with this incredible first-hand account of intrigue, mass murder, and deception?

Brad's thoughts were disturbed by Sean's voice. "Don't worry about running out of tape, Brad. I've got an extra cassette in my pocket."

"Oh, good. I have a feeling we're going to need it."

Ziv cracked open another can of cola. The sound of the tab echoed around the large room, bringing them back to a sense of normalcy from the surreal.

It seemed odd to hear the everyday innocent sound of a tab snapping on a pop can, when what they had heard from Sean made it seem like they were in some kind of dream state—or nightmare state.

Brad found his voice again.

"Sean, I can guess that the point of 9/11 was to create enough fear to justify a war in Iraq? Even though Iraq had nothing to do with 9/11, and indeed didn't even possess weapons of mass destruction? They lied about that, too. Bin Laden was a convenient enemy, wasn't he?"

"Yes, in more ways than you realize. I could go on and on forever about the geo-political landscape that brought the planning of 9/11 to the point of execution, but it's such a maze of subterfuge and betrayals that we'd need three walls just to draw the flow chart. It's nuts. Bottom line, it was done to justify an agenda. And the slaughter of American citizens was considered suitable collateral damage for the greater good. Sick as that sounds, that's how it was justified."

"How were the towers brought down?"

"Nano-thermate, which cuts through steel quickly and without any explosive images or sound. It was simply painted on to the crucial structural members of the towers months before 9/11, under the guise of fire-proofing.

"Magnesium fuses were attached, which were equipped with miniature radio transmitters. Then they were set off remotely in a pre-programmed sequence. All marvellously engineered. The third tower, WT7, the one that wasn't even hit by a missile, was taken down in the same way."

Ziv drained his can of cola, and cracked open another one. Brad could see that his face was flushed—either from all the caffeine he was drinking, or from the adrenaline rush from what they were hearing.

Ziv rapped his knuckles on the table, gritted his teeth, and then growled at Sean. "How the fuck was all this kept secret? You're coming forward now, but why not earlier? Didn't anyone have the guts to blow this open before now? Or before it was even allowed to happen? Jesus!"

Sean lowered his eyes and stared down at the table.

"Ziv, you're right. Nothing I can say about that, at least from my standpoint. It happened. And I sure as hell wish I'd had the courage or the motivation to do this earlier. You don't know how much I wish that. But—I can't live in the past. I can only go forward."

"I can't believe no one has said anything. There must be a hell of a lot of people who know the sordid truth."

Sean nodded. "A lot of people know—but just bits and pieces. Only at the very top do they know the entire story. For example, I've heard rumblings of mini-nukes having been used in the lower bowels of the towers to knock out the base support columns. But, I'm not privy to that and I have no idea whether or not there's any truth to it. I do know that hundreds of people in New York have died from radiation-type illnesses, though, in the years since 9/11. That gives me pause…"

"Has anyone died trying to bring all of this to light?"

A tight grimace came over Sean's handsome face. "Yes. Many people have died from sudden and suspicious causes. The one who came closest to blowing the lid off this thing was a guy named Mitch Joplin. You may remember reading about an attempted bank robbery in New York back in 2003. That was Mitch.

"It wasn't really a bank robbery at all—it was a stunt he pulled to bring in the media. He held the employees and customers of the bank hostage until the media arrived, and had a dud bomb vest strapped to a teller. He was holding a 'dead man's switch.' He planned to make an announcement, but the media that came into the bank were really just a CIA hit squad in disguise. The CIA took complete control of the scene, and made sure that only their fake media team gained access to the bank. They put a bullet through his head before he could say a word."

"I don't recall that. I'll google it. But, why did they kill him? Like, how could they have known what he was going to say?"

"Mitch Joplin was a legendary CIA agent, and had an engineering degree paid for by Uncle Sam. He was also the foremost explosives expert on the CIA payroll. He was almost as much of an icon as Hal Winters was. So they knew he was going to say something, because Mitch was the one who designed the nano-thermate specifications to take down the towers."

"Christ!"

"Yep. He paid for his conscience with his life. Anyway, the story didn't end there. Here's a coincidence for you—another Canadian, like you, picked up the gauntlet in 2009 after stumbling upon the mystery through the adoption of Joplin's dog. The dog had a micro-chip embedded under his skin, which had a coded message on it from Mitch.

"The Canadian was a retired executive by the name of Jack Howser, and he linked up with Joplin's daughter, Kerrie. Together, they tracked down some hidden documents and then just locked them away in legal channels to protect their lives. Basically, they extorted the U.S. government into keeping them alive, threatening that their lawyers would automatically release the documents to foreign media outlets."

"That's an amazing story. Is Howser still alive?"

"Yes. As you can appreciate, he's on the CIA radar. He doesn't know that he's still being watched."

Brad smiled. "Or maybe he does know, and he's playing you."

Sean laughed. "Could be. He was a pretty resourceful guy. Caused the CIA major angst back in 2009. He wrote a novel about his ordeal and published it as a fictional story in 2011. Under a pen name, of course. And only Howser, Kerrie Joplin, and the U.S. government know that the story really isn't fictional."

"Sounds like a fascinating guy. I'll have to look him up after all this is over."

Sean took off his jacket and slung it over the back of his chair. "It's getting warm in here. Back to the story—that Mitch Joplin guy was a perfect example of people knowing only bits and pieces. He was duped into designing the specs for the thermate demolition of the three towers, thinking that it was a safety precaution.

"He was told that it was part of a plan called Operation Avalanche. In the event that certain buildings in the United States were attacked, they could easily be brought down if they were already pre-engineered for demolition. The idea was that the buildings would be evacuated, and then collapsed.

"But when he discovered on 9/11 what the real intention was, it drove him over the edge. All he knew about, though, was the demolition part. He was under the impression that actual jumbo jets hit the buildings—he didn't know about the missiles or the holograms."

Ziv took off his jacket, too, and then lit another cigarette. "How does the Denver airport fit into 9/11?"

"Well, it really doesn't fit in at all. It's a different issue entirely. On 9/11, it was chosen as the safest place to store the planes after they'd served their decoy purpose. And a place to stash the passengers. We couldn't have those planes land at a normal airport, nor could any of the passengers be seen walking around again. They were all supposed to be dead. So, that's where they ended up—but Hal, being the kind of guy he is, wasn't having any of it. He escaped, only to be recaptured in Minneapolis four days later. That's when he was framed for the Mall of America mass murder.

"You know the rest—the tape kept him alive, and he went to a prison in Georgia. Then in 2011, after an attempt on his life, we faked his death and sent him back to Denver. Back to where he was supposed to have been kept captive in the first place along with all the other passengers and crew. Ironic that he ended up back there. Since 2011, he's been our chief flight instructor at Emerald City—"

Brad interrupted. "Emerald City?"

"That's the name for our underground city. Anyway, he's teaching young pilots to fly all the types of planes that he's had experience with. Hal's probably the most experienced pilot America has ever had on its payroll. So, he's been useful to us—in actual flights and in the simulators we have there."

"You're saying that he's actually allowed to fly out of there once in a while?"

Sean nodded. "Every week. Under guard the whole time, of course. He's done a great job for us, and has become kind of a leader amongst all the other residents."

"You call them residents? They're prisoners, for fuck's sake!"

"Yes, they are. And they're even much more than that. Most of them are guinea pigs—being tested physically and psychologically to give us a picture of how life would be over the short and long term in such an underground facility. So we can adjust conditions or treatments accordingly."

Brad let out an exasperated sigh. "Adjust for what? Why?"

Sean hesitated for a second. Then he spoke in a softer voice. "For when the important people arrive."

Ziv jumped in and practically shouted. "What? Who!"

"Anyone America deems worth saving."

"From what?"

"From anything. Any kind of cataclysm: asteroids, solar flares, nuclear winter, an unknown planet coming into our galactic space, the Yellowstone caldera exploding. You name it—Emerald City is designed to allow America to live on, even if it means being underground for decades, if not longer.

"And, Ziv, we're not the only country doing this, I'm sure you know that. There are bunkers all over the world—some private, some government. I have no idea if they're testing them with guinea pigs like we are, but these underground facilities definitely exist everywhere."

Brad put both hands up to his forehead and rubbed his temples hard. "So, the dozens of people from those 9/11 planes are living in this underground city?"

Sean laughed. "It's a much bigger picture than just them. There are thousands living down there—I've lost count of exactly how many. There is an official census that's taken each year, and I think the count taken at the end of last year was 10,000."

"For fuck's sake! How big is this place?"

"It's huge. Construction started about thirty years ago, long before the new Denver airport was even conceived. It stretches now about 100 miles in each direction. It has streets just like up here, train routes, bicycle paths, hospitals, schools, recreation centers, lakes, beaches, restaurants, bars and nightclubs, strip clubs, brothels. You name it. We've even started introducing university level courses. It's four levels deep, and the accommodations are as good as any modest studio apartments up here in the real world. The Denver airport was the final piece to the puzzle. It was built as the main entrance hub to the city, and as infrastructure for the massive airplane hangar that happens to be in the section that Hal is in."

Ziv lit another cigarette, his hand shaking as he did. "Where...did you find...10,000 people?"

"We stole them—from all over the world. A few hundred each year over the last fifteen years or so. From boats, planes, off the streets, kidnappings, kids stolen right from their beds. You've read, I'm sure, about scientists, astronomers, business executives, who all disappeared without a trace. There are stories about these disappearances in the news every year. Usually, that was us.

"Even that Malaysian jet that disappeared over the Indian Ocean— those passengers are in Emerald City. Amongst the passengers on that plane were twenty genius computer scientists who we needed desperately for Emerald City's computer lab. So, we hijacked that plane by remote control and flew it to the island of Diego Garcia. From there, they were brought in a separate transport to Denver. In fact, Hal flew that mission."

"Remote control?"

Sean nodded and took a sip from his cold Starbucks cup. "All jumbo jets are equipped with telematics capability now—designed ironically as a protection *against* hijackings. But it can also be used by us to take any plane we wish to take. And we wanted that one. There will be more."

Brad got up and started pacing again. "So all of these people are just guinea pigs?"

"No, but they're all being treated that way during this test phase. Some will be integral to the society as we move forward and when the elite eventually arrive. The doctors, dentists, tradespeople, nurses, scientists, contractors, teachers, university professors—they will all be essential. But, those who don't have those skills will end up in a different underground facility eventually—or they will just be eliminated if they're of no future use.

"We do have prisons down there right now—some of the people haven't adjusted too well, and we've had crime just like you would expect up here. And some of the people we kidnapped were just bad apples to begin with. Mistakes were made. Hal's in one of those prisons right now due to his escape attempt, but I'll be getting him out of there very soon."

"You have that kind of power?"

"Yes. I'm the CIA liaison director for that facility. Basically, the administrators of Emerald City report to me."

Brad was making notes on a small pad. He didn't want to rely on just the recording. He tapped his pen on the table after jotting down a few more key words, and then looked up at Sean. "What's the power and water situation?"

"Right now, all the power is drawn from the Denver airport, which was built with more power capability than the airport needed. So, it's fine for now until the nuclear power plants are completed.

They'll be deep underground; relatively tiny, but 100 times more efficient than the monsters we have topside. As for water, we have a massive aquifer under Emerald City. Water has been diverted there from other aquifers—one of the reasons why the country is suffering water shortages right now in California and the entire southwest. The water in this aquifer will be more than adequate for a long time, even for the cooling of the reactor cores."

Brad shook his head. "I'm fascinated by all of this. But, I feel violated, too. As a Canadian, I don't have to deal with the incredible bullshit you Americans dish out. The lies and deceptions, and the race to war for the lamest of reasons—or for reasons you just make up.

"This 9/11 thing is just unbelievably twisted, but Emerald City is beyond belief. It's the epitome of inhumane. That you would take innocent people and turn them into laboratory animals—take them from their homes, their families, their friends, their careers, and use them to prepare the perfect underground living conditions for whom you deem the most important people.

"You have no right to criticize Nazism and Communism—what you guys have done is far worse. It's off the charts. I think you're a sick nation, to be honest. And I have to tell you—I think you're one sick man for the role you've played in all of this."

Sean stared back at him with unblinking eyes. Brad could see a profound sadness in those eyes, almost the look of someone who had already given up and resigned himself to his inevitable fate.

"I accept your rebuke. Now, what are we going to do about it?"

Chapter 38

Brock Winters never bothered with disguises. They were uncomfortable, and never seemed to fool anyone anyway.

He had such a distinctive look, just like his dad. Long blonde hair, ruggedly handsome face, broad shoulders, thick forearms, brilliant blue eyes, and a swagger that he could never hide no matter how hard he tried.

So, he just went with it. If people recognized him, then so be it. And he wasn't one of those movie stars who shied away from his public. Because of them, he was a success. And they deserved an autograph if they were respectful about it. And usually they were.

It was the paparazzi who were the rude ones. He never gave them even the time of day, which made things worse for him. They hounded him more because of that. Hoping to goad him into an altercation, and he'd certainly had his share of those during his career. In Brock's mind, they were the scum of the earth—on the hunt for any salacious photographs that might put Brock in a bad light. Or any stories that would paint him as a playboy womanizer.

Which he was, of course—but he really didn't want the world to see him that way. He didn't like the image that he had and, if truth be told, he knew in his heart that blaming the paparazzi was his way of deflecting blame away from himself.

He had all the money in the world, and he could basically do anything that he wanted. And what he wanted most of all was a relationship. But, in Hollywood, good relationships were few and far between. Almost everyone he came into contact with was a narcissist. Empty shells, self-obsessed, as shallow as his beach at low tide.

So, he just played the game. Had fun, never gave much of himself to anyone, because so far, he hadn't met anyone who was worthy of it. He hoped that one day the right woman would walk into his life, but he knew that it wouldn't be in this town. For that, he'd have to live off the grid, give up this stupid business, and start experiencing what was really important.

The sad thing was, in living this fairyland Hollywood existence, he'd developed a warped pre-conception of women. He saw them all just a certain way now. Just pieces of flesh that he could snort some cocaine with, take to bed, and then kick out in the morning, if not earlier.

He never talked to them—not in any meaningful way. It seemed like they never had anything to say, and because of who he was, he never had to talk to seduce any of these brain-dead bimbos into bed with him. So, he never even bothered to try anymore.

Plenty of the women he'd been with had run to the tabloids afterwards. They ate it up. Painted him as a sullen and angry man. A selfish lover who would satisfy himself within a few minutes and then just leave the bedroom to watch TV. He couldn't argue with them— they were absolutely correct. But to see himself splashed that way on the covers of sleazy magazines for the whole world to see sometimes made him sick to his stomach. And even angrier than he already was.

Angry at himself, perhaps, more than at the sluts or the paparazzi. Angry that he'd allowed himself to be caught up in this whirlwind. Sure, he had everything that he could ever want.

Except a lover.

And except his dad.

In his quiet moments, that's who he thought about the most. Hardly ever his mother. She was probably the reason he had such a jaundiced view towards women. He'd wondered many times over the years if she was what caused him to have such high standards as to who he could fall in love with.

Wondered if she was why, until that one magical day when love might finally hit him between the eyes, he viewed virtually all women as just toys. With no more substance than his Xbox.

But, being fair, he also knew that his mother had lived a tough life with Hal. Perhaps that was the reason why she seemed to have lost her self-respect and sense of self-worth. At the best of times, she was frustrated by his absences and secrecy. At the worst of times, she was depressed and lonely, trying to raise three boys with absolutely no happiness in her private life. After a while, she just seemed to give up on herself—and even gave up on trying to inspire her own sons.

But his dad was different.

Brock had never approved of his father's occupation. Even though Hal wasn't supposed to tell anyone that he worked for the CIA, he did tell Brock. He told Brock everything. Brock never understood how this gentle, intelligent man with the heart of gold could blow people's heads off for a living.

When he'd first learned it, Brock had been shocked to his core. Didn't talk to Hal for weeks; had sulked and ignored him. But then he eventually came around. Because being out of contact with his dad was more than he could bear. Even when Hal went away on assignments, he always phoned Brock. Well, he phoned the family, but spent only minutes with his mother and sometimes just a few seconds with his brothers. But Brock was usually favored with a half hour or so.

They had clearly been soulmates. Dreamed of each other, talked to each other in telepathic ways, spoke in their own coded language. They were not only father and son, but buds. And connected in a way that most people wouldn't understand.

Brock finished packing his suitcase and walked into the living room. His driver would be here soon to take him to the airport.

He dropped his bag in the front hall, walked into the kitchen, and poured himself a tall glass of juice. Then he wrapped his signature red bandana around his forehead and placed a black cowboy hat on top of his blonde locks. He had about ten cowboy hats, all different colors, but he tended to wear the black one most of the time. Not because it accentuated his blonde hair, but more because the public thought he was a bad boy so he might as well just give 'em what they wanted.

He knew that deep down he wasn't really a bad boy though—that was just what he'd fallen into. He longed to live a better life, one with more meaning than the one he was living right now.

But, he felt this despair in the pit of his soul. The person who had meant the most to him his entire life was locked up forever. He might even be dead now, Brock just didn't know. It had been quite some time since they'd talked on the phone, which scared him to no end. The tape recording had been stolen, and now his dad had absolutely no leverage left. If it had fallen into the wrong hands, Hal was a dead man.

He was Brock's hero. A true American hero, who had served his country with brutal brilliance, and with humanity and integrity that very few people knew Hal possessed. Most just thought he was a vicious killer. Brock knew better.

Many times over the years, Brock had thought about just releasing the tape to the public—do it at a press conference. With his celebrity status, he would have had no problems gathering a large crowd of drooling press. But he never did—because he pretty much knew how it would turn out.

He would have been branded a conspiracy theorist just like Charlie Sheen. Tagged with that worn-out label that the government and the media just loved to use. Anyone who challenged the status quo or thought for himself, was just a conspiracy theorist. On the other hand, those who inhaled the lies that were being fed to the world were patriots.

But if you spit out the lies, you were a conspiracy theorist.

And once he was thoroughly laughed at, ridiculed and discredited, the tape recording would lose its meaning. No one would believe the shocking revelations that were on that cassette. And, what he feared the most, was that they would then just proceed to kill his father anyway—to make sure there would be no chance at corroboration. A dead Hal Winters couldn't confirm his voice on the recording.

So Brock just left the cassette in his safe—locked away as a wonderful little poison pill. The only thing scuttling their plans to kill his father.

But then it was stolen. And then he started to worry.

Brock walked over to a corner table in his living room. Picked up a framed photo of himself and his dad standing in front of a Cessna stunt plane—the one Hal had used to teach Brock how to fly. In this photo, he was only around fifteen years of age, which would have put Hal in his early forties.

He smiled as he thought of the many hours they had spent up in the air together, soaring like birds through the sky.

And he remembered the skill that Hal had demonstrated one time when he took over the controls. Sending the plane almost vertical, then letting it fall, only to correct it and execute a spin in the air. Then diving towards Santa Monica Bay and practically skimming the plane across the waves. Hal was the most confident and skilled pilot ever manufactured by the American military system, and at one time had even been one of the Navy's Top Guns.

God, I love my dad.

Hal had taught Brock how to be a man—a real man, with the courage and desire to push himself to succeed to the best ability that God had given him. And, despite the fact that his dad was a killer, Brock had never even thought of that when they were together. Hal had always been gentle with Brock, his brothers, and even with his mom.

When they were out together, Hal would hold doors open for others, let people go in front of him in line at the grocery store, pick up parcels for little old ladies and carry them out to their cars. What impressed Brock the most was that his father's occupation never defined him as a person. Never.

Brock was determined not to let his own occupation define him either. Although, he had been slipping in that direction. The drugs, the tramps, the empty lifestyle. He knew he had to catch himself. Hal would want him to. Hal would not want Brock to be defined by the movie star stereotype.

Right now, he knew that Hal would be ashamed of him.

He also knew that the rocketing success that he'd had in his career was due to his father. Hal never told him that—he wouldn't do that. He would want Brock to think he had done it on his own. But Brock wasn't stupid. While he damn well looked the part, he was, without a doubt, a shitty actor. There would be no Oscars in his future. In reality though, he hadn't even had the chance to really act yet. His parts were all action hero types; very few lines, nothing deep, shallow stories.

Brock wasn't naive. His meteoric rise had started almost right after Hal had been thrown into the Georgia prison for the mass murder in Minneapolis. That was far too coincidental. Hal must have made that happen, in the pact of silence that he had struck with the CIA.

Brock wanted a serious acting role more than anything else in his career. Something that would glean him more respect than just a hunk on the screen. He wanted more than just money. He had pushed his agent to get him roles with some substance to them, but the greedy prick just laughed him off. Brock was his steady paycheck—why fuck with that?

He wanted to be as good a man as his dad was. He wanted someone to love him for who he was. He wanted the respect of his peers for being the best at his craft.

And, most of all, he wanted his dad back.

A part of him was convinced that if Hal was back in his life, all of his other dreams would come true. But his dad was the catalyst that was missing—the thing that was making him so angry, so apathetic about life.

Being realistic, Brock knew it wasn't going to happen. He would never see his dad again; he knew that. But, he could get his dad back in other ways. Which was why he was flying to Toronto today to meet with that investigative journalist, Bradley Crawford.

He could help Bradley portray his dad in the right light in his exposé. In the kind of light that his hero dad deserved. And he could help Bradley break a certain story wide open. A story about how planes had never been hijacked on 9/11. That the world had been fooled, and that all those passengers were most likely still alive somewhere.

The tape recording from the cockpit made the deception so shockingly clear. His dad had been at the center of the deception, being one of the airline "captains" that day. And it was clear from the recording that Hal and his co-pilot were as shocked as the rest of the world. In fact, even more shocked, because they were used as pawns in the diabolical scheme.

He didn't know how far Bradley wanted to go, but now that he no longer had the cassette, he would do the best he could from memory to help Bradley recreate the story. And if there was a chance that his dad was still alive, maybe an explosive story written by a famous Pulitzer Prize winning journalist would be the credibility needed to keep him alive. It wouldn't be just Brock, the movie star, holding a pathetic press conference. He'd be standing beside an award-winning journalist who had broken other major stories.

And if Brock couldn't have his dad back, maybe that was the next best thing.

He jerked his head up at the sound of the doorbell. His driver was here.

Brock took one last glance through the expanse of windows covering the back of his house. He loved the ocean, but longed to get out of Malibu.

He had his sights set on Costa Rica—wanted to just pack up and go. Go to a place that was natural and free—free of all the crap. Free of the shallowness and the patronizing. America was a circus, and Hollywood was the trapeze act. Maybe in Costa Rica he'd meet a local Tica—a woman who just enjoyed life rather than all the trappings it offered.

He walked down his long hall, picked up the suitcase, and opened the front door. Greeting him was the smiling face of his long-time driver, Carlos. A Mexican, who was hard-working, honest, and liked Brock for who he was—not the movie star Brock, but just the guy who loved living by the ocean.

They had actually become good friends over the years, and he and Carlos had been involved in more than one brawl with the paparazzi together.

"Hey, Brock. Ready to go?"

"Yeah, let's roll, Carlos."

Brock jumped into the front passenger seat of the Lincoln stretch. He was never one to sit in the back and treat the driver like—a driver.

Brock didn't like pretension and never treated anyone as if they were beneath him. He remembered where he came from and wanted dearly to hold onto that memory. A desperate attempt to hang onto his soul.

"So, Brock, who's your co-pilot today?"

"Gonna fly with Jimmy. You know him—he runs that skydiving school down in San Diego."

"Yeah, good guy. I like Jimmy."

"Carlos, when can you get away for some time off? I know you've got lots of demands on you from more people than just me. But, I'm thinking of buying some property in Costa Rica and could use your advice. Also, I could use your Spanish."

Carlos turned his head away from the road and gave his boss a mischievous look.

"I love taking trips with you. In fact, I think you need me sometimes just to protect that precious ass of yours. You name the date, and I'll make myself available. My social calendar puts yours to shame, but I'll try to squeeze you in somewhere."

Brock laughed and punched him gently on the shoulder. "I think you're the only one who can keep me grounded."

Carlos then frowned at him—in a fatherly way.

"I want you to lay off the drugs, though, if I go with you. And we're gonna meet some decent women, too, not the kind of trash I drop off here for you several nights a week. You need a real woman in your life. Maybe a nice Spanish lady. Deal?"

Brock nodded. "You got a deal, Carlos, my friend."

He looked out the window and studied the beach homes as they drove along the main highway towards Los Angeles International Airport—LAX—which Brock thought was perfect; the airport was the most *lax* in the world in his opinion.

He stared up at the sky. Clear and sunny; not plagued so much today with the famous Los Angeles smog. A good day to fly.

He loved flying—a passion he shared with his dad. He wasn't even close to being in Hal's league, but he was thankful that his dad had exposed him to flying early in his life. It was always when Brock was happiest—getting up there, away from all the crap; just enjoying the great outdoors and the feeling of freedom that flying brought upon him.

Two years ago, he'd bought a Challenger 350, second-hand. It had only been about a year old, but he got it for a cool twenty million—about ten million cheaper than if he'd bought it new.

A beautiful jet, very sleek. It seated eight passengers and with its two jet engines mounted strategically along the fuselage towards the rear of the plane, it was capable of the fastest climb speed of any of the executive aircraft models on the market. This elite jet could accelerate safely to a staggering height of 43,000 feet, and, due to the thin air space way up there, it could fly without refuelling for 3,200 miles.

Carlos turned off and followed the LAX directional signs and then veered towards the private executive jet terminal. "Aren't you glad that your daddy got you into flying when you were just a little boy?"

Brock smiled warmly at Carlos. There weren't many people who he smiled at that way, but Carlos was one of them. "You know it. My passion, for sure. And it's his passion, too. It's the thing Dad loves most in the world." Brock laughed. "Well, after me, of course."

Carlos made a strange face. "Brock, your dad has been dead for four years. You're talking about him like he's still here. Letting go sure has been difficult for you, hasn't it? I've heard you refer to Hal that way before, too—this isn't the first time."

Brock grasped Carlos' shoulder in his big hand, and squeezed. Then he stared out the window at a jumbo jet as it streaked down the runway.

Yes, it was indeed a good day to fly.

Chapter 39

His room looked the same; he was relieved to be back in familiar surroundings again. It seemed as if nothing had been touched while he was away on his little "vacation" in the prison wing.

"Good to be back, huh?"

Hal Winters turned his head and studied the suit standing beside him. He seemed like a pleasant enough guy—neatly combed hair, stylish glasses, wearing a friendly smile on his wide, chubby face.

He'd greeted him at the train station platform just a few minutes ago, and driven him back to his room in a golf cart that looked good enough to grace Pebble Beach.

Hal smiled. "Yeah, it is good to be back. But—why am I back?"

"You've got a friend in high places. Sean Russell called and asked that you be released."

"Hmm…that's interesting. Why? He knew why I was there, didn't he?"

The suit sat down on the edge of Hal's bed and crossed his legs. "Yes, he did. But he said you still have important work to do. You were being wasted in prison."

Hal sat down beside him, took off his shoes, and wiggled his rheumatism-afflicted toes.

"I agree that I was being wasted. Sean's an astute man."

"Look, Hal. We know who you are and we know how dangerous you are. But you do have skills we need. And you also have a positive effect on the residents here. We hope you'll realize that and try to respect that esteem we hold you in."

Hal laughed. "You want my respect? Are you fucking deluded?"

The suit abruptly stood. "What I mean is, you can have a preferred position here in Emerald City for the rest of your life if you play your cards right."

"In other words, you'd like me to just suck it up and be a good boy."

"You don't want to end up back in the prison wing again, do you?"

Hal got to his feet and moved to within a few inches of the suit's face. "Are you threatening me, little man?"

The man backed up. "No—no, not at all. I just want you to look at the big picture."

"The big picture? The big picture is that you've imprisoned hundreds if not thousands of us down here so you can test the lay of the land for your eventual VIP guests. Isn't that the big picture?"

The administrator opened his mouth to say something, then thought better of it.

He was silent for a few moments, then reached inside his suit pocket and pulled out a sheet of paper. He studied it for a second, then handed it to Hal.

"Here's the requisition for your next flight assignment. Sean signed and faxed it in to me. You'll be taking Lieutenant Snow up with you tomorrow. It'll be his first time in that type of aircraft, so give him a good intro. Get some sleep tonight—the first night back in your own bed should be nice for you."

Hal quickly scanned it. "Oh, I'm taking out one of the Stealths, huh? Maybe I can just sneak off under the radar and you clowns will never find me. Wouldn't that be special?"

The suit smirked. "You'll have the usual guard behind you in the third seat, Hal. So, get that idea out of your head."

"I was just fuckin' with you. Get a sense of humor, chief."

"Well, it's hard for me to laugh after seeing the results of what you did to two of your cellmates. And you had those two doctors of ours running to change their underwear after their session with you."

"As you said before, you know who I am...so you shouldn't be surprised by anything I do."

The suit eased back towards the door.

"Okay, I'll leave you to it. Oh, Sean wanted me to pass a message along to you. He says for you to calm down and relax—turn on your iPod and play that favorite song of yours by John Denver. He said it was called *Annie's Song?* Said you'd loved it ever since you made a recording of your son, Brock, singing it at a school concert?

"Also, he wanted me to plead with you not to tell anyone in here about your escape attempt. It would either demoralize them that someone like you failed, or motivate them to try to do something heroic themselves. He wants you to just tell them you were in the infirmary for a few days."

Hal nodded his agreement. "Despite the fact that he's my captor, there's something about Sean that I like. Because the request came from him, I'll respect it. You can tell him that. Now, get the fuck out of here so I can rest up for tomorrow's flight."

The suit hurried out the door, no doubt relieved that his tongue and dick were still intact.

Hal was glad to be alone. He flopped down on the bed and switched on a table lamp. Then held the requisition form up to the light and read it over again.

His flight was scheduled for 10:00 a.m. The plane he'd be teaching in tomorrow was one of the most advanced in the family of Stealth bombers—the B-2 Spirit. Hal loved flying this jet—it was one of the smoothest craft ever made and only eighty pilots on the American payroll were qualified to fly it. He was proud to be one of them, although he couldn't exactly say he was on the payroll anymore.

The jet looked about as much like a bat as anyone could imagine.

It was known as a "flying wing" aircraft—no fuselage or tail. Just two massive wings joined together, humped in the middle for the flight crew. It could only hold three crew members, and normally flew at a height of 50,000 feet, but could also slice through the air just as comfortably below radar ranges.

It was capable of either conventional ordinance or nuclear bombs and had a range of 6,000 miles before refueling. And even then, it was equipped to be refueled in the air.

The B-2 Spirit also employed the long-tested Multi-Spectral Camouflage, which helped keep the jet invisible in the air.

But lately, when he'd flown these things out of Emerald City, they'd been testing an even more advanced version of cloaking. Ironically, developed by the twenty engineers who were kidnapped from MH370. Hal had transported them and their fellow passengers back from the island of Diego Garcia, and the hapless engineers were immediately put to work when they arrived at their new home. Hal hoped that for their efforts they at least got extra dessert at dinner every night.

He put the paper down on the end table and closed his eyes.

He thought about that message Sean had asked the suit to pass along.

Now, why would he say that? That reference to *Annie's Song*? That was a clue Hal had used in one of his letters to Richard Sterling in Coventry, England. The letters that eventually disappeared.

And there was another part of Sean's message, too, that caused Hal to think hard. He said that Hal had made a recording of Brock singing the song at a school concert.

Hal was positive that Sean was talking to him in code in that message. *Annie's Song* was certainly not a favorite song of Hal's, nor was it even a favorite song of his ex-wife, Anne. And he had never recorded Brock singing it at a concert. In fact, sadly, Hal couldn't recall attending even one school concert his kids had been in.

By referencing the title of a song Hal had used in one of his letters, and by using the words *recording* and *Brock* in the same phrase, Hal was positive that Sean was trying to say that the letters, and the cassette recording that had been stolen from Brock's safe, had now been recovered.

Why would he do that? Was he trying to threaten Hal?

He didn't think so. Sean wouldn't have bothered talking in code if that were the case. If he wanted Hal to know he no longer had the leverage of the letters and cassette being in friendly hands or on the loose, he would have just come right out and said that.

And he wouldn't have ordered Hal released from the prison. If the recovered letters and cassette now meant that Hal's life was no longer protected—well—Hal would already be dead. No message would be needed.

Hal had always had a good feeling about Sean, right back to when he'd first met him. That day when Sean had decided to save Hal's life and fake his death in Georgia. Then shipped him off to Emerald City.

No, Hal's intuitive mind was convinced that Sean was trying to tell him that the letters and cassette had been recovered and to reassure him that they were in safe hands.

Chapter 40

The tape recording reached the end and the machine shut itself off. Brad flipped the cassette out and put it back in its case.

They had just spent the last three hours listening—first to the recording of Hal Winters and his co-pilot, Dave, in the cockpit of Flight 175 from fourteen years ago. Immediately after that, Brad played the recording of Sean Russell telling him and Ziv the sordid tale of 9/11 and the Denver airport.

This was the second time he'd listened to the cockpit tape and Brad still felt the same goosebumps rippling down his back. It was an eerie feeling hearing the shock in Hal and Dave's voices when they finally figured out that the entire world thought all the occupants of their flight were dead, supposedly pulverized from exploding headlong through the South Tower of the World Trade Center.

Then hearing Hal's reaction to having his plane guided by the Denver control tower down runway 13A and directed to taxi into a fucking tunnel that opened up right out of the ground.

The shock in Hal's voice, and his quick decision to simply park the plane on the runway apron and evacuate. Then the cool calm in his voice, despite the stress he was under, and how he took the lead over his co-pilot, an Air Force colonel, who clearly couldn't believe what was really happening.

Brad couldn't help but admire the man, the way he showed compassion and concern for his crew and passengers first. Ordering them to evacuate before he and his co-pilot even thought of doing the same. Brad concluded that Hal Winters was indeed one of a kind.

The tape recording of Sean's outline of what happened on 9/11 and what was happening right now in Denver was played solely for

Brock's benefit. Rather than having Sean repeat everything he'd already told Brad and Ziv several nights before, Brad decided it would be best if Brock just heard exactly what he and Ziv had heard.

Brad studied the movie star and wondered what was going through his mind. He looked a little bit thinner than when they'd met several months ago at his house in Malibu. And he looked stressed—at least right now he did, probably because he'd just listened to Sean's voice detailing the shocking truth about 9/11 and the inhumane reality of Denver's Emerald City.

They were all meeting in the same warehouse where Brad and Ziv had met with Sean a few nights ago. They decided this would be the safest place, especially considering that the CIA owned the facility and Sean could vouch for the fact that there were no listening devices.

Brock had flown his jet in to Buttonville, a smaller airport just north of the Toronto environs. Then it was just a quick drive for him across the city to the ramshackle warehouse on Kingston Road.

Brock had been polite when he met Ziv and Sean, albeit sullen. He didn't say much; only that he wanted to listen and help with the story.

But now, as Brad watched him, he couldn't get a read. With the tape recordings having run their course, he expected something to come out of the movie star's mouth. But, so far, nothing.

He looked at Sean and Ziv—they were waiting, just like him. No one wanted to break the silence.

Maybe it was a sign of respect to the son who had just heard once again his father's shocked voice in the cockpit of a plane that was used to trick entire nations into going to war.

And then hearing one of the CIA's top officials talking about holograms, Newton's Law of Motion, and a secret city under the country's largest airport. With how close Brad knew Brock and Hal were, these revelations must have been earth-shattering for him.

Brock Winters was the only one in the room who had a personal stake in Flight 175 and the Denver airport.

Suddenly, he moved. Took off his black cowboy hat and removed his red bandana. Used the bandana to wipe the sweat from around his eyes. Then he grabbed an empty cola can and smacked his massive hand down, flattening it like a pancake.

Brock raised his head and aimed his insanely blue eyes directly at Sean. Then he whispered, "How the fuck do you sleep at night?"

Sean didn't flinch. He just stared right back and didn't even attempt a reply.

Brock lurched from his chair, grabbed the edge of the table, and tossed it into the air. Both Brad and Ziv dove sideways, but Sean went flying backwards with the table landing on top of him.

Brock scrambled across the upside-down table and pulled it off the prone CIA agent. Then he was on top of him, pummeling his face with his fists. After taking several punches, Sean managed to block Brock's arms and throw him backwards against the wall. Then he was on his feet, looking down at the fallen movie star.

Sean turned away and wiped a sleeve across his bleeding nostrils, calmly lifted the table, and righted it back into position again. He walked over to a little fridge and pulled out several more cans of cola to replace the ones that had spilled all over the floor. He placed them on the table.

He went back to Brock, leaned down and offered a hand. Brock hesitated for a second, but then grabbed it and Sean yanked him to his feet.

They all slowly took their seats again. Brad was surprised that Sean hadn't even attempted to fight back. He took a few punches and then just stopped the fight. Brad guessed that someone like Sean, with his training, could have made quick order of Brock if he'd wanted to. But he didn't—almost like he knew Brock needed, and deserved, to get that out of his system.

Brock opened a can of cola and took a long sip. Then he directed his gaze back to Sean again. In his distinctive southern drawl, Brock continued, as if the fight hadn't even happened.

"My dad served his country his entire adult life, doing all the dirty work around the world they asked him to do. He helped overthrow countless heads of state, risked his life for whatever patriotic cause you guys brainwashed him with, and completely lost out on his family life in the process.

"And this is how you repay him? You trick him into participating in a massacre of your own citizens on 9/11, then frame him for a mass murder in a mall? Now you have him locked away in an Oz-like existence under the ground along with thousands of other innocent people. How sick can you guys get? Do you ever know when to stop? Can you stop?"

Sean grimaced. "I understand how you feel, Brock."

"No, you fucking don't! Your father isn't locked up underground, is he? Your father wasn't portrayed to the world as an insane killer of shoppers in a clothing store, was he?"

Sean looked down at the table. "You're right. Wrong choice of words."

Brock laughed mockingly. "Wrong choice of everything, Sean. Did it ever dawn on you that they could do this to you one day? My dad was CIA just like you, and he was a fucking icon, a legend.

"Yet, you guys just disowned him when you were finished with him. What do you think they'll do to you one day when they don't need you anymore? Or when you become a liability? Have you ever thought about that?"

Sean's sad, tired eyes looked up from the table. "I'm not here to do penance. And you're not my priest. You can sit here for days on end punishing me, or we can instead talk about what to do about all this. What's done is done.

"You're not telling me anything I don't already know, Brock, and trust me, you can't make me feel any worse than I already feel. But I'm not going to sit here and do a dance of contrition with you."

Ziv jumped in. "Sean, why are you helping us? The other day you said you had a loved one that helped bring you to your senses. Can you tell us about that?"

Sean shook his head. "No, Ziv, I don't want to. It's too horrible for me to talk about, and I don't think you want to see a grown man cry. I can't save myself by helping you—I know that. My soul is doomed, and it deserves to be. But maybe I can live with myself a little bit better if I help you blow this wide open. That's why I'm helping you."

Brad leaned back in his chair and rested his feet on the table. "We clearly have a big story to tell the world. I've been wrestling in my mind with whether or not we should do that. Whether it's the right thing to do. But I've decided that I can't keep this locked up in my head. We have to tell the story. The problem is, how do we do that? And will anyone listen?"

Sean allowed a wry smile to cross his face. "There may be a way we can make them listen, Brad. In fact, a couple of ways."

Brock folded his arms across his chest. Suddenly, he blurted out, "I want to talk to my dad, Sean. Make that happen."

"I can do better than that, Brock. I'm going to help him escape."

Brock sat up straight in his chair. "What?"

"I'll warn you, it will be dangerous for him. And he'll be all alone on this. But I have a plan that might just work. And there's also a certain something that has to escape with him."

Brock slammed his fist down on the table, knocking one of the pop cans on to the floor.

"No! He won't be alone! You find a way for me to be with him. To help him."

Sean shook his head. "Too dangerous, Brock."

"I don't care. You have no idea how this has affected my life. My success means shit to me. I can't even begin to explain to you how close my dad and I were. But I can't have him risk everything again, only to die alone. You owe me this, Sean. For what you've done to me and my dad. Let me help. I don't give a shit about the danger, and I know my dad won't either."

Sean sighed and sat back in his chair. He looked up at the ceiling and just stared at it silently for a couple of minutes. No one else said a word.

Then he leveled his gaze at Brock again. "Okay. I hear you. It'll be tricky, but we might be able to make this work."

Ziv stood up and leaned over the table. He spoke in almost a whisper. "Include me in this, Sean. I have the experience and skills that Brock doesn't have. Might improve our odds of success."

"You guys haven't even heard my plan yet, and you both want in?"

Ziv chuckled. "You're the CIA. I'm sure it's a brilliant plan; perhaps even as brilliant as what the Mossad could dream up."

"Well, okay. I'll tell you what I'm thinking." Sean pointed at Brad. "No notes, Brad."

Sean used his sleeve to rub away some more blood from underneath his nose.

"It's starting to take shape in my head. A four-pronged plan.

"The first prong will be Brad getting the story out in a preliminary way prior to actually writing the story.

"The second prong—a shocking little demonstration in New York City.

"The third prong will be Hal's escape and he has to take something vitally important out with him.

"The fourth and final prong will involve, in an indirect way, the personal issue I was alluding to, and the horror that has to be disclosed about that."

Sean spent the next hour thinking out loud to the three of them. The only sound was his rich baritone voice, resonating loudly within the four walls of the dingy old warehouse.

But, to Brad, the stunned silence among himself and his two friends was as deafening as a jet engine.

Chapter 41

Brad parked his car on a side street and walked south along Jarvis Street. A seedy area of Toronto, but he expected a location like this considering who he would be meeting and what he was about to do. He took a second glance at his notepad where he'd written down the address Sean had given him. *Yep, should be just up ahead.*

Then he saw the storefront: Universal Technical Solutions. Sean hadn't given him a name, but he had given him a phrase to recite: "I have too many gigabytes and not enough megabytes." A phrase that made no sense at all, but Brad guessed that was entirely the point.

He opened the door of the shop to the sound of a jangling bell. Standing in a glass enclosure, kind of a foyer of sorts, he waited. A scraggly-looking man came out of a back room and walked to the enclosure. He pushed a button, and his voice came through a speaker panel embedded in the glass. He said, "Identify yourself."

Brad pushed a red button on his side of the glass and replied into the receptacle, "I have too many gigabytes and not enough megabytes."

The man reached to his waist and pressed a remote unit attached to his belt. The door unlocked. He held it open for Brad. Without a handshake or a smile, he said, "Follow me."

He led the way to the back of the shop and into a massive room adorned with computers, monitors, and numerous gadgets that Brad couldn't even begin to identify.

He pointed to a chair that was positioned in front of a desk. On the desk was a microphone connected by wires to several processing units.

Brad suddenly felt intimidated by all the electronic wizardry. He had no idea what this place was, and he was here only because his gut instinct was to trust Sean. This step was supposed to be the first prong of Sean's plan.

He sat down and was quickly joined by the stranger, who rolled over on a wheeled chair.

"Do you have your script?"

Brad reached into his suit pocket and brought out the speech he'd written the night before. "I sure do."

The man handed him a water bottle. "Okay, clear your voice, hum a tune, take a sip of water, jerk off and do whatever the fuck else you need to do before you perform your starring role."

Brad screwed off the cap on the bottle and took a long sip.

"I need to know more about this before I do it."

The man frowned at him. The whiskers of his beard seemed to bristle at Brad's assertion, and his eyes were as cold as ice. The man looked to be about fifty years of age. He was well over six feet tall and had long stringy hair, which coordinated with the beard to create an image reminiscent of the hippie era. He squinted and just stared back at Brad with his jet-black eyes.

"What do you need to know?"

"All I was given was this address, that stupid sentence that I had to repeat, and asked to prepare an announcement. I've done all that, but now I need to know what we're doing."

The man sniffed, and then coughed. Both reactions exaggerated.

"I worked with Sean many years ago. Covert stuff. I still do covert stuff, but off the grid now, and totally volunteer. I'm with an international organization called Anonymous. You've probably heard of us and, if so, you already know that I can't, and won't, tell you my name. Everything we do is illegal. And what I'm about to do with you is also illegal. You and I could both do heavy time in prison, if caught. Do you get my drift?"

Brad nodded. "I understand, and that doesn't bother me."

"Sean told me you'd say that. And he probably didn't tell you very much, because there's not much you have to do. You just read out your little speech, and I'll do the rest. Today, I'm just going to record you. No one will recognize your voice. It'll be digitally disguised. Do you want to sound like a man, or a woman?"

"Keep me as a man. And make me sound presidential."

"That's appropriate, considering what we're hacking into."

Brad took another long sip. "All Sean told me was that we would be accessing a national network."

The hippie laughed. "An understatement, my dear sir. We're going to hack into the United States Emergency Alert System. A mechanism which allows the President to make announcements to all citizens over normal broadcasting channels. We'll also be tapping into the Commercial Mobile Alert System, which targets smartphones. No one will be immune to our mischief. The FCC requires all broadcast stations to install and maintain EAS decoders and encoders at their control points. As a result, no matter what TV show, movie, soap opera, or porn smut is being broadcast at the time, EAS broadcasts take precedence. Everything gets pre-empted for EAS announcements. So, for as long as we can maintain it, your voice will be all anyone will hear."

Brad shook his head in amazement. "Have you done this before?"

The hippie chuckled. "Oh, yeah. Many times. The best was a couple of years ago when we made an announcement about the zombie apocalypse. Scared the shit out of people, broadcasting about corpses coming alive and crawling out of graves. We did that just for fun, and to show we could do it. Just last year, we hacked in again, cutting off all prime time shows. But, we didn't make an announcement that time—we were testing out our equipment. It was just dead silence."

"Can't they shut you off?"

"Yes, that's why you have to speak quickly in your announcement, and make sure you get the most important stuff into the speech as soon as possible. No time for fancy words or pontificating. We stay on as long as we can."

"Can you be traced?"

"They try, but very seldom succeed. We're very good at what we do. In reality, the best they can do is cut us off."

"When will this happen?"

"Sean told me it's to go live a week Sunday. I haven't been given a time yet. I'll wait for his green light on that and I'll be on standby all day. He's coordinating, as you know, with two other events: one being something down in Denver, and the other being a demonstration in New York. He's chosen Sunday because of the crowds of people that will be picnicking and frolicking in Central Park."

"Did he fill you in on what we're doing?"

The man nodded. "Yeah. Look, buddy, I may appear to be gruff and unfriendly—I'm not, I'm just cautious and jaded. I like what you're doing, and it's long overdue. At Anonymous, this is the kind of thing we support. We're as illegal as you can get, but sometimes you have to break the law to catch the lawbreakers. That's our philosophy, and we're proud of it."

Brad held out his hand. "Thanks. The world needs more people like you. Will you do me the honor of shaking my hand?"

The hippie smiled. "Sure, Mr. Crawford. Go get 'em."

They shook hands, and Brad unfolded his speech. "Should I start?"

The man punched a button on the console. "You're good to go. Remember, speak clearly but quickly."

Brad leaned forward and put his lips close to the microphone.

He began speaking, clearly and quickly.

Chapter 42

Sean steered the military Jeep through the security zone, and right onto the tarmac of the Laramie Regional Airport, at Laramie, Wyoming. It had only been a quick ninety-minute drive from the Denver Airport in the adjoining state of Colorado.

The weather was perfect, so he expected the jet to arrive at the ETA indicated in the flight plan.

He jumped out of the Jeep, along with his companion, a young Air Force captain named Jeremy Ryder. They walked quickly into the secure area adjoining one of the two runways, and waited.

The captain stood quietly for a few moments beside Sean. Then he shuffled his feet nervously and spoke in a respectful tone. "Sir, do you anticipate any trouble?"

"No, not at all. They're not expecting anything. We'll take them into custody, and then head back to Denver."

"What were they planning to do?"

Sean glanced at the young officer. He was clean-shaven, had bright blue eyes, and was around thirty years of age. Probably as naïve and robotically obedient as the rest of the Air Force clones.

"Son, they're enemies of the state. That's all you need to know."

"Yes, sir."

Then Sean saw it. The gleaming white Challenger jet, swooping in from over the mountains on the horizon. The pilot guided it down onto the runway without even a double-hop.

He marvelled at how smooth the landing was. Brock was one skilled pilot, just like his dad.

The high elevations, updrafts, and mountain barriers created serious challenges for pilots; so much so that most private pilots avoided airports in this kind of terrain.

The plane taxied to the end of the runway, then turned off into the private plane compound area. Within just a few minutes, Brock and Ziv climbed out of the plane and started walking towards the tiny terminal building.

Sean turned to the captain. "Let's go. We'll nab them before they get inside."

They both started jogging towards the two new arrivals.

Brock noticed them first and grabbed Ziv by the arm, pulling him to a stop. He said something to him and they both turned around and started running back to the plane.

Sean yelled out. "Stop right there! We'll fire!"

Brock and Ziv halted dead in their tracks and raised their hands slowly into the air.

Sean and Jeremy caught up to them, and Sean pulled a sheet of paper out of his pocket, scanning it quickly.

He looked up at the two men. "Brock Winters and Ziv Dayan. You are being arrested under the Patriot Act. You have no right to legal counsel until a preliminary hearing is held in military court. At that time, it will be determined whether or not there is sufficient reason to continue to detain you. This officer will now take you into custody under the authority of the United States of America."

He turned to Jeremy. "Cuff them, son."

Jeremy looked puzzled, and whispered. "Uh, sir, do you know who that is?"

"Of course I do. It doesn't matter how famous he is. He's engaged in seditious activities, along with his friend here who is a former Mossad agent. Cuff them!"

"But, sir, this is high profile. I think I need to consult with my commander."

Sean growled at the young officer. "As far as Denver's concerned, your commander reports to me, which means you report to me. Do you understand, soldier?"

Jeremy raised his hand and saluted. "Yes, sir!"

"Cuff 'em. Now!"

Brock and Ziv cooperated by putting their hands behind their backs. Jeremy quickly slipped handcuffs on both men, and snapped them into place.

Finally, Brock spoke. "I don't think you have any idea what you're doing here. This could turn out very bad for you. I know people."

"I'm sure you do, Mr. Movie Star. Do I look worried? Get going— over to that Jeep. We'll be taking a little drive, so you might as well try to relax."

Ziv spit on the ground in front of Sean.

"You're using the Patriot Act to arrest us? That's about as undemocratic as it gets. If you were confident of the charges against us, you'd let us call our lawyers."

"You don't get to call lawyers when you're charged under the Patriot Act. That's the beauty of it. Get moving, Mr. Dayan. We're wasting time here."

*****

The drive back to Denver took about two hours and the prisoners sat silent and sullen in the rear seat, hands secured behind their backs.

Sean guided the Jeep around to a secluded rear entrance of the massive airport. They walked across the driveway and he scanned his entry card at the door.

They stepped into a tiny foyer, which was really just an elevator entrance. He flashed his card again, and pressed a specific button displaying an airplane icon.

The elevator went down, arriving quickly at its underground destination. They exited, and led Brock and Ziv down a long hallway. Sean flashed his card again, and a door opened to an expansive reception area.

Sean turned to Jeremy. "Hold them here."

He walked up to a uniformed female officer seated behind a large counter.

"These are the two new arrivals I filed papers on. Brock Winters and Ziv Dayan. The network should already show them pre-registered."

She looked up at him, eyes wide with excitement.

"Director Russell, is that tall one the actor, Brock Winters?"

Sean smiled. "Yes. Try to control yourself."

She giggled, and turned her attention to the computer.

"Yes, I see that they're signed in already. You've assigned them to this block?"

"Yes. Brock's father, Hal, is our chief flight instructor here. I want these two in the same section as Hal. So, this air terminal block is where they must be. Good for morale. We need Hal motivated and engaged for the important work he's doing.

"Having his son and his friend here should do wonders for his state of mind. The psychologists have already been asked to keep a close eye on them, to see how the interaction affects moods."

"You're the boss, sir."

She squinted as she looked at the computer screen.

"I see we have two empty suites along the same corridor as Hal Winters. Would you like them to be that close?"

"Yes, absolutely. The closer the better."

She performed a few keystrokes, then proudly announced. "Okay, done. I'll have someone escort them down."

Sean winked at her. "You're the best. Thanks."

He started to walk away, but he heard her call out to him in a soft hesitant voice.

"Sir?"

Sean turned around. "Yes? Something else?"

She smiled shyly. "Would it be...improper...for me to ask... Brock for his autograph?"

Sean laughed. "No problem, Lieutenant. He may not be in the mood to agree, but no harm in asking."

Chapter 43

Kurt Bongard was enjoying the day. It was one of those magnificent days that made you glad to be living in New York City. While the city was always busy, and he cursed the traffic just like every other typical New Yorker, a day like this made it all worthwhile. Beautiful blue sky, the blazing sun gleaming off the glass skyscrapers, and all topped off with a nice fall breeze clearing out the usual city smog.

Yes, he hoped next Sunday would be a picture-perfect day just like today.

He drove his Ford F150 pickup truck along the Lincoln Tunnel toll road to the rhythm of a golden oldie by the Lovin' Spoonful playing on the radio. He bobbed his head and shoulders from side to side, singing the catchy lyrics.

Indeed, next Sunday had to be just like today. Because, if it was, it would mean that he would have hundreds if not thousands of people in the audience.

Who wouldn't want to be in Central Park on a sunny Sunday afternoon?

Kurt turned north onto the Henry Hudson Parkway. He could sense that he had a wide smile on his face and thought that it was such a shame no one else could see it.

He pushed down on the power window buttons and enjoyed the rush of the breeze sweeping through the truck. He chuckled, thinking that now some lucky soul might be able to enjoy his soulful singing.

Kurt swung his gleaming white truck east on 97th Street and then south on West Drive. Then he turned off onto a service road and into a parking lot reserved for utility vehicles.

Today Kurt's truck was a utility vehicle. The side panels were wrapped in plastic, identifying it as belonging to New York City Parks and Recreation.

Tonight, back at the garage, the plastic wrap would come off and a new one would go on, transforming the truck into one that toiled for an alarm and security company. Then, Wednesday, Kurt knew that his schedule required him to "start a career" with a local gas company—just for the day.

But, next Sunday, his chameleon truck would once again become a parks and recreation vehicle, and it would be parked back here in this exact same lot.

Except that it would be a lot busier then. It would be, after all, a Sunday. And today was only a boring and quiet Monday. People were far too busy at work and school to be out having fun in the park today.

Which made today a perfect day to do what it was he had to do.

Kurt jumped out of the truck, adjusting his official coveralls and donning his official cap. Then he walked to the back and lowered the lift. He carefully pulled his large wheelbarrow out of the back and lowered it to the ground. It had a custom-designed casing around the top, which snapped on and off. This normally kept dirt and leaves from blowing back onto the ground on windy days, but today its sole purpose was to hide the precious cargo that was contained inside.

He pushed the wheelbarrow at a leisurely pace along the service road and past the tennis courts. He arrived at a grove of trees just northwest of The Reservoir, now known officially as The Jacqueline Kennedy Onassis Reservoir.

It had been renamed in Jackie's honor in 1994, and Kurt thought that sounded a hell of a lot better than just, The Reservoir. Plus, he'd been a fan of Jackie, being that—in his mind anyway—she was the last class act who had graced the title of First Lady. No one since had even come close.

And no one had come close to the caliber of her husband in the Oval Office, either. JFK had been the last truly honest president, in Kurt's opinion. He marveled at how the man had steadfastly rejected the Pentagon's horrific plan to murder Americans and terrorize cities back in 1963—he'd stared them down and torn the Operation Northwoods plan to shreds with his bare hands. In fact, JFK was so horrified that they could even dream up such a diabolical idea, that he fired all of the Joint Chiefs.

Kurt knew in his gut, though, that no president since Kennedy had had the guts to say no to the Pentagon. And of course, Kennedy had paid for his "negativism" several months later with a bullet in the head.

That was probably why, from that day forward, not one single president had found the courage to say no to the Pentagon. Keeping your head intact was a good motivator.

Kurt stopped his wheelbarrow in a clearing just to the north of the tree grove and raised his hand to shield his eyes. He looked out over the massive 106-acre reservoir and the one and a half mile jogging track that encircled it.

Then he gazed south towards the heart of Central Park—the area just east of the Bethesda Terrace. Strawberry Fields was in that general area, too, along with a zoo, picnic areas, amusement rides, and boat rentals in some of the smaller lakes.

Kurt's target was located there, too.

His strong and grizzled hands snapped the plastic cover off the wheelbarrow. Hands that had spent a good part of their lives—the part Kurt wished he had back—flying Black Hawk helicopters. His years in the Delta Force had come to a horrifying end back in October, 1993, a time that had been immortalized in the movie, *Black Hawk Down*. A terrifying movie for sure, but it hadn't even come close to capturing the horror of that time, in Kurt's mind.

The Battle of Mogadishu was the disastrous end to Operation Gothic Serpent. Kurt chuckled as he thought how appropriate that was—the Pentagon had a twisted sense of humor, the same sense of humor they'd exhibited when they named 9/11 Operation Avalanche.

Somalia was just another stupid attempt at regime change—and most of Kurt's comrades in Delta and the Rangers agreed years later that it was nothing short of idiocy to try to change the regime in a country such as Somalia. A country that had been lawless even under the best of leaders. And why even bother to begin with? Who cared? What strategic advantage did it have? Why didn't they just leave these countries the fuck alone?

It had taken Kurt several years to allow the blind patriotism to leave his system, and to stop the gung-ho "Go get 'em boys!" anthem from ringing in his eardrums. The memory of eighteen of his friends being massacred by blood-hungry militiamen was deep in his gray cells now, replacing all of the patriotic crap that he'd been fed when risking his life for one useless cause after another. The beauty of brainwashing was that it faded with time, faded when the brain was no longer punished with the repetitious pounding of orders, commands, and angry rhetoric.

Kurt felt that he was almost a normal human being again now. It might take a few more years, but he'd get there. Well, it was now twenty-two years later, and his grizzled hands no longer flew Black Hawk helicopters.

He pulled the contraption out of the wheelbarrow and set it on the ground.

No, now his hands were flying a different type of aircraft. And this one didn't need a pilot sacrificing his life.

Kurt gave the little drone an admiring once-over. A marvelous little invention, about four feet long and six inches wide. Painted a brilliant white, and shaped like a cylinder. No propellers on this baby, no sir. This one was propelled by liquid nitrogen, basically a little jet engine.

This was not your garden variety drone. Not the type Dad and Johnny could pick up at the local department store. No, this was a Pentagon version—a miniature of the types that were wreaking havoc every day in the Middle East.

The good thing about these drones was that they were small and easy to steal. And Sean Russell had steered Kurt in exactly the right direction to get his hands on this one.

Kurt was glad to be of service—of course he was being paid well for this little assignment, but for Sean he would have done it for free anyway. The cause was a good one, and it was about time. Kurt had always admired Sean's courage throughout the twenty plus years they'd been friends, but this time he was kicking the moon to mars. And Kurt loved being a part of it, albeit just a small part.

He'd managed these little drones before, on some assignments he preferred to forget. And he'd also handled the special equipment these tiny monsters were equipped with.

A hologram projector.

Kurt flipped a button on the side of the drone, which started a whirring noise. Nothing would happen yet, though, until he commanded it to happen.

He pulled a thin console from an inner pocket of his coveralls and flipped open the lid. Turned it on, and punched in some coordinates. Then he tapped his finger onto an image icon—up popped several windows. He tapped his forefinger on the one he wanted, and smiled with satisfaction as he saw it embrace his screen. He clicked Save, and exited back to the main control screen.

Ready for launch!

Today, he would put this thing through its paces, and save those paces in memory for next Sunday. All he'd have to do that day was set it loose and it would remember what to do. Well, he would have to do one more thing on Sunday as well—order it to project the image that he'd selected. He wouldn't do that today, though. The surprise was scheduled for next Sunday, when joggers would be jogging, boaters would be boating, and picnickers would be picnicking. Hundreds of them—and including lower Manhattan itself, maybe a few thousand.

And the beauty of it was, no one would be killed or maimed by this little airborne vehicle like back in Somalia. Or like back on 9/11. People would merely be shocked, perhaps scared, and maybe a bit morbidly entertained.

And hopefully awakened.

The drone would soar over the lake, down to Strawberry Fields, and then on to its final target.

Alice in Wonderland.

Located just north of the Conservatory Water, a statue of Alice stood eleven feet tall, resplendent in bronze, surrounded by the Mad Hatter, the White Rabbit, and a few of her other silly little friends.

The sculpture was erected in 1959 to enrich the visits of children to Central Park—to allow them to experience the wonder of Lewis Carroll's classic story. Alice was the centerpiece of the artwork, sitting on a giant mushroom and reaching toward a pocket watch held by her bunny friend. Peering over her shoulder was the Cheshire Cat, accompanied by the Dormouse, Dinah, and the Mad Hatter.

Kurt thought that Sean's choice of target was pure genius. The irony of having the drone end its journey by smashing into Alice's bronzed head, was perfect. Because the fantastical images of Alice in Wonderland meshed perfectly with the fantastical images of 9/11. Alice in Wonderland was a mirage, a drug-induced journey at worst and a hazy dream at best, that bore no relation to reality.

Just like 9/11 was a mirage that bore no relation to reality. But, instead of being a hazy dream, 9/11 was a clear and vivid nightmare for the people of New York City.

The crashing of the drone into Alice's head was just the tip of the iceberg. Because beyond the tip was a mirage. The powerful hologram projector installed inside the drone would transmit the image of a Boeing 767 jetliner. No one would see the drone—instead, what they'd see soaring over Central Park would be the realistic image of a jumbo jet, so real that most people would duck or dive to the ground. Because this thing would be flying low. Low enough for them to grasp the enormity of it—159 feet in length, a wingspan of 156 feet, and a fuselage almost twenty feet high. They would see the image of a 176,000-pound jet soaring just over their heads, hiding the little drone that was powering it.

And, on its death run, just like the holograms on 9/11, it would swoop down and disappear into its target.

But, instead of tearing into a structural steel tower like a knife through butter, this jumbo jet would crash into Alice Kingsley's head—and then simply disappear.

The Mad Hatter might indeed be angry that day. And perhaps little children would even be lucky enough, in the realm of their imaginations, to hear him mutter in his inimitable way: "There is a place like no other on earth. A land full of wonder, mystery, and danger. Some say to survive it you have to be as mad as a hatter. Which luckily I am."

Chapter 44

"You've probably noticed that we don't have any grocery stores here. All of your meals will be taken in the dining room. We'll be passing by that in just a few minutes.

"The complex is divided up into different blocks. This block is known as the Hangar block, because of its connection to the aircraft wing. And each block has its own eating facilities, entertainment, things like that."

Ziv couldn't resist a comment. "Do you have McDonald's down here?"

The girl glanced into the backseat of the golf cart and laughed.

"No, but I've heard about those places from some of the more recent arrivals. They make really good hamburgers in the dining room, though. And all of the convenience stores also sell things like hamburgers and hot dogs, in case you get hungry in the evening."

She guided the golf cart around some cyclists who weren't staying in the inner lane. Then she turned left and pointed.

"There's the restaurant just down that side street. All of your meals are free, but those magnetic cards I gave you will be loaded with credits when you complete chores. So keep those cards with you at all times. You can use the credits for things like the convenience shops, movie theater, bars, and nightclubs, and—brothels."

Ziv nudged Brock's arm. Then he teased the girl with another question. "Do you work in the brothel?"

The girl laughed. "No, not me. But, there are lots of nice girls there who would just love to meet handsome men like you."

"Are you a prisoner here, or an employee?"

"We like to think of ourselves as *residents*."

"But, you can't leave."

"No, but there's no reason to leave. I have everything I want here. I was five years old when I was brought here. I don't remember much else."

"How old are you now?"

"I just turned twenty-two."

"Your parents?"

"I don't remember them."

Ziv rested his chin on the top of the front seat back. "Weren't they brought here with you?"

She turned her head, and Ziv could see conflict in her eyes—kind of a sad confusion. "I don't want to talk about them, okay?"

"Okay."

Brock had been silent for the entire tour so far. They hadn't yet been escorted to their rooms and he was clearly anxious to get this part of the day over with. Ziv knew Brock was interested in only one thing—seeing his father. So, he sat sullen and silent, barely looking at the myriad of sights they were being treated to.

As for Ziv, he couldn't believe his eyes. Seeing hordes of people cycling along, earphones connected to their iPods, listening to their favorite tunes. Some had smiles on their faces, others just looked stoic.

The tunnel roadway was wide, more than capable of accommodating cyclists, golf carts, and little kids throwing balls around. Each enterprise along the way was brightly lit. The bars and nightclubs were flashing tacky neon, and he even saw one doorway that advertised a casino.

"Hey, what's your name?"

"Wendy."

"Hi, Wendy. I'm Ziv, and my friend's name is Brock."

"I know. I have your registration information. "

"Tell me, how do people bet in the casino? There's no money down here."

"Oh, you just use the credits on your card. And any winnings get loaded onto your card. So, your credits can multiply fast, if you're lucky."

"Are there ever any riots down here?"

"Oh, God no. There's nowhere to go, and most people are content anyway."

"Don't you miss seeing the sun and the blue sky?"

Wendy looked back at Ziv again. "No, not really. I can't even remember what that looks like, except for what they show us on TV and in the theater."

"So, you get to watch TV down here?"

"They select the shows for us, and the movies. No news, though. Except for the news that happens down here, and we get to read about that in the *Emerald City Clarion*."

"That can't be a hell of a lot."

"You'd be surprised. Some things are interesting to learn about."

"Has anyone ever tried to escape?"

Wendy shook her head. "Not that I know of. And if anyone did, they'd probably end up down in the prison."

Of course, Ziv already knew that Hal and two other inmates had attempted an escape, but obviously that news didn't make the Emerald City Clarion.

He rubbed his tired eyes. "How come you're so articulate?"

"We have schools here. I graduated from high school just this year. Might take a degree course next year in biochemistry, when they start those classes in the university.

"Why?"

She looked back at him, puzzled. "To advance myself, of course— to have a future. I can get a better job, and earn more credits."

"And what would you spend those credits on? Male strippers? Gigolos? Booze? Drugs?"

"Oh, no! God, no!"

Ziv couldn't help himself. "Well, what happy stuff would you spend your credits on? You can't buy a house down here, or even a car. You can't fly away on vacation. So, what would you do with more credits?"

Wendy shrugged her shoulders and went silent.

Brock nudged Ziv to get his attention. He frowned and shook his head, mouthing the word, "Stop."

Ziv nodded. Brock was right. He had to admit to himself that his frustration with this sweet girl's naivety had caused him to put her on the spot too much.

She reminded him of the women in the movie, *The Stepford Wives*, and he was finding all of this far too surreal to even believe it was happening literally right under America's nose.

He leaned forward again. "Do you recognize my friend here?"

Wendy pulled a U-turn at a dead end in the road, and started heading back the way they'd come. She swiveled her head and took a good hard look at Brock.

"No, not really. Should I?"

"This is Brock Winters. He's a big movie star."

She took another look. "Really? That's nice."

"You don't recall seeing movies with Brock in them?"

"No. But, most of the movies they show us are really old: *Mary Poppins, Gone with the Wind, The Sound of Music*. You know, nice ones like those."

"I see."

Brock cleared his throat and spoke to the girl for the first time.

"I think we've had enough of this tour. Could you take us to our rooms, please?"

Wendy nodded. "Yes, I've shown you all you need to see for now. If you need more information from me later, just use the internal phone in your room. Press the Concierge button, and you'll get me.

"I can come pick you up and take you wherever you need to go if you can't walk or ride your bike. And there are others who do the same job as me, so if you don't get me, you'll get someone else who's just as nice."

"I'm sure. Right now, I just want to see my father."

Wendy turned her head and stared into Brock's blue eyes.

"Yes, I have no doubt about that. He doesn't know you're here yet, so you can surprise him. Hal is such a nice man—everyone loves him."

She directed her attention back to the road and continued talking.

"Your bikes will be parked in front of your rooms, so you can use those to get around most places. Your dad's room is number twenty-one. Mr. Winters, your room is number nine—and Mr. Dayan, you're in number seven."

"So, I can just walk down and see my dad? I don't need permission?"

Wendy laughed. "Of course! Emerald City is very casual and sociable. You'll make lots of friends here, and you can stay up as late as you want, too; go for walks or bike rides whenever you get the urge. Or go to the bars. It's a very nice atmosphere."

Brock grunted. "Let's hurry, okay? Step on the gas."

She shook her head. "Sorry, but this is as fast as this cart goes. We'll be there soon. Oh, you two will be glad to know that the choices for dinner tonight are roast duck or rack of lamb. Yum! What do you think of that?"

Brock grunted again. "Yum."

Chapter 45

Brock and Ziv walked side by side down the claustrophobic tunnel.

First at a rapid pace, but then Brock felt his feet start to slow the closer they got to his dad's room. He saw it just up ahead—he could make out the illuminated number twenty-one.

Then he just stopped walking and leaned his back up against the wall of the tunnel.

Lowered his head and put his right hand over his left chest.

Ziv gently squeezed the actor's shoulder. "Brock, are you okay?"

Brock nodded. He could feel sharp little pains in his chest, but he'd had those before. Usually every time he had to make a public appearance.

Performing in front of the camera never bothered him, but making speeches and enduring the formalities of Hollywood always caused him stress. And performing live theater usually made him retch.

It was just anxiety and, in the absence of drugs, he knew how to deal with it. Deep breaths and slow exhales.

He lifted his head and stood up as straight as he could. Then breathed in through his nose, held it for a few seconds and let it out slowly through his mouth. Brock did several repetitions of this until he started to feel better.

The chest pains finally subsided and his breathing returned to normal.

"I'm okay, Ziv. Just an anxiety attack."

"Boy, I never would have figured you for those."

"Yeah, I know. The big, confident movie star persona, huh? Believe it or not, a lot of us have this problem. That's why there's so much of a drug culture in Hollywood. Chases the anxiety away.

"If I wasn't in this place right now, I probably would have just snorted some cocaine to make it all better. But—this deep breathing is a much healthier way, and I'm going to try to fucking get used to this from now on, instead."

"Are you nervous about seeing your father?"

"Yep. It's been years, Ziv. I can't even recall how many. He's been in this shithole for four years and I haven't seen him since he's been here."

"And he was in that Georgia prison for ten years before that. I only saw him a couple of times when he was there, I'm ashamed to say. It was selfish of me—it made me sad to see him locked up like that. I didn't consider that it would make him happy to see me. I only cared about how depressed it made *me* feel."

Ziv patted him on the back. "I think that's a normal reaction. Don't beat yourself up over it. I'm betting he understands."

Brock nodded. "I hope so."

"Ready to do this?"

Brock pushed himself off the wall. "Yeah, let's do it."

They finished the walk together, the remaining few steps even slower than before. When they reached room number twenty-one Ziv stopped and wrapped his arm around Brock's shoulders.

"You go in alone. I'll wait out here. When you're ready, come get me."

Brock placed his big hand around the back of Ziv's neck and squeezed gently. "Thanks, man."

He raised his fist and knocked on the door.

A familiar voice answered, in a gruff tone. "Come in. It's open."

Brock opened the door and entered, quickly closing it behind him.

His father was sitting hunched over a little table in the corner, playing solitaire. The music on his radio was playing softly and he didn't even raise his head when he spoke.

"I'm not gonna do dinner tonight, Cliff. Go on without me."

Brock smiled. "I've gone to dinner far too often without you, old man. Time to change that."

Hal looked up and aimed his piercing blue eyes into Brock's

piercing blue eyes. He didn't say another word. He jumped out of his chair like a spry thirty-year-old, and rushed at him.

They embraced for the longest time without uttering a sound. Brock actually lifted his father into the air at one point; he could tell that he'd lost a lot of weight.

But—he looked good, so darn good he couldn't believe it.

They pulled back from each other. Hal planted a big kiss on Brock's cheek, and cupped his face in his still strong hands.

"What on earth are you doing here? Did they agree to let you visit me?"

"No, I'm a prisoner just like you now."

Brock walked over to his dad's little radio and turned up the volume.

He then explained what was going on, how the arrests had been faked by Sean Russell to get him and Ziv into the twisted world of Emerald City. And that Sean had some kind of escape plan that he hadn't told them about yet.

Hal backed up a few paces, and held his arms out wide.

"Let me look at you. My, you look grand! My boy, the famous movie star!"

Brock laughed, and held his arms out wide, too.

"My dad, the famous killer!"

They both laughed together and hugged again. Brock's big, tough dad started to cry. He raised his hand and wiped the tears away from Hal's cheek with the knuckle of his index finger.

"Don't cry, Dad. Everything's okay now."

Hal sniffed and wiped his sleeve across his face.

"I didn't think I'd ever see you again. Thought I was going to just die in here. I tried to escape a while ago, but as you can tell, it didn't work."

"I heard. Not surprised that you would try. Well, you're gonna try again, Dad, and this time you'll have us to help."

"How are your mom and the boys?"

"Oh, they're okay. We don't talk very often."

Hal nodded. "And your career?"

"Goin' good—but it's kind of an empty life. I'm rich, but who cares. No one cares about me, so it doesn't seem worth it."

"I care about you, son. And, someday, someone else will, too. Give it time. Hang out with the right people."

"Yeah, but first we have to get you outta here."

Hal smiled warmly. "I can't believe I'm looking at you—right here, right now."

Brock hugged his dad again, and started crying himself.

"I...had...an...attack...out in the hallway."

"I know you did. I had one myself just before you walked in. Thought you were getting on stage or something in Los Angeles. I felt your pain."

Brock smiled. "We're still soulmates, aren't we?"

"Always will be, son. Just one of those nice things in life. And there ain't many nice things left."

"We'll change that."

Hal frowned. "Brock, I love that you're here, but this is so damn dangerous. Whatever Sean's plan is, it's bound to have some risk to it. I'm used to that, but you're not."

"I don't care, Dad. I have to help get you out of this place. And someone has to break this thing wide open. They can't get away with this abomination—and that's what this is, a cruel abomination."

"It is." Hal shook his head, as if trying to shake the thought away. "So, when do I meet your friend?"

"Right now—he's waiting out in the tunnel."

Brock opened the door and waved Ziv in.

He walked right up to Hal with no hesitation, and held out his hand. "Pleased to finally meet the legend. I'm Ziv Dayan."

Hal shook his hand and smiled warmly.

"I know who you are. Mossad. The bastards killed your wife, but you tracked them down and got them. Good for you—I applauded that day."

Ziv nodded. "Wow, you are tapped in. Yes. That was a long time ago, but it's one of those things you never really forget."

"Thanks for teaming up with my son. Much appreciated."

Brock was standing off to the side while Hal and Ziv talked. He took a real good look at his dad for the first time since he'd opened that door.

Hal looked older than he remembered, but that was to be expected after all these years. But, he also looked a lot better than he'd expected, which warmed his heart.

Hal had kept himself in tremendous shape—not an ounce of fat, shoulders still wide and strong, with arms and hands that looked like they could still tear a crocodile to pieces.

But what he noticed the most was contained within his dad's face—lines that weren't there before, and eyes that seemed to have lost their fire. Still blue as the sky, but they lacked the spark Brock remembered so fondly. Maybe he'd get that wonderful spark back once they were out of this shit-hole.

Suddenly, the door opened and two uniformed officers walked in. Hal scowled at them.

"Don't you fuckers ever knock?"

The lead soldier ignored the comment.

"The three of you must come with us. Right now, please."

Chapter 46

Sean slid his access card through the reader, then opened the door that led him down the long corridor to the hangar area. Using his card one more time, another door opened into the cavernous aircraft storage area. It never failed to amaze him; almost every type of plane imaginable was stored in here. From small private jets to massive jumbos, helicopter gunships to stealth bombers. There had to be at least 100 aircraft stored in here now. The hangar was a mile wide and a half mile deep, and it was always a hive of activity.

This was the maintenance area for the planes, as well as the central control for dispatch. Here was where the planes were prepped for flight, and decisions were made as to which planes would fly.

Unless someone like Sean intervened, of course, which meant the decisions were his and his alone.

He wasn't here all that often though, being based back in Langley, Virginia. So most of the cycles were determined by the crew chief. Sometimes, though, Sean would have a particular type of plane that he wanted tested and put through its paces, so he would e-mail his requisitions in from Langley.

Today, he wouldn't have to e-mail anything—he would just command.

He strode into the dispatcher's office. As soon as he entered, Colonel Matt Weston jumped to his feet and saluted.

"Matt, knock it off with the salute. Why do all you guys keep saluting me? I'm not military."

Matt dropped his hand and a sheepish grin came over his face. "Sorry, Sean. Force of habit. We salute the person in charge, and we're not used to a non-military person being in charge of our military lives."

Sean laughed. "I understand. I'm just teasing you. However, maybe next time you could just bow slightly—or perhaps polish my shoes?"

Matt frowned. "Don't push your luck, buddy!"

"Could I have some of that rancid coffee, Matt?"

Matt picked up the pot and poured a full cup. "Still take it black? And, in this case, since it's been kept hot for four hours, slightly slushy?"

Sean made a face. "Yuk. It'll have to do, I guess."

"So, what brings you down this way again, Sean?"

"Oh, just a little business here regarding a couple of new guests I brought in. Also, we're reaching critical with the tests on "Shroud." I understand they went well on the Stealth bombers in the last couple of weeks?"

"Yeah, Hal Winters took one up just last week as a matter of fact. Test went amazingly well. At an altitude of 2,000 feet the plane simply disappeared. We're continuing to tweak it for lower altitudes. The engineers are going full tilt on that for us."

Sean smiled. "Those guys are brilliant, aren't they? They've taken invisibility to a whole new level—if we hadn't taken those guys off Flight MH370, we'd be years behind the eight ball."

"Roger that! I can't believe how good they are. We make sure they get special privileges here that the others don't get. Room service, things like that—and not just room service for food, if you know what I mean."

Sean nodded. "I know what you mean. Good. Keep them happy. This is the only place in the U.S. where this kind of technology is being tested right now, and it's all due to them."

"What can I do for you today, Sean?"

"Well, I'm flying back to Virginia tomorrow and I want to outline to you the type of flight schedule I need to see carried out over the next few days. Use whatever planes you wish to use until Saturday, to test out the lower altitude cloaking. But, don't bother Hal with any of those tests—he needs a bit of a rest."

"Okay, no problem. I'll e-mail you about how the tests go."

"Yes, please do. But, the big test I want you to prepare for is this coming Sunday. We've never tested this cloaking technology on a jumbo jet before, and it's about time we did that. I want to at least get a preliminary idea as to the level of protection that Shroud gives to a plane that size."

Matt frowned. "Do you think we're ready?"

"Well, we won't know until we try. Hand me the inventory list there, Matt, and I'll pick a plane."

Matt pulled a binder out of a drawer in his desk and handed it to Sean. "We have a great 747 ready to go. That would be a good test."

"No, at this stage I don't want to test a plane with a two-level cabin. We'll try that sort of test later."

Sean scanned the list using his index finger as a guide. He was looking for a specific plane. "Aw, this looks like a good one. Yes, I want this plane, no other. It's been retrofitted already, too—all the seats have been removed, so it's really just a cargo plane. It's lighter now, so it should use less fuel and gain height quicker—which is an important part of testing the reaction time of Shroud."

"Which one do you want, Sean?"

"Write this down, Matt—Boeing 767, Tail number N612UA, manufacturer's #cn21873/41."

Sean tossed the binder back on top of the desk.

Matt was writing on his notepad. "The tail number's been painted over now, you know that, don't you?"

"Yeah, all those 9/11 planes are military green now. But, the tail number might still be displayed in the engine compartment, usually on a plaque. And, the manufacturer's number must also show on the inside of the fuselage. I want to know that the plane you're using is the plane I selected, so just ensure that this is all documented properly."

"No problem. I believe in proper documentation, too."

"I don't want this plane up in the air too long, either, Matt. So you'll have to make that clear to Hal. And, since it will be a short flight, don't forget to keep the fuel in the tanks shallow—thinking no more than twenty percent full? Would be dangerous to have them land back here with almost full tanks. And, don't forget to get one of our Shroud units installed."

Matt's face made a mock pout. "Now, Sean. Give me some credit, huh? No point sending the plane up without the technology. I'm not daft, you know!"

"Sorry—as you know, I'm kind of a detail freak."

"I understand, don't worry. So, what time do you want the flight scheduled for on Sunday?"

"Let's go for 1:00 p.m., mountain time. Doable?"

"Very doable. Leave it with me. And I'll let you know how the test on that one goes, too."

Sean stood up and shook Matt's hand. "We'll do this handshake thing from now on instead of that stupid salute, promise?"

Colonel Matt Weston smiled broadly. "I promise. I'm sick of tapping my temple anyway. It's getting kinda sore!"

Chapter 47

It was a long walk down one more antiseptic corridor until Sean got to the door he wanted. He stopped, then glanced quickly in each direction. Swiped his card and ducked in. Hit the switch on the wall, and the room illuminated. A room the size of a football field, filled to the brim with accordion folders on multi-tiered shelving units.

This room held the personal identification documents for the 10,000 or so prisoners of Emerald City.

He strolled along the alphabetical rows of shelves until he reached the letter D. It took only a few minutes to find Ziv Dayan's folder. Sean reached inside and withdrew his passport, credit cards and driver's license.

His next hike was down to the *W* section, which was pretty much at the other end. He scanned the lower tiers, and then cursed when he realized the Winters would be on an upper shelf close to the ceiling.

Sean wandered along several rows until he found a ladder cart. Wheeled it back and set it up in the W aisle. He climbed to the top, and then pushed himself and the cart along until he came to the files he wanted. Removed the identification documents for Hal and Brock and climbed down the ladder again. He then moved it back to the aisle where he'd found it.

He made his way to the exit and marveled at how quiet and deserted it was in this place. It was a room that people only came to put things in—no one ever came to take things out. Because the people who were documented in this room would never have the need for their passports, driver's licenses, and credit cards again—ever.

Sean was surprised at what little guilt he was feeling about all of this. In fact, truth be told, he wasn't feeling any guilt at all. Instead, he felt energized, for the first time in years. It felt like there was a purpose to his life again, like he was finally doing something that was vitally important. And righteous.

He was well aware that what he and the others were doing was dangerous as hell, but that didn't bother him either. He was desensitized, of course, because he'd been doing dangerous things his whole career.

But, this particular danger felt better—it felt like the right kind of danger. He was risking his life to right several serious wrongs, and if he died doing it he would at least have some kind of legacy that he could look up at from Hell and be proud of. The last thing Sean wanted was to die feeling ashamed of himself.

He opened the door a crack and listened carefully. Then he took a tiny mirror attached to a wand out of his pocket and held it out through the crack. Flipped it in each direction. Good, looked like clear sailing.

Sean quickly slipped out and quietly shut the door behind him. Then he headed off down the hall towards another room. This would be his last meeting before his flight back to Virginia tomorrow.

*****

A soldier was standing guard outside the room, and when he saw Sean approaching he brought his heels together and saluted.

Sean sighed. *Another one.* "At ease, soldier."

"Yes, Director—sir!"

"Thanks for getting the prisoners for me. I'll be spending some time with them now, just to outline some rules and guidelines for while they're in here together. We don't want any trouble, and they have to know our expectations."

"Yes, sir!"

"Okay, I want no interruptions and I'll be putting on the safety lock from the inside."

"Yes, sir!"

Sean sighed once more while he opened the door and walked in. Flipped the deadbolt once he was inside. The three of them were seated around the table, each sipping on water bottles.

Hal spoke first. "Thank God it's you! We were worried that maybe we were blown!"

Sean laughed. "Just trying to test your nerves, guys. This is a soundproof interrogation room, with no bugs. So, we're safe to talk."

Ziv folded his arms across his chest. "We're anxious to hear the plan, Sean. And hoping it's going to work, because I can't imagine spending the rest of my life down this rabbit hole."

Sean took a seat at the head of the table. Then he began to speak, not bothering with any small talk or fanfare.

"You're getting out this Sunday. It'll be tricky, but I think we can pull this off—or, I should say, I think *you three* can pull this off. I've requisitioned a jet to be fueled and ready for take-off Sunday afternoon at 1:00, with Hal as the scheduled lead pilot. There's a two-hour time difference between Denver and New York, so your escape from here will be pretty much simultaneous with the demonstration I've planned for there at 3:00 eastern time.

"They'll come to get you as they usually do, Hal, and escort you down into the hangar. Shortly after they take you down, Brock and Ziv will have to start moving in that direction themselves. Between now and Sunday, Hal, you can show them the door they should be waiting at.

"After you've completed your usual walk-around inspecting the plane, you will need to excuse yourself to use the washroom. And the washroom is just on the other side of that door that Brock and Ziv will be waiting at. You'll have to borrow one of the tarmac crew's access cards.

"Open the door and let these two in. Once they're in the hangar building, they'll have to stay close to the wall and make their way out to the tarmac—staying close to the wall will reduce their chances of anyone taking notice of them.

"Then the three of you will board the plane and take off."

Hal rubbed his chin. "So far, so good. What plane will I be flying?"

Sean was silent for a second or two. "A plane you're more than familiar with. United Airlines Flight 175. You're going to continue the flight that was interrupted fourteen years ago, but you won't be going to your original Los Angeles destination."

Hal whistled. "Perfect. It's been my dream to fly that plane out of this fucking place, and now that dream is going to come true. How did you justify having that plane prepped?"

"We've been testing a cloaking technology, called Shroud. You know about this, Hal—you've tested it already on the Stealth bombers. We haven't yet tested it on a jumbo jet, so that's the excuse I've used to have that plane scheduled for Sunday.

"Using this exact plane is crucial—if we can get it out into the real world again, where it can be identified by its registration and manufacturer numbers, the entire story of how it was supposed to have crashed into the South Tower on 9/11 will get blown to smithereens. It's the ultimate piece of evidence, the monumental smoking gun."

"So, where am I supposed to land this behemoth?"

"You're going to land at Laramie Regional Airport in Wyoming. Only about a half hour flight from here. I've ordered the fuel tanks to be only twenty percent full, and asked that Shroud be connected in advance. Although, in reality, that's just the smoke screen to justify the flight. Don't even bother trying to activate it—it would just be one extra thing to worry about, and we don't even know if it will work on a jumbo anyway. In other words, I don't want you to rely on that technology for the escape. You'll have to wing it—pun intended."

"Understand. Why Laramie?"

"Most of the regional airports in Colorado have a military component—and a few in Wyoming do, too. Laramie is one of the few little airports that doesn't. Should be less dangerous landing there."

Sean nodded in Brock's direction. "And that's where your son's plane is parked right now. I've already phoned the Laramie airport pretending to be Brock, and ordered them to have his Challenger jet fueled, serviced, and ready for Sunday afternoon. So, when you guys land there, you can hop out, into Brock's plane, and then onward into the wide blue yonder."

Brock smiled. "I like the way you think, Sean."

Sean laughed. "You probably won't like the fact that I charged the fuel and service to your credit card. Which reminds me..." Sean reached into his pocket and pulled out their identification documents.

He tossed them into the middle of the table. "Here are your passports and stuff back—hide these until Sunday."

Hal picked out his long-expired passport and other documents, and stuffed them into a side pocket.

"What's the runway situation in Laramie?"

"Two runways—one 8,500 feet, and the other 6,300."

"How about the width? I need 150 feet for a 767."

"It'll be close. The longer runway is 140 feet, and the smaller one is 120. But, there are no obstructions on the sides of the runways, so your wings should have good clearance over the grass."

Hal nodded. "Should be fine. I know also that the seats have been removed from that plane, and it'll just be the three of us riding. Plus, there will be virtually no fuel left in the tanks when we land because you're having them filled to only twenty percent. Basically, the plane will be as light as a feather in relative terms. For a full and heavy 767 I would have needed a runway of a minimum length of 7,000 feet. So, for this plane I'm figuring 6,000 should do it. We'll be fine on either runway."

Sean gave a thumbs up sign.

Ziv crumpled his empty plastic water bottle and tossed it into the waste can across the room. "Sean, what are the rules of engagement? We're going to face some resistance. No doubt about that."

"Hopefully, with some finesse, which I know you two guys have, resistance will be limited. And while they may take chase, your flight to Laramie will be a short one, so there won't be much time for them to do anything."

"Still…"

Sean interrupted. "Ziv, the *rules of engagement* are that you do whatever the fuck you have to do, to get out of here and get that plane out with you. That's the crucial part—that plane has to escape from this place and be back in the public domain. Luckily, you and Hal are equipped to handle assignments like this. I worry a bit about Brock, though."

Brock snickered. "Sean, you must not have seen my last movie."

They all laughed, while Brock made some mock karate moves

with his hands.

"All joking aside, I'll be fine. I'm with these two guys, so I couldn't ask for more. They can order me around and I'll obey. And, hey, I can be head steward on the resumption of Flight 175! I've never played a flight attendant in a movie before, so this will be good practice for me."

Sean stood up. "Brock, I love that you can joke about this. I know you're probably scared shitless just like we are, but you're doing a good job of hiding it."

Sean reached into the back pocket of his pants and pulled out a roll of bills. He threw it on the table.

"You might need this once you're out. Maybe you'll be lucky enough to be in the position of bribing someone instead of killing them. There's a few thousand in that roll—hide it well."

Brock picked it up and stuffed it into his pocket.

Hal ran his fingers through his thick hair, which was still more blonde than gray. "You're aware that they'll assign a co-pilot to me? And that there'll be a guard that always sits behind me on these flights?"

Sean nodded. "Yes. Do what you have to do."

He nodded towards Ziv. "I know that you're a licensed pilot, Ziv, and so is Brock."

Hal chuckled. "This is a 767, Sean. Being just a licensed pilot doesn't mean anything with a plane like that."

Brock shook his head. "I wouldn't have a clue about flying a plane like that."

Ziv jumped in. "I'm rated for jets up to 737s and A320s. Above that, I've had no experience whatsoever."

Sean walked over to the coffee machine and poured himself a cup. Then he turned and faced the group. "We don't have a choice, do we? Luckily, it's a short flight and Hal can probably fly the damn thing with his eyes closed."

Hal cleared his throat. "Not quite, but we'll be fine. This isn't a deal-breaker. What may be a deal-breaker, though, is the weapons situation. We may have to shoot our way onto that plane, and we do have the guard and the co-pilot to worry about, too."

Sean walked back to the table with his cup of coffee. He broke out into a big smile.

"I'm glad you mentioned that, Hal."

Sean reached into his pocket and pulled out a key. He tossed it onto the table.

"Along that deserted tunnel that you used for your escape attempt, there's a door not far from that ceiling vent you climbed through. It leads into a corridor, and then to another door. Both doors unlock with this key.

"Believe it or not, these doors open with old-fashioned keys—the only doors in this wing that do. The second door leads to the weapons room, and we use normal deadlocks instead of electronic for these doors in case of a power blackout. We don't want the guards being in the vulnerable position of not being able to access weapons."

Hal picked up the key and slipped it into his pocket. "This is good. What do we get to choose from?"

"Everything you can imagine is in there. But I want you to take the MK23 semi-automatic pistols. I know Ziv would prefer an Uzi, but they're far too noisy."

Ziv chuckled and added, "But they're very non-discriminatory."

"Beside the rack for the MKs, you'll see a collection of suppressors designed for the MK specifically. Take those, too, as they'll be crucial. If you have to get rough, at least you can avoid drawing attention to yourselves by using silencers. And all the guns in there are already loaded, so you'll have full twelve-round clips in the handles. Take some extra clips as well."

Hal nodded approval. "The MKs are excellent pistols—used almost exclusively by the Seals and Rangers now."

Sean glanced at his watch. "I have to go, guys. Any other questions?"

Ziv stood up and walked over to Sean. "Thanks for this. We know how much you're risking exposing yourself. But one question for you. Back in Toronto, you told Brock and me that your strategy was four-pronged. Do you have the other parts in place?"

"Yep. All set. Sunday will be one busy day with all three events swinging into action at around the same time. God willing, they'll all come off without a hitch."

Ziv counted on his fingers. "One, two, three——what about number four?"

Sean looked down at the floor for just a second or two. When he raised his eyes again he could tell that they'd gone a bit blurry.

"Number four is my prong. It'll follow a couple of days or so after our Super Sunday. You'll no doubt hear about it on the news."

Chapter 48

It was just one of those days. Days that were rare. When everything was just perfect, and day-to-day worries seemed far away. On days like this, it was hard for anything to break the spell, because the depth of feeling in the heart was just so darn stubborn.

Chris Woodley closed his eyes, leaned his head back, and let the rays of the sun penetrate the skin of his face. It felt so good.

Central Park was heaven, a veritable oasis in the center of one of the most vibrant cities in the world. The sun felt so much better here than even in his own backyard.

They had brought lounge chairs with them, but he liked this better—lazing around on the blanket they had enjoyed their picnic lunch on mere minutes before. They'd eaten late, because there had just been too many things to do today. A nice problem to have.

Chris glanced at his watch—just after 3:00. Two more hours of sunshine left—a lifetime. And it was Sunday, so traffic would be light driving home.

No, not even traffic would be given the opportunity to ruin this day.

Suddenly, the rays of sunshine were blocked, and he felt soft hands gently stroking his face. He knew the touch of those hands—they could only belong to one person. He opened his eyes and saw the upside-down image of his wife standing behind him, gazing down at him with an upside-down smile.

He stretched his hands up and grabbed her around the waist. Pulled her down and flipped her forward in a somersault. Sheila landed softly in his lap and Chris wrapped his arms around her, nestling his cheek into her soft, blonde hair.

She murmured in a dreamy voice. "I don't want to leave here today, Chris. It's too bad they don't let people camp out."

"I know. It is idyllic, isn't it? The sun's shining, it's nice and warm, and the kids are having fun. It sure is a good day to live in New York."

Sheila turned around to face him. "What was your favorite part of the day?"

"I think it's right at this moment, looking at you."

She smiled. "Oh, aren't you the sweet talker. Those words aren't going to get you out of dinner tonight, though. You promised to give me an evening out of the kitchen, so you'd better get your mind psyched up to barbecue."

He kissed her moist lips. "Sheila, darling, I always deliver on my promises. But—maybe I could order pizza instead?"

She playfully slapped his shoulder. "No! I want one of your patented barbecue dinners, you lazy bum!"

"Okay, okay. It's just that after a day like this, it's hard to think of actually doing anything."

"It's true, I agree with you on that. So, again, what was your favorite thing today? Tell me."

Chris pondered this for a moment. "I'd have to say the boats. You and I in one boat, the kids in the other. They were so thrilled to be rowing their own boat, and I was thrilled to be your servant, rowing you."

A look of mischief crossed Chris' face. "Which reminds me, I want to row you in a different way when we get home..."

She slapped him again, wearing a mock frown on her face. "You're still as randy as when we were newlyweds."

He kissed her lips again. "You love it."

Sheila kissed him back, slipping her tongue inside his open mouth. She moaned, "Yes, I do."

Chris pulled away and gazed into her sultry hazel eyes. "You haven't told me what *your* favorite part of today was."

"We haven't experienced it yet. It'll be when you grill my steak medium rare."

"Ha, ha. Very funny. Well, it'll taste so darn good that it will indeed be the highlight of your day. So there!"

Sheila rubbed his shoulder. "I loved the puppet show at the Summer Stage. And what I loved most was just watching Hayley's face. She was so enthralled. And after the show she asked me if we could buy her a couple of puppets so she can put on her own shows at home just for us. Isn't that sweet?"

"It is—and we'll have to do that. We'll get her some puppets, and I'll make a stage for her that she can hide behind for her shows."

"Oh, she'll love that."

"Maybe even Josh will be proud of her—but I doubt it. He wasn't too happy about the puppet show, probably because we made him sit and be quiet."

"Well, he's twelve and Hayley's only eight. So, I didn't really think he'd like the show all that much. But it does teach him patience and tolerance, which are good lessons."

Chris nodded. "He did light up though when that stupid rap group was playing at the Band Shell. That's when I myself had to learn patience and tolerance."

"I know, I know. I plugged my ears when they came on."

"But, luckily, both kids enjoyed the Turtle Pond. That was amazing, huh? Seeing all those turtles and fish? Josh wanted to wade in and catch one of them—that's when I had to have a little talk with him about conservation and preserving nature. I don't think he listened too well, because it took a while for him to wipe the pout off his face. I think when we buy Hayley her puppets, we'll have to get Josh some turtles."

Sheila made a face. "I'm pouting now, see? What do I get for my pout?"

Chris rubbed her shoulders. "You get a steak, medium rare, and you get me rowing the boat again later on in bed."

"Well, I guess I'll have to settle for that, then."

They both looked over in the direction of the open field. Josh was playing Frisbee with one of the kids he'd met. Young boys made friends so easily, Chris thought. Sport was the common bond, and he was glad that Josh was athletic.

Josh must have sensed that Chris was watching, because he looked over and waved. Chris waved, too, and then motioned for him to come back to them.

Josh ran over, his face adorned with yet another sulk. He whined, "Dad, I'm playing. What do you want?"

"It's okay—you can go back in a second. I thought your sister was with you. Where did she go?"

"She was hanging with me, but she got bored with Frisbee—as usual. She rode her bike over to that stupid Alice statue." Josh pointed to the east side of the park, a contemptuous look on his face.

Chris looked in the direction of his pointing finger.

"Ah, I see her. Great. You can go back and play now, Josh."

Chris was relieved to see Hayley happily riding in circles around the giant Alice in Wonderland statue. One of her favorite things about Central Park.

She was such a little sweetheart—his little angel. Chris thanked God every morning for the blessings he had. Two wonderful kids and the woman of his dreams. He had a good job, too, but, well, that wasn't exactly a blessing. More like a necessary evil.

This was what was most important—here, in Central Park, with his family.

Suddenly, there was an eerie silence.

It was almost like he was wearing ear plugs. The laughter and excited screams from all the children stopped and the steady hum of adult conversation had abated. Just a stillness now—not even the chirping of birds. And while the disturbing silence only lasted a couple of seconds, it seemed so much longer than that.

Josh hadn't gone back to play with his friends. He was still standing beside them, but his mouth looked to be frozen in the open position, eyes wide with wonder. He was looking north.

Sheila also faced north, and her slender hands were now covering her mouth. And like Josh, her eyes were wide, too—much wider than Chris had ever remembered seeing them.

But, they weren't wide with wonder. They were wide with horror.

Chris followed their eyes. And he couldn't believe what his own were telling him.

Soaring over the Reservoir, heading straight in their direction, was a plane. But not just any plane. This was a monster. A jumbo jet, flying low, probably no more than 100 feet above the water.

And strangely, the plane wasn't making a sound. Which made it even more sinister.

Suddenly, the silence was broken, replaced by screaming and yelling, the sounds of bicycles falling to the pathway, strollers and picnic baskets being tipped over, feet thumping on the ground desperately seeking out escape routes.

It took a couple of seconds for Chris to process what he was seeing. It didn't seem real, couldn't be real.

But, it was.

Chris jumped to his feet and tried to pull Sheila up from her kneeling position. He could feel her body quivering. He slapped her. Once. Twice.

"Sheila!"

She shook her head, but thankfully allowed Chris to lift her. Josh was still just standing there, staring to the north.

Chris pointed to the west. "Sheila! Josh! Run that way! Fast!"

For a second, neither of them reacted. Then, Josh suddenly came alive.

"Dad, my sister!" He turned and started to run in the direction of the Alice statue. Chris reached out and grabbed him by the belt, holding him tight.

"No! Look after your mother! Run! I'll get your sister!"

Josh nodded, took one last glance to the north and then wrapped his arms around his mother's shoulders. "Mom! We have to get out of here! Now!"

Chris was relieved to see her react. She nodded, and even though she still seemed to be in shock, she obeyed her son. He watched as they ran together towards the west end of the park.

Chris spun around and raced to the east.

A jumble of questions were running through his mind. What would a plane be doing over this way? Why was it flying so low? Was this another 9/11?

He glanced back and saw that it was approaching fast. It seemed to have turned slightly, seemed to be following him towards Hayley.

Chris ran as fast as his legs would allow. He'd been a sprinter in college, but that had been a long time ago.

Nevertheless, he summoned that adrenaline now, that feeling of competition.

Pretended to see the tape at the finish line.

And the finish line was Alice in Wonderland.

Hayley was still riding around in circles, intent on making them as tight as she could. Concentrating on her balance. Oblivious to the silent monster that was closing in on her.

Chris yelled. "Hayley!"

She didn't hear him. Hayley just kept riding.

The screams from the crowd were deafening now—he was surprised that Hayley didn't hear them. People were running in every direction, stumbling and falling to the ground, curling up into balls and covering their heads.

Chris kept running.

He dodged a large family doing a group hug, and hurdled over an old man who'd fallen to the ground. He noticed the eyes of the picnickers, all of them reflecting the horror he felt.

Chris kept running.

He was close now. He yelled out Hayley's name again.

This time, she heard him. She stopped and looked back. Then she looked upwards and her mouth opened wide, looking as if she wanted to scream. But, it was just a silent scream—she couldn't find the sound.

Chris took one final look over his shoulder as he ran, hoping against hope that the plane had veered off.

But, it hadn't.

His heart felt like it was going to pound right out of his chest, and his legs felt rubbery—the sudden side effects of what he'd just seen.

He'd taken it all in with only one quick look. The hauntingly silent jumbo jet, with its nose almost running up Chris' ass, was only about ten feet off the ground. It was headed right for Hayley who was standing frozen, stiff as a board, straddling her little pink bicycle.

And Chris fixated on one other strange thing he'd noticed in his last glance. The landing gear wasn't down. The massive plane was going to crash land on its belly, taking him and Hayley with it. Why he thought about landing gear at this point, Chris had no idea. It wasn't as if the landing gear would make any difference now, one way or the other.

Well, if this is the way they were meant to go, so be it. At least his daughter would die wrapped in his arms. They would die together.

Chris dove through the air, hands extended outwards, then curling around his daughter. He felt the trembling in Hayley's soft body as he encased her in his arms; both of them united as one.

They tumbled over the little pink bike and crashed to the ground.

The silent monster arrived.

Then, just as quickly, it was gone.

Like a ghost.

It had been on top of them, absorbing them—and then it simply disappeared.

For that weird instant, Chris sensed that they were enveloped in a sort of fog. Everything became blurry and hazy; almost as if they were in a bubble, assuming he could imagine what being in a bubble was like.

Are we dead? Is this heaven?

Chapter 49

Sunday was a good day to escape.

The tunnels were empty. Just like up in the real world, most people here had Sundays off. Emerald City even had its own church, where services were held throughout the day, finally ending around 5:00 in the afternoon.

Yes, prayer was embraced in Emerald City. The mornings were generally back to back Christian ceremonies, with the afternoons taken up by every other religious celebration imaginable.

No surprise that Muslim traditions were not practiced, and neither were Buddhist or other more obscure Euro-Asian denominations.

Most people who didn't have specific trades or specialties just had boring menial jobs in Emerald City. Having Sunday off was a needed break from the monotony.

Being able to socialize at church with their fellow residents brought back memories of home, and being able to pray in a formal setting was at the very least some small comfort. It seemed to give them hope, and made them feel less like prisoners.

The religious leaders who performed the myriad ceremonies were prisoners, too. To them, however, leading ceremonies down in Emerald City was almost like a calling. If they ever longed to serve a greater cause, this was it.

Above ground, with the world slowly but surely moving away from organized religion; they weren't half as appreciated as they were down here. For most of them, this was the closest they would ever come to being actual real-life missionaries.

All of the priests were well familiar with the history of Jesuits attempting to convert the Indigenous peoples of North America to

Catholicism back in the 1600s; many getting slaughtered for their efforts. The Jesuit Fathers were heroes in their minds, and, in a twisted kind of way, they felt like heroes themselves down in this underground prison.

They had a real cause, a real calling, and they were carrying out God's wishes. Giving their fellow residents some form of spiritual comfort in a captive setting was about as good as it got for a servant of God.

Aside from the non-stop religious services, the other good thing about escaping on a Sunday was that everyone took full advantage of the recreational and entertainment facilities, either after their church service was over, or before their particular service was about to begin. So, basically the entire day was recreational and the tunnels were practically empty. Even the guards were more relaxed on Sundays. Everyone was in a good mood—the beach at the artificial lake was crowded, the amusement park was rife with lineups, and the bars and restaurants were packed to overflowing.

The only recreational spots that were empty were the brothels because this was, after all, a Sunday.

It was 11:30 a.m. Hal led his two comrades down the long, deserted tunnel, and then turned right into the one that he'd attempted his escape from not so long ago. They passed underneath the vent that had almost led him to freedom, and then came upon the locked door Sean had told them about.

"Ziv, you stay out here in the tunnel while Brock and I go in and get the guns. Stand back, away from the door a bit, and kneel down, pretending to tie your shoe laces. We won't come back out through the door until we get the green light from you.

"I'll knock twice from the inside when we're ready to come out—listen carefully for it. If the coast is clear, knock twice in response. If I don't hear you, I won't knock again. We'll wait until you respond. Clear?"

Ziv nodded. "Gotcha. Don't be long, guys. It's deserted here right now, but we shouldn't push our luck."

Hal glanced up and down the tunnel to make sure there was no one wandering around, then pulled the key out of his pocket and unlocked the first door. He and Brock entered a short hallway, which led to the second door. Hal unlocked that one and they slipped inside.

He flipped on the light switch, and they both whistled in astonishment.

Wall to wall guns—almost every type of modern gun imaginable. Pistols, machine guns, sniper rifles, hunting rifles, derringers, and even a few shoulder-held rocket launchers. It was an impressive arsenal, one that could easily wage a small war. One shelf was even dedicated to knives and machetes.

Hal suppressed the urge to run his hands over the array of weapons. For a guy like him, this was like being a kid in a candy store. Seeing all of these guns brought back memories, mostly bad.

But they had been the tools of his trade and he couldn't escape the twisted nostalgia they triggered. He could honestly admit to himself that he'd used most of the brands of guns in this room at one time or another. And even some of the knives.

The machetes, not so much.

He crooked his finger at Brock. "Over here. These are the MK23s."

He walked over to a shelf and chose three pistols. He checked the handles of each to make sure they were loaded, and then grabbed three spare magazines.

Hal stuffed one gun in his belt, pulled his jacket over and zipped it up. Brock slid the other two guns under his belt and stretched his sweater down past his waist.

Then Hal moved further down the shelving unit until he found the suppressors he wanted. He gave Brock two of them, and stuffed one into his front pocket.

"Okay, we're good to go."

*****

Ziv was kneeling in the tunnel, continuously untying his shoelaces and tying them up again.

So far, so good. No signs of life in the tunnel, and he really didn't expect there would be. This one was off the beaten track, and didn't lead to any of the recreational facilities. So there would be no reason for most people to wander down here.

Which, of course, meant it would be tough for him to explain what he was doing here if any guards happened by. Aside from tying up his shoelaces.

He was only about five feet from the locked door, and he listened carefully for the two knocks that he prayed would come soon. They would be easy to hear because it was as silent as a mausoleum in this particular tunnel.

Suddenly, the murmur of voices.

And then he saw them. Two guards rounded the corner from the main tunnel and were headed his way. They had been talking casually to each other, but as soon as they saw him they stopped chatting.

Ziv concentrated on his shoelaces. He figured the best thing to do right now was to put a double knot in one, to legitimize why he was struggling so vainly.

"Hey, what are you doing here?"

Ziv knew this looked suspicious as hell. Here he was just mere feet away from the door to the weapons room.

He looked up. They were right in front of him now, dressed in full uniform, side arms in holsters strapped onto their hips.

"Hi guys. Have a damn knot in my shoelace. Bad ankles—needed to tighten this one shoe, but I can't get the knot out. Are either of you good with knots?"

"Stand up!"

Ziv sighed and obeyed the command.

The mouthy one doing all the talking held out his hand. "Give me your magnetic card."

Ziv pulled it out of his pocket and handed it to him. The soldier scanned it into a machine dangling from his hip.

"I see that you're one of the new arrivals. And, Mr. Dayan, you have an interesting background. Ex-Mossad, it says here."

Ziv nodded respectfully. "Yes, unfortunately. That seems like centuries ago, though."

"It doesn't look like it was all that long ago. You only arrived here a few days ago, too. Why are you wandering around down here?"

"I was just trying to familiarize myself with the surroundings. And trying to keep in shape. I usually jog a few miles each day, so I chose this nice quiet tunnel. At my age, it's hard dodging kids and bikes."

The soldier studied Ziv carefully, clearly looking for any movement in his eyes that would betray him. But, with Ziv's training, he could fool anyone with his eyes, and could even fool any lie detector machine with his ability to control his heart rate.

Seemingly satisfied, the soldier handed Ziv his identification card. "Okay, Mr. Dayan, enjoy your jog. But, could you please do it in the main tunnel? It would be better if you confined yourself to that area."

Ziv allowed himself an inner sigh of relief. "No problem, officer." He knelt down again to pretend to work on his shoelace.

The quiet younger soldier got down beside him. "Let me take a stab at that for you. I've got good strong fingernails."

Ziv protested. "No, it's okay. I'll get it. You guys have better things to do than undo knots."

Suddenly, he felt a sinking feeling in his stomach. Two light knocks could clearly be heard from behind the door only five feet away.

The older soldier's head jerked in the direction of the door, and he yanked his pistol out of his holster. "What the fuck is going on here?"

Ziv's instincts shifted into automatic pilot. His first move was a ferocious head-butt into the young soldier kneeling next to him, sending him reeling backwards.

His second move was a flip from his kneeling position. With the leverage of both hands pushing down, combined with the one foot positioned flat on the floor, he thrust himself upwards, bringing his kneeling leg straight into the air, his foot slamming against the gun hand wrist of the older soldier.

The gun went smashing into the wall, and for one precious instant the stunned soldier seemed to be at a loss to understand what had just happened.

Ziv didn't hesitate. His training had taught him to never leave anyone standing. Two quick karate punches to the soldier's head sent him down hard.

But, the younger soldier had recovered from the head butt. Still on the ground, he grasped onto the grip of his gun and began sliding it out of its holster.

Ziv was like a robot now; executing moves that were hard-wired into his brain.

One of his feet slammed down and trapped the man's gun hand to the floor. The other foot came down hard on the young soldier's throat. He gasped and brought his free hand up in a feeble attempt to pull the foot away.

Ziv leaned down and rammed the knuckles of his right hand hard against the young man's temple, instantly sending him to join his friend in the land of unconsciousness.

He pried the gun out of the soldier's hand, and then dashed over to the wall and retrieved the one that had gone flying. Ziv whispered a prayer of thanks—two guns, but not one shot had been fired. That would have been a disaster, with the sound of gunfire echoing down through the labyrinth of tunnels.

He rushed to the hallway door that led to the weapons room, and delivered his belated reply of two light knocks.

Chapter 50

The three men stood in the middle of the arsenal room, staring down at the two unconscious bodies they'd dragged in from the tunnel.

Hal scratched his head. "Okay, new plan, boys. Strip 'em."

Brock looked up at his dad. "What? Why?"

"We don't have time to debate, son. Strip 'em. You and Ziv are going to don their uniforms. This is actually a blessing in disguise."

Within minutes, the two soldiers were half-naked, and still out cold. The uniforms didn't exactly fit the builds of Ziv and Brock, but they would have to do. Both of them were tall, so the pants were a little short at the ankles. But, hopefully, no one would notice.

"You'll have to carry the soldiers' guns instead of the MKs. Won't fit into their holsters. I'll keep the one MK with me, along with the silencer and extra magazine. We'll each still have a gun, except that yours won't be so silent. But, let's face it, if it gets to the point where you two, who now look like soldiers, have to use your guns, it won't matter anyway whether they're silent or not."

Brock adjusted the military cap on his head, and glanced at his watch. It was 12:15. "Dad, you'd better get back to your room. They'll be coming to fetch you in a few minutes."

"Right. Okay, I want you guys to stay here. Now that you're wearing uniforms, we can't take a chance on someone in authority stopping you to chat.

"Yesterday, I showed you the door to the hangar. Go there no earlier than 1:00. If all goes to plan, I'll do my pretend washroom break and let you in. With those uniforms on, you should be able to follow me freely out to the jet. It'll be fueled and ready out on the apron."

Ziv buttoned up his new jacket, and then slid the soldier's gun into the holster on his hip. "Okay, we're good. Do your thing, Hal. Godspeed. We'll see you in the hangar."

Hal nodded, and pulled the MK23 out of his waistband. Then he slid the silencer out of his side pocket and screwed it onto the barrel of the pistol. Out of the corner of his eye, he couldn't help but notice Brock's face turn as white as a ghost.

Brock gulped and whispered, "What are you doing, Dad?"

"Brock, I want you to go out into the hallway and wait."

Hal sensed that his son knew what was going to happen.

Brock swallowed hard. "Dad, we can just tie them up and gag them."

Hal spread his arms out and gestured around the room. "There's nothing here to tie them with, Brock. Look around."

Brock's eyes were blinking rapidly now. He protested, "But, Dad, they'll probably be out for a long time. We'll be up in the air by the time they wake up."

Hal looked at him sadly. "No, they won't be out for very long, son. They'll wake up in just a few minutes. This is real world. We can't take the risk. I know this is a tough thing to face, but so is this place we're in. If we don't get out today, we'll never get another chance.

"After what Sean will pull off with the other prongs of his plan, this place will be shut down tight. If we get out, we'll save a lot of lives. If we don't get out, we're all doomed, including you two, who were only supposed to be here for a short time. This will become your new home—forever."

Ziv put his arms around Brock's shoulders. "Come on, Brock. I'll go out in the hall with you. Your dad's right. Every brutal thing you've ever done on the silver screen was just pretend. This is the real thing, and we have no choice. Trust me, he'll make it painless for them."

Brock lowered his head and nodded. Ziv gently spun him around, opened the door and guided him out into the hallway.

Once the door shut behind them, Hal grimaced and placed the tip of the silencer up against the forehead of one of the unconscious soldiers. He pulled the trigger to the sound of a gentle spitting noise.

Peter Parkin & Alison Darby

There was a pronounced jerk down the length of the prone body, followed by a sickening stillness.

Blocking out any semblance of emotion, Hal repeated the act for the second soldier.

Then he straightened up and saluted.

*****

Hal was stretched out on his bed when they came for him. He shifted his feet to the floor and stood up wearily. "Okay, I guess I'm going to work again, huh?"

"Yep, another day in the air, Hal. Follow us."

Hal pulled his bomber jacket down as far as it would go, making sure to cover the gun in his waistband.

He'd left the silencer on, so the barrel was quite long. It stretched down under his pant leg onto his thigh, and he prayed the soldiers wouldn't notice the bulge. It was too far over to the left to be mistaken as something else, so if anyone saw the bulge they would surely react. Luckily, his pants were fairly baggy so they should serve to hide it.

They made the familiar trek down through the main tunnel, then down a side passageway until they came to the hangar door. The same door that Hal's son and Ziv would soon be waiting behind. It was 12:50 p.m.

*****

Two jets were parked on the apron, side by side. One was the plane Hal would be flying—the forced continuation of United Flight 175.

The massive Boeing 767. Hal's 9/11 nightmare plane from fourteen years ago, now over-painted in a sickly military green.

Sitting next to it was an Airbus A320. Both planes looked ready to go, with mobile stairs pulled up to the front hatch doors. Hal didn't know of anyone else who was flying today, so alarm bells immediately went off in his head.

He ignored the subliminal warnings—walked out to the 767 and began his traditional walk-around. He inspected the fuel access points under the wings, stood back and examined the fuselage, then walked under the plane and studied the landing gear.

"Hey there, Hal—looks like I'm flying with you today."

367

He glanced up from under the plane upon hearing the familiar voice.

"Ted, glad to have you aboard."

Hal walked up to him and shook his hand.

Ted Banks was a capable pilot, and one that he'd trained on several types of planes already. He liked him—a good kid, and a ranking captain in the Air Force.

"'I've put you in the simulator, but I don't think I've ever actually taken you up in one of these 767s yet. Are you psyched for it?"

Ted squinted into the bright sunlight. "I was, but now I have to get psyched up for the Airbus."

"What?"

"Well, they brought the jumbo out, fueled it up to the twenty percent level, and then the mechanics did their routine tests and checks. They discovered a problem with the landing gear."

Hal felt his stomach flip. "What problem? The landing gear is fully extended and looks to be locked in place perfectly."

"It's probably just one of those annoying warning light things, but we can't be too careful, I guess. So, they've fueled up the Airbus for us, and took Shroud out of the 767 and installed it on the Airbus instead. I know it's not the jumbo test that Director Russell wanted, but the 320 is a pretty big jet and will still be the biggest one Shroud has ever been tested on."

Hal glanced down at Ted's hip and saw that he was unarmed.

He took a quick glance in all directions, then smoothly slipped his hand under his leather bomber jacket. He whipped out the menacingly long pistol and pointed it squarely at the Air Force captain's head.

"I'm sorry, Ted, but it has to be the jumbo."

Chapter 51

"What are you doing, Hal?"

"I'm leaving here today, Ted. In this exact plane—the one I flew in on fourteen years ago."

With the threatening image of an MK23 pointed at his head, Ted reacted by slowly raising his hands into the air. "You won't get away with it."

Hal growled. "Lower your fucking hands. Don't draw attention to yourself."

Ted lowered his hands down to his side. "How do you want to handle this?"

Hal kept the gun levelled at his head. "Who's scheduled to be the guard on this flight today?"

"Lieutenant Dixon."

"Where is he right now?"

Ted jerked his head in the direction of the dispatch office. "Standing over there, near the office. Talking to the mechanics."

"Okay. This is what we're gonna do. I have two friends who will be leaving with me. They're waiting on the other side of the passageway door. You're gonna open that door and let them in. They're dressed in military uniforms. They'll fire up the engines while you and I have a chat with Lieutenant Dixon. We'll let him know that he's got the rest of the day off."

"Hal, don't do this. At the very least, this plane may have a safety problem with the gear. But aside from that, look around. There are at least half a dozen armed soldiers walking around in this hangar."

"Ted, we're doing this, and you're coming with me. My friends aren't experienced with a 767. At least you've been in the simulator. So

I need you."

"What if I refuse?"

Hal jiggled the pistol. "Then I'll kill you."

Ted cocked his head to the side. "C'mon, Hal. You wouldn't do that. We've been friends."

"Ted, do you know who I really am? Who I worked for? What I did?"

Ted swallowed hard. "Yes."

"Then you know I wouldn't hesitate to kill you, right here on the spot. There are two dead soldiers back in the arsenal room right now, who, if they could speak, would attest to that. So—don't fuck with me."

Captain Ted Banks winced and nodded his head slowly.

"When we head over there, this gun will be back in my waistband. But I can whip it out faster than you can blink. Remember that. Any warnings that you utter will cause this gun to be back in my hand. And you'll be the first to go. Don't doubt that for a second—I will shoot my way out of here if I have to, Ted. At this moment, I'm a desperate man."

"What do you want me to say when we're over there?"

"Tell them that Director Russell asked two other officers to go with us today. One as an observer and one as a guard. Remember this one point; you're saving Lieutenant Dixon's life by keeping him off that plane. Because I can't have a guard on there with us. I'd have to kill him once we board. Got that?"

Ted glanced over toward the dispatch office. "I understand. What's going to happen to me?"

"If you prove not to be a threat, you'll live. I need your help—the flight will be a short one."

"Where are we going?"

Hal shook his head. "You don't need to know that yet."

"What if we get opposition?"

Hal smirked. "You just better be one good actor. Your job is to get clearance for us to get off the ground in this plane, and only this fucking plane."

"We have clearance. But in the A320 not the 767."

"Have you been assigned a clearance number to cite to the tower?"

"Yes."

"And a flight number?"

"Yes."

"Well, those are the numbers you'll use."

"We only have a short take-off time span."

"How long?"

"From 1:00 to 1:30."

Hal glanced at his watch. "So, we're cleared to take off only until 1:30?"

Ted nodded.

"It's 1:05. We'd better get a move on. Runway 13 could get kinda crowded soon."

*****

Brock readjusted his military cap, stuffing the last few errant locks of his blonde hair underneath.

He pulled the brim of the hat a little bit lower over his eyes, and then checked his watch.

"It's ten past one, Ziv. Something must have happened."

Ziv was leaning against the wall, hands stuffed in the pockets of his tight military pants.

"Be patient, Brock. These things never work totally to plan, as we've already found it."

They were standing on the other side of the door to the hangar. Brock's throat was bone dry, and the butterflies were fluttering his stomach into knots. Even though this was worse than the feeling he got when he had to perform live on stage, he was thankful that he'd at least been able to suppress the need to retch—so far. They'd already tried swiping the access cards of the dead soldiers, but they didn't scan. Their cards must not have been coded for access to the hangar area. So, they had no choice but to wait for Hal to arrive and let them through.

Ziv put his ear up against the door. "Not a sound in there. That's a good thing. If there were gunshots, we'd have reason to worry."

"Don't even joke about that, Ziv. I sure hope my dad's okay."

"He's a pretty capable guy, Brock. I'm sure he's fine and that he'll be here any minute now. Hey, did you remember to transfer the money and all your identification into the new clothes?"

Brock patted the outside pocket of the jacket. "Yep. Safe and sound."

"Good."

Footsteps coming down the hall!

Ziv muttered under his breath. "Christ, another one."

Brock turned his face away and edged closer to the door. He didn't want to take a chance on the soldier recognizing him.

Ziv whispered to him. "Let me do the talking."

The soldier approached, walking authoritatively towards them. "Hey, guys. You locked out?"

Ziv smiled sheepishly. "Yeah, neither of our cards seem to work. Technology is a pain, isn't it?"

The soldier was tall, husky, and around fifty years of age. By the insignia on his shoulder, Ziv recognized him as being at the rank of major. Certainly not someone who was going to be fooled easily.

The officer frowned. "That's strange. Are you two normally permitted access to the hangar?"

Ziv shuffled a tiny bit closer to the soldier. "We just got reassigned here today. They probably didn't program the cards properly. So, we've just been waiting for someone to come through the door so we can get in."

The major stepped around Ziv and moved towards Brock, who was turned away, facing the door. Brock knew that alone probably looked suspicious, but his worst fear was being recognized as someone the major had seen in last week's feature matinee.

"Soldier, what's your name?"

Brock slowly turned, and raised his hand to cover the lower part of his face. Before he could answer, the major pointed at his wrist. "You're wearing a Rolex? Did you take that off one of our residents, soldier?"

That ominous question was all it took for Brock to react. He knew in his gut that they were in trouble. He should have remembered about the damn Rolex—what soldier could afford to wear a watch like that?

He thrust both of his powerful hands upwards in a lightning move that he'd learned in one of his movie stunts. Both thumbs shot underneath the major's chin and the other eight fingers framed each side of his face. Then he simply shoved up and back with all of his considerable might.

The move caught the soldier completely by surprise, and he didn't have time to even think of resisting. The back of his head smashed into the concrete wall behind him, and his eyeballs instantly rolled upward into his forehead. His body went limp and slid down the wall, collapsing onto the floor.

Brock stared at the prone officer for a second, astonished at what had just happened. He glanced over at Ziv, who looked even more astonished, staring with his mouth frozen open.

Ziv then took a tentative step towards him. "Brock—"

Brock thrust his hand in the air, palm spread wide open. "Ziv, don't touch him! He's still alive and he's going to stay that way. Got me?"

Ziv stopped in his tracks. "Okay, Brock."

Suddenly, the sound they'd both been waiting for—the subtle click of the magnetic door lock being triggered.

Chapter 52

Hal shoved the door open, and his eyes immediately trained upon the body lying on the floor.

He shrugged and gestured to Ziv and Brock. "C'mon, guys. We have to hurry."

Hal pointed at Ted. "This is Captain Ted Banks. Slight change of plans—he'll be coming along as my co-pilot. No time to explain, but Ted knows that if he's not a good boy he'll die.

"So, you two need to walk with purpose along the wall with your heads held high. Walk like soldiers. Get up in the jumbo and fire up the engines. We'll be there to take over in a few minutes."

Hal recognized the insignia on the shoulder of the unconscious officer. He pointed to him and turned to Ted. "Who's this officer?"

Ted looked down at the prone body. He answered softly, "That's Major Rob Diaz. A flight weapons officer."

"Perfect. Give his name as the one who's going to be our observer today. And pick another name for the guard assigned in replacement of Dixon. We need to sound authentic."

Hal directed his attention back to Ziv and Brock. "Get going, guys."

"Dad—"

Hal interrupted. "No time, Brock. Go!"

The two of them headed off along the wall of the hangar, while Hal gave Ted a subtle little shove in the direction of the group of men standing outside of the dispatch office.

As they got closer, Hal could see that only one was a soldier. The other four were dressed in mechanics' coveralls. He glanced at Ted. "Do your thing—and do it well."

They sauntered casually up to the group of men. Ted addressed Lieutenant Dixon.

"Hey, John. Looks like you're going to have the afternoon off. Another guard's been assigned to take your place; Sergeant Malloy. He normally works with Major Diaz, who's been asked to be an observer for today's flight."

Dixon looked puzzled. "That's kind of unusual, being taken off a flight at the last minute?"

"Well, there's another change in plans, too, so today's just an unusual day, I guess. I got a phone call from Director Sean Russell, who has insisted we take the jumbo up today instead of the Airbus."

"But, we already disconnected Shroud and moved it over to the 320."

Hal was impressed—Ted was fast on his feet. "Sean wants us to test the hologram projector instead of Shroud. The projector has already been permanently installed in the 767. But, it's never been tested on it yet. So, that's today's new assignment."

Dixon wasn't ready to relent. "I'm sure we tested the new projector already—a few months ago, I think."

"Lieutenant, our flight window is closing fast. I haven't got time to argue with you."

Dixon nodded. Hal stood quietly behind Ted, ready to react if he saw any sign that he might have to.

One of the mechanics spoke up. He was wearing a cross insignia on his shoulder, which indicated he was the chief mechanic.

"Captain Banks, I can't authorize the 767. There's a concern with the landing gear—you know that already. Some warning lights that were irregular."

"I'll have to overrule you on that, Gerry."

"You can't overrule me. The only one who can do that is the Colonel." Gerry jerked his head in the direction of the dispatch office. "Just pop in there to see him, let him know what you're doin' and, if he's okay with it, you're good to go."

Ted sighed. "Okay, Gerry. No problem."

Ted led the way over to the office. Hal noticed the plaque on the wooden door, with Colonel Matt Weston imprinted on it. Ted knocked on the door. To the sound of a grunted greeting, he opened the door and went in, Hal following close behind.

Once in, Ted saluted.

"At ease, Captain. How can I help you today?"

"Thank you, Colonel. I just need to let you know that Sean Russell wants the 767 to go up today, despite the warnings on the landing gear."

Matt ignored Ted and took a second to address Hal. "Hello, Hal. Good to have you back in the hangar with us. I hope you don't try to pull another escape stunt. We need you down here, and would rather have you here than in that prison."

"Thanks, Colonel. It's good to be back."

Matt turned his attention back to Ted. "Captain, that jumbo is deemed unsafe right now. I can't authorize it to leave the tarmac."

Almost at the exact instant those words came out of the Colonel's mouth, Hal heard the massive engines of the 767 start up. And the Colonel heard them, too.

"What the fuck, Captain?" He got up from his chair and rushed around the desk, clearly intending to head out the door and check out the source of the noise. Hal knew that with the Colonel being an experienced pilot himself, he could probably easily distinguish the sound of the Pratt and Whitney engines on the 767 from the Airbus CMFs.

Hal realized in an instant that he had no choice. He stepped forward, thrust his hand down to his waist, and met the Colonel halfway.

"Get out of my way, Hal!"

A second later there was a bloody hole in Colonel Matt Weston's forehead. He slumped backwards and Hal managed to catch him before the thump of his lifeless body hitting the floor resonated through the walls of the office. Luckily, no one could have heard the gunshot—the suppressor had made it sound as if someone was merely spitting out stale gum.

Hal quickly eased him down to the floor—and then saluted.

He whirled around. Ted was standing with his eyes closed, hands on either side of his head, moving it from side to side as if trying to shake the image from his brain.

Hal grabbed him by the lapels of his jacket and pulled his face to within inches of his own. "Compose yourself! If you want to live, compose yourself! When we leave this office, you have to give Gerry the assurance that we're good to go. Understand?"

Ted nodded.

"Okay, let's go." Hal opened the door and waved Ted ahead of him.

They both maintained the charade of calmness as they strode out of the office. The chief mechanic was the only one there now. The next closest humans looked to be loitering around at the other end of the hangar. Hal was glad this was a Sunday.

Ted waved at Gerry. "No problems, Gerry. The Colonel gave his blessing."

They continued walking out towards the tarmac.

"Hold up a second, Captain."

Hal and Ted turned slowly. Ted asked, "What's wrong, Gerry?"

Gerry had his hand out, palm up, fingers bending up and down. "I need paperwork, Captain. I can't let you leave without the Colonel's sign-off."

Hal sighed and took a quick glance in each direction. Then the gun was in his hand one more time, and it spit another deadly accurate bullet right through the temple of the chief mechanic.

Ted gasped. Hal grabbed him by the arm and shoved him in the direction of the open hangar doors. "Move it! Run—and I mean fast!"

Chapter 53

The seat was the same one he'd sat in on September 11, 2001, that day when he'd brought this exact airplane to a sudden halt on ramp 13A. He remembered it as vividly as if it were yesterday.

The ground opening up before his eyes, trying to suck him, his plane, his passengers and crew into a massive yawning tunnel—which, little did he know at the time, led to a massive yawning hangar.

After that, a desperate race for their lives, a race that led to his co-pilot's head being blown apart. And Hal being framed for the mass murder of ten innocent people in the Mall of America, in a last-ditch effort on the part of his former employers to discredit him rather than kill him.

The cassette tape he'd sent off to his son had saved his life; or more appropriately, bought him time.

Fourteen years of time—useless time, wasted time.

Today, Hal Winters would begin the process of making up for lost time.

Air Force Captain Ted Banks was sitting in the co-pilot's seat. Brock and Ziv were sitting in the two jump seats behind them, which folded down from the wall of the cockpit.

Hal held the yoke firmly in his hand, while glancing at the watch on his wrist.

"Okay, Ted. It's 1:25. We have five minutes left in our departure window. Get on the horn and tell the tower our clearance and flight numbers. I've got the aircraft."

Hal guided the plane up ramp 13A and expertly worked the pedals, exerting enough pressure to ease the massive jet into a gentle turn onto runway 13.

Ted pulled a notepad out of his pocket and put on his headphones. Before fingering the Talk button, he glanced at Hal. "You don't want to do a pre-flight checklist?"

Hal laughed. "You're joking, right? Just get on the horn, Ted."

"We should indicate a flight plan, at least."

Hal chuckled again. "You don't give up, do you? Talk to the tower, Ted. Whether you like it or not, we're leaving right now."

Hal brought the plane to a stop at the foot of runway 13, and then slipped his own headphones on.

He listened in on the conversation between Ted and the tower.

"Tower this is Emerald Nine. Do you read?"

"Roger, Emerald Nine. State your intentions."

"Awaiting clearance for take-off on number 13. Our clearance number is 12888, and our flight number today is E207."

"Roger, Emerald Nine. Your numbers are validated. Await instructions."

As they sat waiting patiently with the powerful Pratt and Whitney engines humming, the jumbo jet's airframe vibrated in its eagerness to leave terra firma behind.

Hal felt a connection to this plane, an affinity—he reveled in its gentle rocking motion. It was almost as if the plane were saying, "I've missed you. What took you so long, Captain? Why did you leave me behind? Take me away from this place."

Five minutes went by without any word from the tower. Brock spoke softly from the backseat.

"Dad, I'm getting a bad feeling."

Hal nodded. Suddenly, he reached over and yanked the notepad off Ted's lap. He scanned it. Then he glared at Ted, fire in his eyes. "You told the tower our flight number was E207. But, it says on your pad E209. What have you done, Ted?"

Suddenly, the headphones crackled. "Uh—Emerald Nine, your departure window has expired. We have incoming now on runway 13. Please clear the runway and return to the hangar."

Hal laughed. "Well done, Ted. Very clever."

He clicked his own Talk button. "Tower, this is Emerald Nine.

Ready for take-off. Thank you for your clearance. And—fuck off."

He whipped off his headphones, and addressed his co-pilot. "Power up."

The massive jet began to move. Ted screamed. "Hal, they said there was incoming!"

Hal yelled. "Ziv, strip off his headphones!"

Ziv didn't wait to be told twice. He tore them off Ted's head and tossed them onto the floor of the cockpit. "I think the Captain wants radio-silence now, Ted."

Ted just shook his head as he held his hands firmly on his own yoke, feet working the pedals in unison with Hal.

The 767 was now racing down the runway, and there was not another plane in sight in this remote section of Denver International Airport. The coast was clear, and Hal's furtive glances upward through the cockpit windshield confirmed in his mind that the threat of incoming was just a ruse.

He didn't need to look at the indicator screen to know that the speed was right for take-off. His superb instincts told him conditions were perfect.

"Wheels up."

Both pilots pulled back on their yokes and the plane lifted gracefully into the sky. It was a clear and calm day, and they gained altitude quickly. As he guided the jet to the north, Hal glanced back down at the Denver Airport, and specifically the dreaded ramp 13A. The huge overhead tunnel door that carved itself out of the ground was still open and, from what he could see from his vantage point, no threatening activity had commenced yet.

Good, we have a bit of a head start.

"Flaps down."

Ted obeyed and punched the switch. "Roger, flaps down."

"Landing gear up."

Ted hit the button for the landing gear. "Roger, gear up."

They all heard the whir of the motor, and the familiar clunk as the gear folded up inside of the bay doors.

"Ted, key in Laramie Regional Airport, Wyoming. Its code is

LAR."

"Roger, LAR. Setting a course 20 degrees northwest. ETA forty minutes."

Hal glanced at the altimeter and saw that they'd reached an altitude from ground of 2,000 feet. Which actually meant they were approximately 7,500 feet above sea level due to Denver's mile-high elevation.

"Set auto-pilot."

"Roger. Auto-pilot set."

"Disengage transponder."

Ted looked at him. "What?"

"Disengage transponder, officer."

Ted reluctantly flipped the switch, now making their flight as close to invisible as possible. At the very least, aside from any military radar with different capabilities, no civilian air traffic control center would be able to tell which plane it was, nor what altitude it was flying at.

"Roger, transponder disengaged."

Hal lifted his hands off the yoke, yawned and stretched his arms out wide. He glanced out the side windows and was relieved not to see any fighter jets flanking them yet. And the sky was clear all around them. Which he expected would be the case—they were flying low, flirting with the angry peaks of the Rocky Mountains. The only traffic they might encounter at this altitude would be small planes and helicopters, and the 767 was so huge that those little aircraft would see them well in advance and give them a wide berth.

Brock must have read his mind. "Dad, do you expect any planes will give chase?"

"Normally, yes. But, in Emerald City, the fighter jets are all hidden underground in that same hangar we came out of. So, they will have to be towed out and then fueled on the apron. Planes aren't left with fuel in their tanks in that hangar—too dangerous. So, towing and fueling will take some time."

Ted piped in. "We'll be sitting ducks."

Hal smirked, sarcasm dripping from his voice, "Oh, come now, Ted. They won't shoot us down—you're onboard."

Ted looked out of his side window. "Sorry about the warning code, Hal. But—I think you understand."

"No apology necessary. A sly move on your part—I would have done the same thing."

Hal sighed and leaned back against the headrest. "Guys, I hear it's beautiful in Wyoming this time of the year."

Chapter 54

Kirk Reid eased his sleek fishing boat along the shoreline of Twelve Mile Lake. He couldn't help beaming with pride every time he went out in this craft. He'd saved up for five years, as he promised his wife he'd do. He never dipped into their savings, or the kids' college funds—he simply gave up smoking and bought two fewer cases of beer a month. He wanted this boat that badly.

Almost every weekend, he came out on this lake, a cold mountain lake that was brimming with trout, pike, and walleye. And because Wyoming was probably the least populated state in the union, the lake was never crowded. He could fish to his heart's content with very little competition.

The boat was twenty feet in length and equipped with four elevated rotator seats—perfect for fighting those pesky fish that loved to swim under and around the boat once they were hooked. And the two captain's chairs in the front allowed for leisurely cruising when the thrill of fishing was over for the day.

He rested his hand on the wheel and turned his eyes away from the water for a second to gaze lovingly at his daughter. Riley was eight years old now, but with the brain of a much older soul. Today, at breakfast, she had asked Kirk to take her with him—the very first time she'd ever expressed an interest in his hobby.

Her older brother, Ryan, was not the least bit impressed. As far as he was concerned fishing was an activity reserved for him and his dad.

Kirk agreed that she could come—in fact, he was thrilled that she wanted to. But, Ryan refused to join them, preferring instead to sulk off to his room.

One part of Kirk was sad about that, but the other part was

ecstatic. This was a rare chance to bond with his daughter. Normally, his wife, Judy, enjoyed that honor, with the two of them shopping together almost every weekend. Well, mainly window-shopping—they couldn't afford much more than that, but it was still an activity they did together, which generally excluded Kirk.

He watched as Riley swiveled around in one of the elevated seats. She'd only been in this boat once before, on the inaugural family cruise. He could tell she was enjoying herself.

She must have had an inkling Kirk was watching her. She stopped swiveling and smiled warmly at him.

Then she looked up to the sky and pointed. "Daddy, look at the plane!"

Kirk directed his eyes skyward. "Yeah, just a little one. Probably only a two-seater. That's one of the things I like about fishing here, Riley. If the fish aren't biting it's fun to just watch the planes."

She giggled. "I thought you said the fish *always* bite here, Daddy."

"Well, a little white lie. Sometimes they don't."

Riley let out a mock gasp. "Daddy, you lied? I'm going to tell Mommy."

"Okay, you do that. And I'll tell her that you borrowed her lipstick last week."

Riley slid her fingers across her mouth. "Okay, my lips are sealed."

Kirk spun the wheel away from the shoreline, and headed out toward the middle of the lake. "Why don't we do some deeper fishing, Riley? We might get lucky and catch some brown trout."

"Whatever you say, Captain." She pointed into the sky again. "Oh, there's a helicopter now. How far away is the airport, Daddy?"

Kirk pointed to the west. "Only about a mile thataway. It's just a little airport, only small planes. But, they're fun to watch, huh?"

Riley went silent for a minute. Then she said softly, "I love you, Daddy."

"Aw, I love you, too, honey."

*****

The Laramie airport was coming into view on the horizon. Hal could see the two runways and he knew that one was 6,300 in length and the other was 8,500.

Even though both could handle this relatively light aircraft—with all the seats in the cabin removed, only four passengers aboard, and practically empty now of fuel—he'd play it safe and land on the longer one.

"Five minutes ETA, guys. Make sure you're all buckled in."

Ted glanced at Hal. "Aren't we going to get clearance to land?"

"Nope. All looks clear, so we're just gonna go for it."

"You can't do that."

"I can do whatever the fuck I want, Ted. I'm the captain."

Brock gazed out the side window. "I can just barely make out my plane, lined up facing out towards the smaller runway."

"Good. I'm going to land on the longer one, and then it'll be a quick jog for us over to your Challenger. I'm looking forward to riding in that little piece of luxury. Maybe you'll let me and Ziv take some turns flying it?"

"Be my guests. I think I'm ready for a nap anyway. Back in Malibu, I'm usually half-drunk by this time."

The jet was in a gradual descent via the auto-pilot. Hal glanced down at the altimeter and the airspeed. "Okay, auto-pilot off."

Ted flipped the switch. "Roger. Auto-pilot off."

"I've got the aircraft."

"Roger. You have the aircraft."

Hal expertly guided the plane on a run past the airport to the north, then eased into a gradual turn to the south, lining up the runway. He pushed the yoke gently forward, lowering the nose, while at the same time reducing his airspeed.

"Flaps up."

"Roger. Flaps up."

"Landing gear down."

Ted pushed the button commanding the landing gear to descend.

"Negative. Non-responsive."

"What?"

Ted pointed at the indicator lights. "No green lights indicated, Hal."

Hal continued on his straight course descending to the runway. He wasn't ready to abort yet.

"Try again."

Ted punched the button again. They heard a slight thumping noise. "Nose gear indicates down and locked. But, the two rear landing gear are still not engaged."

Hal glanced down at his altimeter. Only 250 feet above the ground now and the airspeed was down to 140 mph.

Ziv yelled. "Hal, where's the hatch so we can engage them manually!"

Hal laughed. "Isn't technology a wonderful thing? On these planes, there's no manual option. Only an electronic alternative command button. Try the ALT, Ted!"

Ted pushed the ALT. "No response. Rear gear still not deployed."

Hal yelled, urgency in his voice now. "Aborting landing! Grab your yoke! I'm powering up! Flaps down!"

"Roger. Flaps down."

"Front landing gear up."

"Roger. Front landing gear up."

The 767 was only 100 feet from the ground when it commenced its second climb of the day. Both pilots pulled back frantically on their yokes, while Hal powered up. The jet soared back into the sky.

Once they reached 1,000 feet, everyone sighed with relief. Hal levelled it off and began circling once again.

"If it had been just the front landing gear that didn't engage, we could have still landed. But, with the rear ones disengaged, the plane would have been smashed to pieces. And we could have disengaged the front gear and tried a belly landing on the concrete, but I doubt we'd have survived that either."

There were four pilots in the cockpit, but only Hal was doing any talking. There was, however, a lot of heavy breathing.

He pointed at the fuel gage. "We have to do something soon. We're riding on fumes right now."

Hal completed one full circle and then gazed off to the east.

Suddenly, he pointed, and turned the jet sharply to the right.

"There's our new runway, boys! Assume crash positions!"

*****

Kirk was a happy man. He'd just landed his first brown trout ever—these big guys were so elusive, and almost always prowled the depths. He was so glad he'd decided to take the boat out into the middle of the lake. The action out here wasn't as frequent as it was close to the shore, but the rewards were great for those with patience. And Kirk was a patient man.

Riley was looking on with excitement. "Will Mommy cook that for us tonight?"

"You bet she will, hon. She'll be so proud of us."

Kirk clamped his foot down onto the tail of the monster fish, and started the long struggle of removing the hook from its strong mouth. As he toiled away, an unexpected sound started resonating in his eardrums. A roar. He opened his mouth to try to clear his ears. They were at a high mountain altitude, and he knew that ears could be affected without warning up here.

He looked up from his work.

"Holy fucking mother of God!"

Riley giggled. "Daddy, you swore! I'm going to tell Mommy!"

He didn't answer. Couldn't answer. Just sat there frozen in horror, mouth open as wide as his facial muscles allowed.

Riley followed her dad's eyes up into the sky.

"Holy shit!"

Chapter 55

Vera Woodworth toiled away in the kitchen, preparing tea and goodies for her three best friends. They were already sitting in her living room watching the news, waiting patiently for their afternoon treats.

Vera loved Sundays—the weekly get-together with Hazel, June, and Fran. They would enjoy their sandwiches and cakes, all laid out in splendid fashion on a couple of three-tiered stands.

And then the tea, English Breakfast of course, to perk them up for a marathon of episodes of *The Young and the Restless*.

It was a beautiful fall day in Morristown, New Jersey, but the last thing Vera wanted to do was go outside. Sundays were always a special event, and intended to be spent in her suburban living room.

And, well, all four of them were getting on in years, so staying in was becoming more of a habit for each of them now. More out of necessity, too, because some essential mobility just wasn't possible for them anymore.

They all loved their favourite soap opera—in fact, it was an obsession for every single one of them. But no one wanted to sit through commercials, so Vera always recorded an entire week of episodes so they could watch them all together, free of interruptions.

Every Sunday, they would meet at Vera's for five hours of soap opera glory. It was exciting for each of them: discovering what Victor Newman was up to; debating whether or not Adam and Chelsea would ever get back together; and delighting in the latest disclosures about who was having sex together all the while unknowingly being related to each other.

Titillating stuff, to be sure. The four ladies' cheeks were usually flushed with gloriously crimson embarrassment after each episode, a glow that would linger with them for hours afterwards.

These Sunday afternoon tea parties were a tradition now, one that was unlikely to be broken. Unless, of course, *The Young and the Restless* were ever cancelled. Vera didn't want to think about that. That was just too horrible a thought to even consider.

They usually didn't wrap up their little tea parties until around 9:00 in the evening. Once the marathon soap opera viewing was over, they would sit and chat—usually just trying to predict what would happen on the show over the next week.

Then, next Sunday, they would do this all over again. Vera found that the days leading up to Sunday were rather pointless—she couldn't wish them away fast enough.

Vera carried the treat stands into the living room and placed them carefully onto the large coffee table. Then she hobbled back to the kitchen and returned with the teapot, cups, saucers, milk, and sugar.

"Okay, ladies. Tea is served. Are we ready to watch our show?"

Hazel raised her wrinkled and age-spotted hand. "Quiet for a second, Vera. Listen to this news report."

"...and as the video shows, the large jet swooped down over Central Park while it was full of New Yorkers enjoying a lovely Sunday afternoon. At this point, the authorities have no explanation for what happened, however they are indicating that it was more than likely a terrorist attack. There are reportedly at least a million Muslims living in New York City, and it is possible that several fundamentalist sleeper cells exist."

June shook a crooked finger at the TV screen. "Those bastards are going to kill us all! Just lock them up, that's what I say! And throw away the key!"

Fran chose a nice strawberry tart for herself off the stand. "I don't understand any of this. In our day, we worried about the Germans and the Russians; now it's these Indians and Pakistanis."

Vera corrected her. "No, Fran—it's the Arabs who are doing this."

Fran muttered, "Well, they all look the same to me. What's the difference?"

Hazel raised her hand again. "*Shh!* Will you girls stop yammering for a second so we can listen to this?"

"...said the plane came out of nowhere. Other witnesses report that it seemed to just disappear over the east side of the park. Information is sketchy right now—this just happened and we were lucky to have been here filming at Belvedere Castle. We'll show the footage again now. Clearly, this is a very large plane, but we're not able to identify it yet. You'll see that it comes in very low over the Reservoir, and then turns toward the east. We've been checking with all of our sources and at this point there is no indication of an airplane crash in the New York Metropolitan area, or anywhere else for that matter. What is also shocking about this is that it flew very low to the ground just above people's heads, yet there are surprisingly no reports of casualties. We'll keep you posted as more reports come in."

The video footage played and Hazel yelled, "Look at that plane! Look how low it is! These Muslim pilots are very well trained, my word!"

June poured herself a cup of tea. "We'd better get them before they get us, that's all I can say."

Vera sat down on the corner of the sofa. "Hush. He's talking again."

"...but the authorities are saying that all aircraft at JFK, Newark, and LaGuardia have been grounded. Pilots commanding planes waiting to land are being asked to divert to their alternate airports."

There was a pause for a few moments as the reporter scanned a sheet of paper handed to him. He looked directly into the camera with a look of genuine concern painted on his face.

"I've just been told that police units have been ordered to surround all mosques in the New York area, just as a precautionary move. They won't be entering the mosques, but will maintain a presence outside for security reasons. Viewers may recall that back in the months after 9/11, there were several acts of violence against Muslims as well as vandalism to their places of worship. No doubt that authorities wish to prevent that from happening again."

Fran raised her voice again. "Why don't they just go into those temples and drag them out? Whatever happened to fighting back against evil?"

Vera corrected her again. "Fran, they're not called temples. They're mosques."

"What's the difference? They shouldn't even be allowed to build them here!"

Suddenly, the TV screen went blank.

The ladies sat munching on their pastries, eyes glued to the TV as a red band scrolled across the screen.

It displayed the words:

"This is the Emergency Alert System. Stay tuned for an announcement. This is not a test."

Everyone sat in hushed silence; a silence broken only by the sound of tea cups rattling against saucers.

The headline continued to scroll for a solid minute, then suddenly the entire screen went red.

A man's voice now, an authoritative-sounding baritone, accompanied by the corresponding text of his words on the screen:

"This Emergency Alert System has been hijacked for a very urgent message, brought to you by concerned citizens of the world.

"Today, in New York City, a jumbo jet was seen soaring over Central Park. This was merely a demonstration of holographic technology—it was not a real plane.

"This is the same technology that was used on September 11, 2001, to trick the world into thinking that airplanes hit the Twin Towers, and to trick the world into going to war against Muslim countries blamed for the attacks.

"No planes hit the towers that day—instead they were hit by missiles fired from U.S. Navy vessels, and those very same missiles were hidden by holograms of jumbo jets. Citizens of New York saw an example today of how convincing and realistic these holograms are.

"In addition to the missile attacks, the towers were collapsed by controlled demolition. Nano-thermate was the substance used and it was applied to the structural supports of the towers prior to the attacks.

"The airplanes purportedly used in the 9/11 attacks, along with their crews and passengers, were all diverted that day to Denver International Airport. The people have been living there ever since, in an underground prison known as Emerald City.

"This facility is massive, and actually holds more than 10,000 people at the present time, kidnapped from all corners of the globe. They are being used as guinea pigs—or "canaries in the coal mine"— to test the viability of life underground in the event that the elite of society are required to be evacuated there due to a cataclysm. This facility has been, and still is, a project under the direction of the Central Intelligence Agency.

"As proof of this assertion, something else has happened today, virtually simultaneous with the hologram demonstration in Central Park.

"Three brave prisoners have escaped from this Denver underground facility known as Emerald City, and they have flown out on the very same Boeing 767 jet that the world was told crashed into the South Tower on 9/11. It will be landing somewhere in the western United States; its location will no doubt be reported shortly.

"The Tail number of this jet is N612UA, and the manufacturer's serial number is cn21873/41.

"Citizens and the media should demand that the authorities verify these numbers on this airplane once it is located. It is possible for people to check online themselves to see that these are the exact same numbers of United Airlines Flight 175 that you were told was destroyed in the South Tower on September 11, 2001.

"The world was deceived about 9/11 in a way that was not only unthinkable, but murderous. And wars waged against Muslim countries from these lies—"

Suddenly, the announcement was cut off mid-sentence and the screen went blank again.

Not even the news report from Central Park returned for the ladies' viewing pleasure.

Vera shrugged and picked up the remote. "Well, that was our excitement for the day."

She pressed the button, Recorded Programs.

"Now, let's hope we can watch our show without any more interruptions."

Chapter 56

Everything else was blocked out.

The trees, the sandy shoreline, the blue sky and the sun glinting off the nose of the plane. All of that was invisible—the only thing Hal could see was water, a dark blue magnet that was sucking them closer and closer by the second, to either oblivion or sanctuary.

At that point, Hal didn't know which it was going to be—all he knew was that a crash landing in the lake was the only option they had. They were out of fuel and the rear landing gear was defective.

He'd executed a water landing only once before. While flying a turbo prop for Air America, the nickname for the unofficial CIA drug smuggling airline.

Hal had been flying into Key West from Columbia with a cargo hold full of heroin. Both engines on the old plane had cut out twenty miles from the coast of Florida, and he had no choice but to drop the plane into the rough waters of the Gulf of Mexico. It was a small plane, so it was an easy swan dive. He'd radioed ahead to the eager beavers of the DEA, and they met him with a fleet of cigar boats.

Hal allowed himself a wry smile as he remembered that the DEA agents had been more concerned with the precious cargo than they were about him. After unloading the floating plane that was on the verge of going under, he recalled that they even debated whether or not there was going to be room for him in the boats.

Hal had been fast on the draw though, much faster than they were. And, only at gunpoint, did they manage to clear out a small space on the floor for little old Hal.

This time, there wouldn't be a fleet of boats meeting him. But luckily, the lake looming large in his view was narrow. And, thankfully, it was also long, which was a godsend for a plane this size.

The close proximity of the shoreline should allow them the opportunity to swim for it if they survived the splash landing. But he knew that the water would be cold—even though it was still autumn, he knew that mountain lakes at this high altitude only warmed up to about fifty-five degrees Fahrenheit at the best of times. So, they would have to swim fast to avoid hypothermia.

The plane was crossing the end of the lake now, and Hal skilfully manipulated the yoke to adjust the attitude of the nose. He pushed forward, lowering the jumbo jet to only about 100 feet above the water, then just as quickly pulled back on it to level the plane out of the dive. They were now parallel to the surface of the water.

"Flaps up."

"Roger. Flaps up."

Ted glanced over at Hal. "How are you going to do this?"

"The flaps will slow us down quite a bit. The lake is long, thank God, so we have a bit of space."

Hal then quickly pulled back on his yoke. "Help me, Ted. Pull back on yours."

Ted joined him in the exercise.

"Hal, won't we start climbing again?"

He pointed at the fuel gauge. "No, we're riding on empty now. The higher attitude of the nose and belly will merely help slow the plane down before we hit. Luckily, even without fuel, battery power allows us full use of the hydraulics."

Ted nodded, and took a deep breath.

Hal turned his head and glanced back at Brock and Ziv. He noticed that their faces were as white as sheets.

"You guys okay?"

Neither of them said a word. Their eyes were glued to the ominous sight facing them through the windshield. A dark blue body of water that, from their point of view, probably looked bottomless.

"Guys?"

Brock snapped out of his trance. "Yeah, fine, Dad."

Ziv followed Brock's lead. "Do your thing, Hal. We trust you."

Hal chuckled. "I guess you have no choice! When we get out of the plane, swim like you've never swum before. The water will be very cold. Leave the lifejackets behind—they'll just slow you down.

"When I yell to brace, you know what to do. We're going to hit the water with a lot of force, so put your heads between your legs. And Ted, for you and me, there's no room to bend our heads over, so push forward hard on the yoke at the very last second.

"And I mean, very last second. I'll be pulling the nose up just before we hit, so that the force of the impact will be absorbed by the belly. If the nose is too far down, it'll hit the water first and we'll somersault. So, push forward on the yoke once you hear the water splashing onto the belly. No earlier. I can't stress this enough."

Silence from his co-pilot.

"Ted, did you hear me? Do you understand? We don't want to slam forward and hit our chests against the yokes, so push forward but at the last second only."

Ted swallowed hard. "I hear you, Hal. I'm just in a bit of shock. I've trained to do this, but suddenly I seem to have forgotten everything."

"If it makes you feel better, I've done one of these before. No sweat."

Ted nodded. Suddenly, he pointed through the windshield. "Jesus! Look!"

Hal saw it at almost the same time. A boat with what looked like two occupants, right smack in the middle of the lake.

*****

"Dad! Do something!"

For a few moments, Kirk felt like he was daydreaming. This couldn't be happening—it had to be a dream.

Riley's frantic voice brought him back to reality.

The plane was huge, with a wingspan that appeared to take up the entire width of the lake. And it was almost as if it was flying in slow motion—and oh so silently. The plane seemed to be creeping up on them, aiming right for them.

Without a doubt, with the angle that it was at, the massive jet was going to land right on top of them. It was so close to the water now that the belly appeared to be kissing the gentle waves of Twelve Mile Lake.

Kirk abandoned his half-dead brown trout and dashed to the front of the boat. He turned the key in the ignition, and slammed the gear shift into Forward.

"Riley, lay down on the floor and wrap your arms around the legs of the chair!"

The child didn't have to be told twice. Riley took one last look down the lake and screamed. Then she dove to the floor and held on tight to the pedestal legs of the elevated seat. She didn't even care that the flip-flopping trout's snout was practically in her face.

Kirk spun the wheel of the sleek boat, rammed the throttle to full power, and then turned in the direction of the shore. The bow of the boat rose in the air, but they only moved a few feet. Kirk panicked. He stole a quick glance down the lake while pushing hard on the throttle. The plane was looming larger in his vision now, and it would only be a matter of seconds before it crashed on top of them.

Kirk kept the throttle at full power, but the boat was still barely moving in the water. He could hear the engine straining to its limits.

Suddenly, he knew why.

The anchor!

He'd forgotten about the anchor!

No time to pull it up now.

Kirk shut down the engine, then dashed back to the middle of the boat. He grabbed Riley around the stomach and forcibly yanked her arms away from the mounted chair legs.

Then he swung her into the air and tossed her overboard.

He dove in after her.

Riley surfaced first, sputtering and screaming at the top of her lungs. Kirk broke the surface a second later and quickly slapped her across the face. He yelled at her. "Wrap your arms around my neck! We have to dive!"

She obeyed. Kirk took three quick breaths, the most rapid hyperventilation he'd ever done. Then he allowed for one last glance upward. The monster was close, very close.

He dove.

*****

The forward motion of the giant airplane was already kicking spray up onto the windshield of the cockpit. Hal flipped on the wipers.

In Hal's estimation, they were only about fifty feet above the surface of the water now. At their present rate of descent, it looked like they were going to come right down on top of the boat.

"Brace!"

He pulled back on the yoke, which immediately corrected their downward motion. It was going to be close, but he was confident now that they would miss the boat, probably by just a few feet. At that same instant, he saw the man toss the little girl into the water and dive after her.

He breathed a sigh of relief, then pushed down on the yoke one last time. The nose of the plane responded immediately, and he could sense that the plane was now skimming the surface.

"Ted! Yank back hard!"

Both pilots pulled back on their yokes and the plane made its last nose-up manoeuvre. Hal could feel the upward motion and no longer saw water. All that was in his vision now was blue sky.

The belly of the plane hit the lake hard. The rushing sound of water frothing against the airframe was deafening.

Hal issued one last command. "Ted, push forward! Brace!"

In unison, the pilots pushed forward on their yokes and locked their elbows in place to prevent their upper bodies from lurching dangerously into the control column.

The plane snowploughed through the water for at least a hundred yards before finally coming to a stop and settling down, the friendly lake sloshing against the side cockpit windows.

Hal leaned forward and sighed.

There was a faint moaning sound from the backseats. He glanced back and noticed that Ziv's forehead was resting against Ted's chair back. He seemed to be okay other than being just a little dazed.

Hal then looked at Brock. He flashed his dad a relieved smile—didn't say a word, but found the strength to give him a thumbs up sign.

With everyone distracted, Ted suddenly made his move.

In one swift motion, he clicked off his seatbelt and whirled around. His hand grasped onto the grip of Ziv's pistol and pulled it out of his holster.

*****

Kirk and Riley surfaced, both gasping for breath after what seemed like an eternity under water. The first thing Kirk did was look toward his boat—he was relieved to see that it was still intact and none the worse the wear. The plane had missed it. The vessel was rocking in the waves created by the jet's landing, pulling hard against the anchor that was still resting on the bottom.

He glanced up the lake. The big jet had come to rest about a football field away, and it looked like it was already starting to sink into the depths.

"Riley, swim back to the boat! We have to try to rescue them!"

*****

Hal was too exhausted to react. He was vaguely aware of Ted's sudden movement, and felt the instant panic of knowing that a gun was on its way to being pointed at his head. But his usual lightning instincts didn't kick in fast enough.

Brock's did. As Hal recoiled back against the side window at the threat that was coming his way, Brock's foot lashed out from the back of the cockpit, striking Ted's wrist just hard enough to knock the gun loose.

Hal's own gun was in his hand a millisecond later. The long and deadly barrel rammed up against his co-pilot's forehead. Ted raised his hands, and shouted, "No, Hal! Please!"

Hal's finger was twitching against the trigger. He didn't know why he was hesitating. Maybe it was the stress they'd both just undergone as pilots together—partners in an intense experience that was hard to explain or even define. But—there was something causing him to pause. It didn't even matter to Hal that, if not for Brock, Ted probably would have blown his head off.

He just wasn't eager to pull the trigger.

Hal's life had never been about revenge or retaliation. Whenever he'd killed, it had always had purpose—either he had been paid to do it, or it was to eliminate a genuine obstacle or threat.

This time, he wasn't being paid, and neither was Ted a real threat. Thanks to Brock, the threat was over.

His moment of indecision received divine intervention—in the form of a strong and familiar hand on his wrist, forcing the barrel of the gun up in the direction of the cockpit ceiling.

Brock whispered. "No, Dad. No one else is going to die today."

Hal looked into his son's compassionate eyes, and nodded.

He stuffed the gun back into his waistband, while Brock retrieved the one off the floor that he'd kicked out of Ted's hand.

Ted muttered, "Thanks, Hal."

"Don't thank me. Thank my son."

Hal unfastened his seatbelt, stood up and glanced out the side window.

"I think we're going to be spared a swim, boys. That boat's coming for us. Let's move before this thing sinks."

Hal led the way back to the emergency exit over the wing, on the port side of the jet. He swung the handle and pulled the door inward. At that same instant as the door opened, a hatch door opened automatically along the side of the airframe, about four feet away from the door. A slide popped out and inflated. First, a "step" portion that covered the initial three feet of the wing structure. Then the rest of the thing inflated, which was the slide portion itself, extending down from the step section right to the surface of the water.

Hal put his hand on Ziv's shoulder. He still looked a bit dazed. "Are you okay?"

Ziv rubbed his bruised forehead. "Yeah, I'm fine. I think I'm just more shocked to be alive than anything else. That was one miracle landing you pulled off, Hal. I'm stunned. Thanks."

Hal laughed, stuck his head out the exit door, and looked skyward. "I think we all might have someone else to thank today."

He motioned for his three companions to go ahead of him. "Remember, stand only on the step part that's inflated, near the base of the wing. Don't walk further out onto the wing—it won't hold you."

Hal noticed that the fishing boat had already pulled up alongside the slide. He cheerily waved to the occupants.

"Hey, our welcoming party is here. It looks like we won't even get wet."

*****

They were standing on the shore of Twelve Mile Lake. The four of them had helped Kirk and Riley pull their boat up onto the sand, and now Hal was looking towards the forest. A truck and boat trailer were parked on a dirt road.

Hal pointed. "Is that your truck, Kirk?"

"Yes."

Hal held out his hand. "Give me the keys. We need to borrow it."

Kirk hesitated. Brock reached into his pocket and pulled out the large roll of bills that Sean Russell had given them. He peeled off 1,000 dollars.

"Here, for your trouble."

Kirk must have noticed the pistol in Brock's waistband when he reached into his pocket, because his hesitation ended quickly. He took the money and handed the keys to Hal.

Then he directed his gaze back to Brock—from the gun in his waist, right up to his face.

"Am I going crazy or are you the actor, Brock Winters?"

Brock laughed. "I get that all the time. I can only wish, huh?"

Kirk frowned, not convinced. Then he turned back to Hal. "Where will my truck be?"

Hal ignored the question. "How do we get to the Laramie airport from here?"

Kirk pointed. "Go north on the dirt road for about five minutes, then hang a left onto Hwy 130. Keep going west until you hit Aerospace Drive, then go left again. That'll lead you right into the Laramie airport. Should take you no longer than ten minutes."

Hal squinted as he gazed off into the west. "Well, that's where your truck will be, then. We have another flight to catch."

Hal smiled at the father and daughter team. "Ciao. And—thanks for plucking us out of the lake. We appreciate it."

He jerked his head in the direction of the truck and his three companions followed.

Hal suddenly stopped, turned, and put his hand up. "No, Ted. You can hike to the airport with Kirk and Riley. I don't want to have to worry about what to do with you."

Hal, Brock, and Ziv climbed into the truck and Hal started the ignition. Just then, he noticed a little hand resting on the window frame. Riley was leaning against the door, her innocently pretty face gazing up at him.

"We have to scoot, Riley. Back away, girl."

"I know, I know. But, before you go, Mister, what happened? Why were there no other passengers on that big plane?"

"There were, Riley. At one time, a long time ago—there were."

*****

As Hal was turning the truck onto Aerospace Drive, Brock rested his hand on his father's shoulder.

"Where to next, Dad?"

"I don't know. Nowhere in the U.S., that's for sure! Where is it you've always wanted to go?"

"Costa Rica. Always wanted to live there."

"Perfect. That's where we'll go, then. And the best part is, it's next door to Panama—which is where I have a few million stashed in a numbered account."

Brock laughed. "God, we think so much alike. That's where I have a few million, too!"

Hal smiled warmly at his favorite son. "Gotta love those tax havens, huh? And the good thing is, I know people in Costa Rica, Panama, and even Nicaragua, from a bunch of jobs I did down there in Central America. So—we'll have connections.

"Also, there's no extradition from Costa Rica to the U.S. for political or military matters, and I think what we've been involved in qualifies for that protection. And, Ziv, you're Israeli but also Canadian—there's no extradition to Canada from Costa Rica for any reason whatsoever."

Brock glanced at Ziv. "Do you have any money hidden in Panama,

Ziv?"

Ziv shook his head. "No, the Mossad obviously wasn't as generous as the CIA or Hollywood. I think I'll need a loan from you rich buggers."

Hal frowned. "A loan? You're insulting me, Ziv. There'll be plenty to go around for all three of us amigos, trust me. Life will be good. Well, at the very least, it can't be worse than Emerald City!"

Brock nudged Ziv's elbow. "So, what do you think about hiding out in Costa Rica, Ziv?"

"Sounds like a marvelous idea to me. And it's close to Belize."

"Why? What's in Belize?"

Ziv sighed and gazed dreamily out the truck window. "Just a lady I used to know."

Brock's curiosity was piqued now. "Oh, really? What's she like?"

Ziv looked Brock in the eyes and winked. "Cat Woman."

Chapter 57

Bradley Crawford knew his way around Calgary pretty well. He'd been there many times over the years, doing background on stories and attending journalism symposiums.

He was always impressed with how young and vibrant the city was, not just by the majesty of the glass and steel skyscrapers, but also by the attitude of its million-plus citizens.

The city was known for its "can do" approach to life, and it certainly had plenty of practice at it over the years, what with the boom/bust cycles of a city whose economy depended very much on world oil prices. The province of Alberta was one of the world's foremost oil capitals, and Calgary was the white collar center for the industry.

In fact, the man Brad was visiting today was himself a former CEO of a prominent oil company.

Jack Howser, the pivotal player in the only other serious attempt to expose 9/11, had put the story behind him and moved on with his life.

Despite the harrowing ordeal he and Kerrie Joplin had endured back in 2009 as they followed the clues left behind by Kerrie's dead father, Jack had apparently reconciled in his mind that he was just glad to be alive. He wrote his "fiction" novel and then squirreled his secrets away with several law firms. Secrets that would automatically be exposed once Jack or Kerrie passed away.

When Sean Russell had told Brad about the Jack Howser ordeal back when they met in the warehouse in Toronto, Brad was intrigued. Intrigued that there had been a previous failed attempt to expose the massive deception of 9/11.

And intrigued that Jack Howser had followed the mysterious clues left on a microchip under the skin of his dog, Mule, to actual documents hidden away by CIA agent Mitch Joplin. Documents that proved without a shadow of a doubt that the collapse of the World Trade Center towers was caused by controlled demolition.

This information was earth-shattering, yet it was hidden away. And it would stay hidden until Jack or Kerrie died, which could be many years from now.

But Brad had a story to do right now. He couldn't wait years.

So, he'd placed a call to Jack Howser and identified himself. Luckily, his name carried some weight and Jack knew right away who he was. Brad didn't want to get into a discussion over the phone, mainly because of his recollection of what Sean had said. He'd admitted that the CIA was still watching Jack Howser—which probably meant that they were listening in as well.

All Brad told Jack was that he was working on a story and wanted to have a chat with him for background.

Jack didn't need much convincing—in fact, he seemed intrigued without even knowing what the story was about. Brad thought that was a good sign, and he got the feeling that Jack was just one of those enthusiastic, curious types. Which meant that he was exactly the way he'd portrayed himself as the main character in his novel, Mule. He'd even used real names in the book, which Brad thought was brave, but of course the book had the usual disclaimer about all names and places being fictional even if they represented what seemed to be real people. Brad figured that using real names in the book was Jack's little way of giving the CIA the finger.

He was hoping that Jack might like to give them the finger again.

Brad exited from the Deerfoot Trail expressway and meandered along in his rental car to the southwest quadrant of the city. He veered down a side street off Macleod Trail, and then turned onto Poplar Street. Drove down to number 207, and pulled into the driveway of the attractive but modest wartime-era bungalow.

He could tell that this was a high-end neighborhood, with a good mixture of new mansions and older character homes. Jack's house looked like one of the stubborn holdouts, with newish monster homes on either side of him.

Brad remembered that this area of the city was called Elbow Park, and a lot of the older homes like Jack's would fetch a hefty sum if sold today. Looking down the side of the yard, he could also tell that Jack's home backed onto the Elbow River; a valuable amenity that alone would add half a million to the list price.

Brad sat in the car for a few minutes and reflected on where things stood.

It had been two weeks already since his disguised voice had been broadcast all over the United States through the hacked Emergency Alert System.

Also, that very same day, a bewildering event had occurred in Central Park, with the horrific image of a 767 jumbo jet hologram soaring over the heads of picnickers.

And the day hadn't ended with that—his three friends having escaped from Emerald City in the very same 767 jet the world had been tricked into thinking crashed into the South Tower on 9/11. Due solely to Hal Winters' piloting wizardry, they'd made a miraculous landing on a high mountain lake in Wyoming.

Yet, the mainstream media had avoided covering any of these events. They had all been swept under the carpet, simply through avoidance. The only media outlets that covered the stories were the alternative underground sites, and only a very small population of the United States even bothered to read stories from those sources.

As a journalist, Brad thought this was absolutely incredible. So much for a "free press." They were simply smothered, either through threats, blackmail, or other means. All three events were monumental stories—but they had been ignored.

After the initial hysteria from the local media over the hologram incident in Central Park, the story just simply disappeared. Brad saw a footnote mentioning that an airplane had encountered a mechanical problem and detoured off course from its planned landing at JFK.

Of course, the reports from picnickers that the plane had "just disappeared into thin air" were also ignored and received no further mention after the initial impulsive reporting from journalists on the ground. There were musings all over social media, but hordes of mysterious posters discounted and ridiculed the event to the point that most users of social media probably just got tired of reading about it. And also no doubt questioning in their own minds what the truth was. Brad suspected that a very active strategy had been employed by hidden puppeteers. The sad part was—he wasn't even all that surprised.

It had all just gone strangely silent.

Then the broadcast on the Emergency Alert System—no media outlet gave any serious consideration to the subject matter of the broadcast, despite the shocking assertions Brad had stated over the air.

The EAS broadcast was blamed by government sources on, first, the Russians, and then the North Koreans. FOX News finally came out with the conclusion that the broadcast was simply another attempt by the hacker group, Anonymous, to discredit the United States of America with their conspiracy theory lies. And, of course, Anonymous was then labelled as a domestic terrorist group, one that the FBI would track down and prosecute to the full extent of the law.

And most incredulous of all, the reports of a jumbo jet crash landing into a lake in Wyoming got virtually no mention at all. The plane was not identified either, even though Brad had read out the tail and registration numbers over the EAS broadcast, and warned that a plane had escaped from the Denver facility and could be easily identified as one of the 9/11 jets.

There was no national news coverage whatsoever of this crash landing. There was, however, a tiny news article in the *Laramie Chronicle*—an interview with a father and his daughter who insisted that they had rescued four men from the plane, and that one of them was the actor, Brock Winters.

Brad shook his head in disgust. Journalism had sure changed from what he had studied in university. Now, it was simply entertainment. Nothing of substance was ever reported, unless it involved America or Great Britain in some victorious position with one of their silly trumped-up wars, or unless it involved demonizing countries that were labelled as "enemies." The news was screened and filtered to the extreme, yet the public was still convinced that they had freedom of the press.

And why wouldn't they think that? People don't know what they don't know, and when most of the public relied on the "trusted" mainstream news sources that they'd grown up with—news programs that were branded indelibly into their brains—then they simply believed what they were told. And if they weren't told about it, in their minds, it simply hadn't happened.

This was the conundrum that a journalist like Brad faced. Yet, he was somewhat of an idealist and wasn't yet prepared to give up. Some things just had to be told.

There was supposed to have been a fourth prong to their plan— Sean Russell had told them that was his prong, and that he'd take care of it within a few days after their eventful Sunday. Brad hadn't been in touch with Sean—in fact, he'd avoided doing that out of fear of exposing him. But he thought that by now he would have heard from someone in their little group of five, that the fourth prong had been carried out.

It had been two weeks now—nothing.

And none of them knew what Sean had been planning to do, but he did mention that it had a personal connection for him. Brad figured that since Sean had engineered the EAS broadcast, the fantastic hologram display over Central Park, and the unbelievably risky escape from Emerald City, that whatever he was planning to do was going to be equally spectacular.

But nothing so far. He hoped that Sean was okay. Maybe he'd just decided to cool things down a bit after that eventful Sunday. Sean had been careful to keep himself safely removed from each of the three things that happened, but maybe someone had connected the dots. Brad hoped not. Sean was a brave man—he liked him. And he'd been an absolute genius at planning each of their risky manoeuvres. The man's bravery at risking exposure was the main inspiration for Brad continuing along in his quest to expose this entire horrifying story.

On a positive note, Brad was happy to have received an email from Ziv saying that he, Hal, and Brock were safely tucked away on a beach in Costa Rica. They'd already bought a large house together, dirt cheap, and that life was good so far. Mind you, it had only been two weeks so Brad wondered how long it would take for them to get isolation fever.

Brad chuckled when he recalled the last line in Ziv's email, asserting once again his unassailable right to a byline on Brad's soon to be published story.

Yes, Ziv would indeed have a byline. A good man—and a brave one, just like Sean.

Brad got out of his car, walked up to the front door, and rang the doorbell.

The door opened to the sound of a dog barking and growling. A tall handsome man stood resplendent in the foyer, with a beautiful border collie at his side.

"Bradley Crawford, I presume?"

Brad held out his hand. "And you're Jack Howser."

Jack responded with a hearty handshake. "I sure am. And I recognize you. Have read all of your stories—you've become quite the legend over the years."

"Thanks, Jack. At least I have one fan."

The dog was still growling—just under his breath now, but he clearly wasn't sure about whether or not Brad should be allowed to enter.

Brad knelt down on the front step. "My God! Is this him? Mule?"

"Yep, that's my boy, alright. He'll settle down in a second. Once I pour you a scotch, he'll know that you're a friend."

Brad held out the back of his hand and let Mule sniff it. The dog snorted, then darted back down the hall into the kitchen.

"I think he's accepted you now. He's gone back to finish his lunch."

Brad rose to his feet and smiled. "Jack, it's bizarre for me to meet both of you. After reading your novel, I feel like I know you already. And, Mule still looks like a youngster."

Jack jerked his head in the direction of the living room and Brad followed. "He's incredible. Going on fourteen years old now, but you wouldn't know it. And, I thank God he's still around. Don't know what I'd do without him. He's my little buddy, and he saved my life more than once!"

Brad sat down on the couch, while Jack stood at the bar pouring their drinks.

"I enjoyed your novel. That was quite the hair-raising experience you and Kerrie had, and Mule was certainly quite the hero. Was all of that true, Jack?"

Jack handed him his drink, then sat down in the opposite chair. He smiled and winked. "Of course not, Brad. Didn't you read the disclaimer? It was all fiction."

Brad grinned back. He studied Jack Howser a little bit closer, now that they were sitting across from each other. A very handsome man, and slim and trim. A man who obviously worked at keeping himself in shape. Brad remembered from the book that Jack was an expert in martial arts, so that would explain it. Based on what he knew, he figured Jack would be around sixty years old now, but he sure didn't look it. He also had a full head of hair, but it couldn't hide the noticeable scar that snaked across the top of his forehead.

"Forgive me for staring, Jack, but is that scar on your head from the bear attack you wrote about?"

Jack ran his fingers across it. "Yeah, that's the scar alright. And no problem about the staring. It's a great conversation piece, let me tell you. Makes me much more interesting than I really am."

Suddenly, Mule came bounding in from the kitchen and jumped up on the couch beside Brad. The dog placed his chin on the visitor's lap and whimpered. Brad obliged by scratching the top of his head. "God, what a beautiful dog. And a famous one at that!"

"I think he's accepted you now, Brad. I told you—scotch always does the trick."

Jack took a long sip of the liquid, and then leaned forward, elbows resting on his knees. "So, while it's great meeting a famous journalist like you, I'm naturally curious as to why you're here. And I'm kind of a curious guy to begin with."

Brad laughed. "Yeah, I got that from the book. Well, I'm here for a specific reason. Let's go outside and talk, if you don't mind. Just in case someone's listening in."

Jack frowned. "Sounds serious. Okay, we'll go out in the backyard."

He led the way through the kitchen out to the backyard, then down to the edge of the river where a cedar gazebo stood, complete with padded chairs and a fire pit. Mule followed them and immediately dove into the river, swimming frantically after some kids on a rubber raft.

"That water must be cold!"

"It is, but Mule doesn't care. He's tough as nails. So, Brad, tell me a story—I know you have one. I can sense these things."

Brad started from the beginning and didn't hold anything back. Right from the three people he killed on Vancouver Island, up to that eventful Sunday a couple of weeks ago when the three spectacular things happened within minutes of each other.

He could tell he had Jack's attention. His host had brought the bottle of scotch out with them, and excitedly polished off three shots during Brad's story.

When Brad was finished, Jack just sat there and stared at him for a couple of minutes. Then he looked out to the river's edge where Mule lay drying off in the sun.

Suddenly, he spoke, slowly and softly. "I didn't hear about any of this, Brad. Those three things are biggies, yet there was nothing in the news at all."

Brad nodded. "The Canadian press is bought and paid for, just like those south of the border. They're all in cahoots together."

"It's disgusting."

"Yes, it is."

"So, this CIA agent gave you my name?"

"Yes, he told me about your attempts to expose 9/11 back in 2009, and he's the one who said you're still being watched."

Jack laughed. "I'm not surprised. What's this guy's name?"

Brad shook his head. "Can't tell you that. No one can know, and my story won't mention him either. I don't have to tell you that he'd be in serious peril if it ever came out that he helped us with this. In my view, he's the real deal—a true patriot. Even though he performed his own guilty role in all of this over the years, he finally found his conscience—and his courage."

Jack rubbed the scar on his forehead, and then took another sip of his scotch.

"Christ, tell me about it. Those guys don't fool around. Kerrie and I really feared for our lives back then. And we finally decided it was best not to expose anything—that we'd be better off just bartering for our lives instead. Which we did."

Brad crossed his legs and leaned against the back of the gazebo seat.

"Jack, I feel this burning need to do something about this. I'm a journalist, so telling stories comes naturally to me. But I'm horrified that a lot of good people in high places have done nothing to break this wide open. This is why governments get away with what they get away with—because they know they can. We let them. And the media no longer holds their fingers to the fire. They seem to be manipulated or controlled; I don't know which it is, but it's insidious. We're becoming a society of zombies, believing what we're told, and not questioning the things we're not."

Jack swatted at a wasp. "So, you're on a crusade. Are you prepared for the backlash?"

"Hopefully, I can publish the story before they can do anything to me. I have all the letters from Hal Winters, and the cassette tape from the cockpit. I have the information that my CIA contact shared with us about how 9/11 was pulled off with missiles and holograms. And I will have first-hand testimony from Hal Winters, his son Brock, and my colleague, Ziv Dayan, that this Emerald City in Denver really exists."

Jack swatted at another wasp, then stood up and adjusted the bee-catcher hanging from the rafters of the gazebo.

"Brad, the major part of your story is going to be about this Emerald City place. Because, when you think of it, that's the only part of your story that can still be proven. It's there, in living color. People are imprisoned there. It can be exposed.

"The 9/11 stuff is almost impossible to prove now. The cockpit tape could have been faked and it will be posed that way. Your CIA contact won't expose himself, so you can't use his testimony. That

9/11 plane that crashed into the lake has probably been hauled away and destroyed by now. So that opportunity is gone.

"But, this Denver airport thing is shocking stuff—horrifying. It's a story that needs to be told, and can be proven because it exists. It's right there in Colorado for everyone to see if it can be exposed. But it will be dangerous for you."

"Yeah, I know. Which is what I came to see you about. You have first-hand experience and documents hidden that would be instrumental in exposing the whole goddamn mess, proof that the towers were rigged for demolition. So, 9/11 can indeed be exposed as well as the Denver airport travesty. The protection you negotiated will probably be moot once my story comes out. In other words, once it's out there, there would be no point in them killing anyone."

"Brad, it'll still be dangerous *beforehand*; before the story comes out."

"I know." Brad chuckled. "So, despite that, would you like to be part of it?"

Jack jumped up from his seat and rubbed his hands together.

"Are you kidding? Hell, yes!"

Brad held out his hand. "Deal?"

"Do I get a byline?"

Brad sighed. *Everyone wants to win a Pulitzer Prize.*

"Yes, Jack, you'll get a byline."

Jack's handsome face lit up like a Christmas tree.

He shook Brad's hand. "It's a deal, then. And, speaking of stories, I have a very intriguing video of the JFK assassination to show you. Maybe the next time I see you we can mull it over together. Trust me, you'll need an entire bottle of scotch just for yourself once you watch that thing!"

Chapter 58

Sean Russell loved to eat, especially when someone else was doing the cooking.

He wasn't a fan of his own culinary skills, probably because he never put the effort into doing it right. For one thing, he never had the time, but more to the point, he found it hard to get enthusiastic when he was cooking just for himself.

So most of the time he just picked up fast food, or ate on the run when he was out in the field. Not good for his health, Sean knew, but he vowed to himself that one day when he retired he would make up for lost time. He would take a cooking course and learn how to do things properly. If he knew what he was doing, then it wouldn't seem like such a chore and wouldn't take him so long to do it.

But one problem would still remain, even at that future date. He'd still be eating alone.

Tonight, he wasn't alone, though. In fact, he hadn't been for quite a while now. Ever since he'd rescued Jannat from that CIA prison.

Sean was literally devouring his food tonight. He didn't really know what it was he was eating, but it was delicious. After cooking him unadventurous American food for the last couple of weeks, Jannat convinced him to let her make a traditional Persian dish for dinner. Sean relented, reluctantly. He didn't know quite what to expect, but she assured him he'd love it. Years ago when they were together, she'd never pushed her culture's food on him. Never even offered. Perhaps she was insecure about it back then. But now she seemed confident—and gently insistent.

They were sitting across the dining room table from each other. Jannat cocked her head to one side, and asked, "Well?"

Sean put down his fork. "This was the tastiest meal I've had in a long time. What's in it?"

Jannat laughed. "No way. I'm not confessing. If I tell you, you'll never let me make my dishes for you again."

Sean stared into her beautiful green eyes, and she stared back.

"Freudian slip on your part, Jan. Sounds like you're planning to hang out in my kitchen for a little while longer."

Jannat smiled and resumed eating.

Sean studied her. She'd made a remarkable comeback over the last few weeks. Her hair was full of life and sparkle again, her face and figure had filled back out, and those remarkable eyes held promise once again.

But, most importantly, she'd expressed no desire to leave. They weren't quite back to the way they had been two decades ago, but they seemed to be getting closer every day. They were comfortable talking with each other, watching TV, and had even played a few games of tennis on Sean's private court. She was just as good as she had been twenty years ago—he still couldn't beat her, but he didn't care. All he cared about was that she was still with him.

Her health had improved so dramatically that she didn't even need the nurse any longer. When Sean thought back to how she'd looked in that prison, it was like a miracle. At the time, he hadn't known if he was doing the right thing by whisking her out of that place, but now he was sure glad he had.

Even the risk it posed hadn't bothered him, and it still didn't bother him. It was like a dream come true having Jannat back with him again; something he'd never imagined could happen.

It felt like they had a second chance now and, in Sean's heart, he knew he would never want anyone else. He wanted Jannat Shirazi, and he had no doubt in his mind that he was still in love with her after all these years.

Jannat looked up from her plate and caught him staring. "Penny for your thoughts?"

He blurted out, "I've changed, Jan."

She smiled. "I know you have. I can tell. The risks you took in rescuing me told me a lot. And the things you did with your friends, trying to break the story wide open, told me even more. Twenty years ago, you never would have even considered betraying your oath."

Sean grimaced. "As you know, I wanted to do even more. But, you rejected the idea."

Jannat frowned. "Sean, you were always an idealist, even back when we were together. You tried to make me think you were just a lawyer, but I knew you were working for the CIA. And I really do believe you thought that was a noble pursuit—somehow they'd convinced you of that, and persuaded you that the ends always justify the means. It took many years for you to realize how twisted it all was."

Sean looked down at his plate and pretended to pick at his food.

"Your idea to hold a press conference and disclose to the world about the illegal prison here would have been a huge mistake. And putting me on the podium to tell my horrible story would have been fruitless. That was the idealist in you again. I admire that quality in you, but sometimes it leads you down the wrong path."

Sean nodded. "You're right."

Jannat put down her fork. "I mean, what would that press conference have accomplished? You've seen for yourself how the media completely avoided covering those three big events you orchestrated. You, more than most people, know that the media is controlled by the government. It's a tragedy, but it's true.

"If you'd held that press conference and shocked the audience with the torture prison story, they would have immediately hauled you away. Then they would have embarked on a crusade in the media to discredit you—paint you out as a rogue agent, or someone in the throes of a nervous breakdown. Or, even worse, they would have invented backstories about you, ruining your reputation and your life. You'd cease to exist.

"As for me, you can probably guess what would have happened if I had made a speech accusing the government of imprisoning me, raping me, torturing me, killing my husband in front of me. I would have been demonized as some kind of terrorist, and probably never seen alive again. It doesn't matter that I'm an American citizen—all that matters to them is that I have a heritage that symbolizes what they choose to hate."

Sean didn't know what to say. She was right. And, once again, he was wrong.

"My dear Sean—your idealism finally led you to do the right thing. What you arranged with the EAS broadcast, the hologram over Central Park, and the escape from the Denver Airport, were amazing feats. I'm astonished at what you were able to do, and so proud of how brave you and your friends were. You tried—it didn't work. But, at least you tried, and that alone should relieve your conscience about the past. What you planned to do with the press conference, though, was just suicidal. It might have worked if they hadn't buried the other stories.

"You should be glad that you're safe—none of what you arranged was tied to you. If we did the press conference, though, that would have been the end of us."

Sean gazed into her eyes. "Are you saying that there's still an us?"

"Do you want there to be?"

He got up from his chair and walked around to her side of the table. Sean knelt down on one knee. "Yes, Jan. I want there to be. I know it's too soon for you, but one day I want to kneel like this again and ask you to marry me. And I'll want you to say, 'Yes.'"

"It is too soon, you're right. I feel as if one day I'll want you down on that knee. But, for the moment, I want you somewhere else."

"Where?"

"In the kitchen. It's your turn to do the dishes."

Sean laughed, then leaned in close to her and gently kissed her on the lips. She kissed him back. And he realized at that moment that it was the first time they'd kissed like this in almost two decades. He held the kiss for as long as he could; happily, he could tell that she was attempting the same thing.

*****

Sean was trying to concentrate on a magazine, but his stomach was in knots. He was waiting in the office of his boss, Jarod McKenzie, the director of the National Clandestine Service. Sean used to think of it as an honor to be employed by the most secretive of all the CIA divisions, but not anymore. Now it just made him feel sick.

And adding to the sick feeling in his stomach was now the worry that they knew; that somehow, they knew. And that at one of these meetings, Jarod would tell him that they knew.

Sean thought back to one particular meeting after the eventful Sunday that he'd engineered. In fact, it was the very next day, Monday. He and several other directors were assembled for a crisis discussion.

It wasn't a long meeting at all. With the usual CIA efficiency, they quickly and coldly discussed damage control.

Sean was assigned to the task of salvaging the 767 out of Twelve Mile Lake in Wyoming. So, he sent a team from the Army Corps of Engineers, who had the plane out of there and disposed of at the bottom of the Pacific within two days. He couldn't deny the irony of his being assigned to get rid of the jet for which he'd also planned the escape.

And the director of media relations was asked to explain to the group what was being done to keep a lid on all three incidents. His response was calm and cool—that no one needed to worry, that he'd already been in touch with all of the national media outlets. Issued the order to stifle any stories related to the EAS broadcast, the hologram over Central Park, and the belly-landing of the plane in Wyoming. He'd made it clear to all of the media heads that there would be serious consequences for anyone who gave the stories any air or print time.

His threats had obviously worked.

Suddenly, Sean's daydreaming was shattered by the door bursting open, followed by Jarod sweeping into the office like a tornado.

He rushed over and plopped down on the chair opposite Sean.

He was out of breath. "I'm sorry to have kept you waiting, Sean. What a day so far!"

Sean pretended to be concerned. "Why, what's happened?"

Jarod waved his hand. "Oh, just administrative crap. Congress is giving us a hard time on the budget, so we have to go back to the drawing board. I wish those bastards would appreciate what it is we do, and realize that intelligence doesn't come cheap."

"It's all about votes and getting headlines for their constituents, Jarod. You know that—they're just grandstanding. They always relent in the end."

Jarod nodded in agreement. "Yeah, you're right. But we've got better things to do than pander to those prima donnas. Anyway, that's not why I called you here. Do you remember I was telling you about those Ukrainian nuclear physicists?"

"Yes, they were helping us develop the seaborne shield."

Jarod smiled. "Well, guess what? It's ready for testing. I need you to escort them to San Diego on one of our jets. They want their money, but I told them we'd need to verify first that the test phase is successful before they get one more fucking cent. They're flying here from Kiev on Thursday. I told them that you'll be meeting them, going with them to the naval base, and that their money will be waiting for you to sign off on once they've done their bit."

Sean pulled a pad and pen out of his suit pocket. "What are their names again?"

Jarod laughed. "Don't even try to spell these, just write down the sounds. The tall guy is Andriy Kovalenko, and the other one is Dmytro Shevchuk. Of course, the jerk in charge of Ukraine right now has no idea we're paying his scientists. And Russia's spies certainly have their eyes on these guys, too. The greedy stooges will be traveling here under fake identifications and wearing disguises. Doesn't really matter—they're all ugly square-headed sons of bitches anyway."

"Alright, I'll meet them at Dulles airport on Thursday. What time have you scheduled our plane to leave?"

"You'll be using the Learjet 60, and I've asked the boys to have it fueled and ready to go for you at 1:00 in the afternoon."

Sean stood. "Done. It'll be a relief for you to get this project finished."

*****

"How long will you be gone?"

"Just two nights, max. I'll be home by Saturday."

Jannat reached out and held his hand, feigning a pout. "I'll miss you."

Sean wrapped his arms around her slender shoulders and gave her a gentle hug. Suddenly, he had a thought. "Why don't you come with me?"

Jannat pulled back, a glow in her eyes. "Really? But, I can't fly on that plane with you."

"No, you can't. But I can buy you a ticket to San Diego. I'll be flying out of the Dulles executive jet section, and I can drop you off at Departures in the main terminal. When you get to San Diego, you can take a shuttle out to the Sheraton, which is only half a mile from the airport. I'll meet you there Friday night if I finish early—or Saturday morning at the latest. Then, you and I can fly somewhere together."

"Where will you stay until then?"

"We have our own CIA accommodations at the Coronado Naval Base on San Clemente Island, just seventy miles off the San Diego coast. That's where the test is going to take place, and we anticipate it'll go smoothly, so there should be no delay in me getting to you."

Jannat put her hand on his shoulder and squeezed. "We haven't taken a trip in, what, about twenty years?" She laughed. "Where on earth shall we go?"

"I'll give that assignment to you. You'll be at the Sheraton for a couple of days, so research to your heart's content. You decide, and I'll be your willing travel companion to wherever you choose."

Jannat scratched her chin. "I'm going to need some new clothes."

Sean kissed her on the forehead. "Well, that's your second assignment. San Diego is a great city to shop in, so spend to your heart's content. I'll give you one of my credit cards—you can use that until we get you one of your own again."

Jannat's face was beaming, and Sean's heart was pounding in response to the joy that was lighting up her face. He hadn't seen her this happy since she'd returned to him, and he had to admit that he hadn't been this happy himself in a long time.

"Can you afford the time off work?"

"I have some time coming to me, so I'll just take it."

Suddenly, a crazy thought popped into his head. Crazy indeed, but it felt right.

"Maybe we won't come back."

Jannat took a step back. "Are you serious?"

"Yes, I think I am, Jan."

"What will we do for money?"

Sean shrugged. "No worries, there. I have lots of money stashed away in a numbered account in Barbados. We can access it easily, from anywhere in the world."

Jannat leaned in to him, and wrapped her arms around his waist. Then she laid her head against his chest. "Oh, Sean, let's do it. Let's find some place nice. And safe."

*****

Sean walked up to the government desk in the executive terminal. A uniformed guard was staring at his computer screen.

He flashed his credentials. "I'm here to escort Kovalenko and Shevchuk to Coronado Naval Base."

The guard clicked a few strokes on his keyboard. "Yes, Director Russell. We already took them out to the plane, so you can join them. As soon as you board, the pilots will take off."

"Good. Thanks."

Sean walked out onto the tarmac and climbed the stairs up into the sleek Learjet. He loved this jet and had flown on it many times before. It seated up to ten passengers, so he and his two companions would have plenty of room to stretch out.

The pilots were already in the cockpit. The CIA had a large roster of pilots and Sean knew most of them. They turned around in their seats when he entered.

"Hey, Sean. Good to see you again."

Sean shook the captain's hand. "Sid, it's been awhile."

"Sure has. Do you know my co-pilot, Jeff?"

Sean reached his hand out to Jeff, who shook it warmly. "No, but good to meet you."

"You, too, Director Russell."

"Call me Sean."

Sid picked up his clipboard, and scanned the top page. "Looks like a smooth flight today, Sean, so we'll get going if you're ready. Weather looks clear all the way to San Diego, so you can just relax and enjoy the ride. Should be five hours, gate to gate."

Sean turned to head back into the cabin. "Okay, wake me when we get there."

The two Ukrainians were seated, with their briefcases open. Both were reviewing documents that Sean guessed had something to do with tomorrow's test. He introduced himself, shook both of their hands, and then took a seat farther back in the cabin. He really didn't want to get into a discussion with these scumbags. He was here to escort them, oversee the test, and that was it. Even though the CIA had lots of traitors like these on their payroll and he was used to dealing with them, he didn't have to like them.

He knew this test was important, though. The American aircraft carrier *Dwight D. Eisenhower* had been disabled in the Barents Sea last year. Russian submarines were the culprits, and it was surmised that they possessed an incredibly powerful EMP weapon that the CIA didn't seem to know about. The brass took a lot of flak over that, because intelligence gathering had obviously failed. It was embarrassing for the largest aircraft carrier in the U.S. Navy to be stranded at sea.

So, the CIA tapped into their Ukraine sources and managed to find these two greedy sons of bitches. They had a solution to the problem, a specially designed seaborne shield that would protect naval vessels against virtually any EMP weapon. These guys had been involved in the original design of the Russian technology, so they knew how to defeat it. For a price, of course.

Sean sighed and closed his eyes. Soon, he and Jannat would be flying to someplace nice, and hopefully he'd never ever have to deal with this kind of incendiary bullshit again.

*****

Sean awakened to the unmistakable sensation of the plane descending. He yawned, stretched, and glanced at his watch.

Something's wrong. They'd only been in the air for three hours, and the flight time to San Diego was five hours. They shouldn't be descending yet.

He pushed up his window blind and looked outside. *This isn't*

California. He could see the snow-capped Rocky Mountains off on the horizon.

He got out of his seat and walked to the cockpit door. It was closed, which was unusual on these private CIA junkets. Cockpit doors were never closed, and the pilots usually wandered into the cabin and bantered with the VIP passengers. He turned the handle, but it was locked. Very strange. Sean was getting a bad feeling, and his antenna was suddenly on full alert.

He knocked. No answer. Then he called out.

"Sid? Jeff?"

Still not a sound. He put his ear up to the door. Nothing.

Sean banged with his fists now and yelled at the top of his lungs. He kept up the banging and yelling for a good five minutes until he finally gave up and headed back to his seat, puzzled and alarmed at what seemed very out of the ordinary.

The two scientists looked worried. Watching Sean bang on the cockpit door must not have been much of a confidence-booster, thousands of feet up in the air.

Shevchuk held his hands up in a gesture of confusion.

Sean shook his head and spoke curtly. "I don't know what's wrong. Sorry."

He sat back down in his seat. The plane was flying very low now and seemed to be preparing for a landing. The first thought that came into Sean's mind was that the pilots were incapacitated and that the plane, on auto-pilot, was landing itself. But, that didn't make any sense, because if it was indeed on auto-pilot it would continue along its planned flight path to San Diego.

Sean heard the clunk of the landing gear descending, and the sound of the engines gearing back.

He glanced out the window again. The landscape was very familiar to him now; so sickeningly familiar that the dreaded acid began rushing up from his stomach into his throat.

As the expensive jet executed a flawless landing all Sean could picture in his mind was Jannat waiting for him at the Sheraton in San Diego. And the heartbreak in her beautiful green eyes once she realized that he'd abandoned her once again.

They passed the marker for runway 13, and the jet made a gradual turn onto ramp 13A.

As the plane made its final turn, Sean watched helplessly as the ground ahead opened up before his eyes, revealing beyond it a massive dark abyss.

An abyss from which, as Sean knew more than anyone, there would be no return.